Moonlight and Shadow

"Adding depth to the strong romance is historical personage . . . A fragile peace ending the War of the Roses needs very little to break back into civil war. It is the effortless ability to interweave real people and occurrences into her story . . . that makes Isolde Martyn highly regarded and her books so appreciated."
—*BookBrowser*

"Beautifully written, impeccably researched, and a glowing love story filled with honor, chivalry, bravery, and compassion, it was impossible to put this down . . . A Perfect Ten."
—*Romance Reviews Today*

The Knight and the Rose

"A lovely medieval, rich as a stained-glass window, but as complex as real life."
—Jo Beverley

"The romance clings to life and in the end flourishes . . . Martyn has created a 'fine romance' out of a piece of history."
—*Kliatt*

continued . . .

The Maiden and the Unicorn

MOONLIGHT
and SHADOW

Isolde Martyn

BERKLEY SENSATION, NEW YORK

This is a work of fiction. Names, characters, places, and incidents either are the product of the author's imagination or are used fictitiously, and any resemblance to actual persons, living or dead, business establishments, events, or locales is entirely coincidental.

MOONLIGHT AND SHADOW

A Berkley Sensation Book / published by arrangement with the author

PRINTING HISTORY
Berkley trade paperback edition / September 2002
Berkley Sensation mass-market edition / December 2003

Copyright © 2002 by Isolde Martyn
Book design by Tiffany Estreicher
Cover design by George Long
Cover art by Steven Assel

All rights reserved.
This book, or parts thereof, may not be reproduced in any form without permission. The scanning, uploading, and distribution of this book via the Internet or via any other means without the permission of the publisher is illegal and punishable by law. Please purchase only authorized electronic editions, and do not participate in or encourage electronic piracy of copyrighted materials. Your support of the author's rights is appreciated. For information address:
The Berkley Publishing Group, a division of Penguin Group (USA) Inc.,
375 Hudson Street, New York, New York 10014.

ISBN: 0-425-19328-4

A BERKLEY SENSATION™ BOOK
Berkley Sensation Books are published by The Berkley Publishing Group,
a division of Penguin Group (USA) Inc.,
375 Hudson Street, New York, New York 10014.
BERKLEY SENSATION and the "B" design
are trademarks belonging to Penguin Group (USA) Inc.

PRINTED IN THE UNITED STATES OF AMERICA

10 9 8 7 6 5 4 3 2 1

For my parents, Joyce and Fredy,
with thanks not only for their love but
for nourishing the joy in history that has
been so much part of my life

Heloise's world, 1483

The Houses of York, Woodville, Stafford and Tudor

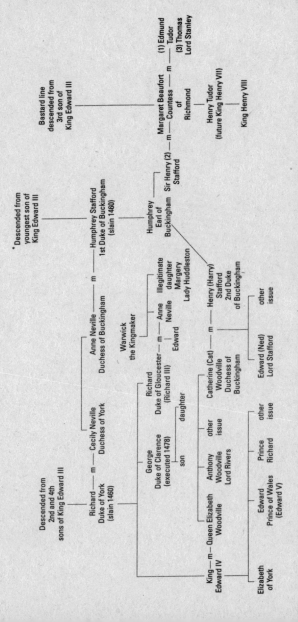

Introduction

Readers of *The Maiden and the Unicorn* will meet some familiar historical figures in this story, which is set twelve years later in 1483.

England is at peace and still ruled by the Yorkist king, Edward IV. He has given the north into the keeping of his competent brother, Richard of Gloucester, whose headquarters is at Middleham, northwest of York.

Wales is being governed by the young Prince of Wales's household at Ludlow under the leadership of the king's brother-in-law, Lord Rivers. This is of considerable annoyance to twenty-nine-year-old Harry Stafford, Duke of Buckingham, who resides at Brecknock (Brecon) in South Wales.

It seems that the old battles between the houses of York and Lancaster are over, or are they? Harry is very conscious of being a Plantagenet and having a distant claim to the throne; over in Brittany, Henry Tudor is waiting for a crack in the Yorkist solidarity; and nearly everyone dislikes the queen's family.

Heloise Ballaster, maid of honor to Gloucester's duchess at Middleham, and Sir Miles Rushden, friend and adviser to Harry, are about to be ensnared in personal conflict as well as a deadly battle for the crown that could destroy them all.

List of Characters

Only those persons marked with an asterisk are fictional.

The Household of the Duke of Gloucester at Middleham, Yorkshire

HELOISE BALLASTER* eldest daughter of the merchant Sir Dudley Ballaster; maid of honor to the Duchess of Gloucester

LADY MARGERY HUDDLESTON half-sister to Anne, Duchess of Gloucester; bastard daughter of Warwick the Kingmaker

SIR RICHARD HUDDLESTON knight banneret; husband of Lady Margery Huddleston

RICHARD PLANTAGENET, DUKE OF GLOUCESTER youngest brother of the Yorkist king, Edward IV; later lord protector for his nephews; future King Richard III

ANNE, DUCHESS OF GLOUCESTER wife of Richard Plantagenet; daughter of Warwick the Kingmaker

EDWARD son of the Duke of Gloucester

DR. JOHN DOKETT chaplain to the Duke of Gloucester

FRANCIS, LORD LOVELL chamberlain to the Duke of Gloucester

SIR RICHARD RATCLIFFE retainer of the Duke of Gloucester

SIR PIERS HARRINGTON* retainer of the Duke of Gloucester

The Household of the Duke of Buckingham at Brecknock, Wales

SIR MILES RUSHDEN* (Y CYSGOD) son and heir to Phillip, Lord Rushden; friend of the Duke of Buckingham

HARRY STAFFORD, DUKE OF BUCKINGHAM brother-in-law to the queen; cousin to Richard, Duke of Gloucester; descended from King Edward III

SIR WILLIAM KNYVETT acting constable of Brecknock Castle; friend of the Duke of Buckingham

SIR RICHARD DE LA BERE retainer of the Duke of Buckingham

SIR NICHOLAS LATIMER chamberlain to the Duke of Buckingham

SIR THOMAS LIMERICK steward to the Duke of Buckingham

PERSHALL servant of the Duke of Buckingham

RALPH BANNASTRE servant of the Duke of Buckingham

CATHERINE (CAT) WOODVILLE, DUCHESS OF BUCKINGHAM wife of Harry Stafford; sister of the queen, Elizabeth Woodville

EDWARD (NED), LORD STAFFORD son and heir of the Duke of Buckingham

BESS Ned's nursemaid

BENET* Ned's servant

BRIAN* archer

EMRYS* Welsh harpist

RHYS AP THOMAS Welsh lord

LADY MYFANNWY* maid of honor to the Duchess of Buckingham; ward of Rhys ap Thomas

THOMAS NANDIK Cambridge scholar and astrologer, formerly in Lord Hastings's employ

TRAVELLER* Sir Miles Rushden's beloved horse

DAFYDD* a superlative mouser

At Bramley in Somerset

PHILLIP, LORD RUSHDEN* Sir Miles Rushden's father

DOBBE* servant to Miles Rushden

SIR DUDLEY BALLASTER* a merchant, knighted by King Edward IV for supporting the House of York

DIONYSIA BALLASTER* younger sister of Heloise Ballaster

MATILLIS* second wife of Sir Dudley Ballaster

SIR HUBERT AMORY* retainer of Sir Dudley Ballaster

MARTIN* groom to Sir Dudley Ballaster

CLOUD* Heloise Ballaster's dun mare

The Prince of Wales's Entourage at Stony Stratford

EDWARD, PRINCE OF WALES (KING EDWARD V) elder son of King
   Edward IV and Queen Elizabeth Woodville

ANTHONY WOODVILLE, LORD RIVERS eldest brother of the queen;
   uncle to Edward, Prince of Wales; in charge of the prince's household at Ludlow

SIR RICHARD GREY half-brother of Edward V; younger son of the
   queen, Elizabeth Woodville, by her first marriage

JOHN ALCOCK, BISHOP OF WORCESTER controller of the prince's
   household; supporter of the Woodvilles

ROBERT STILLINGTON, BISHOP OF BATH AND WELLS a former
   chancellor of England

Others

THE VAUGHANS an English family, based at Tretwr, with a dislike
   of any authority, especially Buckingham's

LEWIS GLYN COTHI Welsh bard

WILLIAM, LORD HASTINGS Lord chamberlain to Kings Edward IV
   and Edward V

SIR WILLIAM CATESBY retainer of Lord Hastings

CECILY, DUCHESS OF YORK mother of Richard of Gloucester; re-
   siding at Baynards Castle, London

JOHN MORTON, BISHOP OF ELY royal councilor; previously a supporter of the House of Lancaster

JOHN, LORD HOWARD supporter of Richard III; later Duke of Norfolk

THOMAS, LORD STANLEY royal councilor; third husband of Margaret Beaufort and stepfather of Henry Tudor

MARGARET BEAUFORT, COUNTESS OF RICHMOND mother of Henry Tudor, a claimant to the throne; wife of Lord Stanley

EDWARD IV, KING OF ENGLAND Yorkist king of England since 1461; oldest brother of Richard, Duke of Gloucester; husband of Elizabeth Woodville; father of Edward, Prince of Wales and Prince Richard

ELIZABETH WOODVILLE, QUEEN OF ENGLAND wife of King Edward IV; mother of Princes Edward and Richard and their sisters, as well as two sons from an earlier marriage: the Marquis of Dorset and Sir Richard Grey

THOMAS GREY, MARQUIS OF DORSET eldest son of the queen by her first marriage

HENRY TUDOR an exile in Brittany; son of Margaret Beaufort; descended from a bastard grandson of King Edward III

DR. ARGENTINE physician to Edward V

DR. LEWIS physician to the Countess of Richmond

GEORGE, DUKE OF CLARENCE late brother of King Edward IV and Richard, Duke of Gloucester; executed by Edward IV

SIR HUMPHREY STAFFORD Welsh Marches supporter of Richard III

TYLWYTH TEG*⁷ faeries and friends to Heloise Ballaster

Prologue

MIDDLEHAM, YORKSHIRE, YULETIDE, JANUARY 1483 Packed like a row of spoons, the maids of honor to her grace of Gloucester snuggled together in the great bed for warmth against the icy wind howling across the moors of Wensleydale. It should have been impossible for a nightmare to insinuate itself amongst them, but Heloise Ballaster awoke as she hit the floor, bringing the candlestick crashing down with her and bruising her elbow on the wooden bedsteps.

The shriek of her nearest neighbor awoke the others and four faces peered down at her from the edge of the coverlet, their braids dangling like a row of bell ropes.

"Your pardon," whispered Heloise ruefully, goosefleshed as she scrambled quickly back up into the high bed.

"Was it him again?" asked someone.

The dream of an armored knight, visor down, thundering towards her with a deadly lance aimed at her breast?

"Yes. And I always fall. Why do I always fall?"

"Mayhap it was not his lance he was aiming at you, Heloise," giggled the worldliest among them. "Maybe there is something you are not telling us."

There was.

Heloise's nightmares always came true.

One

Bring us in no bacon, for that is passing fat,
But bring us in the good ale and give us enough of that,
And bring us in good ale!
Bring us in good ale and bring us in good ale,
For our Lady's blessed sake, bring us in good ale.

YORKSHIRE YULETIDE, 1483 Tankards slammed bawdily upon the trestle tables and the great hall of the Duke of Gloucester's castle at Middleham guffawed with Yorkist laughter as the cockatrice, a gaudy, four-legged monster with the head of a rooster and the tail of a crocodilus, capered round among the revelers. By rights, the legendary creature should have had a pig-like rear but no one could be bothered arguing. It staggered and swore with two voices as someone grabbed hold of its scaly tail.

"Ouch!" spluttered Heloise Ballaster, who was playing the head. She recovered her balance and craned the cumbersome beak round to see which drunken lout was impeding her progress. The merrymaking had become suddenly too boisterous and some of the rowdier youths were trying to discover who owned the cockatrice's legs.

"I'll deal with this knave," exclaimed the cockatrice's tail. Will, the duke's jester, loosened his arms from Heloise's waist and jabbed two fingers out the rear end of the costume into the fellow's nose, and then he squirted the contents of a leather bladder after it. The onlookers collapsed in fits of raucous laughter as the esquire staggered back in humiliated surprise, his face dripping with pudding ale.

"We must end this, Will!" Heloise muttered, lurching away as a reveler tried to peer inside the beak. Thank heaven she wore a black mask as well. Yes, definitely time to make their exit.

This prank was growing far too perilous. God's mercy! If it should be discovered that one of the duchess's maids of honor was prancing in doublet and hose—with a man's arms and face against her waist (not that the jester ever showed any interest in women)—her virtue would be put to the question. Besides, it was not just fear of disgrace that was fraying her wits but a gnawing sense of evil about to happen.

"Shall we make for the great chamber then, mistress? Mistress?"

Heloise did not answer. She swayed as the rush of blood that precipitated a vision flooded her mind. Not now, please God, not now! But it came unwanted—the nightmare image of the duke's son writhing upon the floor, choking for breath.

"Mistress?" Will's arms shook her back to the reality of the smoky hall. He turned her towards the dais, for the great chamber where they had left their outer garments lay beyond the high table—the high table where the duke's heir, a giggling ten-year-old, was reaching out to the golden platter of wafers and sugar-coated almonds. Almonds that could choke a laughing child!

"Jesu!" Fear of discovery—not just of shamefully playing the cockatrice but her terror that the entire castle might shrink from her as a witch—warred with her duty. But how could she risk the life of Richard Gloucester's precious son?

"No," Heloise exclaimed. *"No!"*

The cockatrice hurtled up the hall, its rear staggering, reared up to grab the platter, and tripped. Silver dishes skidded, sweetmeats flew as if magicked, goblets splashed their contents down the sumptuous cloth, the central trestle tumbled, crashing down the steps, and the duke and his guests sprang up.

The music and the laughter stopped in midbreath. Heloise, blanching behind her mask, took an anguished look at the colored shards of costly glass spattering the tiles, and gazed up wretchedly at his grace's astounded face. But the boy was safe. Uncertain, surprised, but beside his father, safe.

Silence, growing more menacing by the instant, surrounded

the grotesque cockatrice. Heloise backed into Will, wishing the floor would swallow her up. For an instant, it seemed to the onlookers that the monster's back and front legs were trying to go in different directions and then the creature shook itself into some sort of unison and hurtled out the nearest door.

"That was impressive," commented a female voice laced with humor. "We shall have to remember that for next year as well."

Lady Margery Huddleston, the creator of the costume, had hastened after them into the great chamber. Briskly, she gripped the painted edifice that had been stifling Heloise and wriggled it free. Already there were raised voices beyond the door.

Heloise blinked at her helplessly, wishing desperately that she might turn time backwards. How could she possibly explain? "I am sorry, madam. I am so sorry." Here was the last person she wished to anger; Margery, the duchess's bastard half-sister, had been a good friend to her.

"They will want to understand." Margery tilted her head towards the great hall. "*I* want to understand! God's mercy, where—" Scanning the chamber, she snatched up Heloise's discarded overgown. "Quickly!" Hastily, she tugged it over Heloise's head, struggling to hide the shirt and borrowed hose just as the door opened.

"Aye, Mistress Ballaster!" exclaimed the jester, crawling with sweating pate and scarlet face from the beast's entrails. "Would you care to explain what in hell you were about? Oh, lordy, here is the judge and jury."

Thirty-one years old, Duke Richard of Gloucester was not a tall man, but, being a brother to the king, his authority gave him extra stature, and at that instant he was looking stern enough to hang a man—or woman. His golden eyes took in the discarded skin of yellow fustian, the scaled, flaccid tail, and rose questioningly to the scarlet-beaked head that his sister-in-law was hugging to her bosom. Margery gave a tiny shrug and the duke stared beyond her to his wife's crumpled maid of honor.

"Close the door!" he ordered grimly.

Heloise's face burned with shame as his shocked gaze fell upon the ungirded gown with its collar slatternly awry, and the loosened ginger legs of the cockatrice puddled around her ankles. Gravely, she removed her mask. At least her accursed hair, bonneted into a coif, was out of sight. They had been so courteous and decent to her, these people, and this was how she repaid them. All the warmth and respect she had sought to kindle in her few months at Middleham was turning to ashes. Controlled though it now was, Gloucester's voice was like a lash to her already bruised morale.

"Since you seem to be the brains of this creature, mistress, perhaps you would care to enlighten me as to why you upset our table?"

Others had followed the duke in—the chamberlain and his grace's chaplain—and she could hear an inebriated crowd gathering outside with the excitement of carrion crows anticipating a killing.

"I thought my lord your son was about to choke." It was the truth. "I was wrong. I beg your pardon, your grace." *Please do not send me home, your grace,* her eyes beseeched him. *Not to the beatings and the anger.*

"How could *you* discern such a thing?" Dr. Dokett, the chaplain, stepped forward, his huge black sleeves aflap with malevolence. "You were at the end of the hall. How could you possibly see?"

"I—" The right words evaded Heloise. How could she tell these noblemen of her premonitions without making them loathe her, fear her? Even Duke Richard, sensible as he was, would send her away. People did not want to hear. It terrified them. Dear God, it terrified her.

Then suddenly there was shouting and the oaken door was wrenched open. The throng crowding its portals separated as Anne, Duchess of Gloucester, eyes awash with tears, pushed through to sag against the doorway.

"What is it?" Gloucester asked, his voice serrated with the edge of sudden fear.

"Our son," whispered the duchess, fingers pressed against her lips. "He choked on a sugared almond but Richard Huddleston turned him upside down, thank God, and he is restored. Oh, my dearest lord." With a sob of relief, she flew across the chamber to the comfort of her husband's arms.

Although Gloucester lovingly stroked the back of his fingers down his wife's cheek, above her head he was staring at Heloise. "When? Just now?" he asked his duchess.

"It was probably the excitement. Foolish child." Anne of Gloucester raised her head cheerfully, knuckling her tears away, and then she sensed the tension around her and recognized Heloise and Lady Margery, snared in the midst of it. "Let us not spoil the feast," she said quietly, receiving a plea from her half-sister. "I pray you, my lords, let us return to the merrymaking."

The duke hesitated, confusion behind his frowning brow. The duchess drew him away, but he was still glancing back at Heloise as the company thronging the dais drew aside deferentially to let their lord and lady pass.

"Cockatrice!" sneered Dr. Dokett, delaying to cast an evil look at Lady Margery and her accomplices. He drove a sandaled foot savagely into the belly of the carcass. "A work of the Devil! And that foul fiend already has your soul! Cavorting shamelessly and you a maid. You should be dismissed!" He hurled the words at Heloise over his shoulder like salt as though she were a demon. And, perhaps, thought Heloise, shaken by the ugly hatred, perhaps she was.

It was a while before the duchess's newest maid of honor left the sullen jester and a pensive Lady Margery Huddleston in the great chamber. With her gown belted and her veil and cap back in place over her coif, Heloise stole out through the side entrance of the great chamber and down the stairs to the torchlit castle bailey. Frosty, smoke-laden air enveloped her but she desperately needed solitude and the shadow of night would hide her.

Climb back into the saddle, Margery had advised, *face them!* But Heloise's usual bravery was at low ebb. The ache of foreboding was still with her, duller now—the certainty that the chaplain would ensure she became despised. All her delight in life was gone. And the alternative to misery at Middleham was to slink back, a failure and an outcast, to a lifetime of recriminations from her father. For just a little space, back there in the hall, safe behind the disguise, she had felt such confidence. But now . . .

Leaning her shoulder against the cold stone wall, she tried to understand. Had the faeries sent her the premonition? But why, if someone else had been meant to save the boy? Or, worse, was she the Devil's instrument? Had her action caused the child to choke? Yet forewarned, how else could she have acted? But the cost, oh, Blessed Christ, the cost! Why could she not have been born ordinary? Even the grinding labor of a kitchen wench was better than this wretchedness; a scullion would sink into her cot too worn to dream. Why have you done this to me? her mind called out in pain. But neither God, the Devil, nor the faeries answered.

She must have lingered outside for longer than she realized, not heeding the cold in her despair, when a young man's voice close by jerked her to her full senses.

"Mistress Ballaster, I have been searching for you." The vapor from the unexpected words hung in the freezing air. The moonlight lit the face of Piers Harrington, one of the esquires. "Why were you not at the feasting, mistress?" A warm hand fastened round her wrist. "Still, no matter, it's my good fortune that you are here now." He might not have seen the cockatrice wreaking disaster, but an accidental assignation was the last thing Heloise could stomach.

"Your pardon, Master Harrington, I cannot stay." She was shivering, with both the cold and her anxiety over how unseemly it would appear if they were noticed—another arrow to be loaded

into the priest's quiver of complaints, especially as Harrington
was the chaplain's nephew.

"What? No reward for finding you, lovely Heloise?" His tone
was slurred but drink had not slowed his wits. In an instant, his
arms were caging her against the wall.

"Another time, sir." Heloise kept her voice amiable and
ducked, but two hands thrust her back. His body pinioned her;
cold stone pressed against her back. This was not the love that
the minstrels sang about. Being fumbled by a wine-reeking
youth? Any maidenly fantasy she might have cherished of a stolen
meeting with some adoring lover perished. Was this reality? And
to think she once had weighed him as a husband.

"Stop that, Master Harrington," she hissed, slapping at his
adventurous hands and dipping her face to escape his breath.

"Damn this!" He snatched at the wire and tisshew veil of her
butterfly headdress that was crowding his face, wrenching her
cap and coif away. Heloise turned into a Fury: fists, elbows, and
toes beat, jabbed, and kicked him.

"There is no shame in kissing a man." He laughed, lunging
in again, and then miraculously there were footsteps and some
unseen force lifted the youth in the air and heaved him aside,
but not before Harrington had glimpsed her loosened hair. The
full moon betrayed her. A stable oath ripped through the air and
he was gone.

"Drink this."

Margery pressed a beaker of mulled wine into Heloise's frozen
hands and tugged the furred wrap closely about her shoulders.
"It was a prank, for God's sake. Her grace will not send you away
for that. And the little lord has sworn to my husband that you
are not to blame. He was laughing at a page's antics when he
choked."

"But the chaplain, my lady. He already thinks me a cursed
changeling. Dear God, I should have kept my own counsel."

"And not obeyed your conscience?"

"I believe this is yours, mistress," interrupted an unfamiliar voice from the threshold. Male arms unfolded and long fingers held out Heloise's damaged headdress and muddied coif. Heloise shyly took the ruined headgear back, not sure how long Sir Richard Huddleston had been leaning against the door frame. She had not met him face-to-face, for he was newly arrived from Cumbria.

"I have to thank you, sir, for rescuing me from Master Harrington," she said huskily. *And saving the duke's beloved child.*

"Think nothing of it, demoiselle." Sir Richard brushed one hand against the other as though dealing with Harrington had sullied his palms. His languid gaze lingered fondly upon his wife before he glanced back at her companion. If he felt surprise or loathing at her witch's hair spread wild and loose, his green eyes gave no sign of it. "There is a messenger come from your father, Mistress Cockatrice."

"Ill news, sir?" She slid off the bed in alarm.

"I cannot say, demoiselle. His grace will speak with you tomorrow." He stepped forward into the bedchamber, tossing his hat and gloves upon the bed. "Your handling of the cockatrice was skillful, Mistress Ballaster, and the eggs"—his wife smiled and the air crackled between the two of them—"were a masterpiece."

"Well laid?" Margery smoothed her skirts skittishly.

"Oh, very."

Heloise had heard such outrageous rumors about this pair: how the king had seduced Margery, the Kingmaker's bastard daughter, and sent her to France as a spy. Could it be true that Richard Huddleston had committed high treason to win her love? Seeing them now together for Yuletide, she could believe it.

"I was telling Heloise this morning about the donkey," Margery said softly. "How it dropped gingerbread in the King of France's lap."

"The donkey of Angers! Oh, surely that was I," answered Sir

Richard, raising his enigmatic gaze to his lady's eyes for the answering echo of his meaning.

Oh, this was love! This was what Heloise desired of life. She felt both privileged to witness the love between these two, and yet bereft, for she could not imagine Piers Harrington gazing on her like this. The realization brought a sense of reprieve.

"Heloise has been afraid to let people see her beautiful hair," Margery was telling Sir Richard.

"I cannot think why," observed her husband. Perhaps his matter-of-fact tone was intended to be reassuring, but Heloise still felt uncomfortable beneath the man's intelligent study.

"The other children used to say I had witch's hair," she whispered.

"And people used to say I was a whore." A trace of pain laced Margery Huddleston's voice. "You must not be ashamed. Your hair is a gift from God, not the Devil. It is what you believe that counts. Now, be cheerful, you do not lack for friends."

Heloise's fear that the faeries had stolen the real Heloise Ballaster from her cradle fled. Oh, the belief seemed foolish now in such sophisticated company as the Huddlestons', but she had been bred on such teasing. First her dreams and then her dark brown hair turning silver like an old woman's. And her father scoffing and saying only a blind man would take her for wife. Well, changeling or not, she would show him. She lifted her chin defiantly and smiled.

"And I should look higher than Harrington if I were you," Margery added, as if she too had the gift of reading minds. "Marriage is not always an answer."

"But merely the beginning of the question." Sir Richard took his wife's hand and drew her to her feet. "Lend Mistress Ballaster one of your caps, my love, and let us see her safely to her quarters."

"Pleasant dreams," they wished her kindly at her door. Dreams? That was the crux of the problem. She was young, accursed, and afraid to dream.

*   *   *

FATTENED ON YULETIDE FARE, HOARSE WITH CAROLING, AND
aching from the carousing, the household—those who were up—
was sluggish and subdued next morning as Heloise followed the
page on duty through the great hall to the Duke of Gloucester's
more private demesne.

The southern-facing chamber was warm from the fire and lit
by wintry sunlight. The Huddlestons, reunited after months
apart on their respective duties, were inevitably together, decorating the windowseat in their silk and velvet, their conversation
in full sail as their infant child, fetched from the nursery, crawled
about their feet.

Closer to the hearth, Richard, Duke of Gloucester, lolled upon
the cushioned settle, with a hound belly up close by and his son
propped against his bootcaps. The pages of a bestiary lay open
across the child's knees.

"But it says here, my lord father, that the stone from a hyena's
eye can make you prophesy if you put it under your tongue.
Does—" The duke's hand shook him to silence as Heloise curtsied in the doorway.

"Ah, Heloise." The Duchess Anne, a younger, compact ren-
dering of Margery Huddleston, looked up from her playing cards.
Leaving her mother, the countess, in midgame, she came across
to stand beside the duke.

Her errant maid of honor curtsied again and waited, feeling
as though she were already on the executioner's scaffold. At least
the chaplain was not present.

"Woman's intuition is a strange commodity," observed the
duke, fidgeting with the ring on his smallest finger. "Expensive,
too, it seems. You have dented my ledger, Mistress Ballaster, not
to mention our best flagons."

"It was out of no malice, I swear to you, your grace." Desperate, she turned her face to the duchess. "Please, I beg you, do
not dismiss me, madam. It shall not happen again."

"It is not why we summoned you, Heloise," Gloucester said

gently. "Indeed we are certain you acted honestly last night and we thank you for your care of our son. No, rather, it is this." He lifted up a parchment from the cushions beside him and held it out to her. "Your father's letter changes matters. Sit down and read it."

With no choice, she sank down obediently upon the tapestried stool and unfolded the parchment. It contained what she feared: in about twelve lines dictated to his notary, Sir Dudley Ballaster was summoning her back. Because her delicate stepmother was with child and since no man had offered for Heloise, she was to come home and become the chatelaine. Home? No, not the home she had left in Northamptonshire, but some castle called Bramley in Somerset which (he proudly informed her) had been bequeathed to him by a friend. She was to go there.

"It seems we must lose you, Heloise. Your father's man, Martin, is bidden to take you home." Duke Richard stood up and kindly drew her to her feet. The boy rose also, straight-shouldered like his father.

Heloise wore her disappointment openly. Free from her father's tyranny, Gloucester's household had given her life order and beauty. But nothing endured. If she stayed, the whispers of her premonition and strangeness would seep out and the servants would be crossing themselves as they passed her by. Her fellow maids of honor had kept silent about her witch's hair but now they would begin to look on her with suspicion; the chaplain would see to that.

The duchess fondly set a hand upon her lord's brocaded arm. "We . . ." She glanced at her husband. "We wondered if you would like us to receive your younger sister when you can spare her. Of course, there is no need to make a decision now."

"I thank your grace." It was a generous invitation. Dionysia was beautiful, normal. Dionysia would soar in the world of Middleham like a comet. "With my father's permission, I should like to send her here as soon as I may." That at least would soothe her father's temper.

"Good lass." Gloucester nodded approvingly. "Well, it is decided that you should leave tomorrow with Sir Richard and Lady Huddleston as they ride south. Best go while the roads are hard with frost."

"You have been very diligent in your duties, Heloise. We have grown fond of you."

"I have been so happy, madam," Heloise exclaimed, the duke and duchess blurring in her vision like a disturbed watery reflection.

"I know what you return to." Her grace's hands framed her shoulders. "I know how difficult fathers can be, believe me." She turned to include Margery in her observation before adding, "And I think you shall be missed, Heloise, especially by a certain esquire, hmm?"

"No, I do not think so, your grace, not after last evening."

Margery came in a slither of silk to curl her arm within her half-sister's. "Heloise is afraid that her unusual hair will repel any suitors."

Gloucester frowned. "Yes, I heard." He glanced warily at the blue velvet cap and the carefully pinned veil that Heloise was wearing. "Silver, I believe." His golden mead eyes lit with kindness. "Surely not so rare as you imagine."

"What is wrong with it? Can I see?" The child's voice chimed between them at breast height.

"Nothing is wrong with her hair," interfered the boy's grandam firmly from her seat at the small table. "But Mistress Heloise wants to be the same as everyone else. So will you when you get to her age." Then she turned the overweight cannon of her fifty years fully upon Heloise. "You will find, young woman, that other worries will chase away such idle thoughts as you grow older. A broken fingernail or tresses that do not curl will become insignificant when you have a house to run and children at your skirts. You will see."

I have already *seen*, thought Heloise rebelliously, biting back a retort, angry that the older woman thought her vain and frivolous. I have already slaved for my father day and night with no smile or word of thanks to ease my burden.

"My lady," she protested, "I assure you I know that hard—" She faltered, not because the countess's attention was back upon the playing cards, but because it was happening again—the blurring of reality and possibility.

It was as if her lungs were bursting. Before her eyes, Duchess Anne's skin was paling. Blood flecked the lady's lips like spittle; the serene eyes were retreating, distressed, dilated, into cavernous sockets; and the world was darkening.

"Heloise! Heloise!" Margery Huddleston's fingers were clamped about her wrist, jerking her back by physical pain into the present.

"I must go," whispered Heloise, her mind shrieking at the invasion, not daring to look at any of the others, lest the vision return.

Go from Middleham, aye, but then what?

Two

BRECKNOCK, WALES, LATE FEBRUARY 1483 Harry Stafford, Duke of Buckingham, rose from his carved chair, dismissing his council with an impatient gesture. His chamberlain, Latimer, gathered up his notes noisily and departed, his disapproval stated in the briefness of his bow. The other councilors followed almost at a tiptoe like husbands back from a carousal. All except Sir Miles Rushden, who closed the door behind them and swung round, his gaze questioning Harry's decision.

"I do not give a cuss if you disapprove, Miles. You are not going to make me change my mind this time," the duke exclaimed, thrusting the lower window's shutters open. Below the castle, the town of Brecknock shivered against the winter gusts. Beyond, the hills rose from the vale like a long green wave and dark tumbling breakers of land heaved up into the shrouded mountains. Rough, raw, the wind from Pen-y-Fan's steep ridge rushed into the room, frightening the papers on the table.

Miles shifted a river-smoothed pebble across to anchor the dispatches and wrapped his fur-edged cote more closely across his breast.

"It is but a small matter to give Ralph the vacant stewardship at Yalding, your grace," he argued, leaning across to take a handful of sweet chestnuts from the pewter salver. He wisely kept to one side of the hearth as he nicked each with his dagger before he pokered them into the embers; the cold draught had sent the fire into a coughing fit.

"No," muttered the duke, glaring resentfully at the distant fog-shrouded beacons. He looked over his shoulder and scowled. "Jesu! Ralph will never make Yalding pay."

"Surely he deserves the chance to prove himself?" Not that Miles had a great liking for this particular servant of Harry's, but Ralph's wife, Eleanor, was efficient and steadfast.

"They have Lacon Farm at Wem. Let that suffice, Miles. I will hear no more of the matter." He struck his fist against the wall. "By the saints, I have had enow of being cooped up here. I need to hunt. Tomorrow! Arrange it!"

Miles inclined his head obediently. He too felt the lack of exercise after the week of rain but for him it never evoked the black despondency that plagued the duke.

"I daresay it is time the realm had another rebellion, your grace," he remarked dryly. "Shall I arrange that too? Although there is the possibility you might end arse up in a butt of malmsey." As had the king's jealous brother George, Duke of Clarence, five years before.

The duke's ill humor fell from him like a loosened mantle and he pulled the casement half to and turned. "Whoreson!" he exclaimed affectionately. "Some wine, if you please."

His friend complied with a lazy grin. Miles was a fine judge of when to let matters rest. The southern Welsh had given him the name of *y Cysgod*—the duke's shadow—but his strength lay in keeping a pace ahead. He knew the Scorpio in Harry Stafford's nature; it was a matter of keeping to the front of the man.

"By the by," the duke exclaimed, "you still have not told me what your father wrote concerning your betrothal with Lady Myfannwy."

Miles frowned as he passed across a cup of muscadelle. He was willing to marry Rhys ap Thomas's ward as part of Harry's political maneuvering for alliances in Wales but at twenty-seven he did not feel it was any longer his father's business, nor was he contemplating this second marriage with particular enthusiasm. His girl-wife, Sioned, and their child lay buried in the cold ground these two years. Besides, his mirror showed how the world saw him and a pitted face would not please a young bride.

"He gives his blessing, and thanks your grace for your care of my fortunes. The other news is my younger brother now has a son. Thank Heaven! Perhaps my parents will give up parading neighboring maidens every time I return home." One of the chestnuts shot across the hearth like a cannonball and Miles coaxed the rest out.

"I shall suggest Rhys bring Myfannwy here in April." Harry juggled a hot chestnut from palm to palm. "A tasty little piece, she is."

And she would bring him considerable lands, Miles conceded. As the heir of a family that had fought for the House of Lancaster against the victorious Yorkists, he needed to improve his fortunes and the alliance with Rhys would be advantageous. He pensively divested a chestnut of its shell; so be it, in April he would take Myfannwy to his bed.

"What is *this* doing in here?"

With thumb and forefinger held as though it were a rat's tail, Harry plucked a tapestried cushion from the settle and swung it with distaste. The Woodville cockleshells, the arms of his wife's detestable family, sprawled across its puffed-up innards. Since King Edward IV had become so infatuated with Elizabeth Woodville that he had married her, the Woodvilles had crept into all the nooks and crannies of power. Marrying an heiress here, an heir there, they had stretched their tentacles across the entire kingdom. Even Wales, where Harry should by rights have had great lordship, was not free of their interference. Nor was the duke's marital bed free either, though Catherine Woodville avoided it as much as Harry did. But she was still a Woodville, the queen's youngest sister.

Estimating distances, Harry dropped the cushion in line with the window and kicked it at the casement. It hit the wall instead and fell with a soft plop onto the oaken chest. The duke shrugged.

"So, what have you in mind to waste the day? Shall we send a bailiff down to Tretower to annoy the Vaughans? Or I could tell my wife I want another son."

Friendship was all very well—Miles ran a hand wearily through black hair that might have passed for a Welshman's—

but sometimes he felt centuries older than Harry, instead of two years younger. He raised his brow at the piniomed parchments hopefully but the duke shook his head.

"There is that sloe-eyed treasure Pershall found for you over at Llantrynach, my lord." Retrieving the cushion, he replaced it before the ducal foot. "Marged? Lives in the lane behind St. Brynach's?" He glanced up and recognized the kindling of interest. "Shall Pershall fetch her over?" At least the girl was eager.

"Yes, why not?" muttered his grace. "And I pray God she will be amusing." He thumbed the Stafford knot upon the goblet. "The seed head of a dent-de-lion has more wit than the last one I bedded."

"And your grace has not forgotten that I leave on Monday."

"My grace has not forgotten, no. But can you not delay? It will be so tiresome without you."

Miles cursed; his leave time was precious. It might take a week to reach Somerset with the roads so miry. "But, my lord, I thought we agreed that I should meet with you at Thornbury." Yes, he should be able to help his father take possession of Bramley and then skirt Bristol and make speed to Thornbury.

"Oh yes . . . well, I suppose you must go." The remark was tepid; the following silence deliberate. Harry's confidence was seesawing again. "I wish I might rip Thornbury apart and build anew. A pox on the king! If only he would grant me the Bohun inheritance, I would have the funds."

Oh, they had ploughed this ground so many times before, groaned Miles inwardly as he perched himself on the edge of the table, nonetheless prepared to listen with his usual patience. If only Harry had not fallen out with the queen, high offices might have come their way and they would both be busy at court, instead of peeling chestnuts in this godforsaken apology for a castle. Mayhap the opportunity would come one day with God's good grace, but meantime he would not be sorry to have a brief respite from Brecknock and its bored master.

And now—because Harry's dark moods had to be endured

else the entire household would feel the brunt—he patiently leaned his chin upon his ringed hand and waited. It was a small satisfaction that the duke's confidences lent him power. But he had no wish to abuse Harry's friendship, nor was he easily manipulated. There were just a few in the household who could understand the bitterness that rose up in the duke like a poisoned, flooded well from time to time—the hatred of the queen, Elizabeth Woodville. Like a constant open sore, the rift with Westminster had begun when Harry, at ten years old, had openly declared his boyish fury at being made to wed not just a girl but worse—the queen's eight-year-old sister. The queen and her brothers had never forgiven him. And, of course, Harry was a Plantagenet.

"I have more royal blood in my little finger than the plaguey Woodvilles can muster in the whole of their ancestry," grumbled his grace, "but I will wager they all were invited to Westminster for Christmas."

Miles refilled the duke's goblet. "No, your grace, Lord Rivers kept Christmas with the Prince of Wales at Ludlow."

Harry looked sulky at the reminder. Establishing the twelve-year-old heir to the throne at Ludlow, with the queen's eldest Woodville brother, Lord Rivers, as tutor, had been calculated to keep not only the Welsh to heel but his grace of Buckingham too. For King Edward, having established the Yorkist dynasty, feared that if ever his enemies gathered strength again, they would seek out Harry for their rallying point. Harry was the last legitimate heir of the House of Lancaster, which was why Miles was safeguarding him. All of Miles's future lay in the value of Harry's birthright and one day, God willing, if ever there was a division in the House of York, Miles would exploit it to the full.

"You and I could have been in that campaign at Berwick against the Scots, Miles. Richard of Gloucester would not have minded me bringing a force to help him. Oh, Christ, Miles, mayhap you should go and join Gloucester's retinue at Middleham. It might bring you more fortune than rotting here in cursed Brecknock."

"What, and break tradition? The Rushdens have always served the Staffords." Someday, Miles vowed, Rushdens would repair their fortunes. One day the wheel of destiny would shift again and he would help Harry topple the Yorkist-Woodville alliance. "Be of comfort, my lord, it will not always be thus. The queen might die before new year—in childbed." It was spoken softly lest passing servants pass the treason on like a contagion.

"Pah, and I can travel to the moon," muttered the Duke of Buckingham, and he kicked the embroidered Woodville arms right out of the window.

THERE SEEMED TO BE A MINOR BATTLE GOING ON, OBSERVED Miles, reining his horse, Traveller, to a halt on a rise some two weeks later and staring in fascination at the full-blooded anarchy that was taking place in the snow down the road. He did not know this part of Somerset.

"That Bramley village, eh?" muttered Dobbe, his manservant, unimpressed. They had passed a castle of rather modest proportions about a quarter of a mile back. Since it had been decorated with a sickening superfluity of scarlet and azure pennons, they had certainly reached their destination, a demesne still usurped by Sir Dudley Ballaster.

The March wind was biting and Miles edged his horse into the shelter of a laneway to their left. His servant, and the two men-at-arms he had brought for escort, followed.

"Do you think someone has forgotten to tell them that we have had peace in England for the last twelve years?" he muttered and sprang to the snowy ground, thrusting back his fur-lined hood and rubbing leather-clad fingers over his darkening chin. He had been looking forward to a shave and a bath, not a skirmish. It was irksome to be summoned to Bramley by his father when he had intended spending the rest of his leave at the family home farther south, in Dorset.

One of his companions chortled. "Well, this is Somerset, ain't it, sir? I am a Hereford man, m'self."

So this was Bramley, formerly his great-uncle's little kingdom. The village looked prosperous enough: its church was steepled, the snow-dappled roof in good repair, and the gardens of the thatched dwellings fringing the king's highway were fenced and planted. The alehouse's summer garland was withered and frosted, but its doors and windows, broad and candlelit in the afternoon gloom, beckoned him like a friendly whore, for it had been a tedious, cold journey.

"Just like Wales. We might ha' saved ourselves the journey." Dobbe mopped his dripping nose with his cuff. The thwack of quarterstaves on shins and grunts as fists met jaws carried clearly in the cold still air and the knot of villagers watching from a sensible distance were adding rude yells to the shouting. "You goin' down there, sir? Show 'em how 'tis properly done?"

His master frowned, slowly making sense of the scene. Jesu mercy, it was his worthy father down there bellowing at a little man with a thatched-roof head—or was it the huge armored fellow he was roaring at? "Well, well," he muttered appreciatively.

Of course feuds still happened in parts of England. Some were local squabbles that had begun during the lawless years of King Henry VI; others were disputes over land ownership, exacerbated by the wars between the great families of York and Lancaster when lands had been attainted and dealt out to loyalists by the victors. Miles knew exactly what the skirmish was about but he had hoped his father would have settled the quarrel by now. He had already glimpsed the bone of the dogfight: Bramley castle—a square Norman tower, a renovated hall boasting scarlet shutters and two chimneys, an encircling wall, a moat with a mill race hard by, a further scatter of dwellings, and a dozen adjacent fields complete with last year's scarecrows. The cozy little fortification had been bought with ransom money earned bloodily by his great-uncle during the French wars of the '40s and passed down to his second cousin, who had died pickled and heirless, bequeathing Bramley not to Lord Phillip Rushden, Miles's noble sire, but to a stranger, Sir Dudley Ballaster. Presumably it was Ballaster who sported the unpleasant haircut and was now shouting retaliatory abuse at Miles's father.

Perhaps it was time to make his presence known. With a lopsided smile at his parent's rumbustious behavior, Miles gave Traveller's neck a rewarding pat and slid once more into the saddle.

"Looks like 'tis over for the day, sir."

In a matter of minutes it was. A score of the combatants, with the armored giant and two limping wretches in their midst, were noisily making their way towards the alehouse but the short man swung himself onto his horse and, with several henchmen and two hounds in his wake, thundered up the road past Miles's party without a second glance at the hooded travelers hunched against the wind.

"Friendly, ain't they?" muttered Dobbe.

The Rushden contingent was dealing with several bloodied noses, each dripping impressively onto the much abused snow, but it was hard to tell what other damage had been done without closer investigation.

Miles swung round to his men-at-arms. "When Dobbe and I are out of sight, go to the alehouse. Pretend you are but travelers. See what you can find out." He kneed his horse to a gallop down the hill.

"Not *pitchforks*, my lord!" he exclaimed in loud disdain as he drew rein. "How very primitive."

"What the—" His father, scarlet-visaged, strode heavily forward with fists raised, the sable serpents on his breast heaving mightily. "By our Lady! Miles!" he wheezed in astonished delight as his son dismounted. "I was not expecting you until morning."

"It seems I should have brought my full armor, my lord." He had thought to find Bramley already in his father's hands.

"Ha, we almost had 'em, my young hawk." The older man's

embrace was still vigorous but he seemed more stooped than when they had parted last summer. The dark, once lustrous hair was liberally flecked with silver and, though the strength was still there in the aquiline nose and determined mouth, the older man's chin was dewlapped from feasting too richly. More disturbing was the labored breathing that betided weakening health.

Masking his concern, Miles clapped his sire on the back. "You will not be entertaining me at the castle, I think, my lord father." He nodded in greeting to the Rushden men. "Not exactly a victory, I see." It certainly would not do to count bruises or missing teeth.

"Did you note Ballaster?" Lord Rushden sniffed and glared disgustedly up the street. "Rode past you. Strutting little cock! Carpet knight!" He spat, and added in the hushed growl he always used when criticizing the House of York, "Got his tap on the shoulder for supplying old King Ned with arms and a loan during Warwick's rebellion. Godsakes, the man's father was a crossbow merchant in Bristol."

"And does Ballaster play the shopkeeper?"

His father sneezed. "Aye, when he is not playing at being a nobleman. 'Pon my soul, lad, you should have seen this swaggering varmint sticking his chest out like a pigeon and proclaiming, Ooohh he had supped with the king and my lord Hastings. Should be a law against wretches with no breeding acquiring land. Next thing we shall have ploughmen representing the shire in Parliament." He sniffed again, rubbing at his moustache with his forefinger. "Mark my words, we shall have a hard time getting Bramley from this dog's arse. Tie us up in the courts for years if we let him. You might have a word with Duke Harry, Miles. See if he can do anything to resolve matters in our favor."

"I suppose the place is worth it," muttered Miles, anticipating a pile of lawyers' bills. His family's fortified manor house was much more to his taste, and he wished he were there now instead of standing on an icy sward in cursed Bramley. His father already had two castles and both needed repairs. Why did he want this one? Miles glanced towards the retainers his father had led up from Dorset. Most of them were stamping and blowing on their fingers to keep the blood flowing. Miles was not feeling warm either, and his father sneezed again, a hand to his throat as if it irked him. "So where do we honorably retreat to, my lord?"

"Retreat? Watch your language, lad. Seized one of the outlying manors yesterday. Gives us a base at any rate. I daresay you are hungry." Lord Rushden whistled for his esquire to bring his horse. "Think I am coming down with an ague, lad. My throat's as rough as a carpenter's file."

"And when is the next battle?" Miles asked with tolerant affection. "Cockcrow?"

"Ten, tomorrow, but a small matter. Yon fool has challenged me to combat. Whether he thinks it will settle matters, God knows. I reckon that whoreson wouldn't know a charger from a packhorse."

"Combat?" Miles's dark eyebrows rose, his amusement vanishing. His father might have earned his knighthood at the battle of St. Albans, but that was some twenty years back. "You are surely not going to fight the fellow?"

"No, of course not," exclaimed his father, flinging an arm about his shoulders. "Now that you are here, *you* are."

Three

It was one thing to acquire a castle but it was quite another to be accepted by the nobility. And if your grandsire had been a crossbow dealer and your father had gained his temporal power by swaggering around London, buying himself a baron's younger daughter, donating liberally to royal funds, and doing disgustingly well in the world, then you were definitely to be ignored. What made matters worse for Heloise and her younger sisters after they settled into Bramley with Matillis, their timid stepmother, were the tidings that Phillip, Lord Rushden, cousin to the previous owner, was disputing their father's right to the castle. He had already journeyed from Dorset with an armed force, seized one of the dwellings in the nearby manor of Monkton Bramley, and was trying to collect rents from her father's villagers by coercion. Vowing vengeance, Heloise's father, Sir Dudley Ballaster, had taken every able man and was gone down to Bramley village to put a stop to such effrontery.

Sir Dudley's daughters were used to their sire charging off in a pother as if he had been stung by a gadfly, and Matillis, who was scarcely older than Heloise, was too dreamy to be anxious, so they gathered in the solar, the castle's warmest chamber, and deliberately busied themselves with Dionysia's departure for Middleham.

Growing uncomfortable from the huge fire, Heloise gazed forlornly at the thick glass panes dribbling with moisture. The chamber smelt stiflingly of woodsmoke, beeswax, and the lavender perfume that her stepmother had dabbed on too generously that morning. Heloise's day had gone ill: her father, expecting her to be more omniscient than God, had scolded her not only for the red cloth left in the laundry, which had turned his underdrawers rosy, but also for the hole in his boot sole and her youngest sister's cut knee. A wonder he did not blame her for the Rushdens!

With a sigh she rearranged the fireguard, then dutifully knelt again to finish pinning Dionysia's hem, but her discontent was epidemic. Their old nurse, darning by the window, was muttering about her eyesight, and at the small table, despite Matillis's attempt to hold the peace, Heloise's youngest sisters were growing peevish, squabbling over scraps to clothe their dolls.

"Are you nearly done, Heloise?" asked Dionysia with a seventeen-year-old's impatience, draping an uncut sweep of emerald satin across her perfect bosom and squinting to see what a lock of her golden hair looked like against the green.

"How can I finish this if you fidget so?" Heloise chided, trying to make the hem flow gracefully into the short train so that they could start sewing on the embroidered border.

"Pah, a few rucks will not show when the border is on. Can we set this lower?" Dionysia poked discontentedly at the broad band of honey-hued silk that edged her bodice and reassessed her reflection.

"No, Didie, we cannot. It took me all last evening to shape it." Heloise rose wearily to her feet; picking off the wisps of thread that clung to her fine wool skirts. "I have never known a fabric to slither so."

Behind her, Nurse set the darned woolen stocking aside. "Them Rushdens," she declared with a tone that promised gossip, and all the sisters turned towards her. "Slitherin' is what put me in mind of it. The Rushden serpent story." Matillis, unused to these utterances, looked perturbed but Nurse continued: "They say that over two hundred years ago in the days of King Edward Longshanks, the Lady Dyota Rushden cuckolded her husband by making a pact with the Devil."

"What does 'cuckolded' mean?" asked Lucretia, the youngest at ten years old, who was subsequently dispatched from the chamber to find a nonexistent bag of mending.

"What kind of pact?" whispered Dionysia as soon as the door closed.

"The fiend lay with her as a serpent."

"Better than a bull," muttered Heloise, wondering just how snakes mated. "Would it not have been more sensible for the Devil to keep a human form?"

"Perhaps he likes variety. I should prefer a swan myself," giggled Dionysia, glancing around as if Lucifer ventured out of Hell to note her name.

"Please go on, Nurse," urged Clio, thirteen years old, still smirking at the petty victory over her younger sister.

"And in each generation ever since that day"—the old woman lowered her voice—"there has been a Rushden with the soul of a serpent."

"No more, Nurse," protested Heloise. This talking of the Rushdens was stirring up unease—a foreboding—not exactly that something calamitous would happen, but rather, that Fortune had shifted the wheel and a change had occurred.

"It's no gossip, bless you, my darling. There's wicked black serpents on the Rushdens' insignia to prove it." The old woman was well versed in the heraldic flauntings and *genealogia* of her betters.

"Hmm, that story is not in the least original." Heloise picked up Lucretia's doll from the small table and plucked at its veil. "The Plantagenets claimed to be descended from the Devil much further back than that. Mayhap we should invent a legend to give ourselves respectability."

"Do we know any lusty swans?" Dionysia flounced across to tuck her arm through Heloise's and beam at Matillis. "Or fiendish serpents? A fiend for Heloise to match her elfin hair."

"I think you are mixing up Jupiter and the Devil." Matillis crossed herself for good measure. "And no more talk of the Rushdens."

"I just pray Sir Dudley thwacks them right out of the shire." Nurse grabbed another stocking from her basket. "Them Rushdens are said to be murderous thieves to have truck with and the heir as ugly as sin and a cold-hearted knave withal, but leastways your father has a temper on him hot as Tewkesbury mustard and it will be a brave man who will cross him."

"Or woman," muttered Heloise.

Nurse set down her mending. "You poor sweeting," she clucked. " 'Twas not fair you took the brunt of it this morning. Well, never you mind, there's a good man out there somewhere for you, mark my words."

"Is there, Nurse?" For once, Heloise did not hide her feelings. "Must my fortunes depend on finding a husband? I hate the way the world is tilted so that fathers and husbands have all the authority. They treat us as though we are breeding stock to be sold at market." She might have added more but the horns sounded and a chorus of barking heralded Sir Dudley's return.

"Well, I am back," he exclaimed, striding into the silent solar some moments later, two grinning hounds, reeking with pond water, at his heels.

"Yes, we can see that, sir," muttered Dionysia, swishing her new skirts out of the dogs' path. Heloise stepped in front to shield her and shooed the beasts to the hearth where they settled appreciatively. At least her father could have ordered the servants to sluice them down but he clearly had another matter foremost in his mind, for he was wearing a familiar, smug expression that usually boded ill. Warming his hands behind his back at the fire, he beamed at them like a general about to announce a victory.

"You would have been proud of me, my wenches. The bailiff was right. We came across Rushden trying to force rent from the villagers and when I demanded he depart, he had the hide to call me a scoundrel and a disgrace to the shire. It was so close to the alehouse that half the village heard him. There was nothing for it but to toss my glove at him." His eyes lingered on his new wife. Matillis was beaming admiration—at least on the outside.

"You challenged him to combat!" Heloise stared at her parent in disbelief. His anatomy could hardly be described as muscular. Puny might be a better word.

"Indeed, I did." Sir Dudley's grin was as gleeful as the Devil's signing up a soul. "That man is a traitor to the king's grace if ever I saw one. Scratch the fellow and I will wager you will find a Lancaster sympathizer. The cur looked daggers at me when I said I had King Edward's favor and had supped with Lord Hastings. Just because I was knighted in a palace, whoresons like Rushden think they can sneer at me. Well, tomorrow at noon that plaguey fellow shall learn that I am not a man to bear insults lightly."

"Lord Rushden never picked up the gauntlet, surely?" Heloise exclaimed.

"Indeed he did. Went as red as a cock's wattle with every jack man of 'em watching and agreed to meet me tomorrow at the edge of the wood outside the village of Oakwood, a mile from here. Potters Field, it is called. You need not gape at me like that, all of you. Rushden's sword is rusty in its scabbard, mark my words. The fellow is at least sixty. Stooping and stupid."

Useless to tell her father this was utter lunacy. Humiliating a baron of ancient noble family! Oh, not only would this intensify the quarrel over Bramley, but it would send all the local nobles flocking to Rushden's banner. The Ballasters would be shunned like lepers. Oh, why must he bluster so? Challenging an enemy to personal combat belonged to the make-believe world of Sir Lancelot.

"You had better put in some sword practice after dinner, sir," Dionysia suggested lightly, her covert glance at Heloise implying she thought their father would find some excuse before the morrow. But this issue was more than skin deep; not only was it about old nobility versus new money, it was political too.

"Pah, you do not imagine that I shall fight Lord Phillip. Sir Hubert can be my champion, of course."

"Will Sir Hubert agree to this?" Heloise queried. Her sire's retainer was a galumphing, good-natured old carouser with the frame of a colossus and the brain of a caterpillar! Oh to be sure he would!

"Aye, of course, and don't you go a-meddling, trying to make him say no, girl! It is about blessed time he paid me back for all the ale and victuals over the years."

It was despicable of him to load his quarrel onto poor Sir Hubert. This was not a matter of little boys playing with wooden swords. "Please, sir," Heloise protested, risking a scolding. "I have a fearful feeling about this and it is foolish to . . ." She faltered as the humor ebbed from her father's face.

"A fool, am I?" He snatched up some discarded sewing and shoved it at her. "Keep to your stitching, girl, and mind your manners." Thrusting up her hands defensively, she winced as the needle in the fabric jabbed her. "Changeling!" he sneered. "No wonder her grace of Gloucester could not find a suitor for you. You want to take care that Holy Church doesn't get to hear of your babblings and lock you up."

Or worse.

"Giving your opinions," he continued, "sticking your nose into men's affairs, mouthing tomfoolery. At least she"—he grabbed Dionysia's wrist and jerked her towards him—"*she* has the sense to keep a still tongue in her head and please a man." Then his foul temper abated, his breathing steadied. He gave his new wife a reassuring glance but there was no kindness for his oldest daughter. "Go and talk to the faeries, Heloise. Ask them if they will have you back."

"PICKLED AS A SOUSED HERRING," MUTTERED MARTIN, SIR Dudley's groom, next morning at dawn as he stood gloomily with his master and Heloise, staring down at Sir Hubert's great bulk snoring on the straw of the byre. "Sir 'Ubert couldn't slay a flea between his thumbs let alone bestride a horse this morning. What's to be done, master? On my faith, I've tried burnt feathers and slappin' 'im but we'll not have 'im sober in time." As if to add emphasis, the rooster pattering on the tiles above their heads opened his throat and shrieked.

For answer, Heloise's sire picked up a pail of water and hurled its freezing contents at the knight's head, but Sir Hubert merely rolled over like a happy dog.

"God damn you!" fumed her father. "This is your fault, girl! You should have kept the old fool sober." He strode out into the yard. "Bring my breakfast to my bedchamber and announce that I have been taken ill with the measles."

"But our family honor . . ." Horrified, Heloise grabbed up fistfuls of her skirts and hurried along beside him.

He halted to glare at her. "What if I truly had the measles and were fevered and delirious?"

"That would be acceptable, sir." She shivered, wishing they might finish the argument indoors.

"Amen to that. I truly have the measles."

"Oh, sir." Martin dutifully snatched off his cap to address his employer, delaying him further. "Forgive me sayin' so, but folks'll say you are craven if you do not fight this mornin'."

"Then Bramley shall close its ears to the gossip. You will inform the household I am contagious, daughter. Now see to my breakfast!"

"But if you eat heartily, sir, they will think—"

"Cease whining, you useless creature, and make sure the beef is not overcooked at dinnertime nor the mustard runny."

"I know my duty, sir," she flared and slackened pace lest he cuff her.

"Fie, your mother's father would turn in his grave at such behavior," muttered Martin, shaking his head at Sir Dudley's back. " 'Tis not the way of the nobility."

"I know it." Heloise led Martin into the warmth of the kitchen, her thoughts skittering over the consequences as she gave orders to the kitchen servants for breakfast. The groom was right: once the gossip rippled out, her sisters would fetch no husbands, poor Matillis would be shunned, and they would never

ever find acceptance among the Somerset nobility. She rubbed her hands before the fire, wondering how she might amend matters. If Lord Rushden was elderly, she would wager her best gown that he would hardly be spoiling for a fight on a bleak morning. It was fit to snow again out there.

"Try the pottage, mistress," pleaded their head cook. "The master threw it over poor Thomas yester morn."

Heloise took a long-handled spoon and dipped it into the pot suspended over the embers. "What if I dress in Father's armor and go in his stead?" she whispered to Martin and paused in her ladling. Could she? Dare she?

"Nay, mistress," he protested, clapping a hand to his balding pate, but the outrageous idea tempted Heloise as she set a small loaf of fresh white bread beside the bowl upon a wooden platter.

"But, Martin, it might serve."

The groom hastened after her as she carried the tray into the great hall and waylaid her at the foot of the wooden staircase leading to her father's chamber.

"Godsakes, mistress, a gentlewoman cannot do such a thing."

"Why not? I have my father's inches and if I keep the visor down, no one need know. I will write an apology here and bear it with me so you may carry it across to Lord Rushden at the field and there is an end to the business, save"—she glanced towards the upper room—"Father will have me beaten for it but . . ."

The groom looked as though he was struggling against an apoplexy. "If you are discovered," he spluttered, the wooden banister wobbling precariously. "The scandal, mistress. It will be worse than cowardice. Your honor—"

"Since my father tells me I shall never find a man to offer for me, it does not worry me, but you are right, we must take care to keep this secret. What matters is that my sisters shall one day find worthy husbands and escape his temper."

"But what if you have to fight, mistress?"

She sensed the faeries listening, hidden high in the beams of the hall, and felt no disapproval. "It will not come to that." Besides, she had watched combat practice at Middleham with the other maids of honor, and years ago Sir Hubert had let her test the feel of a sword and shown her a few tricks when he was teaching her cousins. Her instincts told her this was right. Even sensible Martin was wavering. "Will you help me, Martin? Set out my father's armor, saddle Sir Hubert's destrier, and come with me as my esquire? Oh, please . . . and pray you, say nothing to my father. Will you do it?"

"Aye, mistress, fool that I am."

"DOES NO HARM FOR A NOBLEWOMAN TO KNOW WHAT A HUS-band must carry into battle," Sir Hubert had once said to the giggling Ballaster maidens when they had been trying on his plumed jousting helm. But today it was not just the helm. Inwardly Heloise trembled like a maiden about to be sacrificed to a dragon; outwardly she pretended serenity as Martin gradually buckled on piece after piece of steel over the quilted brigandine and leggings. Not all the pieces matched, but with one of the servant's tabards tugged down over her chest and hips, only an expert would have noticed.

Save for her heels, every clattering inch of her was encased in metal, from shiny insteps to the polished gorget about her neck. She felt extremely protected until she tried to move and found her limbs stiff, slow and weighted as if her body were remote and it needed a carrier pigeon to reach her fingertips with the message to bend her gauntleted fingers round Sir Hubert's sword handle.

"If this t'were a tournament, the winner might demand your armor and your horse," Martin clucked after fastening the old knight's belt about her. They had guiltily made extra holes in the leather to keep it from slipping down over the tassets that encased Heloise's thighs. "Easy now." His young lady was wobbling precariously on the small upturned barrel and he steadied it so she might step across into the saddle.

"There will not be any tournament," Heloise muttered.

"Don't you change your mind, mistress, after all this labor."
He heaved her leg across the shiny leather and then handed up
the helm. "Aye," he said, noting her grimace, "riding astride will
be strange for you but I'll keep good hold of the leading rein
and Chivalry's a valiant beast."

She lowered the helmet over her coif and clanked down the
visor. Instantly the wintry world was reduced to muffled sounds;
her vision to a horizontal slit. The inside air about her face was
damp from her breath yet stifling, and she swiftly pushed the
grille up again, preferring the chill wind on her cheeks. So this
was what it felt like to ride into battle. God help her, it was like
carrying three large sacks of grain. Well, such torture might be
preferable to being pierced by a fatal arrow on the bloody fields
of Wakefield or Towton, but this was agony.

BY THE TIME THEY EMERGED FROM THE WOODLAND TRACK,
the clouded sky was tinged with orange, promising sleet to im-
pair Heloise's vision even further. And they were late. Unfamiliar
with the roads, they had missed the track to Oakwood and had
to turn around. Potters Field proved to be a fist of cleared land
thrusting into the woodland at the edge of a common. No doubt
Lord Rushden had chosen it for its flatness. A ditch drained it
on one side, a hedgerow edged it on the other, and a small scatter
of bleating sheep were glaring at the horsemen that huddled
within the fringe of oak and hazel. To the side of the track just
before it ventured into the wood stood a dilapidated hovel, and
tethered to the small broken-down manger propped against its
wall was a donkey. A plump little man, clad in a long houppelande, emerged from inside, rubbing his hands up and down his
forearms to keep warm. Seeing Heloise, he hallooed the Rushden
company, and they immediately rode out into the open.

As she identified her foe through the grille of her beaked visor,
Heloise found her courage ebbing. Lord Rushden sat straight-
backed in the saddle, his formidable visor already down. Even

though she knew the steel shell hid a crabbed and elderly man, her enemy looked unnaturally huge, terrible, and incredibly defiant. The black rondels on his argent surcote seemed to be taunting her like arcane eyes across the meadow, and then as Heloise drew closer she recognized the circles' imperfections—they were coiled serpents. Two of his henchmen were laughing at his groom's efforts to shoo the unshorn sheep through the gate to the side of the meadow. The fat man caught at his stirrup by the hovel but her enemy took no notice; his gaze was firmly fixed on her.

"Take him the apology, Martin."

The groom grimly ran across the grass that separated them. Heloise saluted haughtily as Lord Rushden raised his head from scanning the parchment, and then she gasped. This was the nightmare at Middleham when she had fallen from the bed! The black knight! Of all the fools in Christendom! God protect her! She had invited herself to her own death!

In a daze, she watched Martin running back to her as if he were a creature no longer of this world. Lord Rushden's answer was already in her mind.

The groom's eyes were round as turrets, his fear great. "Says it be too late for an apology. 'Pon my soul, mistress, you have to tell 'im who you are."

She shook her head. This was meant to be. At least if she died, there would be no more complaints, no more beatings. "I acquit you of all blame, Martin."

Because it was not a proper jousting field, there was no wooden tilt to keep the horses apart. Heloise took the wooden lance, swallowed nervously as she kneed her charger round, and then rode to the edge of the field. She had one last chance for survival. If Lord Rushden knocked her from the saddle, she could pretend that she was stunned and mayhap there could be an end to it. She moistened her lips and signaled her readiness. Her enemy saluted her mockingly and lowered his lance. The Rushden groom raised a kerchief, and as he cast it down, Heloise spurred forward, with a prayer to St. Catherine. She instinctively swerved as the malevolent lance came at her. Her own weapon went astray, missing Rushden entirely, and she quickly withdrew her feet from the stirrups and, as if hit, toppled off the horse into the deep grass the way her cousins had taught her to fall. All breath burst out of her as she crashed in an untidy sprawl. Her nightmare had not told her what came next.

Her head was still ringing as the thud of hooves returned. Lord Rushden dismounted and clanged purposefully towards her. She blinked up at him through the slits. He was not pointing his sword to her throat! Plague take it! He was waiting for her to fight him on foot.

Groaning inwardly, already badly bruised, she turned onto her knees, awkwardly staggered to her feet, and reluctantly drew Sir Hubert's sword. Rushden made an assault. That Heloise parried it was a miracle. It happened twice and he began to circle, forcing her to stagger and turn to keep him in her sight. He was assessing her, exploring her speed, mobility, skill, and each blow became more testing. Cursing beneath her breath, Heloise made a lunge but she found it hard to raise the sword with sufficient strength to bring it down upon him. He was taller than her and moved aside easily, not with an old man's lumbering gait but with a younger man's energy. If only it were over, she prayed, as he began to tease her, making feints here and there. And it was beginning to snow, marring her sight further. She felt like a hapless beetle fronting an agile ant. Each sparking blow as her foe's blade struck hers jarred her whole body.

"Where did you learn the use of arms, dotard, in the market?" jeered her enemy. The malicious serpents on his breast blurred as she reeled at his voice. St. Catherine protect her! This was not the blustering voice of some ancient, but the strong, mocking tones of a far younger man. Blinking back tears of fury and frustration, she cast her wooden shield away, clasped the sword handle with both hands, and swung the blade with all her strength, but the stranger parried it easily. His blows grew lighter, playful, as he drove her back.

His taunting laugh as she almost tumbled backwards over a molehill made Heloise break her silence. With a fierce whoop of female anger, she charged at him. For an instant he dropped his guard, and her blade caught his helm. She might have taken further advantage of his surprise, but sweat from her brow blinded her and weariness and cold were addling her mind. More was unbearable. She crumpled to her knees and the world vanished.

MILES GRABBED OFF HIS HELM AND FLUNG IT ASIDE AS HE KNELT down in the long grass. He cautiously lifted off Ballaster's helm only to rock back on his heels in astonishment. He had fought a boy! The linen coif framed a young face and no hint of beard sat yet upon the frozen downy cheeks. Certes, a very pretty boy, more suited to the choirstall than a destrier's saddle. Cowardly Ballaster! Sending a codling to fight. If only he had guessed earlier, for it called his honor into question. Should word of this leak out . . .

"Stay back, all of you," he roared as his people and the fat barber-physician came running. He needed to protect his foe's identity, not to mention save himself from ridicule.

"Sir!" It was the leech, venturing closer, anxious for business.

"Stay back, I said! You there, give me a hand."

Snowflakes glistened on his adversary's lashes as Miles and the Ballaster esquire carried the youth into the dark windowless hut. God's rood, the lad's armor probably weighed more than he did! They laid their burden on an old palliasse set on a wooden frame. Miles stood back frowning as the esquire crouched, anxiously feeling for a pulse in his young master's neck. Reassured, the fellow unclad the boy's hands and began to chafe them.

"He will live," Miles asserted derisively, drawing off his gauntlets. "Who is he? Ballaster's son, I suppose." The esquire did not answer but the lad did—with a groan. "Wait outside, fellow!" Miles snarled, nudging the door open with his armored shoe, and he stood there while the esquire edged past him uneasily. "So, are you groggy, boy?" Miles taunted, fastening the latch. It amused him to stay in the shadows, to deliberately make himself formidable. "You are fortunate I did not run you through."

"Who are you?" whispered the youth, straining to see in the gloom.

"Sir Miles Rushden." Pacing across to the ancient hearth, Miles turned his back on the lad with a menacing rattle of hauberk. He knew how to frighten his prisoners. "Your family is occupying my inheritance."

He almost heard his captive swallow. "Are . . . are you going to ransom me?"

Miles swung round arrogantly to see that the youth was now leaning on one elbow, staring miserably at the ground, shoulders hunched. Circumstances warranted frightening him further. "Oh, no, boy." Miles's voice was laced with contempt. His foe evidently had no understanding of the rules. "I cannot be bothered. Perhaps I should just give you to my men for a beating."

The prisoner's head whipped up defiantly. "Then you are no true knight."

Inexplicably, the taunt stung Miles, bringing the blood to his cheeks. He had been playing on the lad's fear, determined to teach him a lesson, but young Ballaster did not lack courage even if his father did. "Why did you take your father's place?"

"He was sick, so he chose Sir Hubert in his place. Sir Hubert was a mercenary at Nancy."

"The siege of Nancy was a defeat," retorted Miles witheringly. "And what happened to the legendary Hubert this morning? Did he suddenly vanish in the night?"

"He was sick too," the boy admitted, staring at his toecaps.

"Ha! Or drunk."

The coifed head jerked defiantly. "Where is *your* coward of a father then?"

"Do not be insolent with me!" Miles snarled, watching in satisfaction as the boy recoiled. He strode to the door and halted. "I should take my belt to you." He fingered the buckle, his pause perfect as his young enemy's jaw gaped. "Save that I want my breakfast and it would take too long to strip you to your arse." For a few heartbeats, he waited menacingly and then he unlatched the door and slammed it back against the wall so that the whole dwelling shuddered. With a powerful hand, he grabbed up Ballaster's esquire by the collar as though he were a discarded cote and dragged him inside. "Take your young master and be gone!" he growled, loosing the man so violently that the fellow went sprawling towards the boy.

"It is not his fault." The youth put a steadying hand out to the terrified fellow and the pair of them turned their faces to Miles, uncertain and fearful whether they should try to leave.

"What are you waiting for?" Being malevolent was quite amusing, but now he was weary of playing the tyrant. The servant replaced the youth's gauntlets before he helped his master to his feet then he hesitated, a-feared to pass the grim silhouette half-blocking the threshold.

The boy—Miles could see now how narrow-shouldered he was—unsteadily set his hand on the esquire's sleeve. "Pass me my helm, Martin." The husky young voice was in command, but the groom's hands shook as he obeyed.

The boy took the helmet calmly, his leather fingertips smoothing the plume, as if he derived calm from the action. His eyes shimmered as he cocked his chin proudly. "If we ever meet again, Rushden, it will be I who will take delight in it, believe me." With that, he bowed his head, not out of humility but so he might set the steel helm back on.

"Oh, I am trembling already," mocked Miles, highly amused. He jabbed out an arm to block the boy. "Tell your yellow-livered sire that if he must ape his betters and play the knight then he had better learn the rules. I do not fight children." He patted the steel cheek of the visor. "But if you cross me again, lad, as I said before, I shall take my belt to you."

"I am trembling already." His own words were hurled back at him with such sarcasm that Miles was hard put not to laugh and prod him further. Now the varmint thought himself reprieved, he was showing the insolence of a tiny lapdog yapping at a wolfhound.

Leaning against the doorway, arms folded, Miles watched with the lazy grace of a victor as the loser was helped clumsily into his saddle. The visor jerked round at him as if the eyes behind it were etching his enemy's face into memory. Miles curled his fingers in an insolent farewell and the lad angrily touched his spurs to the horse's flanks and galloped away.

Someone gave an obsequious cough at his elbow; the leech had come seeking payment. "You were not needed nor were you bidden here," growled Miles.

"A very unusual combat," persisted the man, lurking like a distasteful smell, as Traveller trotted over at Miles's whistle. "It will make a good story in the alehouses."

"The point of all this, Master Surgeon?" Miles asked irritably.

"The point, Sir Miles? Ah now, anyone in their right wits could see it was not Sir Dudley Ballaster you fought."

"No," muttered Miles dismissively, anxious to shed the armor and warm himself before a fire. "It was his son. The boy was incompetent. What of it?"

The man's eyes glittered with the prospect of a bribe. "But Sir Dudley Ballaster does not have a son," he said.

Four

Garbed as a servant with scuffed boots, a brown, wide brimmed hat, and a shabby cloak hoicked over a worn broadcloth jerkin, it was easy for Miles to talk himself past the gatekeeper at Bramley Castle next morning. Fortune had already played his friend in this foolish enterprise, for he had passed a party led by Sir Dudley on the road and perhaps the servants would be less vigilant in their master's absence. Mind, he knew he should be carted to Bedlam for taking such a risk. His excuse to his father was that he would scout out the weaknesses in their enemy defense but in truth, sheer curiosity drew him—that and his own guilt. He doubted he had fought a maid, but certainly if he had and made matters worse by playing the swaggering bully afterwards, then he had breached his own code of chivalry and needed to apologize to salve his conscience.

He halted in the shade of the small barbican and appraised his surroundings. The great hall with its flanking snow-capped tower was at least two centuries old but long windows had been let into the southern wall and turret chimneys added. Adjoining the old solar was a more recent two-storey building—bedchambers, judging by the feather beds stuffed out over the sills for airing. So the wars in France had been lucrative. Huzzah for Great-uncle Rushden, the old pillager! Well, perhaps it was worth fattening a few lawyers to keep Bramley in the family.

The squabble of little girls reached him from an upper storey and he could hear voices in the buttery. An excuse was pregnant on his tongue should anyone challenge him. He would declare that his master was on fire with love—an irony that—but there had to be one daughter that was passing fair and worthy of seduction. If that did not work, he would play gormless and mumble that he had come to the wrong castle, but so far only a stray cockerel parading out of the hedge—a hedge laden with curiously rose-tinted underlinen—had dared to shake its wattles at him.

Although the air was chill enough to redden noses, the sky was as blue as our Lady's robe and the sunlight was already berating the frost rimming the grass and bestowing cheerful warmth upon his back. Enjoying his adventure, Miles whistled like a cocksure servant and skirted the west side of the building. A kitchen garden and an orchard, bristly with winter boughs, lay beyond the stables.

He was hoping to find fault, but good housekeeping was much in evidence. Ballaster's servants were diligent: no horse dung dirtied the courtyard, the firewood was stacked sensibly, and although the air smelt of woodsmoke from the hall chimneys, there was no odor of a stinking midden or byres that needed a good sousing, and he would not have noticed the dovecote particularly except that a dusting of damp droppings showered him as a fluttering bird landed with a clap of wings.

"Whoopsy!" A maidservant emptying a bucket from a casement nearly caught him midship. Miles touched his hat to her and she simpered, making great play with her bodice as she closed the window. At the stable door, he slowed, wondering if he might safely estimate how many stalls were occupied, but a burly stablehand stepped forth, wiping his hands clean upon a rag, and challenged him.

"Your pardon, I was a-lookin' for someone to 'elp me. I 'ave a message for one Mistress Ballaster." He hoped the rustic accent was not overripe and humbly touched his forelock to add authenticity.

"Which one?" barked his accoster.

Miles gaped dully and shrugged. "Dunno, friend, 'ow many be there?"

"Well, one of 'em's over there." The man jerked his thumb towards the garden and waited. "Well, go on wi' ee. She won't bite."

Under such brawny scrutiny, Miles had no choice but to let

himself through the wicket gate. Beyond a tunnel arbor festooned with sweetbriar, a yellow-haired demoiselle with a basket on her arm was scattering bread crumbs on the path.

"Yes?" At first she could not be bothered to turn her head.

"Good day to you, mistress." She was devastatingly pretty but he dared not stare. Eyes humble, he clumsily tugged off his hat and lifted his fingers to his forehead in an incompetent salute. He had tousled his hair to hide the careful trimming.

"Well, fellow?" Shrewd eyes that he had never glimpsed before assessed him rapaciously from his dusty toecaps to his damaged face. It was hard to know whether she was as old as sixteen but she looked as knowledgeable as Eve.

Eyes downcast, he began to fumble in the breast of his doublet. "I 'ave a message from my master, Sir Miles Rushden, for your brother. 'Tis friendly."

"My—" She bit back her words and rose, shaking her skirts. "Indeed," she murmured, glancing down as if to give herself thinking time. "I have heard Sir Miles attends his grace of Buckingham. Is it true?"

"Aye, m-mistress." Not a bad stammer, he thought, pleased with himself.

Her fingertips steepled. "And shall you be returning to the duke's household with Sir Miles, fellow?"

"Y-yes, mistress, three days hence."

The rosebud mouth drew together speculatively. "You would not be Miles Rushden in disguise, perchance?"

By the saints, she was sharp-witted. "My m-master did say s-sommat about riding over here this day."

"Indeed," she muttered, and, lifting her skirts jauntily, started towards the hall.

Miles lifted a hand to retrieve her attention. "Where do I go, pretty mistress?"

"Oh, down that path. My brother . . . and sister . . . are there. They are quite inseparable." Not bothering to explain, she hastened away, humming. So the leech was wrong, there was a son, a bastard son perhaps.

The well-trodden path led to a splintering, weatherbeaten door, unlatched and ajar. Replacing his hat, Miles stepped through and found himself amongst shiny-trunked pear trees dappled with snow. A startled woodpecker flew past him with a yaffling cry as he followed the trodden grass southwards down the rise.

Christ protect him! Miles froze as a shrouded figure rose up, like a ghost from its moonlight grave, at the far end of the orchard and then, his breath subsiding, he chided himself as it lowered itself again. It was a woman who was very slowly and painstakingly brushing the snow off sacks that lay around the footings of some half dozen bee skeps. Miles glanced about him for young Ballaster but, save for the eerie beekeeper, he was alone. With misgiving, he moved forward, quiet as a hunter, towards the apiary.

The woman was murmuring to the bees, her long unbleached cotton skirt sweeping across the thin carpeting of snow. A veil full of snags and catches hung from a reaper's broad-brimmed hat, and though the gauze shrouded her almost to her thighs, it did not hide the firm curves of her breasts. The boy's sister?

Heloise did not hear him. Rather she heard the change in the humming. She knew instinctively it was Rushden. Although yesterday's taunts still made her seethe, she had carried his armored image to her pillow like a medallion, sinfully make-believing a world where her father had no governance and Rushden, no longer sinister, lifted her onto the saddle before him like a lover. If only her fantasy were not a shadow. Life was not the *Romance of the Rose,* she reminded herself; it was letting a scarlet cloth loose in yesterday's washing and going without supper as penance. And this brigand was no better; he too had threatened her with a beating.

What in God's name did this man desire now? To deliver another tongue-lashing? And why was he clad in such an ancient riding cloak? He was lurking warily, well beyond the perimeter of the hives, but watching her with the stealth of a cat stalking a songbird. Heloise was gleeful at his uncertainty. This was a better combat yard for her mettle, for if he came too close or spoke in anger, a thousand barbed defenders clad in gold and nut brown livery would rise up to protect her. A sense of reckless excitement plucked at her.

"Lady—" Miles lifted his arm cautiously in greeting but the woman put a finger to her lips with an imperious gesture and carried on as if he were no longer there. Not daring to raise his voice, he took a careful stride closer, his body tensing, and waited. Ignoring him, was she?

The drone grew louder. Several bees, disdaining the cold, were coming at him. Could insects sense fear? Who was the patron saint of bees? St. Ambrose? Miles swallowed nervously as one bee tested the coarse wool of his cote. A second landed on his glove, but he stood behind the girl now.

Her movements were languorous and controlled. With great calm, she nudged one of the wicker skeps more firmly onto its stand. The disturbed insects flew up angrily, risking the frosty air. A few settled on her straw brim and one darted up beneath the gauze. With a blow of her breath, she nonchalantly shook it out and looked up at Miles from behind her veil, waiting. For what? For him to make the wrong move? Suddenly understanding froze him.

He *had* fought a girl! For an instant he knew shame, wanted to blurt out an apology like an embarrassed youth, but then he felt the tendrils of his hair stir as a bee moved across onto his cheek. His flesh crawled. The thickness of the veil was not enough to hide the gleaming eyes daring him to panic.

"Afraid?"

Miles barely heard the soft whisper. He was thinking of yesterday: *If we ever meet again, Rushden, it will be I who will take delight in it, believe me.*

No! His lips formed the word and beneath his cloak, his muscles clenched. Merciful Christ, he had just walked blithely into her trap as if he welcomed punishment. *Would* she drive the swarm against him? Desperate to run, he forced himself to stare down the sly scrutiny, to fight his terror, but the horror filled his brain, he saw himself panicked, screaming, his breathing blocked, his face and neck jabbed by— *No,* his mind snarled at her, *no!*

The sorceress journeyed slowly to the next hive, taking her basket with her. Miles took a step slowly back, then another and another until he found himself beyond the coned village and its vindictive keeper. His breath returned to normal but the insects had not left him. The beekeeper was watching him, faceless behind her veil, as she brushed the snow from the last hive. He sensed her silent laughter and glared back. *Now we are even, lady, but next time you will be on your back. . . .*

Oww! As if she had slapped him, the last bee panicked and stung his cheek. Cursing, Miles turned his back and leaned against a rough-barked trunk, taking great gulps of air. Swiftly tugging off his gloves, he strove to pinch the base of the sting to ensure no more venom oozed in nor any barb remained.

"Did one of my bees *need* to die for you, fellow?"

Fellow! Miles looked round, his feelings raw. Still veiled, she stood quite close. A small peleton of concerned insects patrolled around the cover of her basket but her concern was for the dying insect in the palm of her glove.

"No," he answered hoarsely, watching her lay the small warrior upon a snowy bough.

Reckless behind her gauzy armor, Heloise stared up with triumph at her enemy. She had him confused, annoyed, and vulnerable and she wanted more. Here was no irksome stripling but a man, pleasingly proportioned, with midnight hair and eyes like quicksilver. Last night's sinful fantasy came back to her: this knight unhorsed, tumbled unhurt upon the grass as she had been yesterday, and her leaning over him, her hair unleashed, her fingers touching the strong line of jaw, smoothing back the tousled dark hair. He was looking at her and . . .

The Rushden serpent was looking at her! And with a fascination that sent excitement shimmering through her like sparks of fire. Her mind, left momentarily open like an unlocked door, felt the savage blaze of desire rip through him. God's mercy! Panicked like a frightened dove, she took off through the trees.

"Wait!" he called out, and hastened after her.

No, this was lunacy but . . . Grasping a medlar trunk to steady herself, she squared her shoulders then walked on.

"I suppose you have made a reconnaissance of our defenses, Sir Miles?" The words were tossed back at him bravely.

"I came to learn the truth." He overtook her round an apple tree.

"You have a sword, Sir Miles. I am sure you can whack the truth to its knees if it suits your purpose."

Miles winced. "A philosopher as well as a beekeeper. You *are* a spinning top, lady. Was it you yesterday, Mistress . . . ?"

"Heloise," she said unhelpfully, with a sideways step so a branch played chaperone between them. "Yesterday? Oh, you mean the wretched boy you threatened to strip and give to your men for a beating. Shall I summon my servants to do the same for you?"

White teeth gleamed. "Did I promise that? Your pardon, Heloise." The breathy way he said her name wreaked damage to her self-control. "You have a man's courage, Heloise!" He grabbed the bough as though he would thrust it aside.

"What, not a woman's?" Angered, she darted away, skirting the next tree.

He followed like a hunter and, when Heloise turned, halted before her on the snow-dusted slope. Male, strong . . . within a hand's-breadth. And life had pitted his soul, not just his face. She could sense the ancient simmering fury in him.

"Does your face hurt you, sir knight?"

"No." A deeper answer rimed Miles's breath. The world

hushed for a moment and he could no longer breathe. He knew
her clear gaze probed his features, as if she were trying to peel
back the layer that disfigured him. He tensed, discomforted, and
then . . .

And then she set back her veil. Dark lashes shyly lifted and
lovely, troubled, hazel eyes looked up at him, her glance settling
upon his swelling cheek. There was no unwelcome pity, no noting of the scars he carried like a brand. His breath eased out
slowly, misting the air between them. Somehow her gloves fell
softly to the ground and his hat joined them.

"Stay still, sir." The girl's hand was gentle against his chest,
her breath fragrant upon his chin, as her cool fingers examined
his burning skin.

Stay still? Miles was utterly enthralled, hardly able to drag
his gaze from the soft lips so near his own and yet . . . Was he
bewitched, lured here by magic? The young knight, the vengeful
beekeeper, and now this young woman with an angel's smile,
were they all facets of one gem? Glass jewels flashed at him,
masquerading as moonstones in the silver caul that hid her hair.
Why did she not wear it loosened to show her maidenhood? *Who
was she?*

The questions must have been brazen in his stare for her eyes
widened in surprise. The straw hat dipped. Shyness, he presumed,
but then she lifted her face and he was glad to be wrong.

"You won this bout and rightly so." Miles captured her hand,
lifting it to his lips with courtly grace. "But do not imagine this
is over, mistress," he warned, reluctantly letting her fingers slide
free. "There are subtler ways to take a castle."

The infinitesimal pause in her breathing appeased him. "But
surely in any campaign you risk capture, sir."

"True, mistress." His grin was predatory. "But such peril
makes the victory infinitely more desirable."

Her answer hurtled a cannonball through the courteous banter. "For you maybe, but not for the poor wretch who broke his
wrist two days ago in this quarrel. No, nor your father's man

whose eye is blinded. God's truth, sir, you are welcome to Bramley and—and its—"

"—blushing underskirts?" he added roguishly.

Hurt flared; he deserved a thwacking but she surprised him with a shimmering, self-deprecating smile. Cruelly, raised voices echoing from the courtyard spoilt the delicate truce between them.

"You showed audacity in coming here, Sir Miles."

"A fox in the Ballaster hen coop? Yes, time to go, I think."

Aye, he must, he knew; it was madness to become entangled further. He would not play Jason to her Medea. God knew, this enchantress's humor changed like a weathercock.

He kept pace as she hastened up the slope but then she faltered, clapping a hand to her ribs as if in pain. The beautiful eyes glazed over and her body tightened like a lute string. Another facet, Miles thought, roused at imagining her beneath him so, but this was no trickery; she was clutching his sleeve, her doe's eyes wild.

"Go back! Home, yes. Tell your father he is needed at home!" And she started hurrying through the trees.

"Come back!" Miles shouted. What had she meant? Why . . .

He was close in pursuit when Mistress Ballaster misguidedly glanced back. Her long skirt snagged beneath her pointed shoe. Miles tried to catch her, but his boot heel slid upon the icy ground and he tumbled sprawling down on top of her. With maidenly embarrassment, the girl hastily twisted, trying to drag herself swiftly free from the tangle of sleeves, but one of Miles's spurs had snared in the hem of her undergown.

Then the world went wild. A half score of men with cudgels burst through the gate.

The maiden's nimble fingers extricated him but a cage of boots barred his escape. Ugly stares examined his clothing for signs of disarray; surliness surrounded him, seething, threatening to boil over into violence. Knowing the picture they must present and cursing himself for a fool, he clambered from his hands and knees with as much dignity as he could muster. Although he was tempted to draw his dagger against their cudgels, he might as well have brandished a daisy stalk at the louts. With bravado, he reached down a gallant hand to the wench and said a prayer to whichever saint was good at calming virgins. The plea must have worked, or else Heloise Ballaster was possessed with more common sense than most spinsters.

"No, I can shift for myself, sirrah." Her voice was calm as she rose gracefully. "What else was it you wanted to ask me, fellow, before I slipped?" It was gracious of her, sparing him any blame.

"Aye," muttered the most bull-necked of the pack salaciously. "Wot was ee goin' to ask 'er?" Growling, the Ballaster retainers closed in like a royal bodyguard, fencing him from their princess. Their fists were edgy, ready to smash him to a bloody pulp.

"No!" Her sovereignty was brandished calmly. "Put away your cudgels, all of you! Can you not see, he is *only* a messenger." Miles, used to brandishing authority, winced at her mockery. Was he being taught another lesson? Brushing her hands clean, she was waiting, her hazel eyes laughing at him. "Well, fellow?"

When the words surfaced at last, his voice sounded alien to him. "My master says . . ." One of the servants muttered behind the girl and hurt sparked across her madonna face. Would she be punished for this later? Miles swallowed and chose his answer with even more care. "My master says, mistress, that he will have his lawful inheritance from your father yet and that he knows full well who is the bravest of the Ballasters. Tell him so . . . I pray you," he added swiftly, remembering his disguise.

"I shall tell him." Displeasure lined her voice but gratitude glimmered in her eyes. Then she clapped her hands like a good chatelaine. "Two of you, see this man off *our* land, and back to work, the rest of you. I thank you for your care of me."

"Aw, mistress, can't we give 'im a right dustin' and tip him down the well?"

A feminine glance perused the prisoner consideringly and mischief flared fleetingly in her eyes before she said with a little sigh,

"Oh, no. Now if it were his *master*"—she paused for emphasis—"well, then, that would be different," and the impertinent wench turned on her heel.

Miles stared after her, his mouth a hard line of suppressed fury, his mind reeling from bewilderment. One instant she was being solicitous, the next taunting him. And what had been that strange babble about his father needing to go home?

"Come along, you!" A rough hand shoved Miles and he was prodded from the orchard with a bunch of servants sniggering in his wake. They marched him behind Mistress Ballaster across the bailey, and he did not know whether he was glad she was still in charge, or shamed that she intended to watch him being ignobly ejected from *his* father's property. When the fair girl and two children ran giggling to join her, his mortification was sublimely terrible.

"Your dovecot needs cleaning!" he snarled in valediction, his voice raised to reach her, and for thanks received a booting across the drawbridge.

HAVING CUFFED HIS GATEKEEPER AND, IN THE SOLAR BEFORE supper, lectured his daughters on suitable behavior when accosted by strangers, Sir Dudley—who was still blithe from his miraculous recovery—repeated his warning to the entire household from the hall dais, dwelling somewhat emotionally on words like *theft* and *virtue*.

Heloise refused to eat in the great hall but she listened to her father's words from behind the solar door, ashamed that he was intent on sullying Sir Miles's reputation. At this rate, every gossip in the shire would be sniggering at Rushden's escapade. Why was her father doing this, knowing that it might bring the full wrath of their enemies? Miles Rushden would be angry and she needed him to leave. His very presence had mocked her, arousing a hunger for the fruits of life—a future denied her because of her despised hair. Her dreams at Middleham had been a warning; Miles Rushden was dangerous, especially for her.

*   *   *

"LET ME SEE THE BAILIFF'S LETTER, SIR!" MILES FLUNG THE REINS
to Dobbe and strode after his father into the house they had
requisitioned at Monkton Bramley. He had just returned from
his confrontation with the witchgirl to find his father preparing
to depart for Dorset. His mother had been injured.

"Letter's on the bench there," muttered Lord Rushden, strap-
ping a leather flask onto his belt. "With God's grace, I'll make
good time if I leave now."

"Christ Almighty, Father!" Miles looked up in disbelief. "She
has broken a rib."

"Aye, I always said that horse would throw her one day." A
loving hand clapped his shoulder. "Godsakes, Miles, you have
gone as white as a corpse."

"Where is the man who brought this?"

"Round the back in the byre. Rest easy, lad. Your mother will
mend."

The shapeshifter, Heloise Ballaster, had been right. Twice!
Predicting she would best him on their next encounter and now
this—his father needed urgently at home. No, this was utterly
insane. How could she possibly have known?

Miles found the messenger dozing on the straw. "Did you tell
anyone of your tidings on the journey here?" he demanded, shaking him awake.

"N-no, sir. I came directly."

"And no one waylaid you?" Goggling, the man shook his head
and Miles released his collar.

"Changes matters, of course," his father was saying behind
him, "having to return to Upton Stafford. Pity we never had a
cannon here, we could have bombarded Ballaster into surrender.
No need for you to come back to Dorset, Miles, seeing as you
have to return to the duke, but you could snip this rooster's tail
feathers in the meantime."

"Of course." Miles tried to collect his shattered wits. "I need
not leave here till Sunday, but yes, I will create such hell for

Ballaster that he will rue the day he set eyes on Bramley."

"That's the spirit, Miles. Go over to Norton Magna and collect the rents, then send the rest of the lads on to me with the money."

"How much did they collect? Wait till I lay hands on that whoreson. I'll geld him! Nail his feet to the floor while I do it, too!" Sir Dudley paced before the hearth in the great hall.

Sir Hubert, sober, received a warning glance from Heloise, who sat with a distaff by the fire, and cleared his throat. "I know the king has given you his good lordship, Dudley, but have a care. Old Rushden has been boasting that his son is high in Buckingham's favor."

"Bah! That incompetent," Ballaster muttered, careful that none of the servants would hear him. He took a goblet of wine from Dionysia and sipped it irritably.

"Ah, but you don't run foul of any great lord in this life, unless you haven't a sparrow's fart of doing otherwise. Cut your cloth, Dudley, to match your arm. As to young Rushden, we might give him a beating yet, I daresay."

"Heloise would not like you to do that, sir." Dionysia darted a look at her sister.

"Go to, Didie!" Heloise shifted painfully. The truth of her caller's identity had been beaten out of her and she regretted her treachery. She would not forget that Miles Rushden had braved the bees to speak with her.

"Ha, never tell me you found something to pity in the pock-marked scoundrel," scoffed her father. "Offer to mend his face with fennel juice, did you? Pah, women! Didn't he threaten to strip away your tassets and take his belt to you at Potters Field?"

Heloise looked away, with a prayer of thanks that the bees had stung Miles Rushden—and would they please set upon her father.

"Stop worrying, you goose." Dionysia slid her arms fondly about her sister's neck. "This serpent of yours is shortly returning to his duke. In three days' time he leaves for Wales. He told me so himself. I have my skills at extracting useful information from unsuspecting men," she added with a purr.

"Now there is meat for the digestion." Sir Dudley's eyes were gleaming of a sudden with malicious interest.

The room blurred, their voices faded as Heloise felt the pain and anger of a roped creature. She saw their enemy lying face-down between the ruts of a stony road with blood upon his temple. "Jesu mercy," she whispered, needing air. Her father was destined to kill Miles Rushden.

Heedless of the cold, of her silken slippers, useless against the stony ground, she rushed out the door and across the courtyard to rest her cheek against the cold bark of the birch tree that grew there. Her breath was vapor, her tears like tiny moonstones. Above her was a dark sky with its sprinkling of silver tapers in the heavens.

"Take him away," she whispered to the faery folk. "You must! Please!"

Five

It was an ambush—a rope taut across the bridle track at fetlock height. His man Dobbe, catching it first, went crashing down in a thrash of hooves. Miles glimpsed it too late to draw rein. All he could do was spur Traveller across the ditch alongside the road to avoid the harm. A branch grazed his temple but his horse staggered as a dozen masked rogues rose whooping from the undergrowth to drag him from the saddle. It took effort to roll free but he managed to cause havoc with his dagger, sending one of the ruffians to his Maker, but there must have been a half dozen still coming at him like hunting dogs while the others scrambled up to attack his men. Swords and pikes forced him back into the gully. Ditchwater lapped his toes, mud sucked at his heels, and grasping weeds tentacled his spurs. Before he could draw his sword, a net of thick rope fell across his shoulders. Half-blinded, he gave a roar of fury, thrashing out as they hauled him to the road. A fist drove into his belly and he staggered, bent double.

"Mind his valuables!" bawled someone.

"Aye and have a care to his face, remember," cautioned someone.

"The Devil's been there before us by the look of him." A cruel hand grabbed his hair and jerked his head back. "There's more holes in this 'ere face than a coney warren, and no mending neither."

A vicious blow caught him beneath the jaw and the world disappeared.

By the time his wits recovered, his head was slapping against a horse's sweating flank like a loose stirrup and there was a rag stuffed in his mouth. When they yanked away the musty hood covering his face, it was the glittering windows of Bramley, reflecting the dying sun, which mocked him. The chimneys with smoky tendrils might have been the sulphurous oozing caves of Satan's demesne and Sir Dudley, laughing fiendishly at him from the doorway, could have been the Lord of Wickedness himself. In the stables Miles was hauled from the horse, and the gag yanked out, but before he could demand news of his men, a bucket of water slapped him straight in the face and he was locked into a small whitewashed room.

Icy water rivulets ran down beneath his camlet shirt as Miles slammed his hands against the door, calling down curses and yelling until he was hoarse and could shout no more. Finally he subsided against the wall and sank to the floor, his bruised body shuddering, his arms across his breast like a wobbly St. Andrew's cross. A candle flickering upon a narrow table lured him to struggle to his feet and stretch out frozen fingers to its timid warmth. Beside the table legs sat a ewer and napkins, and lying across a small bench were dry clothes. He ignored both. Mud clung to his ripped hose and his doublet was soaking and filthy but he would be damned if he would cooperate.

Someone was rasping open the doorbolt. Miles swung round, his hand going instinctively for his missing dagger. A curtain of grizzled hair valanced his visitor's bald dome, settling in hanks across massive shoulders and framing a florid face that hinted at a surfeit of feasting—the giant he had glimpsed in the village. Flabby lips grinned amiably down at him. "I am Sir Hubert Amory." Of the siege at Nancy. Miles stayed unimpressed. "Ha!" the colossus exclaimed, withdrawing his hands from behind his back to wave a wine jug and two goblets. "Thought you might have a thirst on you, young man." He swaggered unsteadily over to the bench, set the jug on the table, pushed the clothing to one side, and plonked himself down as if he were about to carouse in a tavern. "Not ready then?" he asked, filling the goblets with a generous hand.

"Ready? For *what?*"

Before Miles could grab him by the lapels, the old man

whipped out his dagger with a surprising swiftness for a drunkard. "Style not to your taste? I should hate to see you brought low by the cold, my boy. Nigh killed his grace the king last winter." Miles dazedly watched the tip of the rondel run adroitly beneath an already clean nail. "It is like this, Sir Miles: you can wash and dress yourself in clean raiment or we shall do it the faster way—empty a few more pails of water over you until you sniffle yourself into compliance. Or is your lordship waiting for servants to help you? That can be done, too. They are a bit rough but they will peel you mother naked quicker than a dog can piss."

"Get out!"

"No, my boy, I am sitting right here until you decide which way it is going to be."

Miles furiously began unlooping the buttons of his ruined doublet. "I do not know what game your master is—"

"Friend, lad. Sir Dudley is a friend and I owe him the favor to have you nice and clean with no more trouble. Nearly fought you at Potters Field, it seems, but I drank too much. Castilian soap there, lad, in the dish, and a jar of some sweet-smelling stink for you to swill over yourself if you've a mind to it. Where was I? Oh aye, poor little Heloise. I would never have got myself drunk as a lord if I had realized what would happen. Doing this for her. She really takes this family honor rather hard. But it is not the clothes that make the man—or the woman either. Values, my boy. Values!"

"If that is the case," muttered Miles, untethering his sodden hose before he shed the rest of his garments, "I wonder you keep company with the likes of Ballaster."

"Go back a long way, we do. He paid my debts and gave me a roof over my head again. I was drunk in the gutter every nigh—"

"Spare me the minutiae!"

"When did you have the small pocks, lad?" the older man asked as if it were a mutually agreeable topic.

"Two years ago," Miles muttered sullenly, toweling himself dry. His ruined face was not a subject that he liked to discuss with anyone, let alone this old bibbler. He had come to terms with his appearance; what others made of him was their affair. With an oath, he pulled on the fine lawn shirt and Holland drawers then sat down, scowling, to negotiate the woolen hose. One leg was scarlet, the other blue, a fashion he detested.

"That's what I mean, my boy." The dagger waved in the air for emphasis. "You are the same man beneath the skin whether scarred or no. Pretty, were you?"

"God keep me, would you just—" Miles buried his foul language in a gulp of surprisingly good wine before he slid his arms into the gypon.

The old man chuckled and lapsed into silence, watching him as he tied his points fore and back and stood to secure the rest of the laces. The unpleasant daffodilly doublet Ballaster had provided barely fastened across Miles's breast but the velvet was of good quality. The popel trim, castbotons, and satin panels were overdone. The sleeves could have been somewhat longer, but, feeling more civilized, he tugged down the gathered shirt cuffs and knotted the laces of the embroidered Rennes collar. Still cold, he was glad of the cote. Its split sleeves hung to knee level in a froth of summer squirrel fur.

"Satisfied?"

"Oh, very splendid. You could pass for a servant at the court of Il Magnifico himself or even for a lord at Windsor. Try the hat."

Miles snatched up the ruby velvet cap. A brooch weighted the liripipe that hung down the side to chin level.

Sir Hubert opened the door and held up Miles's riding boots. The clean leather reflected the candlelight; the spurs had been removed.

Miles pulled them on and felt restored; now he might have some chance of escape. "What is this foolery?" He gestured to the abundance of satin songbirds festooning his breast. "Am I to be released from a flampayne pie to sing to Ballaster's daughters?"

"Never thought of that," chuckled the old man, scratching his neck. He still kept his dagger in his other hand. "He is ready, my lads!" he announced to whoever waited beyond the door. A horn was sounded in the yard.

Ready for what?

WAS IT HELL OR ELYSIUM THAT AWAITED HIM? HE WONDERED as the doors of the great hall were thrust open before him. Viol and shawms burbled unheeded in a corner; the dark red floor tiles shone with a patina that told of recent cleansing; and the pleasing smell of charring pinecones was laced with the delicious aroma of suckling pig, which wafted from the kitchen passageway to pluck at Miles's appetite. Above his head, a wooden chandelier, as large as a cartwheel, sent candlelight capering over the high, beamed ceiling and dancing upon the long, mullioned windows. Decorating the great fireplace mantel and embarrassing all the shields, which neatly surmounted crossed swords at intervals along the whitewashed walls, were the cursed Ballaster arms— no doubt newly acquired at great expense—three industrious-looking bees. Miles glared. They should have been rampant with their stings out.

On three sides of the hall, the tables were draped in white cloths and set for feasting. The servants, still arranging salvers and carving knives upon the sideboards, cast covert glances at their master's prisoner, who was beginning to have some sympathy with a Christmas goose smelling the heat of the oven. A door briefly opened to the solar above the wooden balustrade, loosening the sounds of female laughter and a waft of steamy air that hinted at baths seductive with rose and lavender. Miles, resplendent in clothes he had not chosen, began to perspire in his finery.

"Rushden, welcome." Striding from a chamber at the tower end of the hall, Sir Dudley glittered fulsomely, every sumptuary law defiled; the jeweled buttons on the old rooster's mustard demi-gown would have bought two destriers. If Ballaster was so rich, why did he need Bramley except to prate that he owned a castle? He could have built himself one in fashionable brick as the king's chamberlain, Lord Hastings, had done at Kirby Muxloe. "It is an honor for us to entertain a man so high in the esteem of the noble Duke of Buckingham." Sarcasm sauced the courtesy.

Entertain? And what was he supposed to do in return? His belly growling with hunger, Miles ignored the proffered hand but took the goblet that was brought to him. His host tapped his own full winecup gently against it. Miles smiled, drank it to the dregs, and hurled it at the nearest Ballaster arms. It deposited a small dribble of Bordeaux upon the shield, fell with a clang, and disappeared between the table legs.

"You have an excellent aim. We shall feast soon," exclaimed Sir Dudley. The grin beneath the beaked hat stretched with inexplicable affability, considering his guest's ill manners. "But weightier matters first. This way, Sir Miles."

There was little choice but to be shown into what appeared to be a counting room. Several manor rolls were propped in a corner as if they had been quickly tidied off the table to make room for the contract pinioned down upon the baize cloth.

"You will sign this, please, Sir Miles." A command, not a request. "It gives you Bramley as my daughter's dower."

Dear God, his misgivings were right. They did not want to geld him; they wanted to marry him. Christ Almighty, he could not let this upstart destroy his future, or wreck the alliance with Rhys ap Thomas. Incredulous that he—the Duke of Buckingham's right hand—should find himself in such a predicament, Miles squared his shoulders and stared down patronizingly at his captor. "You jest, man."

Sir Hubert and several others of the Ballaster affinity had crowded into the chamber behind him. Miles stared at them as if they were creatures of a nightmare. Could he have fallen from his horse and cracked his skull? Christ help him, he must get out of here. He had his life's plans already drawn. "I am not marrying into your accursed family," he asserted loudly. "Bear witness, all of you!"

"Did a mouse squeak?" guffawed someone at the back.

Since Sir Dudley was bantam-sized, Miles made full use of his superior height to menace him. "Do your worst, little man," he sneered and swung round to address them all. "It is against the laws of England to force any man or woman of constant character to marry against their will. *Primus,* I am already betrothed"—an exaggeration, but never mind—"*secundus,* any marriage made at swordpoint can be annulled in a church court; *tertius,* no banns have been called on three successive Sundays or holy days; *quartus,* there has to be a willing bride; and—"

"Firstly," interrupted Ballaster, "I prefer to use English when I am talking business. *Firstly,* if you had been here you would have heard the banns being called on three consecutive days. Granted, they were not Sundays, but they were called before sufficient witnesses. Secondly, the bride will be here at any instant; thirdly, any marriage that is consummated is valid and this one will be; fourthly—"

Dear God, was there a full moon or were his brains addled? Would he wake up from this nightmare sane and happy in his bed? Surely they could not make this valid!

"Marry one of your breeding?" Miles scoffed. "I should like to be assured of a bride who is likely to bear me sons not daughters." Within an instant he grabbed Sir Dudley, wrenching his arm behind his back, and drew the man's jeweled dagger. The sharp steel edge pressed dangerously against the aging skin. "Release my men and bring them here!" he snarled at the old giant.

"So nice in manners," commented his host with a smile, holding very still. "Sir Hubert, my dear fellow, pray tell our men to slit the throats of this lordling's men and convey the bodies in a cart to the highway."

Sir Hubert hesitated as he reached the threshold. "Pity. They seem fine fellows and loyal withal." It was not a bluff. A half score of men stood between Miles and the door. Escape was futile. With an oath, Miles flung his prisoner at the human barricade and hurled himself after him but his blade went flying. Strong arms viciously thrust him back before Sir Dudley, and a goose-feather quill was pushed between his reluctant fingers.

"Shall I tell you where to put this?" bawled Miles, breaking free and flinging it skiddling across the parchment.

"Young man, I am offering you what your lord father covets. It will end the feud between us."

"No," snarled Miles, finding it hard to think in a straight line with the heat and the wine befuddling him. Eyes watched him on all sides with unconcealed menace.

"Oh, this grows tedious," muttered his host. "Let him sign it in the morning. The *perche en foile* will be overdone and the sauces cold if we delay much longer. Bring him to the chapel."

Chapel! Miles grabbed the candlestick and set fire to the contract.

The retainers seized his cuffs and ankles. It took all their strength to force him sideways and get his kicking limbs beyond the doorway before they could carry him—spread-eagled like a traitor about to be drawn and quartered—out into the courtyard. He was set down clumsily on his feet before the priest on the chapel doorstep. They had to hold him upright now, his mind was reeling so.

"Where is the bride?" roared Sir Dudley. "The wench will be feasting on dried bread if she delays much longer."

The tasteless merriment of tabors broke upon the night air; the musicians danced their way out across the torchlit yard, followed by the beautiful daughter garlanded in flowers. For an instant the man in Miles was not displeased. Was this his bride? The girl stopped before him with a fulsome curtsy, blonde hair floating in a golden cloud. No! This mare would have to be kept in a costly stable and exercised in blinkers on a short rein. The wench gave him a dazzling smile and stepped aside.

An angry, defiant Heloise Ballaster appeared behind her,

flanked by two little girls bearing silken flowers. Pale and straight as a lily she stood, the centers of her eyes large, dark, and wild like a night creature's. They were going to handfast him to a sorceress.

"No!" exclaimed Miles, turning in a hedge of steel, his mind seething like one of her beehives. "God's mercy, no!"

"Come on, Heloise!" bawled Ballaster and hauled her forward.

The girl was rigid and a trace of tears still lingered on one cheek. For an instant, pity clouded Miles's thoughts and his gaze touched lips he had not yet tasted and slid to her graceful neck and the shimmer of breasts where a samite bodice sewn with pearls tantalized him to unclothe her with his imagining.

She was putting a spell on him again. Why was her hair not loosened like her sister's, like a bride's, to proclaim her virginity? Why was it cauled in a jeweled net with the garland of gold leaf blossom lapping her forehead?

Miles struggled to keep his sanity. "I am . . . am . . . not playing the cuckold, Ballaster. You cannot foist your daughter's by-blow onto me."

The words jabbed her. The girl lifted her face, her eyes wide with shame, and backed away horrified into a wall of servants.

Ballaster grabbed her by the wrist and thrust her towards Miles. "Accuse me of what you will, young man, but not that. It is you who have amends to make. You think this marriage forced upon you? It is done to make good your betrayal of my daughter's honor. You took her maidenhead at Potters Field and then three days ago you had the insolence to come and ravish her in my orchard."

"No!" thundered Miles but he faced a peacock's tail of accusing faces. "On what evidence?"

It had been merely an instant that he had been alone with her in the hovel and Godsakes, she had been clothed in steel. As for the orchard? He frowned, his right hand trying to find his aching temple, turning his head with effort to outstare the hazel gaze that fixed him now, remembering the soft body that fell upon his, the hum of the bees—Could he have—

"There were witnesses, Sir Miles."

"Aye," came a chorus of some half-dozen voices. "An' there was grass stains and blood upon her skirts."

"No, no." Miles rubbed his hand across his forehead. "This— this is utter fab-fabrication. M-mistress, have you no voice?" The girl wretchedly glanced towards her father but the face she turned on Miles was like our Lady's, fair, compassionate, and silent, only her eyes compelled him, willing him. To what?

He dragged his gaze away to reason with the onlookers. "How much is he paying you for such lies?" Swaying, he swung round on his captor. "Will you kick these poor wretches from your door if they do not dance to your piping? Is there no one here who is not venal?" His voice grew louder in desperation as he turned to the chapel door. "Chaplain, upon your immortal soul, I beg you, bring out the Gospels and I shall swear I never ravished her. Lady! Tell them for the love of God!"

Heloise shook, her bare shoulders turning to gooseflesh in the freezing air. She stood dazed and weak, as if her father's fingers, iron around her flesh, were all that held her upright. She had been threatened with the rod and, despite Dionysia's attempt to smuggle her food, had received no sustenance save watery ale and a little bread for three whole days. The wine she had foolishly accepted just before coming down the stairs was dousing her common sense.

Was this so very wrong? Would this stranger make a worse master than her cunning father who was winding him in like a hooked fish, drawing him to land inch by inch? Oh, he was fine and lordly, her bridegroom, the borrowed splendor glinting in the torchlight. Better living than dead upon the road, but she saw the dried blood beading the graze upon his brow and felt the breath of destiny. She knew the full fury in Miles Rushden and that it would spill over, scalding her.

"Lady, tell them!"

The kindly shadows hid the dints in Rushden's face and she

glimpsed how handsome he had been—the high-boned cheeks and lordly, angular features declared an illustrious Norman ancestry—too good for her, despite her mother's noble blood. No, this was not the match she had envisaged for herself—a miserable marriage made within a circle of bared steel.

"I c-cannot marry Sir Miles, Father, a-against his will."

"Lady." Her bridegroom's voice was a purr of thanks, the anger briefly scabbarded.

Her father only laughed. "See how he plays my daughter like a lute."

Heloise closed her eyes, her spirit screaming with disgust. She wanted to flee from the despot who had sired her, and seize whatever rope of escape was flung to her. But not this way! Not by spoiling this young man's future. This was folly! Yoke herself to an enemy, one who already despised her for her merchant blood, a man who would use the good lordship of the Duke of Buckingham to annul the marriage instantly? No! For where would that leave her? Neither maid nor wife, her honor questionable, her name a scandal. Oh, she should not have detained this stranger in the orchard, she should have conducted him to her father's presence and spoken to him before witnesses.

Her eyes snapped open as fingers, compelling and powerful, curled about hers. "Lady, you must swear to the chaplain that I never defiled you!" Miles Rushden drew her so close, he could have easily kissed her mouth. "Swear it!" As if he felt her trembling in his grasp, his voice gentled, "Dear God, mistress, the bees would have stung me to death if I had laid one finger on you." They were almost breast to breast. The charm was momentary, dangerous, and Heloise, not yet loved and tried in the tournaments of the solar and bedchamber, experienced the unexpected, unreasonable stirring of sensuality.

"How can you do this?" she exclaimed to her father, shaking herself free from the brief mental enslavement, although the man still held her and she felt the burning pressure of his fingertips and the strength of the mind behind the eyes that compelled her gaze. She could not help but look up at him again. Moistening her lips nervously, she sought out the courage she needed. *Stand up for yourself,* Margery Huddleston had warned her.

"Be at ease, Sir Miles. I will not have you!"

"Thank you." Satisfied, he let her go instantly.

"Heloise!" Her father grabbed her. How many years of tyranny were within that one breath? Roped by their hands, bowed down by fate, Heloise tried to pull free from both and run, but she was threatened with disinheritance and Dudley Ballaster's threats were shafts that always found their mark.

Miles knew he had lost. He read the despair in her eyes. The little knight, for all her bravery the other day, was frightened of her father.

"I—I want her examined." He folded his arms haughtily but inside he had never felt so helpless in his life. "It will prove she is a maid." It was his final bid, a last coin of reason to be tossed upon the table.

The girl gasped, trying to free herself, but her father's smile was nasty. "As you wish, Sir Miles. Examine her yourself."

"No," exclaimed the wench, blanching even paler with fury and outrage. "I shall not permit—"

"Be quiet, girl, can you not see our guest is worried that we may close the door on the pair of you and accuse him afresh? Well, lad, our repast grows cold but if—"

Heloise Ballaster, with a quick twist of wrist, broke free, her breathing fast. "Chaplain, I beg you—" She flung herself on her knees on the step before the priest, her palms in supplication.

"My son," the chaplain asked Miles, "*were* you alone in the woodcutter's hut with this young woman?"

"Yes, but . . . only for an instant."

"Pah, more than that," said someone.

"And were you or were you not alone in the orchard with Mistress Heloise, sir?"

" 'Ad 'er on the snow, 'e did," chirped in another unwelcome voice.

"Yes, but again—"

"Again, indeed. My son, I sincerely advise you to do the right deed by the young woman you have carnally known, especially as her father is agreeable to the match and has offered you the disputed manors for her dowry. Let us proceed."

"What did you tell your father? That I raped you among the bee skeps?" Rushden's lip was drawn back in a snarl. "What did it take? A small cut and a few drops of blood upon your petticoat?"

Heloise struggled to rise but her father had her by the shoulder. "Stay where you are, daughter!"

"Kneel down, my son." Miles folded his arms and stood there, his chin raised. "Kneel, lad!" A well-aimed boot slammed into the back of his knees and he found himself on his hands and knees, wincing in pain. A gloved hand grabbed him by the hair and hauled him into a kneeling position.

"Good lad," whispered Sir Dudley and a dagger pricked the skin beneath his chin.

The chaplain swiftly read out the question but Miles kept silent.

"There are plenty more ways to make you say the right words," whispered his determined father-in-law. "We could slice your horse's fetlocks and make sure your servants go shriven to Heaven before morning. Satan got your tongue, lad? Say it!"

The words were pricked out of him. A huge roar of laughter buffeted him and Sir Dudley let him go. The chaplain quickly demanded the bride's answer.

"Agree to this, mistress," Miles threatened the shivering girl beside him, "and you shall think yourself wedded with Lucifer himself."

"Do you think me a fool?" she ground out, her breath uneven.

The priest, becoming annoyed and peevish, repeated the words for the bride a third time. The crowd held their breath.

Heloise stared stubbornly ahead, but someone gave her soles a hefty kick and as she jolted forward, her lips parted to protest, and a voice said swiftly, *"Ego te vole habere—"* A cheer went up. Dionysia had her fingers across her lips as she leaned down to adjust her sister's dress. "You will thank me later," she whispered.

Her reluctant bridegroom was struggling to rise in fury but her father set a firm hand upon his shoulder.

"Repeat that," said the chaplain, nodding to Heloise, his eyes darting behind her warningly at Dionysia.

Heloise's head jerked up. If Didie spoke the promise, did it mean that Rushden would be married to her?

"Heloise," warned her father, his voice heavy with threat.

"Heloise, please," whispered Dionysia.

Her mind was whirling rapidly. There must be no question which sister this man had married. No legal wranglings. Dionysia's future must be safeguarded. With such beauty, her sister could marry a wealthy, powerful Yorkist lord.

Heloise's voice was clear and unfaltering when she finally obeyed:

"I will have thee, Miles, as my husband for the rest of my life and do hereby plight my troth . . ."

The man beside her cursed. "You shall regret this. Upon my soul, you will!" His wrist was grabbed ungently and his hand was guided forcibly to place a ring on her fourth finger.

"It shall be annulled, never fear," she whipped back. "I have as little pleasure in this as you."

They were pushed into the chapel for one of the fastest masses Miles had ever heard. This household was not only corrupt, it was almost godless.

"Bring on the bride ale!" exclaimed Sir Hubert, as they hauled across to the hall. Some optimistic fool flung a green garland about Miles's neck. He ripped it away.

Heloise, who had once attended a wedding at Middleham where the bridegroom had tenderly kissed the bride through a garland, felt deprived of all earthly joy. A trothcup was brought to her new lord. The wine must be welcome to his ebbing spirits though not the manner of it. Rushden raised it mockingly to salute her.

"To your perdition, sweeting!" he said, and dashed its contents in her face.

Six

"You will thank me for this one day."

Heloise, shrinking from her father's voice, found her chair surrounded by the household women hovering excitedly, like agitated butterflies, to escort her beyond the solar to the best bedchamber. It was a relief to quit the company of the silent man who had been seated beside her through the feast but a torment knowing that they would shortly haul him struggling up the stairs and thrust him into bed with her. She remained seated, staring unseeing at the delicacies on the bridal platter that neither she nor Rushden had touched. Her body was sticky where the red wine thrust at her had made shameful rivulets upon her gown and run like blood between her breasts. The musicians began the erotic shivalee with its sensuous drumming.

"Heloise, come," urged Dionysia, bending over her shoulder.

"Oh, why did you do this, Didie?"

"Because it is the only way of escape and I love you too much to leave you here," her sister responded quietly. More loudly, Dionysia exclaimed, "Come, all is ready for you."

"I will see you in Purgatory, sweetheart," Rushden told her, breaking his silence. His dark-fringed eyes were furious, his smile icy, as he rose to his feet.

Uncertain whether he intended to privily murder her or discover some other torment to feed his revenge, Heloise lifted her chin. "I should prefer to go to Hell alone."

"Oh, take 'em both up," exclaimed her father. "I've had a bellyful of his sour manners." He eyed the untouched food with miserly regret. "Set the platter in their chamber. Mayhap, son Rushden, you will have an appetite on you after you have played the man."

Rushden's fist missed her father's jaw by a whisker and the

sole of his boot sent the board from its trestles, heaving the huge salt, the platters, and the goblets. The dogs rushed at the tumbled repast and the hall rose in consternation.

Gulping back tears, Heloise took to her heels and ran up the stairs. She grabbed the wooden bar behind the solar door and tried to set it across before the others could reach her but her little sisters ducked in beneath it, giggling.

"Oh, what is the use," Heloise cried in despair at the huge human torrent bearing Rushden towards her like a hapless log. "No, please!" she cried as Dionysia pushed her backwards into their father's bedchamber. His splendid bed, with its green tasseled celure and David and Bathsheba frolicking on the costly tester, was now a torture. Quilted silk pillows made her tremble.

"Tame him. Bell him," purred Dionysia.

"Take off his horns and stroke his tail," giggled someone else as the women surrounded their victim, plucking at her belt and kneeling to untie her garters and roll down her stockings. Was this what it felt like to be attacked by carrion birds?

"Where is his tail, then?"

Someone hushed her youngest sister.

Leading the male procession, the chaplain stepped in to sprinkle holy water on the sheets and her new husband was carried awkwardly through the doorway like an unloaded coffer and set up beside the wooden bedstairs. Outside on the wooden landing, Matillis lingered, wringing her hands, and the minstrels fiddled frantically.

Sir Dudley pointed a finger at the bridegroom. "Remember, you are not setting foot outside this chamber until the marriage is consummated."

Rushden laughed. "If I have enjoyed your daughter already, as you allege, then this"—he waved a hand to the bed—"is quite unnecessary."

"Oh, I applaud your clever tongue, lad, but I like to see things through."

"Have you not meddled enough, Father?" exclaimed Heloise

from the circle of women, slapping their hands away.

Her parent ignored her, standing at the foot of the bed like a tourney marshal while Rushden's escort, bruised and black-eyed, grabbed at the man's clothing as if they were enemy soldiers robbing a dying commander of his armor. Heloise's assailants recommenced their task as if it were a race.

"Make sure they are mother naked," Sir Dudley chivvied, rubbing his hands gleefully. "Then let us see if a Rushden stallion can mount a Ballaster mare. Into bed with 'em."

Miles was shoved alone between the sheets; the girl had not yet arrived there. Between the moving rout of skirts and sleeves assailing her, he momentarily glimpsed a slender waist which gracefully flared into white hips that beckoned touching, and, below, a pale shimmer of narrow heel and shapely calf. The corner cressets were stifled and the chamber dimmed as they plucked off her headdress. The bed glinted, like an altar betwixt two candles, and he waited for the priestess. Fair like her sister, he thought at first, regretting that he dared not run his fingers across that silken skin, and then he blinked in disbelief as they pushed her backwards to the bed. The girl's hair was grey. Like the Loathly Lady! He had been bewitched and wed to an old woman. Primeval superstition quickened his heart.

"No, I will not bed a witch!" he roared, crossing himself and struggling to quit the bed. "By sweet Christ, Ballaster, is this the only way you can find a man to mate with her? I will not bed a witch."

There was a gasp of horror and a dreadful, ugly silence followed as if a spell had frozen every one of them to stone. Appalled at himself, Miles wished he might scrape the words back up but they lingered on the air like the appalling stink of vomit. The woman's silver head turned. With relief and disbelief he saw that the complexion framed by the aged hair was still delicate and tender but her look of tormented fury slashed him like a whip. He recoiled against the pillows, remembering the hushed whispers of his childhood that Jacquetta Woodville had bewitched

King Edward, lured him to the forest, and forced him to marry her eldest daughter when by rights he should have wed a foreign princess. And now it was happening to him.

The body of a siren, but her hair . . . The witch-girl had turned and was gazing at her sire in horror, unaware that the moonlight curtain of her hair had parted and a taut breast was jutting through. This was enchantment indeed, subtle, enticing; Miles's spellbound gaze drank in her beauty like a thirsty man, enjoying the indulgence for a fleeting, lustful moment. Each curve was deliciously seductive; the tips of her unnatural hair, which hid her womanly parts, beckoned his eyes. He felt his own senses responding and reasserted control over his instincts, knowing that Ballaster was watching him like a smug magician, confident that he would be bewitched enough to slide between her thighs before the dawn.

Heloise saw the fear and contempt in Rushden's stare grow hot with lusty interest and with a gasp realized that every man in the room was leering. She could only set trembling arms across her body and lower her head so that her hateful hair at least hid their faces from her. Her anger spent, she was shivering from the growing chill and trembling at the burning desire that flickered in Rushden's eyes. Not until now had she believed that he might actually lie with her.

With an effort, Miles forced himself to look away and sensed the ancient fear stalking through the men. Carnal desire and superstition writhed in the very air. Christ have mercy, what demons had he released? How long had the girl been hiding her fey hair from the men? The sea of suspicious faces needed to be calmed. He would not wish a woodpile lit beneath Heloise Ballaster.

It was an effort to coax his mouth into a semblance of humor. "My, Ballaster, a pretty changeling, then, if not a witch. Did your wife sleep in a toadstool ring the night your daughter was conceived?"

God's rood, worse and worse! Now he was labeling her mother

a whore who had frolicked with an elfish lover, and gluing cuckold's horns on Ballaster's forehead.

"Set back the covers. Daughter, get into bed." Ballaster's cheeks were dark, his voice terse. One of the old besoms clucked approval at Miles as the sheet was whipped away from him and the bawdy gests began to restore normality. The magician was not smiling. Miles felt Sir Dudley's derisive stare note the recent bruising. Hardly any pock scars spoilt his body. "Hail damage, sweet knight," his previous mistress had teased between kisses. It had only been his face that he had deliberately marred in guilt and anguish.

"My daughter's body is unblemished, as you have so thoroughly observed for yourself, Rushden." Miles swallowed at the just accusation. "I warrant her hair is uncommon but she would not have been able to stomach the mass if she practiced the black arts. As to her mother's honor, slander that further and I will score through my daughter's dowry. Now set your naked leg against my girl's! *Do it!*"

Cursing, Miles eased himself sideways and touched anklebone and calf against his witch. He felt her shudder as if he had burnt her.

"Bear witness, all of you, that their naked flesh has touched. This is the way of handling royal weddings by proxy," Ballaster told the gawking household before he flung the bedclothes back. Everyone applauded, ignoring the swift jerk beneath the covers as the protagonists moved apart.

"Leave us! Go!" Heloise grabbed the sheet and swiftly drew it to her collarbone. "Go!"

The chaplain stepped forward and gave them a very hurried blessing, with an extra one for Heloise's fertility, much to her annoyance.

"That's done, then. Bring away the bridegroom's clothes, you ribalds." Sir Dudley jerked his head at Dionysia to gather up her sister's tumbled gown. "Now remember, lad, you are not going from this bedchamber until you have performed your husbandly duty and, daughter, you will behave like a good obedient wife. Acknowledge this man as your lord from now on and do your duty to please him. Attend to her, young man, and beget your heir. I want a grandson."

Rushden lunged forward, fist clenched, but her father, stepping back, merely laughed. "You grow predictable, young fellow," he scoffed. He waited until everyone had trooped out the door, except Sir Hubert, who lingered to blow Heloise a kiss and bow nobly to Rushden before her father pushed him out and, following him, loudly locked the door.

Heloise's cheeks flamed. Must she succumb like a meek slave to a man who had threatened to beat her for putting on armor and loudly labeled her a whore and her mother a harlot? Never! She had a little courage left—save, her body was shaking now, beyond her control—but, Jesu mercy, she now feared this stranger who had been given lordship over her.

Wrapping himself in silence, Rushden attempted to draw up the coverlet but it was woven of stiff metal threads and heavy brocade. With a curse, he slid out of bed. Heloise yelped in surprise as he yanked the unbleached blanket from her, draping it round him like a bishop's cope. Then he strode across to the small table.

"Are you hungry?" The nonthreatening, commonplace inquiry made her realize that she had been holding her breath. Her body lost some of its rigidity.

"Yes," she whispered, catching hold of the words tossed to rescue her temporarily, wondering if she could wriggle out of bed, taking the sheet with her.

"Stay there. I will bring the platter across." A sensible solution but hardly reassuring. She felt tethered like a bait, wondering if this Rushden mastiff might take a bite out of her at any minute.

He set the plate between them and hoicked himself up onto the bed again, carefully keeping a fold of the blanket across his thighs. The rest of his covering was permitted to fall. Heloise peeped sideways, aware of arm muscles that would take more than her two hands to encompass and a broad triangle of back, which had stretched the borrowed doublet at the seams. Strong, elegant hands tore off a piece of bread and set a slab of cheese upon it. He took a mouthful hungrily, his fine white teeth tearing the crust free before his stare rose from the silver platter to examine her and he drew the back of his hand across his lips.

Clutching her sheet firmly, Heloise reached out for a Lenten tartlet. Its casing was sticky but it smelt divine to her starved senses and she suppressed the temptation to attack it ravenously. They ate in silence. The nourishment restored her spirits and she stole a covert glance at her new husband's profile. Instinct told her the hate lit by her father had abated somewhat. The gentleness of the candlelight hid the scars on his cheek and showed her a face of strength that might have graced Camelot or Aix, but his strong chin and hawk-beaked nose unnerved her, and the stubborn edge to his mouth she knew already. And she had vexed his ambitions.

Yes, Holy Church had linked them, making her his property for eternity unless he found the legal means to unlock the invisible chains from both their wrists. But that was for tomorrow. It was the hours of darkness stretching before her now that made Heloise anxious. She had been given to this stranger, like the repast that lay between them, to enjoy or disdain as he pleased. A stranger, albeit no ancient creature with December skin and foul breath, but a man who knew more of women than she did of men.

She licked her fingers thoughtfully. At least her hunger was not so great now. A small sigh of satisfaction escaped her and her companion paused in his own eating and looked at her for the first time that night without being disagreeable or stern.

"This can be annulled." His words were reassuring but his fingers reached out and lifted some strands of her hair, testing the texture.

"I—I am not a witch," she told him at last, her voice husky, sounding foreign to her hearing.

"No? How disappointing." A slow smile lit his face, his steel grey eyes teasing her tortured senses. He let her hair fall but it seemed a long moment before he looked to the platter and selected a sweet pastry. Heloise's heart was drumming with ill speed.

"I thought you much younger at Potters Field." That, she supposed, was the nearest she would receive to an apology.

"I am almost twenty."

A frown tempered his amazement. "I thought the blonde maid was the eldest. And you are still unwed?" he continued. "Why? Because of your hair?" He watched her fingertips tangle themselves in the silken silver threads against her cheek.

"I had no desire to wed. You or any other." That did not please him. Did witches wed? At least married women covered their hair. Some urge arose—a desire to reassure him that she would keep her hair hidden so as not to shame him—but the words died on her lips. There would be no future with him. She watched the blanket trail behind him as he left her to stride across to the wine jug. Yes, he would leave.

He filled the goblets set out for them, not asking her will but making the decision for her in husbandly fashion. "It will restore you," he told her, bringing the winecup across.

"Yes," sighed Heloise, and drew it to her lips. She watched above its rim as he lifted his.

"We have a dilemma, you and I, mistress," he said eventually and emptied the vessel far too rapidly. Agile thoughts flickered like tapers behind the alert gaze, his body tense and purposeful as he ran a thumb across the goblet's smooth perimeter.

"What do you suggest, sir? That I change you into a sparrow so you can fly out the window?"

Rushden's eyes glimmered wryly. "Witty but not very practical—if you are not a witch, that is." A wave of laughter from downstairs mocked them. "We are both resolved on annulling this marriage. Is it possible?"

Was the wine abusing her senses further? "Yes, of course, sir, if you petition his holiness the Pope straightway, and I imagine that his grace of Buckingham would—" And she must write to his grace of Gloucester.

He was holding up a hand to silence her. "Lady, I do not mean that. Believe me, I shall do everything within my power. What I meant was—" He looked about the room as if the mislaid words had rolled beneath a cupboard. "What I need to know is, are you a virgin?"

Her cheeks burned. "What if I say no?" A spontaneous verbal thrust, revenge for his earlier insults! The reckless reply snuffed out the goodwill in him. His gaze coldly apprised of his response and she felt her breathing grow uneven.

"Then we shall grow old together in mutual hate."

"I might be lying."

"You might be lying, yes, either way." Then he added, "Mistress, I have said some very hateful things in your presence. You are intelligent enough to understand why. Can we at least be honest with each other for a little space?"

Of course, Miles decided, he could put her to the test, hold her wrists against the pillow above her head and discover the answer. What, and come near ravishing her? No, touching must be avoided at all costs and he meant her no harm. As if she read his thoughts, the girl slid a hand beneath the sheet and withdrew a rondel dagger, which she must have hidden earlier beneath the mattress or bribed a servant to do.

"Lay a hand upon me and I will make a eunuch of you," she snarled, then spoilt the effect by adding in astonishment, "Why do you laugh at me?"

Knotting the wretched blanket tighter, he walked across to the spy hole in the wall and languidly leaned into the tiny embrasure that squinted down upon his feasting enemies. "Not drunk enough, I fear." He looked back at her across his shoulder, his mouth still twisting in amusement at the weapon in her slender fist. At least she held it properly. "What if you had lain on my side of the bed?"

The lady's lower lip quivered but her grip tightened. "I—I should have thought of some way to obtain it. Rolled on top of you and seized it that way."

Her innocence had Miles doubled with laughter. "You *are* a virgin," he asserted cheerfully, relieved that no one had defiled her, and watched her lips part in pretty indignation. "Yes, Mistress Ballaster?"

Heloise nodded sulkily, wondering how he had deduced it.

"Well, that is a relief. We shall obtain our annulment after all. You could have spared me the bother of guessing." He kicked aside his ridiculous train and tried to lecture her as if she were an army. "Now attend me, mistress. For the future, we must ensure we neither meet again nor compromise each other in any way until an annulment is received."

"And for the present?" She lifted an impertinent eyebrow. Tightening the sheet about her only emphasized her breasts as she reached out for another savory. "My father says that you will not—"

"—be given my clothes back until I have pleasured you." He served her up a roguish smile that had thieved hearts. "Yes, how do I avoid that dilemma?"

"Geld you?" teased Heloise, waving the dagger like a fan.

"Ravishing you is a sweeter prospect." A delectable proposition, if only the wench were daughter to a Welsh baron, not Ballaster's spawn. "Do you think you could put that thing back beneath your pillow? I know you enjoy the weapon in your hand but it unmans me."

"Good." Heloise grinned at Rushden as if he were a friend, but it was most unseemly behavior to speak so—especially to a man. Or could one do that with a husband? Was this what marriage could be like? If so, she rather liked the prospect. The wine must be addling her common sense, she decided, knowing that if she seduced Miles Rushden, he would probably strangle her before morning. "I think the wine is getting the better of me," she admitted, spiking a piece of cheese with the blade. "I have eaten nothing these last three days. I—I was locked in my chamber."

"I am sorry to hear it." Rushden was running his hand along the casement sill, noting the lock of the door, the thickness of the panels, eyeing the ceiling. "There has to be a way."

"Try the chest."

He threw back the lid. "I was hoping. Pah, it is all sheets and coverlets. Some of them laundered by you, judging by the blush of them!"

Heloise ignored the taunt. "We might knot them to make a rope and anchor it to the chest. I should not trust this." She shook the nearest bedpost. "We had to replace these because of woodworm and I doubt the joints would hold. Knowing my father, he will post a half dozen sentries. Could you make a skirt of sorts and pass for a woman?" The look she received was not happy.

"Upon my soul, woman, are you crazed?" Miles had forgotten her unworldiness. The solemn almond gaze questioned innocently and he clenched his jaw and turned away. His covering was loosening and he retrieved it hastily with a curse and tucked it methodically about his waist so he looked less like a younger version of Elijah and more like a villein competing in a summer sack race. The folds threatened to trip him. "Oh, the Devil take the thing!" he yelled and sat down heavily on the bed, feeling as sulky as the brother of the Prodigal Son. And then the bed threatened to heave him off.

"Mistress, what in—?"

Taking advantage of his distraction, Heloise had burrowed beneath the sheet, trying to free its ends so she might not be confined to the bed. It was no use, especially with him anchoring half of it. She struggled to turn beneath the cover and emerged bedraggled and red-faced from her exertions.

"If it is not too much trouble, sir, would you kindly loosen the sheet so I, too, may have some freedom?" He had an unholy grin, she discovered.

"Of course. Try now."

Glowering at him, she eased up the sheet, still trying to keep herself modestly covered. She sternly gestured him to turn his back.

"Is there likely to be needle and thread in the chest?" Miles asked, once her maneuvers had been completed. "You could sew me something." Now the rustling had ceased, he glanced over his shoulder to see how she had taken the suggestion. He needed her compliance and of a surety she had been trained in such skills.

"What are you expecting? A houppelande with lined sleeves?"

"A tunic?" He wore his most cajoling expression, one that had earned him a few exquisite adventures in haylofts.

"You jest. And, no, there is no needle here." She had managed to stand but the sheet was so tight about her that it hardly rendered her mobile, and he saw that the dagger had not been sheathed. It took him a swift stride and a sharp, painful twist to seize it.

"Now, mayhap, we can put it to less bloody use." He tossed it on the bed, jerked the blanket from his waist, and spread it like a cloth upon the floor. "Stand on it!"

His bride was rubbing her wrist. No doubt she would have been eyeing him sourly if she had not been so inhibited by his nakedness for her face and pretty shoulders blushed rosily.

Trying not to imagine what the rest of her skin was doing, he grabbed her forearms and jerked her forward. "Stand there! I need it taut. Godsakes, you are married now." Then, with an oath, he grabbed her pillow, shook free its covering, and slit half the seams. "Keep your eyes closed if you must, but hold up your arms." She yelped as he dragged her hand from her sheet and tugged the fine linen over her head. It would have been tempting to enjoy her nakedness as the sheet tumbled round her ankles. Heloise Ballaster squeaked, opening her eyes. With a fumbling hand, she swiftly pulled the pillow cover over her thighs. He spared her modesty, turning to hack at the silk cord that held back her father's expensive bedcurtains. For a moment he fingered the heavy fabric and then turned. "Here!" He dumped the fistful of cord into her astonished fingers.

She looked up into his appraising eyes and felt no less naked; the fabric was tight upon her breasts and strained across her thighs. "Thank you," she said huskily. This man was now her master; a man who wanted her yet loathed her. She held her breath, knowing that like two serpents his destiny coiled with hers.

"A perfect Delilah," Miles mocked and then regretted his cruelty. No, this was no sultry, worldly whore. For an instant, he let the memory of his first wedding night stir from the recesses of his mind; his bride, innocent Sioned, sweetly blowing the candle out and expecting to sleep. "Oh, God!" he whispered now, grinding his fists into his eye sockets. But this virgin was not Sioned. This was squat Ballaster's daughter, even if she was a willowy faery maiden. "Devil take you, would you . . . would you mind standing where I put you!" It was beyond his strength of will to ignore her slim ankles and alluring legs as he tidied the fabric.

"You are doing it wrong." To his surprise, she knelt beside him, careful to keep her gaze upon the task, and they discussed the business as diligently as two tailors. Then she told him how to hold the wool cloth tight against the bias while she drew the dagger blade through it. It was not easy and the cut edge looked as though it had been attacked by giant moths. The man made no complaint but took the blade back from her and made a crescent rip in the center of the rectangle. "Excellent," he muttered, sawing the blade down at a right angle while she held it taut, "all we need are a couple of sheep and we can go to Bethlehem."

At least he had a sense of humor. She could have been locked in with a dour, choleric lout. Heloise shut her eyes as he rose. A pat on the cheek made them snap open. He was laughing at her and he did look like a model for a Nativity painting. The tunic reached to his calves and he had belted it with the emerald cord.

"It tickles damnably. I hate to imagine what a hair shirt must be like. No, I think I know."

Miles's hair shirt was Heloise Ballaster, staring at him now with her fawn's eyes. For an instant he forgot the unearthly hair.

"Is Lord Rushden still at Monkton Bramley? Shall you go there?" she was asking.

He remembered her warning to his father and his expression tightened defensively. Behind his back, he crossed his fingers against her. "My father has gone home. My mother . . . needed him. I shall rejoin his grace of Buckingham." He must have read surprise in her face for he added, "Oh, were you expecting me to return with a small army at my heels? No, I shall not embroil my father, though he shall hear of this."

"I am glad of it," Heloise answered gravely. "There has been enough blooding. Two of our men were injured and one of yours died for this folly."

The fierce intake of breath frightened her. Rushden strode to the window and slammed his hand against the wall so violently that the whole room trembled. His strong shoulders became rigid, and he lifted his face.

"Poor Dobbe. God save him. He served me since I was a child," he murmured, and his fingers found her dagger. She felt it was like treading on a layer of ice to wait on his uncertain temper; say the wrong words and the man's hatred might crack his fragile courtesy. She held her tongue, hardly daring to breathe. The minutes dragged before he raised his head and swung about. "There must be some way out."

She jumped as he violently thrust aside the curtain that hid the garderobe.

"Jesu forbid, s-sir, you cannot go down that!"

"True, lady, it would be like stuffing a badger down a rabbit hole and I would lief as not be mired further by your family." Grabbing the handle of the oak chest, he heaved it across to the casement. Before she could protest, he sprang onto it and drove his heel through the window.

The chatelaine in her winced at the bent spikes of ruined leading. Cold air rushed in to quiver the candles and pucker her arms. "Would it not have been simpler to open it?"

"Not when your father padlocked the handles, Mistress Goose." Half of him disappeared to inspect the roof. "A marvel! The dogs are barking but no one is willing to investigate. Brrr!" He sprang back lightly onto the floor. "This is the hard part." He grabbed her discarded sheet, anchored it with his foot, and ripped off a small strip. Then his sable head lifted, his eyes glittering with menace, like the serpents of his house.

"W-what do you mean?"

"This!" It took less than a blink to bowl her back across the bed. Miles turned her, an elbow muffling her face into a dimple of the feather bed while he dragged one thrashing arm behind her back and knotted the rag about her wrist. Then letting her breathe, he hauled the gasping, disheveled girl up against the closest bedpost and tethered her like a witch to a stake. "Scream if it helps."

"You hellspawn!" Heloise twisted, trying to free herself, but it only tightened her bonds. The candle in the glass lamp, suspended in chains from the upper bedrails, wobbled precariously and she stilled in panic.

"I think we need a fire to entertain your father while I escape." Rushden laughed as he bundled bedding from the chest into the remainder of her sheet and set it upon the windowsill. "Now, if this were a troubadour ballad I might whistle up my horse and spring down upon his back, but I think that would ruin my chance of fatherhood and snap my spine." He came across to her and lifted the candlestick from the small table. The sputtering flame menaced her. "I could set fire to the bedclothes, Heloise, my witch-wife." Playfully tossing the dagger, he caught it deftly by the handle. "Your father cannot feed you to the dogs if you are bound, be thankful for that. Adieu, lady. And never come near me again, if you value your life." Yet as he reached the chest, he turned, all mockery gone. "I doubt I can free my horse. Look after him, lady, his name is Traveller."

An instant later, he set alight the bundle and hurled it flaming from the casement—dear God, he meant it for the kindling stacked outside the kitchen! Then he hauled himself out onto the roof.

Heloise was hoarse when the key finally turned. Old Hubert, three sheets to the wind, staggered in, with Dionysia at his heels. As tipsy and useless as windfallen apples, the Ballaster servants, shooed from the feast, rolled into the courtyard. Heloise—once they cut her free—ran out barefoot, shouting for fire brooms. The kitchen was in flames.

Seven

 Her father threw aside the rod and stood, arms akimbo, glaring at his weeping daughter.

"If you had done your duty, Rushden would be eating out of your hand. Pah, you do naught but cost me money, girl, and for what? Your reputation rent beyond repair, the kitchen burnt to ashes, us cooking in the open air like heathens, the man beyond our reach, and his devil of a horse kicking everyone who goes near it." He paced and turned. "And the whoreson thinks he's won, I'll wager. Well, I shall write to the king's grace and my lord of Gloucester this very day." He beat his palm into his fist resolutely. "Aye, and you shall confront Rushden in the common gaze and make him acknowledge you."

"And he will deny it," Heloise whispered, knuckling away her tears. "I will not crawl to such a man like Rushden. He says I must never come near him again."

"So he can annul the marriage, you daft fool. Oh, stop your snivelling. Listen to me!" He grabbed her chin. "We saw him examining the goods. He fancied you and so he might again." She tried to pull away, detesting the flared nostrils, the angry broken veins that ran beneath his skin. "What choice do you have, girl? If the Rushdens will not have you, you are of little worth to me." Letting go of her, he strutted to the window. "To be plain, Heloise, it is your choice whether you starve. Obey me and you leave for Wales with servants. Disobey and you leave alone and penniless."

"You would disinherit me?" Her body hurt as she struggled to her feet, staring at him in horror. "For my sweet mother's sake, you cannot—" Be so cruel? Oh, he could, she did not doubt it. What argument would move him to be merciful? "God's truth, sir, can you not see that Miles Rushden is hungry for far more than Bramley? It was not my looks last night that he rejected but my blood. We are beneath him, sir, can you not understand that? The Rushdens want nothing to do with the likes of us."

His fists hit the sill and he turned abruptly. "Never, never let me hear you talk that way, babbling like a loser! You grab what you can, girl. You drive your fist in the teeth of the world and you win. He has his price."

"Money does not buy respect or love," she exclaimed defiantly and held her breath. He had never given her either and nor would Rushden.

"Love," he sneered. "Love is silk, love is velvet, love is extra. You have too much of your mother in you. Dionysia would see this matter differently. She would hunt Rushden down." Reaching the door, his hand paused at the ring handle. "Martin shall see you to Brecknock. You may take a maidservant, your mare, and a pack ass, and the young cur's stallion can go on market day to meet my losses."

Rushden's horse? What had he called it? Traveller?

"Give it to me."

"Not on your life, girl. That beast is worth a small fortune. Now, pack! For by my life, I wash my hands of you."

MUST SHE GROVEL BEFORE RUSHDEN LIKE SOME HEATHEN CONcubine and beg him to bed her? Never! She had some courage left.

After her father had gone, Heloise sat miserably, her fingers clasping her forearms, cursing him for his heartlessness, then she bestirred herself and bathed her tear-swollen eyes. Her hands were clumsy with cold for she had been denied coals for her chamber as punishment.

This was hard, to struggle against the despair dragging at her like weights. She swore she would not sink into a deep well of self-loathing. Beggars and lepers had worse lives, she told herself, and what of the damned souls facing the Devil's pincers in Hell for the next millennium? There had to be a safer path for her to follow, one that led her from her father's hatred. If only she could return to Middleham. Facing the chaplain would be easier than pleading with Rushden.

"Which path must I take?" she sighed to the faery folk and unfastened the window to let them through. Only the piping of a winter robin busy in the hedgerow answered her. Swallows might leave like summer traitors but old Rob endured the cruel rains of winter and kept Yuletide in England. Surely she had as much courage as such a tiny bird?

At least the key was not turned upon her now. Trying to keep her poor bruised back as straight as a battle standard, Heloise walked stiffly down the stairs, drawn in loneliness to the stable, to seek the other creature that was the scapegoat for her father's wrath.

"Mistress." Martin looked up from examining a cut on her mare's back fetlock, wiped his hands on the backside of his jacket, and came round to greet her.

"Christ ha' mercy, Martin, what is wrong with your face?" But she realized as she spoke. Dear God, was there no end to the damage Rushden had done to her and hers?

"I dabbed on honey liquid, like you allus said, and ice from the water butt. We chased young Rushden into the orchard, mistress. 'Ad him cornered nicely but then 'e whacked off one of your bee skeps with a trellis pole and toppled the rest of 'em. Bees flew at us, they did, like bloodthirsty Furies, and 'e got clean away. Won't be no honey this year."

"My poor bees."

"Aye, dead from cold or stinging." He unhooked a plaited wisp as he spoke. Her mare, Cloud, shook herself at the prospect of her winter coat being brushed and gave a frightened whinny as the horse in the stall at the far end kicked fiercely against the wall. The building shuddered so much that one of the hackneys knocked into his manger in distress. Even the placid sumpters shifted fretfully. Last night's smoke must have made them all unsettled, thought Heloise, hushing her gentle horse.

"I hear you did not fare so well, either, mistress." The groom's glance slid furtively to her back. "By the by, Sir Hubert let Rushden's men go, mistress. Leastways I suspect so, only don't go telling Sir Dudley. Old fellow unbarred the cellar. After more liquor, I suppose. They must have sneaked off during the hurly-burly with the fire. Dangerous man, Rushden, not for a gentle soul like you, Mistress Ballaster. I don't like to brag about bein' right, but I allus said you ought not to 'ave gone to Potters Field an' now see what's come of it."

"Rushden's horse, Martin?"

"That's 'im now, mistress." Hooves slammed again. "Angry, aye, and hungry. Won't let any of us come near 'im." Just like Rushden at the bridal feast. "The master says 'e's to be taken to market. We shan't be sorry, neither." He led Heloise down past the stalls. "Put 'im in the far one, we did, to prevent young Rushden taking 'im."

She was not disappointed. Like its owner, the stolen stallion was in its prime and just as touchy. True, Traveller was a little untidy with winter shagginess, but his steel grey coat gave promise of becoming as snowy as the Duke of Gloucester's destrier, White Surrey. Being a palfrey, he did not have the height and breadth of the duke's horse, but to Heloise he was just as magnificent.

A bold yet not unkind eye bid the groom keep his distance, then the huge lip curled and the nostrils flared. Martin grabbed Heloise to safety as the animal reared and brought its hooves crashing against the shuddering barrier.

"It'll be a fool or a brave man who tries to lead that one out."

"Let me speak to him alone."

"No, mistress, see 'ow dangerous 'e is. I know you've a way wi' creatures but this one's a devil in horse skin." Seeing as how she was adamant, he finally ordered away the stable hands who had gathered round them.

"Traveller?" Heloise took a step closer. "Traveller, I have to talk to you."

Wary but intelligent eyes watched her. She burrowed a hand into the manger and held out some oats on her palm. The stallion shifted his weight onto his back haunches, ready to spin out of her reach or to rear, but curiosity urged him at the same time to take a step forward and stretch his neck out almost within touching distance. It took a little while to explain to him what her father intended. In an unhurried voice, continually holding the stallion's gaze, she told him what he must expect next day at the markets and what she feared might happen to her.

He was listening, watching her fully. One of his companions wickered in the next stall but Traveller's concentration never left Heloise. As the soft, even cadences comforted him, he bowed his head and took the oats. Heloise leaned forward and blew very gently into his nostrils and a huff of breath came back at her and a gentle touch, soft as fustian, brushed her nose. She slowly straightened and set her hand upon the splendid forehead, smoothing him beneath her fingertips, up to the base of his ears and gradually down to his nose. He was still tense, uncertain. She told him she understood his panic and that she had felt like this last night with his master.

In a soft whisper, she assured him he was beautiful. With her other hand, she felt for the bolt and drew it free, never withholding her stare as she stepped inside his stall, praying he would not sense the thin ache of fear beneath her hope. He turned, still eyeing her movements, facing her. Like men, stallions liked nothing better than flattery and he listened intently to her telling him how noble and clever he was as she rubbed his long nose and moved to one side of his head.

"See how easy it is, vain one, you do not want to listen to a woman at first and then gradually you grow more sensible." With gentle fingers, she teased a long ear, running her fingers up its silken casing, and then she firmly slid her palm caressingly down, under his gorgeous mane, up his withers, and across his back.

The great head swung. Soft horsy breath huffed in her ear and a velvet nose nuzzled her neck with a whinny.

Stroking him, she sang the sad words men said Charles of Orléans, imprisoned in the Tower of London, had penned in lonely exile. The plaintive farewell was for a beauteous lady or maybe his beloved homeland of France. Heloise improvised for Traveller and made up or hummed the phrases she could not recall.

> *"Farewell now my darling dere,*
> *Farewell most wisest and so manly,*
> *Farewell my love from yere to yere,*
> *Farewell kind, courteous and true.*
> *However I fare, fare well you,*
> *I take my leave against my will."*

Her cheeks wet with tears and she knuckled them away. The horse regarded her thoughtfully, as if he sensed his happiness depended on her.

"I am not going to let my father sell you," she whispered with sudden conviction, sensing the faeries had crept along the rafters to listen. The moment had become special and magic, and she must listen to her heart. "No, I shall take you with me. We shall go out into the world together."

She had fallen in love with Rushden's horse. At least it was a beginning.

"Heloise!" Dionysia hurried towards her. "We have a visitor! Lady Huddleston, her grace of Gloucester's sister. She has been in Somerset visiting her manor at Sutton Gaveston. And, Heloise, she says I may journey north to Middleham with her straightway and Father has agreed. Oh, Heloise, be happy for me."

"I am, truly."

"Maybe she can help you—you know, intervene with Father."

"Does the sun rise in the west, Didie?" But silently Heloise raised her face to the rafters where the faeries were hiding. Maybe her prayers were answered.

"IT WILL NOT WASH," MARGERY SAID SOFTLY. "OH, MY DEAR Heloise, even if I could take you back to Middleham with us tomorrow, your problem will still be out that door waiting for you." Yes, male, hostile, and likely to kill not kiss. "I have never met any of the Rushdens. I believe the old lord was pardoned for fighting for the House of Lancaster and has kept his nose out of trouble since. They are certainly of very noble lineage."

"And they do not want a crossbow merchant's daughter ruining their purity." Heloise set the bedcover back. "Thank you for listening, my lady. I have been cudgeling my brain to think of a way out of this, some means to survive, but I had best let you get some sleep." It had already been impertinent of her to knock on their visitor's door after the rest of the household had gone to bed. She had been sitting in her friend's bed since nine of the clock explaining.

"No haste," Margery replied, shifting her pillow and easing her honey braids free. The young hound sprawled across her feet upon the coverlet rose from its slumber and came to lick Heloise's wrists. "Look, you are no coward, Heloise. I think you really should demand some help from Rushden."

"I expect he thinks I bewitched him." Heloise tickled the dog's back above its tail.

"Did you?" No malice, merely curiosity and good humor laced Margaret's question, but it warned Heloise that others might ask with less goodwill.

"No." She laughed. "But it was strange, the morning after the fight at Potters Field, I was thinking how satisfying it would be to be revenged on him and suddenly he was standing in the orchard as if I had summoned him."

"Hmm . . . are you sure you could not bring him to heel as a husband?" Margery murmured with the sleek smile of a woman blessed by love. "You know, I ran from Richard Huddleston for a very long time but he was always there like the Devil waiting for my soul." She heeled the heated brick across to her friend.

It was not extra warmth that drove betraying color into Heloise's face. "I had rather be damned than to beg for crumbs from that knave's plate." Rushden would probably haul her out to a woodpile and light a fire under her. "Oh, my lady"—her fingers twisted in her despised silver plait—"I was hoping to return with you and throw myself on their graces' mercy, but I suppose the duke's chaplain has convinced them I am a freak who consorts with demons. . . ."

"It sounds like you nearly did." That brought a bitter smile. "A moment." Margery rose and, to Heloise's surprise, opened the bedchamber door briefly as if she feared an eavesdropper. "One must be careful," she declared, coming back to lean over the cradle where her tiny son was sleeping. "And what I have to say may shock you and I should not like it repeated. We need not worry about Alys here." She twitched the blanket higher over her maidservant, who lay snoring on a trundle, before she pushed her dog out of the way and slid back into the bed. "I think it might please their graces better—and the king also—if you went to Brecknock and forced Rushden to acknowledge you."

"The king!" Heloise stiffened.

"Not only because Rushden is now your lawful husband but because it would be, well, interesting to have an intelligent gentlewoman in Buckingham's household." She gave Heloise a measuring look.

The king and Gloucester would be pleased if she would . . . *spy for them!* Heloise stared at her older friend through a different glass. "You *were* an informer," she breathed. The gossip had been true.

"*I* was not." That truth was delivered sharply. "I was sent to France by King Edward in secret to deliver some special letters, and it was not immoral, I was trying to prevent a war."

It seemed wise not to prod for further confidences. Spy? Inform? This was a Pandora's box. "But, madam, what use could I be in Brecknock? It is so far away."

"Can you not see it is common sense for any great lord to keep abreast of what is happening all over the kingdom? For my part, I know little of Harry, Duke of Buckingham. Indeed I have only rarely set eyes on him but he bothers me, the way he keeps himself apart. Is it out of pique or disinterest?"

"I have heard he spends most of his time in Wales."

"Indeed, and there are Welshmen who dream of rising up against the English."

"And Englishmen who still hate the House of York," muttered Heloise. God forbid that Sir Miles Rushden was one of them!

"Exactly, and if ever the king's enemies rally again—which God forbid—Buckingham might be persuaded to claim the throne. He is a Plantagenet, of legitimate royal blood; his grandsires supported the House of Lancaster, which would make him most acceptable; and he is reputed to resent his marriage with a Woodville." She steepled her fingers, tapping them together, as if her mind was fired with possibilities. "Yes, it would be useful to know what is being said these days at Brecknock."

Of course, decided Heloise, it was only to be expected that Margery, who had been at the heart of great matters during her father Warwick's rebellion, might be tempted to smell rats in perfectly innocent pantries; she probably missed the excitement. But King Edward was a strong king, so what could go wrong?

"The realm seems quite safe, madam. Forgive me for arguing, but we have had peace for twelve years or more, and the king has two healthy princes to succeed him, not to mention my lord of Gloucester and his son too."

Margery sighed. "The English chronicles are full of treason. Have you ever seen the heads on London Bridge? I know all about rebellions, believe me. And it is only five years since Clarence was put to death, but I will say no more on that."

"B-but would my lord of Buckingham have informers at Middleham, my lady?"

"I have no doubt of it."

They were talking about a different England, one that Heloise had only glimpsed. One that frightened her. It was as if Bramley and the manors she had grown up on were but a little world, scarce higher than the grass, while high above her head, the giants of England, the dukes and earls, played other games. Why seek her help? Gloucester must already have an agent dining at his cousin Buckingham's table. No, this was not her business.

"My lady." Heloise stirred finally. "I am flattered that you think I am trustworthy to serve in such a manner but it would be very easy for an enemy to fabricate evidence against me." Gathering her wrap close, she drew back the bedcurtain on her side and slid her feet to the floor.

"No, wait," protested Margery, gazing at Heloise's braids. "I . . . I understand your vulnerability. Forget what I suggested. Listen, there has to be a solution. Surely if you have the peace offering of Rushden's horse to return to him, the man will be a cur not to be grateful for that, so why not go to Wales for that reason alone? Or is your intuition warning you against Brecknock?"

"No." The oaken bedpost was smooth beneath her fingers as Heloise stroked it. "It is being friendless that bothers me. A man can easily obtain respectable employment but it is not easy being a gentlewoman and I cannot keep that state for long. My father will never have me back after Rushden has turned me away."

"Then you *will* go to Wales."

"It seems I have no choice."

"Then let me give you a gift that may bring you comfort." Margery padded across the room to a wooden jewel coffer that sat upon the small table beneath the casement. "A charm for the courageous cockatrice and valiant lady knight." She tugged a gold chain with a key from beneath her nightclothes and unlocked the casket. "Here." A unicorn brooch, small enough to be a hat badge, gleamed upon her palm. "Take it, Heloise. Wear this in Wales if ever you are in desperation."

Was this just a token to give her courage? Or did Gloucester have an agent already at Brecknock who might help her?

With a wry smile, Heloise lifted the brooch. "You mean some-one will nudge a cartload of straw beneath my window in case I have to jump?" she asked.

"Exactly, but only if the roof is on fire and you cannot— Have I said something wrong?"

"No," spluttered Heloise, but her merriment stilled abruptly. Strength emanated from the snowy enamel, tingling her fingers. The fabled beast's eye glinted at her, reminding her of Traveller. "Thank you," she said softly.

"I had a St. Catherine brooch once from the king himself." For an instant, her friend's face was shadowed and then she shook herself back into the present. "I wish my husband were here to advise us. A groom and a maid are insufficient escort. You will need some well-trained men-at-arms. I could spare two of my escort to protect you from all those lawless Welshmen."

"Two! Oh, Margery, how shall I repay your generosity? I have a few jewels my mother left me. Would you take those for surety?"

"Nonsense. Now, it could take two weeks or more to reach Brecknock from here. Do not go by way of Gloucester but take a ferryboat across the Bristol Channel to Chepstow and seek ad-vice there about the best road. When is your father sending Rushden's horse to be sold?"

"Two days hence."

"Then you leave that day and you demand the horse."

"Demand?"

"Yes, my lady Rushden, after all, it is your husband's prop-erty."

"My husband's," repeated Heloise, as though it were a new prayer still to be learned. "Yes." It was an empowering thought.

"Now to bed with you, cockatrice." Kind arms embraced her. "You have friends, remember that."

"I have one more favor. Please, will you watch over my sister at Middleham? For all her mischief, I love her dearly."

"I rather think she can take care of herself. Now sleep well. Wales is waiting for you, Heloise!"

HARDLY! HIDING BEHIND A DAMP MIZZLE, WALES WELCOMED the travelers with the enthusiasm of a scowling, underpaid servant, as the oarsmen raised their blades dripping from the grey water of the Bristol Channel, and the ferry barge was roped to the quay. Heloise had expected to make the crossing earlier but the ferry passengers had been forced to wait until the Severn bore had run its course, and now Chepstow looked scarcely worth the effort. A great castle high on its cliff above the river stared blankly down at the salt-sprayed disembarking passengers. The scent of sour ale wafted from the tavern at the end of the quay, adding to the stink of what must have been someone's day-before-yesterday's unsold catch, which was festering forgotten in a wicker putcheon with a ragged tomcat trying to claw it forth. If the rain had brought out the rats, the ferry's arrival drew the inevitable touters, prating of ale, whores, and dice. A one-legged beggar hobbled among them, rattling his bowl and cursing a pitifully young strumpet for distracting his customers, and beyond them a drunkard spewed his innards on a warehouse step. Heloise had been to ports before but well chaperoned with her father in command. True, it was a miserable March day, but the English wharfergers loading the panniers of salmon and sea lamprey onto carts did not whistle as they labored, as the Bristol men did, but swore and cursed. This, then, was Wales.

Efficient and sensible, her escorts sought out a reputable horse-lender and learned that to reach Brecknock, they might ride west to Newport and hire a guide to Abergavenny, or else travel up the Wye to Monmouth. Heloise decided on the latter as the safer choice.

The track, hedged for the most part with budding beech and hazel, followed the valley northwards. In the upper town of Monmouth, they sought to hire a guide and found Hoel, a balding, prickly local ("Neither Welsh nor English, look you, but a Monmouth man and proud of it") who began every one of his utterances with *"Yn affodus,"* which Heloise learned to her cost translated as "unfortunately" and meant she would have to delve deeper into her purse.

Monmouth, so proud that it had birthed the hero of Agincourt, had also spawned an oversupply of Saturday stalls that sold medallions and crudely hewn cameos of Henry V with his monkish haircut, as well as a variety of enamel hat badges (that would have pleased many a secret sympathizer with the defeated House of Lancaster) and small metal knights on horseback to take home to pampered sons. Heloise bought one of these to send back to Margery's babe for when he was older.

On Easter Sunday Heloise's party heard mass and rested. At dawn next day Hoel led them out across the drawbridge over the Monnow River to journey along the Frothy Valley. Fewer cutpurses perhaps but dawdling cows aplenty. Enduring lanes of dung, they called at prosperous farmhouses, where they bought cheeses to exchange for the goods Hoel had told them to buy in Monmouth for barter. The little English spoken was barely intelligible but Heloise paid attention to the lilting cadences and by the end of the second day had even learnt a few words of Welsh.

With a fresh audience, Hoel was as full of stories as a pond with frogs after rain. It passed the time, except he put Martin so in fear of Welsh faeries, the *tylwyth teg,* that every time an evening shadow quivered, the poor man jumped.

By Abergavenny, Heloise was growing fearful for another reason. In two days she would be confronting Rushden. Maybe he was not so mighty in Buckingham's household as he claimed and the duke might give her testament a fair credence. The small unicorn pinned to the collar of her gown gave her courage but the brooch also reminded her that the Huddleston men would quit her company very soon. She would be an outsider and her foe considered her a witch.

"EDRYCH MAS!"

Hoel tensed like an arching cat as armed horsemen and a half dozen ruffians on foot burst yelling out of some woods ahead of them on the road north of Crickhowell. What were they? Horse thieves? Prayers to St. Catherine and St. Christopher were speedily on Heloise's lips as the men rasped out their swords and formed a protective circle about her.

"Can we outride them?" she muttered, swiftly kneeing Traveller round. The River Usk sealed any escape to the west. Trees grew thickly up the hillside to the right. That left the way they had come.

"I doubt it" mouthed the older Huddleston man. "Godsakes, Welshman," he growled at their guide, "open your mouth and say something useful for a change."

Hoel let rip a speech of voluble Welsh and punctuated it finally with a spit upon the grass. His new audience, for the most part bearded, and lacking any insignia to show their allegiance, glared back with blatant hostility.

"That was useful," Heloise commented dryly. "What now? We all go back to Crickhowell for oatcakes and a good rubdown?"

"Wel!" One of the brigands understood her and laughed, kneeing his pony forward and raising a leather gauntlet to thrust back his riding hood.

Astonishingly, Heloise beheld a woman! One of indeterminate age, for the creature's complexion was as brown and speckled as a milkmaid's and the unruly dark hair snared back like a horse's tail showed a few glints of silver. A fur-skin cote protected her upper body from the wind, half hiding a brown leather tunic that covered her to her thighs. A riding skirt, hitched high, left her boots unencumbered. One did not have to be Welsh to know

that her vehement language as she circumnavigated them was
interrogatory. Their guide answered with a shrug and the woman
halted, facing Heloise.

"Where are you going?" she asked bluntly in understandable
English.

"Who asks?"

"The lady of Tretwr."

"Tree Tower?" Heloise sounded out the word. "I never heard
of it." She looked round at her Welsh guide. "I thought by now
we were in the demesne of the Duke of Buckingham."

Hoel sucked in his cheeks and of a sudden found the opposite
tree branch worth studying.

"Stafford!" The woman spat, wheeling her shaggy pony about.
"He merely thinks he rules. I will ask again, woman: state your
business."

"It is of a private and delicate nature," Heloise answered with
intended haughtiness and let Traveller dance impatiently beneath
her.

"So someone's fathered a brat beneath your girdle, eh?"

"No." Amazement made Heloise smile without fear. "Do I
look as though I would let a man take advantage of me?"

A spark of admiration gleamed in the narrow eyes studying
her. "Aye, if it pleased you." As the woman's keen gaze slid over
Rushden's stallion, Heloise pressed her lips together in fear and
adamance, ready to grab her dagger from the sheath stitched to
the saddlebag; she had traveled too far to be bested now.
"Whither are you bound then?"

It was tempting to be discourteous but it would achieve little.
"Brecknock Castle."

"Of course, and your horse too." Mischief glimmered in the
woman's expression; fingers stroked a dagger's spiral handle.
"You have to pay a toll for crossing our land."

"Of course, the point of this little encounter." With a suspicion that Hoel might have had some arrangement to bring his
travelers through the illicit toll, Heloise opened the purse on her

girdle and drew out two rose nobles. "These you shall have but I should not advise you to snatch anything else. I have friends who will not be pleased to hear of it." The woman's eyes had noted the jewelry she wore and she frowned.

"To be sure," she said, holding out her palm for the coins; then she gave an order to her men in Welsh and laughed, adding in English, "I wish you joy of *y Cysgod*. Tell Duke Harry you met me—if you dare open your mouth to him." She spurred away before an utterly puzzled Heloise could answer.

"Tree Tower?" echoed Heloise, her heart settling back to normal rhythm as they took the road again. "Do the Welsh nest high in these parts?"

Hoel ignored the jest, his feathers still ruffled by Lady Vaughan, and did not speak until they were into open country. *"Nawr te, arglwyddes,* that is Tretwr."

It was unbelievably stylish. Heloise had expected a Norman keep, and there was an elderly round one squatting in the backyard like a forgotten relative, but it was the stone house in front that took her breath away. A window, surmounted by an arched molding and flanked by arrow embrasures, looked out from the front of each wing and attached between them was a splendid gatehouse, three storeys high, whose huge double doors stood open, giving Heloise a glimpse of a fine courtyard surrounded on four sides. The chimneyed hall looked out to the south across a walled garden. From horseback, she could glimpse trellised arches.

"Wfft! This might look pretty, see, but those are murder holes above the door," muttered Hoel testily. "Let us hasten past, lest they string us in a row for beans to climb upon. *Yn affodus,* Black Vaughan's ghost still rides although he has been fourteen years in his grave. His three lovely bully sons have seen to that. Keep the legend alive, they do. And the women are no better. Their mother, Elen Gethin the Terrible, shot a man at an archery contest in cold blood, *gwelwch chi."*

If the Welshman was expecting her to turn white as a miller's apron and tremble, he was disappointed. "Why?" she asked, biting her lip, not daring to wickedly ask if Elen had been actually aiming at a bull's-eye butt.

The guide's brows rose in surprise. "An intelligent question, Englishwoman. To settle a score, it was—because the man had killed her brother." As if he sensed that she was not frightened enough to please him, he added crossly, "Glad you have come into such lawless wilds?"

"It thrills me exceedingly," she countered dryly, "but let us follow your advice and press on."

God protect them from further harassment by any other local villains, she thought. If Lady Vaughan could make her own laws, then the Welsh Marches were not so crushed beneath the English heel as Heloise had expected. "Do all women in Wales behave so?" she asked Hoel, curious to know if women here were permitted more freedom.

"*Gwaethaf modd,*" he muttered and then had mercy on her. "*Yn affodus,* yes!"

Eight

One could believe it was sheep not Englishmen who ruled Wales, for the silly beasts were as numerous as maggots on a carcass—noisy, too, with their new lambs. They decorated every hillside and with sheer dithery malevolence blocked the road wherever possible. It was wild and handsome country—like Miles Rushden, yet to be tamed. Great breaths of April clouds were tossed above the Black Mountains, one instant shadowing the terraced moorland, then cockily showering the riders and apologizing with a rainbow. Hoel led them north to Talgarth, a village with a ruined fortress not far from the broader highway that ran betwixt Hereford and Brecknock, and now she no longer needed a guide, Heloise paid him off.

At Bronllys next day she delegated the Huddleston men to hire a byre where they might hide Traveller from Rushden in case she needed the horse as bargaining. Just as she set her foot in Cloud's stirrup for the last stretch to Brecknock, her maid confessed with sobbing gulps that she and the youngest Huddleston man had sworn a trothplight and please might she return with him to Lady Huddleston? Heloise enviously gave the wench her blessing and left her with her lover. *Yn affodus!* Brecknock might sneer at her for arriving without a maid.

The Brecknock road led with Roman straightness along a broad, level valley. Fruitful desires were opening the whitethorn thickets and yearning seeped through Heloise as though the sap were rising in her, too, but a stark future lay ahead. What use daydreaming of a knight who would adore her or Rushden as a princely dark lover? The real man was going to be angry, cornered, and ruthlessly dismissive. She would need every ounce of courage to face him.

As they drew closer to Brecknock, other mountains, visible

and invisible, climbed the horizon to the southwest, barren and formidable, and Heloise was glad that Brecknock proved not to lie in their shadow but in friendlier farmland on a meeting of roads where the River Usk coiled north. But Brecknock was not welcoming. Carrion crows perched upon a gibbet, freshly occupied by a stinking corpse. Crossing herself and making a prayer for the dead youth's soul, Heloise kneed Cloud on, fearful lest a vision come to her.

There were dwellings now, and the riders passed over the town ditch and through the Watton Gate, fuming at the iniquitous toll. No spires or towers showed them where the town's heart lay so they slowed the horses to a walk behind a Benedictine monk who was humming plainsong as he led his ass along the eastern side of the marketplace. Heloise did not tarry, or let Martin try his raw Welsh on any stallkeepers, for now the castle could be plainly seen at the northern end of the town and a miserable rain was setting in.

And a humble little castle it was, too. Were they in the right town? Surely this could not be the dwelling of a duke? Plumes of smoke rose from within the fortress's walls, but no pennons decorated the towers. It was not a good omen and Heloise observed with a heavy heart that the town did not nestle close to its protector like a camp follower, but seemed to be trying to crawl away from its master's vigilance. Maybe that was because yet another river, narrow and unfamiliar, severed the castle from its charge.

The monk turned off purposefully through the town's northern gate and Heloise was left to face her hazardous future.

"Will you grab the nettle now, mistress, or shall we seek lodging and return tomorrow?"

"Oh, Martin, say a prayer for me." Heloise bit her lip and rode forward, trying to keep her courage high. What could they do to her that her father had not done already? At least the castle drawbridge was down but so too was the portcullis. It looked as welcoming as Rushden would. A nettle indeed! He would recoil from her with icy hauteur and what should she do then?

"It is not what I expected." She took Martin's hand and slid stiffly from Cloud's saddle to stare forlornly up at the rose sandstone barbican. She had anticipated something of Middleham's splendor but this seemed like a poor kinsman in comparison. The loops and slits hinted at a dark, cold Norman interior. Beyond the grid of the portcullis, the bailey was as empty as a larder plagued by mice. Little money had been spent here and her heart sank. If Buckingham was hardfisted, he would have little patience with her woes.

"I think this may be the lesser entrance, mistress, but no matter." His belly gurgling as noisily as the river, Martin rapped at the porter's window. "Ho! You asleep in there?" He politely ushered his mistress farther into the shelter of the arch and smote the shutters again with his riding crop. Egglike, they burst open and a rough-chinned, hairless fledgling poked his head out.

"My lady," he exclaimed in a cheery English voice, "we were not expecting you for another two days. Welcome!"

Creaking machinery urged the portcullis up and a fleshy porter in a tabard half-scarlet, half-black, stepped out onto the drawbridge, gave her a gap-toothed grin, and whistled a pair of stable boys to fetch in the laden sumpter and mud-spattered Cloud. "Her grace will be pleased to hear that you have arrived safely."

Heloise made a surprised face at Martin. Who were they expecting? Obviously a stranger, since the porter did not know her face.

"She will?"

"Aye, my life on't," chortled the gatekeeper, "but she ain't here at present. Over Eastertide she been at Lady Darrell's, 'is grace the duke's mother, with the little demoiselles and the babe, but Lord Stafford is here. An' 'is grace will be back Wednesday. Now don't you be standing' there a-freezin', my lady. I'll send a lad straightway to tell Sir William that you are here. Is your maid tarrying behind, my lady?" At least the man asked the obvious as discreetly as he could.

"Alas." The expected guest crossed herself with melancholy devotion; the gatekeeper could draw his own conclusions. He did, and drew breath to press her for details but her small silencing gesture was sufficient.

Well, thought Heloise, with a quick thanks to St. Catherine as she stretched out her ungloved hands before the porter's brazier, she was into the castle on a lie but at least she might have a chance to speak privily with Rushden.

"Those bells sound close by." She offered the porter a friendly smile; new friends were useful and she might need to leave the castle hurriedly.

"The Priory of St. John the Evangelist, my lady." So that explained the monk. At least she might seek a night's shelter from the hosteler if the castle turned hostile. "We have Dominican brothers too, my lady, at Llanfaes, across the bridge, over the Usk." He pointed southwest. Brecknock, then, lay within a carpenter's square where the Usk and this lesser stream intermingled. It did no harm to get her bearings.

"Sir William will see you now, my lady."

As she followed the servant across the silent courtyard, she realized Martin was right: a larger gatehouse with a drawbridge faced the Usk. Maybe the castle looked grander from that approach. The youth led her past a roofed well, not towards the old Norman keep squatting, gaunt as a hungry anchorite, on its high mote to one side of the bailey, but up a small flight of steps, through a porched doorway, and into an unheated great hall set against the southern curtain wall.

She shivered, longing for the bright, tapestried walls of Middleham, but the page ushered her into a counting chamber where a generous fire crackled blessedly. This must be the castle exchequer or the receiver's room. Folded letters were tucked or hanging over the lower of the two wooden wall rails and sealing wax seals dangled on broad bands of tape above. Ledger boxes and parchment rolls were stacked upon the shelves behind a cheerful, well-fed man in his forties who sat before a baize-draped

board with a leather-strapped courier box at his elbow. Seeing
her, he closed the inkwell, dropped his pen into a wooden jar,
feather down to protect the quill tip, and came round to hold
out two hands to clasp hers in greeting. Why was she being so
vigorously welcomed? she wondered. An impression of sky blue
eyes and a peppery mane of hair stayed with her as she lowered
her eyes modestly and curtsied.

"Lady Haute. What a long journey you have had. What do
you think of our hills, wild, eh, compared to Kent?" *Kent!* Saints
preserve her, she had never set foot in Kent, not even to make a
pilgrimage to Canterbury.

Rapidly plumbing her memory, she managed a breezy answer.
"I suspect that our cherries are as good as your mountains, Sir
William."

He bowed charmingly over her hand. "And have they repaired
the Akeman Road outside Cirencester yet? You could have lost
a horse and cart in some of those holes before Christmas."

Dear God, yes, it was the old Roman route, but from where?
St. Albans put his hand up for a mention, but little else came
to her. How dangerous would it be to lie? "Actually I—I journeyed up from Chepstow. I had . . . have . . . a good friend in
Somerset I desired to see." She smiled amiably, wondering who
on earth this Lady Haute was. A noblewoman, so certainly not a
midwife or a wet nurse, but was the lady wed or widowed? Thank
God the duchess was at her mother-in-law's with her children.
It at least gave some respite. And who was this man? What
standing did he have with the duke?

"Sir William . . . ?"

"Knyvett, madam, of Buckenham, Norfolk. Acting constable.
Ah, Bess, my sweet, do not hover there. Close the door and come
and greet my lady."

Another challenge to be faced? But there was no sign of recognition, merely shy politeness as a thin young gentlewoman
came across the rush matting to curtsy.

"Is it not wonderful that my lady is here ahead of time, Bess?" Again, that puzzling hint of relief.

"Indeed," the girl agreed sweetly, nervously tucking a wisp of nut brown hair beneath her coif. "Yes, indeed, we are so pleased to welcome you, my lady."

Why? Had they a dragon this Lady Haute was supposed to tame? Had Heloise sprung from the cauldron of her father's unpredictable governance into an equally dangerous fire?

"Bess is— Ah, Limerick." A snowy-haired man in a long houppelande that lapped about his old-style pointed shoes came in to greet her. He too was smiling. Worse and worse, thought Heloise.

"Lady Haute, may I present his grace of Buckingham's steward, Sir Thomas Limerick." Bess caught his eye. "Oh, and this demoiselle is Lord Edward's nursemaid."

A *little* dragon? Heloise took a deep breath. "Your porter mentioned that Lord Stafford is here," she ventured, wondering if she had found the right key to the gate. The statement could be construed as polite conversation if nothing else. There was a rapid exchange of glances between her hosts.

"Mulled wine, Bess," Sir William exclaimed. "Now, Lady Haute, Bess says there has been a brood of mice in the chamber set aside for you but we have put a mouser in there for the last two days. Toss him out if you have an aversion to the fellow." A human or four-pawed mouser, she wondered, warming to Sir William's affability.

Over wafers and between sips of comforting wine that seeped down to warm her icy toes, Heloise began to edge the door of knowledge open. Her hosts were at pains to praise the Duke of Buckingham's eldest son to her but as their comments became more fulsome, she began to deduce that Lord Edward also had horns and a spiked tail. In short, Lady Haute was to turn him into an angel. No wonder the duchess and the other children had sought refuge at their grandam's. And where was the child's father and the rest of the household?

The steward enlightened her: "His grace of Buckingham is at Thornbury with others of his retinue but we expect him back this week." Thornbury! That was in Somerset, hard by the Bristol Channel. Dear God, all this while Rushden had been but a few days' ride from Bramley. Dionysia had it wrong. Her quarry had not been on his way to Wales at all, and incredibly she had arrived ahead of him. Well, she must make the best of her advantage. Kind St. Jude, the saint of hopeless causes, was lending a generous hand in her affairs. *Two* dragons! If she did her best, maybe she might make some allies before she faced Rushden's anger.

CASTLES WERE FULL OF INFORMATION IF ONE KNEW WHERE TO uncover it, and Bess, anxious to please the lady appointed over her, was a pantry of tidbits and morsels. As they traversed the hall and climbed the staircase that led to the nursery and bedchambers, Heloise learned that the duchess suffered from megrims, was easily worn out by her children, and exchanged letters with her royal sister twice a month, and it was the queen who had graciously recommended Lady Haute. The duke and duchess rarely kept each other company now that they had produced four children. His grace hunted a great deal with his friends. Friends? Oh yes. Unfortunately Bess showed excessive interest in one of his grace's knightly companions but it was not Rushden and Heloise decided wisely not to squeeze any gossip out of her since she assumed that a respectable married noblewoman should not display interest in unattached noblemen, and she did not know her new status. Was Lady Haute a married woman or a widow past mourning?

She tiptoed her way through conversation at supper with anecdotes of her recent travels, deftly diverted Sir William from a discussion of hostelries on the London to Canterbury road, and finally excused herself, duplicitous but unscathed. She did not like lying to these people. They would feel betrayed once Rushden unmasked her deceit, but perhaps there was a way to prevent that happening; if the little dragon liked her and she built up a treasury of goodwill before Rushden's return, miracles were possible.

THE YOUNG WELSH MOUSER THAT BOUNDED OUT OF ONE OF the chambers partitioned off from the nursery was sleek, gelded, and white-stockinged. The rest of him was shining black except for a slash of white between his ears and down his nose. At least he was welcoming, but where was the other little beast in her charge?

Bess pointed to the other door and lifted a finger to her lips. "I thought you had enow for the day to weary you, my lady. I would not be in a hurry to meet that one if I were you. That's the garderobe there behind the arras, when you need it, and I have set clean water for washing in your bedchamber. If you have aught for cleaning or pressing, I will send them out to a laundress in the morning."

Heloise thanked her for her thoughtfulness and began a dutiful inspection of her new realm. Inside the ambry was a wooden fort, a baby cannon, painted boards for table games, and a box of foot soldiers. In the other corner, she lifted the lid of the brightly painted wooden chest to discover a little sword and buckler, a tiny longbow, a crick ball, and a gaudy top.

"Very tidy, Bess," she said pleasantly, pausing to run her fingers over a hobbyhorse's leather mane. Traveller! Tomorrow she would send Martin back to Bronllys to ensure the horse was properly cared for and let Margery's men return home.

"You should see it on a rainy day. Not an inch of floor to be seen and everything hurly-burly. And this is only my lord's nursery. My little ladies have their own quarters close by her grace's bedchamber but if they are all playing here together, as sometimes happens, it is bedlam. And here is Benet, Lord Stafford's manservant. Make your bow, Benet." A shambling, moon-faced fellow came out from the nursery, bowed awkwardly, and took his leave again at a nod from Bess. "Do not be a-feared of his squinty eyes, my lady. A mill short of a grindstone, that one, but stout-hearted."

As they enjoyed wafers and hyppocras together before the fire, it was hard not to answer the questions that the younger girl snowballed at her in honest curiosity. Heloise sidestepped them as best she could by asking her own and was relieved to hear that Bess slept on a truckle bed beside the child. Thank goodness! It promised a rare privacy and would avoid the sleepy confidences that came from sharing a bed. Benet slept in the child's chamber too. He might be simple, Bess assured her, but he was as loyal as a dog, and would willingly fetch the water for the child's bath and perform all the menial tasks.

Heloise's narrow chamber contained a truckle bed. Along the opposite wall a clean towel hung from a wooden rail above a small cup board. Upon it she found a pewter ewer, a jug of water, a jarful of pumice powder, and herbs for sweetening the breath. She hung her gown up on a wallpeg, said her prayers, and crept gratefully between the sheets, nestling her soles against the wrapped, heated brick, unable to believe her good fortune so far. Perhaps it was her destiny to come to Brecknock to look after the duke's son. She hoped that was why Miles Rushden had been catapulted into her life. If she did her best, maybe she might make some allies before she faced his dark anger.

Mercy Jesu! She stifled a scream as a creature landed on the bed beside her, but it was not a rat. A confident purr coaxed her hand out from the blanket to tickle the short soft fur at the base of his pointed ears.

"You are supposed to be under the bed catching . . . things . . . not up here with me," she pointed out, as the feline's volume increased beneath her fingertips. "This is not wise, master cat. You and my hair do not go together. People will gossip." Like most males, even gelded ones, he took no notice and burrowed beneath the coverlet. Oh, well, thought Heloise, I had rather sleep with you than Sir Miles Rushden. "Since you are Welsh, I shall baptize you Dafydd in the morning and if there are any mice around, they shall stand your godfathers."

Thinking about Miles Rushden robbed her of sleep, but by early morning she had her weapons primed and ready; she would make a success of handling the child and then she might have the artillery to battle her husband. At dawn she must have fallen into a heavy slumber for Bess came in and shook her awake. Seeing the superstitious fear in the girl's eyes at the unusual color of her braids, Heloise hastily reassured her and made her promise not to gossip. Thank God, Dafydd had not emerged from his snug hiding place for a naming ceremony.

"Oh, before I forget, my lady, Sir Thomas said to give you this." Bess held out a sealed letter. "It seems you made better time on the road than your carrier." The parchment was addressed to the duchess from the real Lady Haute.

Heloise thanked the girl and closed the door. With trembling fingers, she broke the seal, scanned the florid writing and nearly gave a whoop of joy. Eleanor Haute craved her grace's forgiveness but she and her husband were both badly smitten with the measles and as she had no wish to infect Lord Stafford, she would be delaying her journey until the contagion had passed.

"Thank you," whispered Heloise gratefully to any saints and faeries who were listening. A few precious days!

Fingers of sunlight were cheerfully poking through the shutters. The world was waiting for her. She ran to the window, leaned across the cold embrasure and lifted the latch to a view that took her breath away. Distant hills rose up beyond the woods. The highest peak was the hue of gorse and a laurel of light cloud hung gauzily around it like a victor's wreath.

Moist warmth gentled the air. Her heart lifted; she could smell the fertility of the earth, imagine the young corn shoots unfurling beneath the dark red furrows and the creatures hidden in the trees and burrows stirring after their long winter sleep; her being reached out, rejoicing with them.

*   *   *

THE FAIR-HAIRED CHILD LED IN TO MAKE HIS BOW WAS SO beautiful that for an instant Heloise could not believe that the household thought him an ogre. He was clad like a tiny nobleman but the slashed, hanging sleeves edged with winter squirrel were unsuitable for a child and the cost of the mustard-hued brocade fabric of his doublet, which no doubt had to be kept from spills and mud, would have fed a ploughman and his family for a year. He took off his soft-crowned hat, bowed as gracefully as a courtier, and then spoilt the effect by folding his arms defensively and standing feet astride in a perfect imitation of Sir William Knyvett. The slightly winging eyebrows lent his face an elfish intelligence and perhaps this too made the servants fear him. Heloise knew too well how those sorts of suspicion hurt.

"Thank you, Sir Thomas." She opened the door for the high steward and offered a semicurtsy. He accepted the hint and with a warning glance at his lord's son swept majestically out.

"So, Lord Stafford, it is clear to me," declared Heloise, "that you do not need a lady to govern your hours, but I do need to make a living. You look rather boring. Are you?"

The blue eyes stopped their assessment of her quite abruptly and his gaze swung back up the tawny velvet folds of her high-waisted traveling gown.

"My mother is prettier than you."

"Of course. She is a duchess. Duchesses are supposed to be prettier than anyone else except queens—and princesses. Do you always carry eggs in your hat?"

The small face crinkled derisively at such stupidity.

"There!" Heloise pointed. "Where is my mirror? Let me show you." The swift placing of the little freckled egg that her smallest sister had solemnly given her for a keepsake was easily achieved. Thank the saints, the child's brim was upturned and fastened with a brooch. "Here." She rubbed the silver mirror against her skirt and held it before him. "A swallow's egg. It must have fallen from a nest. What a pity you did not know, you might have hatched the fledgling against your chest." Small fingers felt for the egg and beheld it suspiciously but he made no accusation. He dropped it down into his sleeve and Heloise wondered what other treasures wriggled below the fur. One of his sleeves certainly seemed to possess a life of its own. Dafydd had also noticed the twitching and prowled over to investigate.

"What have you hidden in there?" asked Heloise. She dumped the disgruntled cat outside the door and turned back to the child. "I do like frogs. Or is it a mouse?" Better now than in her shoe or the bottom of the bed.

Annoyance twitched the precocious little mouth. Muttering, he burrowed one cuffed hand down into the split and drew out a toadlet. Heloise held out her hand and he solemnly tipped it onto her palm, where she gently stroked it with her fingertip and waited for it to escape. It took strategy and coordination for the pair of them to catch it, and crawling on hands and knees towards each other, both calling out instructions, took the sharp edge off the tension between them. But a knock on the door spoilt the adventure. It was Bess bearing a beaker of a urine-hued brew.

"Your physic, Lord Edward. Drink it down like a brave lad."

"It is foul. I hate it!"

"What is in this, Bess?" Heloise smelt it and took a sip. "Uuugh, lungwort!"

"Bravo, my lady. Never mind, poppet," the girl declared as the boy jerked his head away from her expected ruffling, "the woodbine will soon be out and you can have a remedy from that instead." She took the cup from Heloise and held it out. The child ignored it; anyone could see he was working himself into a temper. In an instant, he was red and gasping for breath. Bess thrust the cup back at Heloise, then knelt down and grabbed the little shoulders. Shaking him did not help and patting his cheeks was little avail.

Heloise set the concoction down with deliberate clumsiness. "Oh, I have spilt it." The tantrum instantly ceased but he was still short of breath.

"It happens every time he is thwarted, my lady," Bess explained later after she had led him away to his tutor, "and every time he exerts himself. He can behave correctly when it suits him but he is a sniveling little monster most of the time."

"To gain attention?"

"To get his own way, my lady. Takes after his father, I reckon, for there are plenty of folks would say so when their tongues are loosened from a bit of drinking."

"What happened to the last governess of the nursery?"

"Oh, got herself into the family way within a month, or leastways that was her excuse for leaving. I hope you will stay longer, my lady."

Not if her so-called husband got wind of her presence, sighed Heloise, but if she could make herself indispensable at Brecknock before Buckingham and his retinue returned, then she might be forgiven her duplicity. Yes, Lord Stafford was a little devil. The deceptive angelic hair might darken to honest brown as he grew to manhood but that sulky chin strongly hinted that he would become an unpleasant master if no one took him in hand now. At least she had the authority to order a change in Lord Stafford's meals and medicines. The rest of the day, she distracted him whenever he threw a breathing fit. By nightfall she was exhausted but so, too, was the little boy. He went to bed right willingly, to Bess's amazement. Now if she could only manage Rushden the same, thought Heloise—and blushed. No, bed was not quite what she had in mind.

Her initial private success with the child was not repeated in the hall next day. The crux of the matter slyly put his tongue out at her then whinged and balked at his food through dinner on the dais. By the end of the meal, Heloise could see why the welcome she had been extended was becoming tepid. Sir William and the others had been hoping she would make permanent changes to the child's nature. "If you behave, then I will arrange an adventure," she whispered behind her hand.

The small tyrant licked his spoon consideringly. "What sort of adventure?"

"A surprise." The small elbows edged slowly off the table, the question mark of a back straightened, and his toes ceased causing earth tremors below the great salt.

But, what surprise? She had but a few days until Wednesday when the duke and his retainers were expected and she needed to rebuild Sir William's confidence in her. She began by taking the boy to the ducal kitchen after his tutor had given him leave. The child's eyes goggled as she bid him examine rabbit nets, mortars, and jelly molds, turn the spit, ladle off the fat from the large cauldron, smell the different spice jars, and sniff the basket of dried toadstools for the morning fire lighting. It taught the child to count his blessings, for some of the tasks were loathsome; one scullion, stripped to his waist, was cleansing greasy vessels with steamy hot water and salt; another was struggling to scale a large perch; and the master cook, annoyed to have his realm invaded, made a great play of hacking a carcass going down for salting, to affright the little noble.

Ned giggled as Heloise tied his long sleeves in a loose knot behind his back, but when she tucked cloths in the top of his stomacher and her platelet belt and pushed up her sleeves, he goggled at her. He, Lord Stafford, was to make pancakes? Soon she had the small kingdom of the kitchen under her domain, fetching bowls and whisks and joining in with instructions for their little overlord. In the afternoon, Heloise bade Ned show her the castle garden and there they moistened a barrow of mud and designed a castle fit to rival Beaumaris. It subsided rapidly. After dinner they made bows and shot at the butts. The following morning they attempted to make a crossbolt with glue, parchment, and steel, equipped with little fur tails to tell which way the wind was blowing. A pity there were insufficient flax strips to make a decent string; her father would have been ashamed of the miserable result, but it entertained the child. They crept to the stables in the early hours of Sunday morning and saw a foal born. On Monday afternoon they made a candle shaped like Salisbury steeple and pressed woodcuts onto it.

"A chandler's trade!" tut-tutted Sir Thomas Limerick, called in to admire the child's handiwork, but he smiled and patted her hand.

"What harm in understanding how others must live, how the world runs?"

"It runs on greed, Lady Haute. Those with riches do as they please, the rest labor."

"But you will admit the child is more manageable."

"For the nonce, yes, my dear, but things will be different when his grace returns."

Desperation hardened her resolve.

"Sir William," she asked after prayers on Tuesday morning, drawing the knight to the fire that now warmed the hall from a central hearth. "I know this might strike you as an outlandish notion but I think part of Lord Ned's problem is boredom. He needs an adventure beyond these walls. I should like your permission to take him into Brecknock this morning." Her host's face was indecipherable and she added earnestly, "I think it is important that he understand how everyday transactions are made. He will be lord of this demesne one day, God willing, and must understand how to negotiate a fair price. Oh, I know he will have officers to do these things but—"

"I think it an excellent suggestion," he cut in.

"You do, sir?" She clapped in delight.

"Whoa, my lady," he exclaimed laughing, catching her hands in one large fist. "Let us think this out. My lord of Buckingham has enemies aplenty in Wales. Two hundred years since we conquered these valleys, but the accursed Welsh still resent it."

Surely the Brecknock people would not harm a child? The town seemed no more dangerous than any English market town and she had heard no Welsh voices as she passed through.

"Then perhaps we shall go in disguise."

"Homespun, you mean?" When he saw she was serious, his

frown deepened. "Ah well, it may serve." He paced to the casement and stretched, his hands on his waist, while she waited. "Do it," he said at last. "My lord duke will not like it but hopefully no harm will come to the pair of you. I shall send a couple of doughty archers with you."

"Only if they follow at a discreet distance."

"Hmm, a winsome stranger like yourself will raise a few brows. The boy has been little seen. As long as he keeps a still tongue in his head, but . . ." He tugged at his ear, a plethora of doubts clouding his face.

"Oh, please, Sir William, I shall take good care of him. Please let me do this before his grace returns."

Although he gave consent with misgiving, Sir William thrust a fistful of coins into her hands with unlooked-for generosity.

The frightened child threw a tantrum at the suggestion that he must walk to the town and mix with commoners. While the two men sent to escort her muttered and stamped their feet like impatient tethered horses, it took Heloise the best part of an hour not only to coax her little lord into wearing meaner apparel but also to convince him to leave the castle. Ned sniveled and grumbled down the stairs, pulling back at her hand, and she nearly gave in. Then, as they crossed the bailey, he wickedly sprang and skipped, jerking her hand and jumping his whole weight on her arm.

"I am not a bell rope! The whole idea of this is to enjoy our disguise." His governess drew him out of sight into the porter's cell. "They will know you are a nobleman for sure if you behave so." Sullen eyes regarded her from beneath a scowling brow. He had acquired the knack of making his eyes half disappear beneath his upper lids and it gave him the look of a baby demon gargoyle.

"And if the wind changes, I shall look like this for all my life," he chanted nastily.

"Which is, of course, not true." Heloise believed in honesty but then spoilt her principles by saying, "I shall very likely sell you to a blacksmith if you misbehave and you will spend the rest of your days in a sweltering smithy hammering horseshoes, or maybe I might apprentice you to a beggar. Your angel curls might earn some extra groats."

"My father will have you hanged if you sell me," he muttered.

"Pah, no one will buy you anyway. Besides, I should miss you."

He glanced up at her. "Truly?"

"Yes." Like a chill wind. "Now you are to be plain Ned and I shall be your mam. So what say you?" He pouted like a waterspout. "My lord, if you draw attention to us, the Welsh might thieve us, hold you in chains for ransom, and feed us naught but leeks."

She briskly marched him across the Honddu Bridge like any housewife on her way to market and they overtook a pardoner and a woodman, spiky with kindling across his shoulders. It was reassuring to know that the two archers were following behind at a sensible distance but Heloise's instincts told her the child was in no danger, and it was so wonderful to be free of fortress walls.

Her clothes had been chosen with care—a plain russet gown, borrowed from one of the women servants, and a calf-length cloak against the cold. Her hair was piled under a simple cap and she wound a veil over it and round about to scarf her throat. The purse, heavy with Sir William's bounty, hung strapped to her belt at the front, not at her hip where it might be easily cut. Lord Stafford's clothing was a simple tawny tunic but beneath it he wore a quilted doublet to keep him warm.

Brecknock lacked the distinctive high street that ribboned many of its English counterparts; instead it had two main streets that ran from Castle Gate to Watton Gate. Heloise followed the traffic of carts down Shepe Street and found the market, bulging away from the main concourse, dominated by the Bothall and a chapel. Then her mind began to spin; she saw flames flickering from the thatches and the blackened stones.

"Come." The child tugged at her hand. "What is the matter? You have gone all sickly."

The gabled roofs and walls returned to normality; the squeal of a pig being branded a few paces away was uncomfortably real. "I—I felt . . . would you like to light a candle?"

"Pooh, not mass again."

"No, but lighting a candle would be the proper thing to do, Ned. This will be your town one day. See, St. Mary's—is it not?—lacks a tower. Perhaps you or your father might pay for one. Let us go in and see where you would build it. You may give me your opinion."

The duke's son made an obligatory prayer and then inspected the ceiling while Heloise knelt. She said nothing to St. Catherine, feeling that the saint had vindictively answered her prayers already, but she sent a plea to the saint who watched over Brecknock to have a fire peleton ready on the day her vision came true, and she lit a candle to St. Miles of Padua that he would soften his namesake's heart towards her. The disadvantage was that the saint was well known for helping people find what they had lost. "Please do not let Rushden return yet, please," she prayed.

Outside the church, she taught the little lord to discern the genuine needy from the cunning beggars and insisted he cast a penny in the begging bowl of a legless man. Ned wanted to make an examination of the poor wretch's rag-covered stumps to make sure they were authentic and she had to swiftly yank him towards a market stall which sold sugared almonds, sweet licorice beetles, and tiny marzipan apples. Not only did she promise him a sugar pig on the way back if he behaved, but she bought it to show sincerity and tucked it in the drawstring bag upon her arm.

In the next hour, his new governess taught the duke's son how to bargain for some comfits for Sir William and a ribbon for Bess. The marketplace was her schoolroom and the stall-keepers her counters and building bricks. The child's cheeks

turned pink from the south wind but his eyes were bright with
new experience. True, he grabbed her skirts in his fists and hung
on fiercely as they watched the dancing bear—such a large creature that Heloise felt it would be good to cling to someone too—
but she bravely held out an oatcake to the alien creature and won
Ned's admiration for her courage. Even her archers were beginning to enjoy the outing, especially when she allowed them to
enjoy a pot of ale on the western side of the market, where the
better taverns and the more prosperous merchants dwelt. There
was entertainment here: a traveling juggler frightening the children with his flaming breath, and a dog dolled up with a lady's
cone and veil tied to its head that leapt through a hoop at his
master's order. The man had a puppy too but it was fearful of
the crowd and would not perform. Shamed by its disobedience,
the owner lashed its hindquarters, confusing the poor thing further.

"Stop that!" exclaimed Heloise, grabbing the whip from the
astonished man's hand. "It is doing its best to please you, you
cruel lout! Can you not see that?" Then she realized she was
drawing attention. "Oh, here, I shall buy it from you." She tipped
the remainder of her money into the greedy, dirt-rimed palm.
"Tie Bess's ribbon round its neck, dearest!" she ordered Lord
Stafford.

The mouth of the heir to his grace of Buckingham was gaping
but mercifully the little fellow did what he was bid before the
dog made off. Heloise caught it up over her shoulder—all paws
and tongue—and whisked Ned out of the crowd. She halted at
the bench outside the tavern, greeting the archers as though they
were acquaintances, and set the wriggling creature down.

"Ain't you something, my lady," muttered the older man beneath his breath, squatting down to let the small dog lick his
hand. He fed it a piece of his pie.

"May I have him?" pleaded Ned, tugging Heloise's arm hard.

"But you already have a sugar pig."

"Oh, please, *please*."

"I do not think it a good notion, dearest," she answered gravely, sitting down on the bench and drawing him onto her lap. The pup was attacking her toes. "I rather think its hair would make you cough."

The child wriggled round, making a saddle of her thighs, and fastened his sticky fists around her neck. "Please, my lady. You may have the sugar pig but please may I have her." The cock-eared little creature was nipping at his heel but he laughed, showing no displeasure.

"I shall think on it," Heloise promised solemnly. "If you manage not to have any more coughs or sniffles for the next two days, I may agree."

One of the archers whistled and was caught gazing at the heaven with a disbelieving expression. "Do you take wagers, Brian?" he asked his companion softly as the boy slid off Heloise's lap.

AS SHE HAD VOWED TO HAVE NED BACK AT THE CASTLE LONG before four o'clock supper, they turned homeward, picking their way slowly up the high street that ran towards the castle on the easterly side of the market. Heloise carried Ned. Brian, the older archer, had gestured an offer to take the child from her but she was adamant that the two men should keep their distance. A mistake, for the child grew heavier by the moment and the little dog was whining to be carried too.

It was then that townsfolk ahead of her swore and scattered to the doorways. A half dozen horsemen in sallets and brigandines whipped their horses urgently down the street, spattering mud as they galloped past. Heloise cursed roundly and one of the hindmost riders laughed.

"Whoresons!" a lilting voice bawled after them and there was an answering growl of *"Saeson, y diawled"* from the crowd and a contemptuous spit of saliva on the cobbles. The sibilant whisper of Welsh and unease made her apprehensive. She shared the people's anger. Perhaps these were local ruffians like the Vaughans, come to drink and make trouble. She began to hurry and the archers moved closer.

The horsemen made a rapid circuit of the town and must have met up with riders who had gone counterwise, for suddenly a dozen of the knaves galloped forth from Shepe Street. Still clasping Ned, Heloise shrank back against the wall to let them pass but the foremost man yelled at her two archers and skidded to a halt, blocking her way. The others joined him, forming a semi-circle of leather and sweating horseflesh about her. Ned awoke and started screaming in genuine terror at the huffing nostrils of the horses. No trouble now, she prayed, anxious for the boy's safety, not like this, with half of Brecknock looking on and Ned's dog whining ludicrously at her toecaps. But the men surrounding her looked as ill at ease as she.

She was cut off from the archers. Anyway, they would be no match for these armored brigands. Then she realized that each man-at-arms wore a span-wide badge, a loose yellow knot, across their hearts. The badge that the castle servants wore upon their sable and gules tabards.

"Go away!" Ned shouted. "Take the horses away!"

A horseman clothed in black leather hose and short doublet, with the hood of his riding cloak shielding his head against the increasing rain, imperiously edged his steed into the circle. Heloise was conscious of the chain of authority glimmering across his shoulders before his gloved hand thrust back the grey hood. Disdainful eyes beneath haughty dark brows stared down upon the child, then the man's mouth tightened in annoyance and he glanced into the crowd as if seeking someone. It was no use waiting like a fearful, tiny bird for the shadow of this hawk to pass. Miles Rushden's steed threw up its head and showed its teeth, and Ned began to scream and scream.

*   *   *

"DRAW BACK!" THE GIRL WAS DEMANDING. "CAN YOU NOT SEE you are terrifying him?"

They had found Harry's boy, thank God, but where was the erring new governess of the nursery? Had she recklessly consigned the duke's heir to a maidservant while she gossiped or bought some pretty trinkets? Miles had been unprepared to discover that the sticky-faced, exhausted burden bawling against the wench's bodice was Lord Edward Stafford. He knew the other voice and yet . . .

Miles's gaze no longer lingered on the child, it rose exploratively over the girl's uncovered throat and was held by the troubled beauty and unlooked-for, bewitching familiarity in the creature's face. He put a thumb and forefinger to eyes that had seen too many miles and looked again. It *was* his *de jure* wife who stood there absurdly with mud spattering her skirts and a mongrel cur stringed to her wrist.

HELOISE BARELY HEARD THE HISS OF RECOGNITION FROM THE people at her husband's coming. The earth shook uncertainly beneath her feet and it was not just because the great hooves of his horse shifted restlessly. Pinioned beneath that gaze, she prayed, breathless, with all the strength she had, that he could not possibly recognize her—but the man's expression had already darkened. The stallion protested as the grip on the reins abruptly tightened. Disbelief, disgust, and anger flashed across his ruined face and then, as he remembered the waiting, watching soldiers, a visor of control slid down and he was their leader again.

"Sir." Brian the archer had shouldered his way through and now stood at his stirrup like a petitioner. "Be easy, sir, naught has gone amiss."

Had it not . . ., fumed Miles, but his men were waiting for his orders. "Take the cur!" he commanded, with a jerk of his head.

Heloise watched as the archer slid the string from her wrist. He gave her a wink of reassurance, but her entire being was centered on Miles Rushden's anger. She thanked God they had an audience; he could not abuse her here—or could he?

"*Lady* Haute?" The lift of eyebrow conveyed his mockery as much as did the disdainful quirk of lip. A smile no deeper than the travel stubble on his cheeks told her that she had never looked less like a noblewoman.

"The mud is from your men's hooves, Sir Miles," she retaliated, and then realized the enormity of what she had just said. In a few words of wild defense she had turned his taunt into a recognition, made him a conspirator to her deception in front of the Stafford soldiers and in the common hearing. He drew breath, jaw clenched, and she alone guessed how much he was battling to contain his fury.

Sweet Christ help her, this was not how she had intended this meeting. She had imagined a few words with him privily, a chance to explain her circumstances, make him understand before she dared to ask for help, advice, whatever he would be prepared to give. She could only stare up at him now, bereft.

The great horse he rode frisked, impatient for its stall, and had to be reined round, but it gave its rider a chance to leash his temper. One of the burlier soldiers broke the silence, coughing in amusement at his superior being bested. A woman in the crowd sniggered and a stone skidded among the horses' fetlocks.

Miles's expression tightened and his soldiers officiously swiveled round with menacing glares at the townsfolk. The closest onlookers edged away.

Witch-maid! The Devil carry him to Hell if he knew what to do now. How dare she stand there, lovely despite her shabby, ill-fitting gown, with Harry's son in her arms? The deceiving, greedy vixen! Tracking him to Brecknock! What was she after, payment to hold her tongue? Surely her father already had more gold than Midas. What, then? Public acknowledgment that she was now his wife? But why the assumed name? Surely it was the queen who had recommended Lady Haute. What other game was she playing? He stared at her, perplexed, and then, realizing that they were causing a spectacle, he swiftly saluted the duke's grubby heir.

"I give you good day, my little lord. His grace your father has returned and desires your presence. Come!" He beckoned Ned to mount before him but the wretched infant shrank back, cowering at the horse's impatient hooves.

"I will take him." Sir William Knyvett, red-faced and hardly dressed for riding, spurred into the circle. "There is no harm done here, Rushden," he announced, clearly to reassure himself. No harm done! The heir of the Duke of Buckingham appareled like a tinker's bastard, and his slatternly one-night wife here to demand her rights. *No harm?*

Sir William's arrival shook Mistress Ballaster out of her daze and her cunning returned.

"No, of course not. Please be at ease on that, Sir Miles." Enough sweetness to choke a man. God forgive her! Then the dissembling strumpet inclined her head graciously at him as if they were meeting at the palaces of Westminster or Eltham. Her glance rose to his but instead of a challenge or pathetic beseeching, the wench's eyes were guileless. The Devil take her, what a player! No wonder she had already deceived Sir William into employing her. Miles was so speechless that it was she who nodded to the archer to assist her.

"Let's be having you, my lord." The man lifted the unprotesting child from her arms and passed him up onto Knyvett's saddle, where the whelp lolled back against Sir William, sucking his thumb scornfully at Miles.

"May I leave you to bring Lady Haute, Rushden . . . Rushden?"

"My pleasure, Sir William," he answered with feeling and turned a predatory face towards his wife.

Nine

Heloise had no more intention of riding back with Miles Rushden than mounting a broomstick. She ignored the arm he held down to her. "Thank you, Sir Miles, but I cannot sully your saddle. It is no distance, I should prefer to walk."

"Oh, I'll swear you would." The gloved hand waited menacingly. "You will come back with me now, *my lady.*" His voice, low and dangerous, offered no escape. He raised his stirruped boot to make a mounting block for her. Cursing silently that they were still an entertainment, she reluctantly set her left foot upon his and took the proffered hand. His hands, tense and fierce about her waist, settled her before him, and then he kneed his horse about. The people drew back, hushed and outwardly respectful, to let them pass. His men followed. An apprentice whooped, someone else jeered, and again she heard the hiss of words she did not understand.

Biting her lip, Heloise sat as stiffly as she could, trying hard to avoid any part of her body touching his, but the reins and arms encircled her too closely for her peace of mind. The memory of that shameful night at Bramley came vividly back to her. She had imagined dealing with him in a formal manner, not in this enforced intimacy with his elbows against her breasts and his breath upon her cheek.

"Lady Haute," Rushden sneered, adding in a growl for her ears only, "and what have you done with her? Pushed her into a river?"

"No, she— Sweet Christ, look out!"

With an oath at his stupidity, Miles reined his steed out of the way of an alehouse pole. One of the soldiers behind them chuckled at his distraction. No, here was not the time for settlement but later it would be a pleasure! He stoked his anger fur-

ther, remembering the final humiliation of that wedding night—
of fleeing barefoot across the icy ploughed fields to smite upon
the priest's door at Oakwood shivering as he pleaded to borrow
attire from the sexton so he might return to his father's house.
It was Christ's mercy that he had not died from cold.

"You need not be a-feared," his armful said soothingly, as if
she were sympathetic to the discord of feelings jarring him.
"They do not know I am me."

The obscure, *female* explanation mollified him not at all. "No,
by God, but I do! Believe me, when I have done with you,
mistress," he continued through clenched teeth, "you will wish
you had never been born."

"I expect you would like Traveller back."

He was too angry to listen properly. "A plague on that, mistress! I want you out of my sight and out of my life!"

"But—"

"I will deal with you, madam!" He spurred the horse up Castle
Lane to jolt the meaning into her head.

The stupid, gummy grin that the porter gave "Lady Haute"
as they galloped over the drawbridge was enough to turn an
honest man's stomach. With a curse, Miles drew rein beside Knyvett in the crowded courtyard and was disgusted that the stable
boy who ran up to take his bridle was also wearing a smile for
Mistress Ballaster as if she had bestowed a livery on him. Had
the slut bewitched every man jack of them? He dismounted to
a distinct hush. Godsakes! Just when he thought he had put
leagues between himself and Heloise Ballaster, here were half of
Harry's retinue gawking at the pair of them.

"Got yourself a wet nurse, sir?" guffawed someone.

Miles gave the man an archer's two-finger gesture and turned
to deal with his passenger. His tarnished wife had made no attempt to wriggle down. In fact she seemed bewildered by all the
wagons and packhorses being unloaded about them and the flush
across her cheeks and throat proclaimed her shame. He had little
choice but to set his hands about the wench's high waist and

feign indifference as he dumped her down. His hands, however, held her longer than they should have. For an instant she wobbled precariously, like a slowing spinning top, before she rallied her wits and slithered swiftly from his clasp to take the sleepy child from Knyvett.

"You goin' to put Rushden to bed too, darlin'?" chortled some wit.

Miles laughed, but inwardly he was fit to throttle his witch-wife. Not only was she a disgrace to her rank dressed as she was, but the heart-shaped face and the brat clutched to her breast bestowed a Madonna-like purity the dishonest piece did not deserve. It should have been Sioned standing there in his life, with their little boy in her arms.

"Been frightening her, Rushden?" Knyvett was running his thumb across a smudge of dried tears on the wretched creature's cheekbone and pinching her cheek like a foolish dotard. "Your quarrel should be with me. I gave permission."

Miles peeled off his gloves. "I leave it to your conscience, Knyvett."

"No incident occurred, Rushden."

"Not for want of trying, it seems." He deliberately blocked Mistress Ballaster's way, mainly because he wanted to be difficult and it seemed a temporary measure to keep the lid on his temper.

"Where's my puppy?" demanded the boy petulantly, rousing his face from the girl's bodice, and the large archer materialized like an obedient sheepdog to wind the string around the sticky fist.

"Your pardon, sirs," Heloise cut in breathlessly, "I—I must have Lord Stafford bathed straightway." Preferably before his father saw him! She was desperate to escape the stares of the throng about her. Not only was Rushden clearly itching to upbraid her, but Brecknock had suddenly become unfamiliar, peopled with strangers, and she was bone weary. Ned seemed to weigh heavier with every step as she navigated the barrels and the coffers, making for cover where the hawks who ruled this alien world could not fly at her.

"Lady Haute!"

A new voice assailed her before she had taken a few paces. The jingle of spurred boots on the cobbles hastened. She faltered and turned.

A profusion of freckles, almost obliterating the milk white complexion beneath, spattered the handsome face of the youngish man who had followed her. She was aware of hair the color of mace lapping back from a high forehead and secured at his nape with a leather string, of snowy sleeves bursting out of slashed velvet sleeves, and the expensive embroidery, the golden knots in militant downward rows upon his doublet. Blue eyes glittered with a mercurial mischief that made the man hard to decipher.

"Surely this cannot be my son?" This duke did not have the calm authority of Richard of Gloucester but his tone carried the insolent freedom of high rank. He probably expected her to be humbled by his attention but Heloise was tired of the chilling wind, the meandering rain, men, and fathers in particular. Although Miles Rushden might frighten her, she was not in awe of his betters. Living in Gloucester's household had cured her of such inhibitions.

"Is this my son?" he repeated.

"I suppose he must be," replied Heloise, her normal composure irritated, and blushed, realizing she had just cuckolded the Duke of Buckingham's manhood and spattered the virtue of the queen's sister. "I—I mean if you are my lord of Buckingham then—"

The duke's expression did not change; clearly he had learned not to show his emotions. He glanced over his shoulder, knowing they were observed: "The *lady* asks if I am Buckingham?" His gaze astonishingly singled out her husband, but the rest of the Stafford retinue paused in unpacking, invited to observe her mortification.

Rushden briskly detached himself from his men, his whole

demeanor as purposeful as a hunter. With a sinking heart, Heloise realized that the true confrontation, the humiliating unmasking she had hoped might take place in more favorable circumstances, was upon her now.

Miles stopped short, delaying his intention to proclaim his unwanted wife a calculating, mercenary baggage. What on earth was Harry making of her? Incredibly, despite drying mud bedaubing the wench's hem and the honey stains bespecked with dust upon her bodice, the picky Duke of Buckingham was eyeing Mistress Ballaster with the covert cunning of a horse dealer out for a bargain.

Possessiveness unreasonably overwhelmed Miles; Heloise Ballaster was his to deal with how he pleased and he wanted neither interference nor interest shown in her until he had made up his mind how to be rid of her without the entire castle listening in.

"Am I the duke, Miles?"

"Yes, your grace, so please your lady mother."

Harry turned his head at the sudden formality starching his friend's voice. "How reassuring." With a chill smile that promised the girl further conversation, the duke turned on his heel and strode away.

Heloise let out a quiet breath, and because the bailey was still a mess of people, managed to look her powerful enemy in the face. Tired and chastened, her courage was vanishing as the truth sank into her weary mind. Miles Rushden had been no braggart at Bramley; he was indeed the Duke of Buckingham's trusted friend and henchman. Ned came to her rescue. He rearranged himself around her, demanding attention, and a flicker of irrational pain, dislike even, showed briefly in Rushden's face.

"You shall be called to answer for your actions later, madam," he told her coldly and jerked his right hand in dismissal. Well, women could emulate such hauteur too and with a curt nod, she hoicked the child higher and marched away. It was then that the puppy, still ribboned to Ned's wrist, decided to demolish her dignity by depositing a steaming coil upon the cobbles. Rushden, thank the saints, had already reached the steps to the great hall and did not see.

Guffaws of masculine laughter burst from the soldiers close by. Another time Heloise would have shrugged cheerfully; instead she hastened towards the nearest bolt-hole. It turned out embarrassingly to be the entrance to the garrison guardroom and a couple of soldiers caught gossiping in the passageway gaped at her, their expressions turning swiftly predatory, but old Brian had tactfully followed her in. Chuckling, he once more lifted the child from her arms and escorted her towards her quarters as if she were the one who needed a nursemaid.

Bess, bless her, had a fire warming the nursery and a small cauldron of hot water steaming over the glowing coals. The door to Heloise's bedchamber had been kindly propped open, so that too was cozy. How wonderful to surrender Ned into Bess's capable hands. Fragile and thankful to be alone, Heloise crept onto her bed and wept softly into her pillow. Sleep must have claimed her briefly for she dreamed of a large man fishing and laughing while the clouds above gathered into a seething miasma, before a tiny hand shook her shoulder.

"Mistress Bess has a ewer ready if you wish it. I've had my bath." The child left her and closed the door.

Slowly she bestirred herself, unleashed her hair from the coif, and lifted the ewer to the floor, chiding herself for letting the water cool.

"Why is your hair silver?" Ned interrupted, returning at an inopportune moment.

Dripping with soapwort, Heloise parted the silver strands and surveyed the crinkled, bath-pink child crouched opposite the basin. It was hard to converse intelligently, kneeling with your forehead upside down in a basin. He repeated his question in case she had water in her ears.

Heloise sighed, wrung her hair, and wrapped a flannel cloth about her head.

"Yes, Ned, silver and different from yours and Bess's. Have

you noticed people are afraid of anything that is different?"

"Like my father because he is a duke? Or Benet because his eyes are crossed?"

"Exactly. And because my hair turned this hue when I was a girl, people fear I am of the elfish folk."

"I should like to have a *dewines* or one of the *tylwyth teg* for my governess." His puckered smile was beseeching.

"No." Heloise shook her head. She could not tell him of the frightening, unasked-for visions.

"Oooh, could you be a changeling and not know it? I wish I had been one, then I could do mischief at night, turn the milk sour, and frighten people." He touched her damp hair. "It feels the same as mine."

She kissed her fingertips and transferred the kiss to his little nose. "Can we keep this a secret, sweetheart? I do not like people to know, only those I love."

"And do you love me? I am not afraid of your hair."

"I am right glad of that, and yes, I believe I do love you, my little lord."

Tiny arms slid about her neck, stroking her wet hair back behind her ears. "Thank you for taking me to the town. Shall you get beaten?"

"No, not anymore," she said firmly. "Now, shall we take supper in the nursery?"

His reluctant governess was halfway through coaxing buttered leek into him while she unfolded the tale of the Loathly Lady and Sir Gawaine, when Bess knocked to inform her they were both to attend the duke before supper. Heloise felt sympathy for defenseless rabbits and wondered which might prove her greatest enemy now: the fox-haired duke or his heartless shadow.

THE LAVENDER DAMASK OVERGOWN WAS ELEGANT BUT NOT subversive, Heloise hoped as she tugged the matching cap down over her coiled braids and made the wire framework that propped her veil comfortable about her ears. Angling the silver mirror

back from her, she decided that the gown's sloping collar with
the respectably high inset of silk across her breasts surely bespoke
neither wantonness nor ambitions above her station. If she could
only survive the talons tonight. With a deep breath, she squared
her shoulders and set out for dangerous open meadows.

An astonishing change had taken place. Now that the duke's
retinue had returned, the great hall was almost as grand as Middleham's. All the candles and cressets were alive with light, logs
were burning in the main hearth, tapestries and painted arras
hung upon the walls, and a long white cloth, its folds stylishly
pleated about a pace apart, covered the board that sat across the
dais. And as was usual in great lords' households, messes of bread,
each sufficient to serve four, were set at intervals. The delicious
smell of roasting meats laced air perfumed with pine.

The hall usher was placing the knights and men-at-arms but
there was not a gentlewoman to be seen.

"Lady Haute?" The duke's chamberlain, Sir Nicholas Latimer,
introduced himself. "From now on you are to be seated there."
He pointed his wand of office to a place not far below the dais.
"But his grace will speak with you in the great chamber first."

Interested faces watched as she was conducted through the
hall and up the steps to the door behind the dais. She had hoped
she would be scarcely recognizable as the emburdened nursemaid,
but one of the esquires giggled and said, "Woof," and a knight
gave her a wink and a friendly, canine "Grrr."

She should have had her hackles raised. His grace of Buckingham, with his leather-slippered heels resting carelessly upon
a small table, had already chastened a weeping Bess and was
primed like a crossbow to shoot bolts into her self-esteem as well.
The younger girl drooped before him like a penitent, tearful-eyed
and hands piously clasped. Sir William was there too, standing
akimbo at the casement, his back huffily turned and thumbs a-
twiddle. Had his grace been berating him too or was it the well-
stacked fire that had heightened the older man's color?

"Lady Haute." The tone was mocking. Ringed fingers directed

Bess to step aside and make room for the new prisoner. If this had been Middleham, his grace of Gloucester would have taken Heloise's hand courteously; this duke remained seated. She curtsied; it was one of her best—and wasted, since he did not acknowledge it.

"You are younger than we expected."

"I have sufficient grey hairs, so please your grace."

Buckingham's expression remained inscrutable at her impertinence and he rose irritably and paced to the hearth, fingers slapping against knuckles behind his back. There was a sense of player about him, Heloise realized, and wondered how long he expected her to quiver in servile trepidation before he turned to deliver a coup de grâce. "I believe, however, that I have established a satisfactory understanding with your son, my lord," she informed his back in her most cheerful manner.

"Satisfactory understanding," he echoed scathingly, swinging round to face her. Heloise waited for the blast and it came with excellent timing. "Taking my son where there is risk of infection." He let that sink in and continued in chilling tones: "Wasting good money on trinkets and some pesty cur when our castle is overrun with a plague of puppies already."

"That may be true, my lord," she countered, "but Lord Stafford did not wheeze a single time at the market and Bess has bathed the little dog most diligently and combed out all its fleas. Has Ned spoken with you yet? He was most anxious to tell you about the sword swallower."

A swift sideways glance came at her; Sir William sucked in his cheeks and displayed a sudden artistic interest in the gilded ribs of the ceiling.

"Sword swallower!" Buckingham folded his arms, intending, no doubt, to stare her down. "Would you by any chance be telling me my business?"

"Yes, your grace." Investing in another curtsy, Heloise raised candid eyes to discover that he was not looking at her.

"What do you say, Miles? Shackle the lady in our best dungeon with a score of Brecknock's largest rats?"

Her husband left the doorway and stepped past her skirts. The smooth cut of his unembellished grey doublet made Buckingham's hectic brocade and glittery buttons fulsome. "Oh yes," he answered dryly, "as many as will make her merry," and half-seated himself upon the table, one of his splendid hanging sleeves almost touching her knees.

"Rats have feelings too, your grace," answered Heloise recklessly and stood up unbidden. "Do you need to punish them as well?"

But the duke's amusement had been merely stubble deep. "Dear God, my lady, are you seriously expecting me to surrender my son into your seditious keeping? You will have him wishing to be a silly ploughman."

Heloise shook her head. "I did consider ploughing might keep him occupied for half an hour but no, I do not think that is a good notion, so please you."

"Ploughing," echoed his grace ambiguously, exchanging looks with her husband. Sucking in his cheeks, he turned to face the fire again, leaving Heloise confused as to whether she was being indulged, condemned, or merely laughed at. It also left her almost nose to nose with her enigmatic husband.

Why had he not denounced her? Was it because he feared for Traveller or did he believe she would tell his duke about their marriage? She raised an eyebrow at him as much as to say, If you are going to set a noose about my neck, make haste; but Miles Rushden was not studying her like a highway brigand waiting to commit an assault. There was confusion behind his cold grey eyes, as if he were trying to make sense of her, to find evidence of the slattern. He had not seen her dressed like a lady before—but then she remembered her wedding gown and blushed. His chin rose in triumph as if he had drawn blood, and she stepped back, abruptly sensing not just his lazy enmity. Her eyes cursed him, but the musk he wore pricked her senses as he drew his gaze slowly up from her feet, sliding over the damask like a hand finding a path upwards, touching but not touching. She was waiting as the shadow reached her lips, and her body stirred unforgivably at the game he was playing to insult her.

The duke turned, fingers rubbing across his well-shaven chin. "You are pardoned this time, Lady Haute. Obviously Sir William and the nursemaid here did not make my orders clear."

Bess hung her head and Heloise reached out, drawing her close, but Buckingham was unimpressed by the show of female unity. "Miles, in God's name, find some means to imprint it on these silly creatures' brains that certain measures have to be observed for the safety of us all. Let us be very clear on one thing, my lady governess. You are not to take my son from the castle without my authority. Mine or Sir Miles's." His ringed hand clapped Rushden's pouched shoulder. "Do you understand me, madam! You put my son at considerable risk taking him into Brecknock. Is that not right, Knyvett?"

The older man coughed, nodding at the verbal jab. "Aye, not wise of me to permit it. Plaguey Welsh!"

Did it not depend on how the Welsh were treated?

"I assure your grace the English and Welsh stallkeepers seemed very happy to do business with us and . . ." Heloise faltered as the duke's cynical gaze told her what a mirror did not—that any young woman of reasonable looks could gain attention.

"How long have you been at Brecknock, *Lady Haute*?" Rushden took his turn at scything her self-confidence.

Her chin lifted. "A week."

He unfolded his arms and moved round to flank the duke. "Then, of course, you are omniscient on Welsh affairs, my lady. Our pardon for trying to correct you."

Her telltale skin flamed crimson in the uncomfortable silence but then Bess's stomach noisily pleaded hunger and the duke wearily gestured them out. "Take your places in the hall, mesdames. I find you amusing, Lady Haute, but learn to accept advice."

Rushden followed Heloise out onto the dais with an indifferent face but his words were aimed to irritate. "How many children have you had, my lady? Six, is it not?"

Heloise glanced sideways at him as she reached the edge of the dais; he was baiting her.

"Enough babes to know that Lord Stafford needs both love and an understanding of when his behavior is unacceptable," she retorted, sweeping ahead. "But I am sure you at least try to set him a good example, sir," she added witheringly. "Come, Bess!"

Supper—especially as she loathed eels—was a torment. In respect of their returned master, the servants Heloise had become acquainted with no longer jested as they served. Bess was clearly awed by her superior's courage in answering the lords of the castle in their own coinage. The younger girl made a noble effort with gossip, running her memory along the faces who sat opposite as if they were a row of rosary beads. Heloise tried to give a semblance of being entertained but a few covert glances at the dais told her that her forward demeanor was being discussed by the men who sat there. Under their scrutiny, she ate very little and spoke even less.

At least her husband had not given her disguise away yet; she was sure of that. Thrice she discovered him watching her, and swiftly looked away, her breath catching. It irked her to be so dependent on his concealing her true identity but she must win more time. It was not just her own security that she feared to lose; Ned would feel himself betrayed if she ran away and she wanted the duke to see the new cheerfulness in his son.

After Buckingham rose from the board, the hall slowly emptied. Instead of Rushden following the duke, he came down to where the women sat.

"Attend me, mesdames," he ordered officiously and strode off down the hall, expecting them to follow.

"That man is trouble with an illuminated *T*," muttered Heloise, snagging her gown on the edge of the bench as she rose. "Is he aught but a knightly page boy to the duke?"

Checking to ensure no one else had heard, Bess giggled at her outrageous disrespect but sobered swiftly, her fingers working to unsnare the fabric. "Pray do not be crossing swords with him, my lady, and we'd best not tarry. He is the duke's sword arm. Y *Cysgod*, the Welsh call him."

"E Shisgod? And what does that mean?"

"The Shadow, my lady, and he is to be feared."

THE BAILEY, DUSKY IN THE TWILIGHT, WAS HAZARDOUS; THE grooms had not finished shoveling the yard clean and it was necessary for Heloise and Bess to choose their path with care, for the windows of the hall, lit from behind, gleamed magically but offered little illumination. Rushden was waiting, arms folded, his whole stance impatient and imperious. Beside him stood a servant with a flaming torch held at arm's length so that no sparks would fall upon their clothing.

"Dear me, Sir Miles, are we to have a tour of the dungeons to sober our *silly* heads?"

"A ducking stool might be more appropriate. Over here, if you please, mesdames." He indicated an empty two-wheeled cart, and frowned as a cat, black as coal save for the splash of white down his muzzle and shirtfront, sprang up to mew for attention between the wooden banisters. "What do you see, madam?"

It was not easy to notice anything in the flickering light. Heloise picked up Dafydd and arranged him purring against her shoulder as she examined the shafts. "What are we looking for, sir?"

"Deliberate damage."

Heloise stooped and instinctively ran her fingers over the nearest wooden spoke. She heard his hiss of breath as she fingered the saw cut but fearing it might reinforce his suspicion of her sorcery, she deliberately explored the other spokes before she returned to the damage. "Here."

"Aye, that is the Welsh for you. God knows how far it would have got before it tipped its load. There is more." He dismissed the torchbearer and led them into the lower floor of a tower, some sort of harness store. A pair of servants dicing by a brazier sprang up to salute him, rapidly pocketing the dice. Rushden ignored them and they thankfully slunk back out of sight.

"See this." The duke's friend grabbed a handful of leather girth straps set aside for repair and carried them into the light of the horn lantern.

"All hacked through," whispered Bess. "By our Lady, sir, I had no notion."

"It is only eight years since the last rising. So, you can see how well they love us, Bess. Now do you understand why Lord Stafford must not be put at risk?"

A mutual concern. Heloise nodded gravely, meeting his stern perusal. No doubt he had been expecting some feckless answer, for his expression lightened for an instant, and Heloise remembered their confrontation in the orchard with a sense of loss. If only her father had not intervened, they might have become friends instead of enemies. Dionysia had dismissed Miles Rushden as pockmarked, something that Heloise had hardly noticed. Goodness, in the poor light now, the scatter of scars hardly showed at all. She saw instead the strength of purpose in that jawline.

Rushden's fingers slid meaningfully along the strap, raising his voice so that the men might hear. "If it is someone from the castle, the consequences . . ." There was definitely something attractive about men who enjoyed power, maybe it was that edge of danger in challenging such a man's intelligence and authority. "Lady Haute, are you listening?" Rushden's supercilious look had been replaced by an anxious scowl as if he feared she was going to announce some dire revelation like she had at Bramley.

"Yes, indeed, sir. But why would anyone bother to wreak such mischief?" she asked as he tossed the leather girths back on the pile. "It is not as though Welshmen will ever gain their independence now and I cannot see as how they are hard done by."

"The prophecy of Myrddin. Merlin, in our tongue."

"Merlin? King Arthur's Merlin?"

"Certes, my lady. The Welsh believe greener grass grows apace in Brittany. Some Welshmen see Tudor as a second Arthur who will lead them to a golden age."

"Tudor, you mean *Henry* Tudor?" Heloise owned to amazement. The descendant of the bastard line of Lancaster! Surely it was unthinkable. "But Tudor is a child still."

"Not anymore. He is only a year or so younger than his grace our duke." Rushden allowed his words to sink in then added, "And *Ned,* mesdames, is of Plantagenet stock. After the king's kinsmen, he has a claim to the throne and must be protected."

"Well, no harm came of today, sir," muttered Bess. "Lady Haute had two of the archers with her. Your pardon, but I must needs say, sir, that since my lady's coming, Lord Stafford has been as good tempered as a dog with a bowl of bones to gnaw."

"So long as the bones are not poisoned, Bess," Rushden answered sternly, and held open the door for them to leave.

Heloise lingered. "I promise you, Sir Miles, I shall guard Lord Stafford as though . . . as though he were my own son."

The wall cresset flared momentarily betraying a sudden sensitivity in his face as though her words had pained him, and then the pewter gaze turned quicksilver. "Perhaps I speak out of turn, but should you not be home in Kent, providing your lord with sons, madam, or have you given him an heir and a second son besides?"

"I trust I am here with my husband's blessing, Sir Miles, but, in truth," she continued with a sigh, including Bess in the conversation, "I wish most heartily that I might speak with my husband this very instant, and tell him how it is with me."

"Sometimes we cannot have what we should like." His double meaning might have gone unmarked but as Bess looked back at her with compassion, Miles Rushden indulged himself by bestowing upon Heloise a summer gaze that spoke of a shared bedchamber and a licensed view of her nakedness.

How dared he! She was no wanton harlot! Why would he not

let her speak with him and explain? Or did he plan to keep her in torment like a caged wild bird? She must have trembled with anger and shame, for the younger girl's arm came about her. "There now, my lady."

"I am well enow, Bess." Her heart frantic, she leaned back against one of the upright beams and saw now that she had Rushden anxious. Did he fear she was having another premonition? Within his sleeves, the man had his fingers crossed against her but his eyes were also on her belly as if he feared she had come to Brecknock to foist a by-blow upon him. Surely he did not suspect that she had taken a lover since their unhappy wedding night! It was definitely time she sorted matters out with him.

"I thank you for your time in explaining the need for vigilance, sir. Come, Bess."

MILES TARRIED LONGER ADMONISHING THE DICE PLAYERS, BUT when he strode out into the bailey, Mistress Ballaster was still there. "Pray go on to the nursery without me," she was saying, "and make sure Ned is abed, not tormenting poor old Benet." Bess unfortunately did not dally.

Miles scowled. Now what did Mistress Ballaster have in mind? A promise in some out-of-sight corner? Weeping or seduction? At least a grovel?

He called out, "Lady Haute, I thank you for your assistance tonight. Good night to you." With a desperate longing for a score of torches and an audience of hundreds, he kept a healthy distance between them, gave his sorceress a curt nod, and headed for the steps of the great hall.

She hurried after him. "Sir! I have a further matter to raise with you." Yes, he knew what that was.

On the bottom foot of the steps, where there was more traffic, he half-turned, his dark frown warning her to stay away from him. "There is nothing to be raised, I assure you, madam." Color suffused her cheeks at his insult but she stood her ground.

"We have to talk. You must understand. . . . *Please.* I want to explain."

"Enough, madam!"

Heloise sped after him, overtaking him on the top step. "Sir, you can at least—"

Her husband did not turn until he had reached the great hall where they might be observed; only then did he pause. Heloise let go the fistfuls of her gown, smoothed the damask and her temper.

"Will you give me a hearing at long last?" she asked him, smiling as if they were sharing amiable banter.

His mouth curved slightly but his eyes were hard as lodes-terres. "Admire the tapestry, madam."

"Oh." His meaning caught; she gazed up at Diana changing Actaeon into a stag. *Sensible goddess!*

"Now suppose you tell me how much money you intend to extort from me."

"Are you worth so much?" She stared pointedly at the bee harvesting the forget-me-nots and then lifted her gaze to the oak tree where a nightingale perched, the symbol of cheerful, indus-trious womanhood. "I would like to remain as Lord Stafford's governess."

"You, a nightingale! Keep looking at the tapestry! Godsakes, so that is it. Inveigle yourself into everyone's good graces and then expose me as a heartless cur."

"That is a monstrous suggestion." She turned from him, as if about to flounce away, then changed her mind, and swept back to his elbow, her fingers daintily masking her lips as she said through her teeth, glaring at the crouching Actaeon, "I do not blame the Welsh for wreaking what petty havoc they can."

That drew blood. He was conscious of them being watched. "I remind you, madam, if you cannot manage to obey our rules, you had best . . . *leave immediately!*" He saw her right hand clench but she was too wise to make a spectacle of the pair of them. The fingers straightened. "That is sensible," he added in a calming voice, treating her like he would Traveller. "Keep your anger sheathed."

Had she been glaring at him, he might have sprouted antlers too. "Do not patronize me, you hellspawn, or I shall tell the world this instant you are my husband."

"You truly want that?" he scoffed, with a sweep of an arm as if he was explaining the symbolism of the squirrel in the hazel bush behind Actaeon. "Surely you want to be free of me? Look at the tassels!"

She stooped to study the decoration that dangled along the lower border. "Of course I do." That was said with bushels of feeling as she straightened. "Diana had sense!" she muttered. "Perhaps I should put horns on your head."

He fingered a woolly thistle. "Dearest, darling Heloise," he began, his tone nice as poisoned honey, "if you are here to ensure that Holy Church never severs us, I will make your life with me so delightful that you will wish yourself beset by all the plagues of Egypt—simultaneously! Now buzz away. We have been standing here long enough."

Heloise bit her lip and managed to stanch her temper, convinced that she still held the upper hand. Surely he would have unmasked her otherwise. He wanted his freedom and she was sure he wanted his horse. "And Traveller? I have looked after him for you, and saved him from being sold. Give me fair hearing and you shall have him back."

He feigned indifference but Miles did not tell her he would whistle outside every stall and byre from Brecknock to Hereford if need be to find his beloved horse. "Lady, I have already replaced him and I shall certainly replace you."

Ten

"His grace is asking for you, sir." Heloise let her breath out as a young henchman interrupted them. With an officious nod, as if he had merely been speaking with her out of duty, Rushden paced off to the great chamber and she was left with a boyish knight whose exuberant grin through straw-colored hair reminded her of Ned's puppy. A possible ally?

"Sir Richard de la Bere." He introduced himself with a flourish and pulled a waggish face at the tapestry. "Poor old Actaeon."

Heloise cocked her head to one side. "No, pity the unfortunate goddess."

"Why?" He hailed the panther and ordered a cup of perry for her.

"Why, Sir Richard? Because Diana must stay chaste now. She has cut off her nose to spite her face, for Master Actaeon is a handsome lover and she has spurned him."

He laughed. "I say, that's a refreshing philosophy, Lady Haute." With a kindly arm, he led her to the fire. "Good health, my lady! How was your journey here?"

She was telling him about Hoel's foibles when the duke came down into the hall with Rushden at his side. The pair of them strode off purposefully out into the bailey like two dogs off on a night scavenge. It was tempting to linger with de la Bere but somehow the conversation had turned to hunting—clearly his passion—and the servants were pointedly snuffing out the candles, so Heloise pleaded weariness. Her new friend—involved in tracking a hart through Stockley Wood—looked disappointed that she did not wish to hear of his final triumph, but let her go.

Compared to Middleham, Brecknock's stairs and passages were meanly lit and Heloise took care climbing the spiraling stone steps to the next floor and cautiously contemplated the evil passageway. The night before, a rat had raced ahead of her. She was reminding herself to always carry a taper when a gloved hand swooped across her mouth and a relentless arm dragged her struggling into a small hidden chamber behind the arras.

"Hold still, damn you!" her legal owner snarled after she jabbed her elbow fiercely into his chest. Physical fear subsided into healthy annoyance but her heart was still galloping like a horse stung by a gadfly and her skirts were so intimately entangled with a stool that she was forced to cease trying to kick Rushden's shins and hang on to his sleeves instead. He let her go with an oath. A flint rasped and the room about them flickered into detail as he lit a single candle set in a wall cresset. They were in a small, paneled chamber off the chapel; Heloise caught a glimpse of the shrouded altar before her captor locked that entrance and dropped the key into the fringed purse on his belt. Then he set the bar across the door he had just hauled her through and surveyed her with the satisfied expression of a dragon that had returned to a cave to gloat over its hoard.

"When I mentioned we needed to talk," muttered Heloise, tugging her bodice straight, "I did not anticipate it would be such a struggle." With her headdress looking like a dislodged chimney pot and hair tumbling down over her right ear, any attempt to look grave and earnest would not wash. "Are you expecting me to kneel and confess to horse theft and extortion?" She indicated the prie-dieu, the only other furnishing in the room, save for the toppled stool and a crucifix on the wall.

"Now that would be a wonder," Rushden answered, leaning back against the door. "You have only a few moments to state your case before my patience wears through. I advise you not to be wasteful."

"Is this tête-à-tête not unwise, sir?" She righted the stool and picked up a fallen prayer book, smoothing its bruised pages regretfully before she fastened the clasps back together. "It takes few moments to conceive a child. I should have thought you would have engineered a peacock tail of eyes to witness our argument and keep our conversation chaste."

That ruffled his tail feathers no end. "I am waiting, Mistress Ballaster."

"Well . . ." She replaced the book on its oblique shelf, marveling that her weariness had so swiftly abated. "In a nutshell"—she steepled her fingers—"I have been banished from Bramley and now have neither income nor prospects outside these walls, thanks to you and my father." Pacing to and fro like a lioness in the king's menagerie, she added, "And I would be the last person to deny Dionysia her chance to find a worthy husband, so when—"

"The point of this," he interrupted tersely, slapping his hand on the top of the prie-dieu.

"The point is that my father sent me here against my will, and before I knew it I was installed as Ned's keeper complete with keys and napkins."

"Just like that?"

"More or less." She sat down upon the stool. "Sir William Knyvett would have bussed me heartily he was so pleased to see me."

"I can believe it." A priest might have granted her absolution by now but Rushden was hardly likely to send her out with a benediction and a few Hail Marys. "You still have not told me how you dispensed with Lady Haute."

"Well, it was marvelously fortunate. The poor lady wrote to say she was indisposed with the measles. You see, fortunately, dear Sir Thomas Limerick sent me up my . . . well, her . . . unopened letter." She peeped up cautiously. He was looking surprisingly mild-mannered but that was a sunny day that would not last long. "You really must appreciate, sir, that had I explained who I really was at that precise moment, it would have made things extremely difficult."

"For me?" he offered sarcastically. "You were so unselfish, thinking of my sensitivity in such matters."

"Yes," she agreed helpfully. "I realize that this is putting you—"

"I seem to remember before we last parted in such, shall we say, inconvenient circumstances, that I hinted to you that I never wanted to set eyes on you again."

"And here we are." Her dimpled grin was only skin deep.

He was smiling too, his laugh a politeness. "And here we are." He straightened up from the prie-dieu and his expression changed so rapidly that Heloise sprang up from the stool and stepped back, her heart thumping.

"So what are we going to do about this?" he asked, advancing with dragonlike purpose.

She shrugged helplessly as she read the desire in his eyes to incinerate her. "Nothing, sir?"

"Nothing!" That halted him. His gaze smoldered at her nonchalance, but to her relief he paced away from her and set his hands to the bar. For a moment she thought the interview was at an end but he was merely bracing himself, as if touching the tangible solid wood might bring comfort and restore common sense.

"I seem to recall explaining to you"—he swung round to confront her like a lawyer arguing his case before a jury—"that it was essential that we never spend a night under the same roof until the annulment was granted." He gestured to the excess of painted stars above their head. "Yes?"

Heloise nodded apologetically, giving the ceiling a cursory glance. "But this is a rather large roof," she pointed out, including the entire castle in her remark. The man gave a hiss of angry breath, but she pressed on: "Sir, you only spoke to me at all tonight because his grace commanded you." True, he had little choice; if he avoided "Lady Haute" like a plague-ridden village, some tongues might have wagged, but that observation was better stored away. Instead she continued quietly, "So you see, I imagine it is possible for us to avoid each other completely with almost no effort."

His quicksilver eyes regarded her scathingly. "Are you such a simpleton? If you remain here, mistress, I have access to you."

The meaning drew the blood into her cheeks and, as if to thrust the words fully into her mind, her husband coldly let his glance rise from her little pointed toes, hover in unseemly fashion upon her breasts, and halt upon her lips, which she parted unwittingly beneath such scrutiny. Something which seemed to begin beneath her ribs like a slow vortex was whirling downwards to her thighs. This man knew too well what lay beneath her clothing. She turned away from that insolent study before she was tempted to stare and give him brazen coin for coin.

Access, yes. Miles felt himself tempted. This silver-haired enchantress was a hand's-grasp away, beseeching him with waif's eyes; her body was a tantalizing sheath to be broken, to be seduced into granting him admittance. It would be so easy, so satisfying to tug away the silken panel that lay across her collar and free those pert breasts for lovemaking. He felt himself hardening and swung away from her, gripping the prie-dieu as if it exuded some holiness that might assist him against her witchery. He had to be rid of her. Her presence disconcerted him, creating fractures in the wall he had erected against emotion. If he permitted it, her lies, her disguise, would be like ice freezing into the cavity of friendship betwixt him and Harry, pushing them slowly apart.

Heloise guessed he was exacting a silent revenge for the shaking administered to his careful world and was sorry for it. Brecknock could give her safe haven for a little space if only the harbormaster's watchdog would let her stay. What would happen if she did step across the pace of world that lay between them to nestle against that arrogant backbone? And suppose she trailed a gentle touch across the glimmering knuckles and up his velvet sleeve to his shoulder to tangle her fingers in the soft, black waves and coax Rushden's face down to hers? Would he kiss her or curse her? No, she must risk nothing. Along that sinful path betwixt hand and lips lay folly and Heloise knew better than to steal what could never be hers.

The man had turned his face to her, waiting. It was necessary to soothe the hackles down and slide a makeshift collar round his neck until she could work out the answers herself. Stroking the fingertips of one hand up and down the back of her other hand, held fisted against her breasts, she tried for an answer to placate him. It cost her, but being conciliatory was far more crucial than losing her temper.

"If need be, I shall submit to an examination when the annulment arrives."

His reply astounded her: "Shall you indeed? We should both be fools to rely on that."

"You whoreson!" The unladylike word was out before she could leash it and it took all her power to fight down the urge to knock the Rushden hawk nose crooked.

Seeing such temptation whorling her fists, Miles swiftly stepped back out of harm's way. "Such fine manners, Mistress Ballaster." He let his mouth curl haughtily. The girl's base blood showed. "I am merely being practical, woman, if you would bother to listen. There are other ways to lose a maidenhead besides lying with a man; riding horseback for instance can rip the evidence of virginity."

Heloise's defiance slackened. He was perfectly right even if the indelicacy of the man in mentioning such matters shocked her.

"So let us be clear on this, you shrew. I am ordering you to leave Brecknock by Thursday or I shall have you taken back to your father by force, make no mistake. You may ride home muzzled in a cart for aught I care." He did not mention Myfannwy would be arriving.

Heloise leaned wearily back against the wall. She did not want to return to the little empire ruled by her father; she was going to have to fight with every weapon she had to keep some hold over her destiny, and she could not see beyond Brecknock. "I think you are making rather heavy weather of this, sir." He looked fit to explode at such an understatement, but she continued, "I should like to retain my position here." The proclamation made her feel good and she straightened up and announced the rest of it: "In fact I intend to. The duke's son needs some affection in his life. I have seen beggars' children given more love—"

Laughter in the passageway outside stifled her peroration as Miles flung up a warning hand. A young woman's inebriated giggle and a man's soft winning tones rippled past and ebbed beyond their hearing. When the silence again lay between them, Heloise picked up her skirts decisively. "Since it is not wise to be seen or *discovered* conversing with you, sir, especially in private, would you mind if we end this delightful audience?" She swept to the door and stood regally for him to open it.

With an ill will, Miles hoisted the bar from its brackets, wondering why he was giving her more time. "We shall speak of this again. Do not think yourself out of the wild wood yet, mistress."

Heloise ruined her triumphant departure by asking in wifely fashion, "Oh, did you remember to write to his holiness?"

"No, I might manage it in a year's time," he exclaimed witheringly, his fingers still controlling the door latch. "Of course, Pope Sixtus *and* Bishop Stillington *and* my lord of Canterbury. Anyone I have missed? The king? The Ottoman emperor? Yes, now, there is a thought, and the poor heathen fellow has a different wife each night while I have difficulty dealing with the one foisted on me. Good night, madam! Forgive me if I follow you at a distance but I wish to ensure you find your way to your bedchamber unravished."

"So considerate," purred Heloise, grateful even if it was self-interest rather than gallantry which fueled his thoughtfulness. She waited while he robbed his purse of the chapel key and lifted the candle free.

Keeping a cautious distance like an assassin, Miles followed her. She went the wrong way twice and had to be whistled to and signaled with the candle so that by the time she reached her

door, he was ropable and close to suspecting her of leading him
on a tour of the entire living quarters out of sheer revenge.

He plundered an ambry and drank a cup of muscadelle, angry
that he had been drawn into the wretched girl's conspiracy.
Moths had more sense; at least they investigated a flame before
it consumed them. And he was the one person in the entire
household who had claimed any recognition of Lady Haute. If
the real widow arrived, Harry would want to know why Miles
had deceived him. And Lord Rhys ap Thomas was arriving on
Thursday. Damnation upon it! Curse her! Curse everything!

His bed was occupied when he finally flung himself down on
it. Dick de la Bere amiably rolled out of his way and asked whose
skirts he had been lifting.

LIKE A DOG WITH A BONE TO BURY, RUSHDEN WAS CERTAINLY
trying to be rid of her as discreetly as possible. Next morning as
Heloise was leaving the castle chapel after mass, the porter,
having taken great pains to make the delivery himself, handed
her a letter. She tucked it briskly beneath her belt, whisked Ned
back to the nursery, and locked the letter into her jewelry coffer.

Thank all the saints she did. When she finally snatched a few
moments' privacy, she read the letter and discovered it purported
to be from Lady Haute's husband, requesting his wife to return
at once. The orange seal on the parchment was different from the
previous one and rather indistinct. Yes, she realized, it was a
letter from a husband: hers! "Rogue!" she muttered and tossed
it on the nearest fire. She was not going to spin away when
Rushden cracked his toy whip. God smite him! How long would
this game endure?

And what was worse, she had been commanded to take Ned
to breakfast with his sire. To hear about the sword swallower?
The duke's interest in his son was the only glimmer on a dark
horizon, for she guessed that dear friend Rushden would be listening, too, and sending vengeful promises to her across the
trenchers and the Paris napery.

The duke was breakfasting at the small table in his bedchamber and Heloise, having delivered his son, was bidden to wait by the door—near enough to remove Ned if he disobeyed, far enough to be disregarded and hear nothing. She felt like a sentry as the servants came past with platters and it was embarrassing, too; Ned tucked his legs around his stool leg, blew on his pottage, and prattled happily. Several times the duke stared across at her, and her husband, dining with them and ill at ease with the child, glanced over his shoulder occasionally, but offered no pleasantries.

Heartily sick of studying the scarlet-and-gold-caparisoned bed, the costly carpets, the pedestaled astrolabe, and the collection of lidded golden goblets studded with gemstones, marching across the cup board shelf, Heloise observed that his grace of Buckingham matched his bed. He was buttoned tightly into a scarlet doublet stitched with panels of yellow silk crisscrossed with golden cord. Yet for all his flamboyant splendor, there was an elegance in his companion that was much more powerful.

Rushden's black cote's slit sleeves rustled with a lining of grey taffeta every time he set his cup to his lips. Heloise's gaze was drawn immodestly to the lazy stretch of his shoulders, the way the white pleated collar of his shirt was half-hidden by glossy hair, black as midnight. You need a barber, she silently chided his proud profile, and then blanched as he suddenly tugged at a fingerful of hair and squinted sideways at it. This is definitely against the teachings of Holy Church, Heloise chided herself, or was it mere coincidence? Could the man be made to feel a tickling in his right kneecap? One of Rushden's ringed hands slid down across the woolen hose of his left leg. Hmm. Then she tried to make him sneeze, without success, before she sensibly gave up. It was wrong to mock the magic; the faery realm might punish her for succumbing to such frivolity.

His grace of Buckingham finished his gillysops in wine, dabbled his fingers in the proffered rosewater, and scraped his chair back, but it was Rushden who spoke to Heloise. "I understand you have received bad tidings from home, my lady Haute." He wiped his hands on the napkin and flung it back across the page's shoulder.

"Oh, nothing of consequence, Sir Miles," she answered grandly, "but thank you for your concern."

Rushden's jaw tightened.

"Your husband does not miss you?" Buckingham was being helped into his cote by his servant Pershall.

What else had the queen's letter of recommendation told the duke, she wondered in panic. "Not a bit, your grace, except he fusses occasionally about matters that are easily remedied." She gave her real husband a quick smile and looked back at the duke. "I do not complain, my lord. He leaves me to manage my own affairs so long as I do not interfere with his pursuits."

"Elderly, is he?"

"Somewhat older than I, your grace, and . . ." She pursed her lips, looking towards Rushden. "And his understanding is not what it was." A hit indeed, for Miles Rushden picked up his meat knife, fingering it lovingly.

The duke turned from the hand mirror held by his servant. "My son has been telling me his breathlessness is almost vanquished."

"A few infusions, tried and true," Heloise answered warily.

"Good." His grace did not offer a verdict on her governance. Certainly not a man to put praises in her alms dish. Observing Ned eyeing his long sleeves mischievously, he languidly felt them for protuberances and, finding none, ruffled the boy's curls. "Off with you!" Dismissed, Ned scampered back to Heloise, bowed to his father and Rushden, then tugged her swiftly out.

It was Rushden's sleeve that had received the earthworms. He silently handed them to Heloise later and strode off before she could apologize.

MISTLETOE! THAT WAS IT, THOUGHT MILES, NOTING AN INcongruous tangle of greenery on a healthy tree branch still un-

furled for spring, as he rode out with his men-at-arms to
Llangorse to investigate some trouble stirred up by the Vaughans.
Mistress Ballaster was sinking her tendrils into him like mistletoe
and looking so pearly white and pretty that every man at the
castle was stripping her bare. Godsakes, the Tretower rogues were
easier to deal with than the cursed wench. He tried to concentrate
on the road, wishing he had Traveller back. Maybe he needed to
whistle outside every byre and barn he passed. Where could she
have hidden him? Perhaps he should interrogate the balding esquire who had been with her at Potters Field.

To Hell with Heloise Ballaster! If only he could forget what
lay beneath the layers of skirt, the froth of veil, and the strip of
fur that had edged her neckline this morning. Here he was on
the outskirts of Llangorse now and his mind should be on his
errand, but no, last night's temptation was still with him, reminding him he did not just have a familiarity with this particular wench, he actually owned her. That was, if he wanted to—
and it was not impossible. The thought was tantalizing and an
incredible nuisance. Just when he was telling himself it was necessary to be honest with Harry and have the wench sent packing
back to her outrageous father, a part of him that had not been
overworked of late was urging him to amuse himself. You own
the goods, said his sinful side, you could at least examine them
further before you send them back.

It was at that point that he and his men were attacked by the
Vaughans.

HE SHOULD HAVE KEPT HIS MIND ON HIS WORK, MILES RE-
flected as they later galloped back, bruised and victorious, towards Bronllys. But he had a drawstring bag of dues clinking
safely in his saddlebag and when Thomas Vaughan had taunted
him about the new mare with foal that he had lately acquired,
he had forced the cur at swordpoint against a tree out of earshot
of his men.

Vaughan had needed little persuasion to tell him the rest. It seemed that an English noblewoman had rode upon Traveller into Wales and it was common gossip in the valleys that she carried Rushden's babe.

MAYBE SHE SHOULD GIVE TRAVELLER BACK TO RUSHDEN AS A peace offering, reflected Heloise, leaning against her bed as though it were a misericord. Dafydd was rubbing an ear against her elbow for tickling. Yes, and while she was at it, have Ned's dog secretly burnt at the stake to trumpets, followed by universal rejoicing. She sadly turned over the remains of her best leather shoes. The wicked creature had also ripped the leather thongs off one of her wooden pattens, put teeth marks across the other, demolished a garter, chewed the end of an embossed leather belt, and shredded a corner of her feather bed, before being smacked soundly on the nose. With a deep breath Heloise charged like a tourney champion into the nursery only to discover her charge's rear end halfway out the window, and the sound of horns filling the courtyard.

"It is my lady mother!" exclaimed Ned, wriggling in past the window mullion with his gypon and his hose nearly parting company, "and there will be presents!"

THE ENTIRE HOUSEHOLD SPILT OUT ACROSS THE COURTYARD like an upturned milkmaid's bucket and then, according to their rank, were swept back up into lines, like counting beads, by the clucking chamberlain, Sir Nicholas Latimer. Heloise, superior to the falconers but inferior to the treasurer, abandoned her line to reprimand Ned, who, polished and sponged, was hopping up and down the steps like a well-dressed flea.

Diminished by the glory of Duke Harry and his son, Heloise felt safer yet no less anxious. What if the duchess had met the true Lady Haute at Westminster or Windsor? One consolation, Heloise reflected, winding Ned's sleeves tightly round her gloves so he could not bounce, was that if she was unmasked, Miles Rushden would face a few unwelcome questions as to why he had pretended to recognize her as Lady Haute. Where was Rushden? She was curious to know which row of bowing heads he had slid onto, for he did not seem to hold any actual office other than friend and confidant. She glanced around her but the man was absent. Perhaps he was looking for his horse or harassing some poor villeins for taxes they could not afford.

CATHERINE WOODVILLE, YOUNGEST SISTER OF THE BEWITCHingly beautiful Queen of England, was twenty-six years old and rather disappointing as she stepped down with her little daughters from her chariot. Her forehead was fashionably plucked so it was impossible to see if she had the same family ash blonde hair that was supposed to have stolen King Edward's heart. Judging by her russet traveling gown, it seemed as though the duchess cared little for fashion or else the duke was mean with her allowance. Maybe she had merely given up competing with her gorgeous sister—Heloise knew the feeling.

Not only sumpters laden with panniers clopped into the bailey, but cart after cart wobbled in. An astonishing collection of long-haired aging men and youths crawled out with stiff limbs from beneath the wagon awnings, clutching rebecs, hurdygurdies and all manner of instruments. Only elderly men and young castratos! The duchess was a careful lady, thought Heloise, observing that Duke Harry was viewing them with exasperation. They regrouped and began to play as her grace hoisted her skirts to her anklebones and fastidiously sidestepped the puddles.

The Duke of Buckingham stood, hands on hips, with Ned now loose beside him. Far from greeting his wife with any affection, his grace exclaimed, "God help us, you have not bought another hobbyhorse," as a brightly painted toy (this time with a gilt mane), was unstrapped and presented by a servant on bended knee to Ned.

The child took his manners from his father and his face puckered into sulkiness. "Where are my stilts? You promised me *stilts*!"

With a tight smile, Heloise marched up behind the child and plucked his hat down over his eyes. "Bow and kiss your mother's hand! *Now!*"

Ned shoved his hat up and rolled his eyes upwards at Heloise in his best demon imitation, but he gracefully presented his mother with a charcoal drawing—of the castle, the sun, a flower, and a very vicious-looking portcullis. The duchess took it as she might a posy from a village child and drifted along the rows of officers, expressed her hope that Heloise had not found Brecknock too cold, and took herself straight to her bedchamber with a megrim.

Anxious to convince the duchess that she was competent, Heloise had her lies queued up, but neither she nor Ned was given an audience. Thwarted but not yet acquitted, she took her grace's lack of interest as a rebuttal.

"I am not impressed," she muttered to Bess, who shrugged unsurprised.

The duchess finally sent for her after dinner. As Heloise followed Ned across the carpets and the furs to make her curtsy to the background chords of shawms and flutes, she felt like a lacewing having its wings pulled off; the noble ladies of the bedchamber were busy estimating the worth of her clothing.

With testimonials fresh in her ears from Sir William, Duchess Catherine was amiable to Heloise. While they picked over Ned's brief history in obligatory fashion, the little knave quarreled with his siblings and had to be removed by Bess. The duchess did not blame Heloise for his rudeness. Perhaps it was the way he always behaved to get any attention from his mother. It was only when an aging Welsh harpist was summoned in to play, that Heloise was able to stand back, thankful that the interrogation was over.

No, not quite. It was now time to become acquainted with Ned's little sisters, admire his baby brother, suffer the nurse's condemnatory stare, and nod to the other children's nursemaids. When she finally retired to the edge of the chamber with her persona intact, she was considerably relieved. The saints must be feeling generous. Neither Duchess Catherine nor any of her female entourage claimed to have met the worthy Eleanor Haute before.

"Are you at all musical, Lady Haute?" the duchess called out to her, with more enthusiasm than when they had discussed the nursery minutiae.

"Yes, your grace."

Ned, who had been allowed back in, tried to clamber up her skirts, pleading with her to sing her grasshopper song. Music was clearly a means to please her mistress further and acquire a well-placed ally, so Heloise modestly sat down on the stool in front of the duchess's cream leather toes and sang a love song.

> "Oh, sleep, my lord,
> My earthly treasure,
> Sweetly doth the nightingale sing,
> For in your love,
> Is all my pleasure,
> And all my joy is of your making.

> "I will keep guard,
> Against the long night,
> Sleep now sweetly, loving friend,
> That in the morning,
> You may kiss me,
> And our love shall know no end."

OUTSIDE, MILES, NOW WASHED AND GROOMED TO KISS HANDS, hesitated to interrupt whoever was singing so exquisitely. Duchess "Cat" had found yet another voice and a new palm to press coins into. That would please Harry like a burr in a saddlecloth. But the singer was a woman, not a castrato. Miles frowned and leaned back against the stone wall. The music slid beneath the door, invading his hard-edged heart, and the sweet, crystal voice gouged at his soul.

> *"Oh, that I could*
> *Heal the deep wounds,*
> *Ah, Sweet Christ, were it not so,*
> *God in mercy,*
> *Love thee always,*
> *In love, my life—in death my woe.*
>
> *"I kept my love,*
> *Against the long night,*
> *But at dawn Death took my friend.*
> *Lonely am I,*
> *In the sunlight,*
> *Oh, Christ, your pardon on me descend."*

"Miles?" De la Bere's large paw was shaking his shoulder. "Music caught at your gut, man?"

Watery grins were not one of his best accomplishments. "It is no matter, Dick. A little sadness. It will pass."

"Look to the future with Myfannwy, eh? You will have another child before long."

"Yes." The weary fingers that rubbed across his chin touched again the damage they had wrought in penance.

"Let us go in then. The song is over."

But nothing was over, for it was a familiar, slender young woman who sat on the stool at the duchess's feet, not with her skirts spread in a violet leaf but in complete self-abeyance, white hands neat upon her lap and her knees close together like a dreamy child lost to the world. As the applause surrounded Heloise Ballaster, he watched awareness flicker back into the hazel eyes. Then she saw him and rose, ashamed. He had intruded on part of the deception.

"Sir Miles, we do not often see you here." The song had animated Duchess Cat as always. "The music drew you?"

"Yes, the music." He denied himself the temptation to look at Heloise, suppressed the raw pain the song had roused in him, the yearning, the sense of loss. Was there no end to Mistress Ballaster's accomplishments? She would be even harder to be rid of if Cat became her buckler—and she had won other hearts. Miles looked in disgust at the dotardly adoration wreathing the blowsy face of the old Welsh minstrel. No, she must go! In a few days she had shaken his steady world. He dared not give her longer.

"Was it the figs at supper, Sir Miles?" the millstone about his neck asked sweetly some time later. The others in the room were safely distracted by the new psaltery that the duchess had bought in Hereford.

"Your pardon, Lady *Haute?*" An iron bar would have looked friendlier.

"Why, you seem quite out of sorts, Sir Miles." Heloise was speaking to her toes.

"I have no need to talk to you, madam," he muttered, raising his hand as if he stanched a cough. She was hard put not to laugh. Next he would only be communicating by sliding coded letters penned with onion juice into her palm.

A blast of hand organ and pipes together permitted him to retaliate. "You know how I manage to keep my sanity, madam?" He was staring straight ahead now, trying to pretend they were not speaking together, but he no longer sounded ill tempered. "By thinking of ways of bringing about your demise. Strangling is at the top of my fist."

"Well, you shall have to do it in the common gaze, sir," she cooed, "since we are never to be alone."

"That ruling, my dear Lady Haute, is only to avoid ravishment not murder."

"Ah, but theoretically you could do one, then the other or even—" His exasperated frown shamed her into silence.

"Are you ever quiet, Mistress Ballaster?" Miles observed witheringly, deciding it would be absolute heaven to throw her across his knee. "I assure you, murdering you slowly will give me all the satisfaction I require."

He glanced sideways but the lady had lapsed into pensive silence. "By the by," he announced with pleasure, "I forgot to tell you, the bargaining is over. I have Traveller back."

IT WAS A SMALL REVENGE, BUT FORCING THE DUKE AND DUCHESS to watch Ned and two schoolroom companions perform a tiny interlude in Latin in the solar before supper was giving Heloise no end of satisfaction. She had insisted that all the parents endure the spectacle. While Ned's tutor and Bess organized the chaos behind the settle where the tiny, excited performers were crouching, ready with handsacks stitched with eyes and mouths, she ushered in the reluctant audience.

"You speak Latin, Lady Haute?" Rushden, ever shadowing the duke, greeted her a few moments later as she stood near the door with Sir William.

"*Eheu!* Worse than my French but better than my Greek. Do not go, sir. Please watch." She meant it kindly.

"No, such things pain me."

"You may be a father one day."

She expected him to toss a jest for her to catch, but his adamance had a pained edge to it. "They are beginning. Excuse me."

Sir William, having overheard the exchange, managed a warning afterwards. "Think you should know something, Lady Haute," he muttered, pulling at his long earlobe. "Rushden lost his wife and only son to the pestilence. Boy would have been Ned's age, had he lived."

So that was why he avoided Ned. "Sweet Jesu, forgive me." She crossed herself. "And was he with them when . . . ?"

"Ah, there's the rub, my lady. He was ill himself with the variola when the news was brought to him. Caught it traveling back from here and was abed at Newport for a week. The tidings made him crazed."

SO RUSHDEN DID HAVE A HEART BENEATH HIS ARMOR, HELOise, moved to pity, thought sadly as she stole past a sleeping Bess and snoring Benet to check on Ned and found him dreaming happily, thumb in mouth, a cloth donkey cuddled beneath his arm.

Dropping a kiss upon Ned's cheek, she thought of the other child, whose death had been announced at some indifferent inn in Newport. How cruel for his poor father—she imagined Rushden lying in a simple chamber, his face scarlet, beaded with the *vesiculae* like evil droplets of sweat. Had a servant brought him a letter or spoken the tidings? Some instinct made her open her coffer and take out the ring that her father had snatched from Rushden for her nuptials.

Dear God! Her head began to spin. *No!* she screamed, sinking to her knees, her palms pressed to her eyes, but the vision came: a younger Rushden with the tears trickling down his poor crusted face, in rage tearing the letter again and again and again and hurling it into the fire. *Spare me! No more!* she protested, stumbling back to the nursery, but the unseen power forced her mind to watch as Rushden sank to his knees and, with a bestial howl of fury, dragged his nails down, down across the blisters.

The fire was almost dead in the hearth when Heloise finally uncovered her face and raised her face to the crucifix on the wall. Shakily she rose to her feet, smudging the tears away, and tried to busy herself stoking the embers. Her hands trembled as she shredded the herbs to make an infusion for Ned's breakfast. She should leave Brecknock, put an end to the lies—go from Miles Rushden in peace!

"My lady."

Heloise nearly dropped the pan in the fire.

The old harpist, Emrys, was standing in the doorway, enjoying the fact that his sudden appearance startled her. "Your voice, *arglwyddes,* was given as a blessing," he declared, stepping in unbidden, making no apology for finding her with a wrap over her underkirtle and her hair plaited for bed. Before she could stop him, the man set his harp down and prowled straight through into Ned's bedchamber. She followed anxiously but he merely cast a glance over the child and the other two sleepers, his creped smile soft and ambivalent.

A finger on his lips, he drew her back into the nursery, closed the inner door, and perched himself on the three-legged stool beside the hearth. Then, without a by-your-leave, he began to tell her in a voice, beautiful and undulating, of his beloved Welsh music, of the broth of the cauldron of the goddess Ceridwen whence came the powers of Taliesin, and his people's dreaming. So entranced was Heloise by the legends that an hour passed swifter than clouds across the moon's face, before the old musician took up his harp and played for her.

Emrys's singing voice was cracked with age like ancient glaze but once it must have been strong and a delight to man and maid. He began to teach her, speaking slowly in his own tongue, then singing the phrases and bidding her repeat them. It was impossible to remember the Welsh at first but he coaxed each verse from her over and over again and then he sang with her, and Heloise wove a descant over and beneath his melody.

"*Arianlais,* there's nice it is," he said finally, his eyes misty in the light of the sputtering candle stub. "Indeed it is a pity you are not Welsh and a male child, for indeed I could make a bard of you. The great Taliesin himself would have written gladly for such a voice as yours." He rose. "The hour is late, see, but can you come to the town tomorrow even? You shall hear such music."

"The town, Master Emrys! I fear permission would not be granted."

Wiry thick eyebrows came together in a frown. "There are other ways to leave this place. Say you will come, *arglwyddes.* We have a visitor coming to the town, one who wears the mantle of the wondrous bard Dafydd ap Gwilym, and a wreath of oak leaves upon his brow. Lewis Glyn Cothi, my lady!"

Clearly she was supposed to be impressed. "But is the great Lewis not coming to the castle?" she countered tactfully. "I am sure her grace would be pleased to hear him."

"Ah, no, Lewis will not play for the English, not since the men of Chester gave his hide a drumming. Not forgiven them, he has. Though mayhap he will come when the lady Myfannwy weds, for he is supposed to keep a reckoning of lineage and play at such feasts."

"Myfannwy?"

"Aye, Rhys ap Thomas's ward." Another name that was supposed to strike her with awe. "Our noble Rhys is coming to discuss her dowry arrangements. But, tomorrow night, *bach.* Surely you can leave these swaggering English bullies and the child for a few hours? The tall wench can mind him. Why not, a little adventure, see? Oh, come, *arianwallt,* and sing what I have taught you tonight."

"What was it?" she asked with good-natured suspicion. "A lament?"

"Of course, for a land that is flattened beneath the heel of the *saeson.*"

"*Saeson?*"

"It is our word for Englishmen."

"Englishmen! Of course! That is what the people were muttering when the soldiers came to fetch me from the town."

"We will have you speaking Welsh in no time." He pinched her cheek with an old man's mischief. "Come and hear our fine music. You shall be safe from fumblings, I promise you. I shall not quit your side nor leave you to be plucked by sweaty lads, though they would make a fine woman of you." And what was that supposed to mean?

"I cannot afford to anger his grace." But it was tempting to leave the castle again.

"Nor shall you. We honor such gifts as yours in Wales, *arglwyddes.*" The crinkled gaze dwelt on the silver fibers scarifying her shoulders. "Ask the *tylwyth teg* and send me your answer."

Heloise stared at him in utter delight and felt the soft tendrils probing at her thoughts.

"Never run away, *arglwyddes,* see, else you will never find your heart's desire."

"SIR." MILES SWUNG ROUND AND FOUND IT WAS THE COLTISH nursemaid, risen early, curtsying to him. Bess drew herself up gravely, tossing back her nut brown braids. "I am not one to blab, sir, but I think you should know that Master Emrys came and played for my Lady Haute late last even. I heard him ask her to visit the town."

"Did he now? And what did she answer him?"

"Neither aye nor nay. One of the Vaughans' ruffians is to be hanged today at East Gate, is he not?"

"Aye, for sheep stealing," he answered somberly. "Emrys has no love for the Vaughans but if he pesters Lady Haute again, bring me word; and, Bess, it would be in your interest"—his fingers tapped this belt purse—"to keep an even closer eye on my lady—for her own good, of course. Let me know anything out of the ordinary."

Yes, a quiet word to the sentries and the porter might be advisable. It was about time he quietly plucked out this thorn in his flesh. When Lady Eleanor Haute left the castle, it would be forever. He would personally winch the drawbridge down and kiss her good riddance.

"What the—" He looked down. A black and white mouser was rubbing against his boot cuffs. The hair upon the nape of Miles's neck prickled as the creature purred and arched.

"Oh, that is my lady Haute's cat. He must have followed me down. Come, Dafydd."

Miles ran a finger around his lawn collar as if it were choking him. Could Heloise know they had been talking about her? Two white antennae rose on either side of the feline's brow. Miles stepped back abruptly, and, inconvenienced, the cat stared up at him unsmiling. All cats looked so, but the moment Bess had taken the beast away, Miles untangled his small cross from the lacing of his shirt and muttered a paternoster.

*   *   *

HELOISE SHOOK THE OUTER DOOR OF THE NURSERY THAT morning. She was expected at mass. Had Benet thought her gone already, and turned the key? The duke and duchess would be displeased if she was not attending Ned. Was this a trick of Rushden's to discredit her? Might there be accusations that she feared to enter God's house? Rustling her skirts in annoyance, she paced to and fro and then she quickly unclipped the veil wire from her ears. Detaching part of the gauze so it would not be damaged, she squeezed the wire together and slid it into the lock. It took an eternity of jiggling and a variety of attempts before the tongue drew back and she was free.

The entire household save for the guards on the towers were already in Sir Nicholas's chapel as she tiptoed in rosy-faced, her butterfly veiling less than perfect. Whenever the congregation rose or knelt, she zigzagged her way between the throng to Ned. Her thoughts were on anything but God.

"Where were you?" Ned asked in a whisper that could have raised an entire graveyard.

"Hush!"

Rushden glanced behind him and for an instant looked as startled as a disturbed thief.

The chaplain announced he was calling the banns for the third time of the marriage between Sir Miles Rushden and Lady Myfannwy. "And if there be any reason why this man and woman should not be wed, let him give forth his arguments."

Oh, Jesu! As Heloise took a deep breath, the woman next to Rushden screamed and a large spring toad, no doubt hired at great expense, scattered the front rank of notables. The chaplain's Latin accelerated as the servants set up a hue and cry and the poor cleric looked extremely relieved to bless and dismiss the pack of them, including the toad.

"Did I ever say life at Brecknock was tedious?" muttered the duke. "Lady Haute, remove Lord Stafford and have Benet use the rod on him."

"No! No! It wasn't me!" bawled Ned.

"Of course it was not," exclaimed Heloise, anxious that he should avoid a breathless fit, "and I should like to know who locked me in." Her glance flickered across Miles Rushden's face as she looked about her challengingly but all save her husband had already found Ned guilty on that as well.

His help came unexpected though exceedingly suspect. "I believe we should trust the word of a future duke, my lord."

His grace's eyebrows rose, as if he was surprised by his friend's sudden championing of the child. "If it was not Lord Stafford . . ." With an iron stare the duke examined the faces of the other children, including his daughters. "I expect the culprit to make a full confession and apology to the chaplain, and if anyone else makes a mockery of God's house, the punishment will be severe." If he was expecting his duchess to endorse that sentiment, he was disappointed. "Come, madam!"

With a permissive glance from her grace, Heloise crouched down and coaxed Ned from his mother's skirts. With tenderness, she trickled a friendly finger down his scarlet face and poked the tickly spot beneath his arm before she rose and declared: "This morning we are going to learn about approaching difficult beasts. Sir Miles! Perhaps, sir, you would grant Lord Stafford a few moments of your time."

Rushden, delayed from disappearing in the duke's wake, could not have looked more surprised if she had metamorphosed into a *crocodilus*. His answer was curt: "Talk to the marshal, madam."

"Oh, do go along, Sir Miles," Duchess Catherine said irritably and, ignoring her waiting lord, swept off to the nearest stairs.

With Ned's hand in hers, Heloise nodded to Bess and waited for Rushden to escort them. Marry Myfannwy! Of all the secretive, lying whoresons! And he was looking as sinful as a satyr after an orgy—or so she guessed, having little knowledge of such things.

"I wish you to take us to Traveller, sir," she declared briskly.

"Do you now!" Rushden's lips were a tight pleat of annoyance.

"Or we can go toad hunting if you prefer." *The viper was marrying!*

"Ohhh, please," exclaimed Ned.

TRAVELLER WHINNIED A WELCOME AND LOOKED UNDECIDED AS to where to bestow an affectionate snuffle. Perhaps for sentimental reasons, he chose his master first, with a watchful eye on the witch-girl's purse. Perfidious beast!

"Now perhaps . . ." Miles's demon lady turned, with steel beneath her purring tone. "Perhaps you could encourage Ned to feed him." With an experienced hand, she scooped a handful of oats from a sack and held it out. Oh, wounded, was she? What was this? Another trial by ordeal? "It might help to lift him, *sir.*" The word was icy.

Miles took a deep breath. "No." He wanted to run.

It was the child that broke the impasse, stealing the last few paces from Bess to wind the knight's hanging sleeve about his hand. "Sir," he said, with newfound humbleness, "I *should* like to try."

For the first time since his son's death, Miles felt small hands upon his shoulders. It should be Phillip in his arms. Phillip should have lived. Tears threatened to choke him. He swung the boy abruptly towards the wall so that Mistess Ballaster could not see his hurt, but the child had. Ned was straining back to read his face. "Sir, was it you who set the toad loose?" The winter cold between them was thawing fast.

Miles made himself look at the little boy. "Yes," he whispered, adjusting his grip.

"Why?"

"Because . . . because Brecknock can be dreary. Now do not blab on me to Lady Haute and . . . and come and meet Traveller. He will not hurt you. Trust me." A small arm anchored itself around his neck as he took a pace nearer to the stallion's stall. "See, Bess and Lady Haute are not afraid, Ned. Lady Haute is not afraid of anything."

"Not even toads, human ones!" muttered his wife with feeling.

"Will you let a woman best you?" whispered Miles. "Come on, Ned."

Did she have to stand there like *his* governess while he tried to talk courage into Harry's child? Must she beam so sunnily at the grooms and stable hands?

Now he had to endure the entire stable adding its pennyworth of thought and winking at the women out of turn. Thankfully the child finally managed a quick pat of Traveller's chest and jerked back. At least the stallion had behaved responsibly, as if the horse understood the small human's fear. Perhaps the witch would let him go now, or did she intend to create a scene that would keep the gossips busy?

"I pray you take Lord Stafford to feed the old dun liard or one of the gentler sumpters, Martin," she was ordering her groom. "Go with them, Bess."

So Mistress Ballaster intended to snatch a few words about his other wedding? Well, if she misbehaved, he would have to put a swift end to the conversation. Strangle her now while no one was looking.

Heloise, surprised that Rushden was content to stroll very slowly along with her behind the others, was more than eager to set loose the quarrel between them. "How in God's name can you marry?" she asked through clenched teeth.

"Ah, so this is why we are idling among the wisps and the brushes." He idly flicked a dormant broomstick. "How did you manage to get out?"

So this cur had locked her in. It was tempting to belabor him with the broom head; instead she sucked in her cheeks and glared at his knee-length hanging sleeves. "Have you other familiars in there? Cockroaches, lice?"

The grey eyes narrowed but his tone was pleasant. "No more than usual." He clicked his tongue at his spare horse as they passed. "Children teach us so much." Then his gaze pinioned her. "I would not have let Ned carry the blame, believe me."

"And if his grace had not listened?"

"I know my quarry, lady. It is what I am good at." They were close enough to where Ned was being lectured by the marshal. Close enough and apart enough to talk privily. "Perhaps I should explain that this marriage with Rhys ap Thomas's ward is part of a latticework of alliances to augment the duke's power in Wales." How very condescending of him to enlighten her.

"Oh, I see." Heloise resisted the temptation to fold her arms and glower.

"Do you? I hope so. The match is of importance to his grace. He will not welcome meddling." The knifepoint was beneath the words.

A merest shrug showed her indifference. "By all means go and beget heirs with Lady Myfannwy—eventually." That brought his head up—defiantly. Still trying to disarm him, she added, "I still cannot see how you marrying will help the duke."

"By marrying this heiress, I acquire further lands in Wales and since I am his retainer, I am sworn to support him as my overlord."

"He wants Wales?"

"No, he *needs* Wales." Miles looked about him for some means to teach her and, with a cautious glance to make sure the others were occupied, uncovered a sack of sawdust as if he were demonstrating the quality. "Look, here is England, see!" He crouched and drew an outline. "King Edward and the Woodvilles have much strength in the south. The royal chamberlain, Lord Hastings, holds the Midlands, and the king's brother Gloucester dominates the north."

The lady leaned down close to his shoulder, holding her veil back. "And my lord of Buckingham seeks to control Wales for himself?" The perfume she wore wove like a comfortable leash around his neck.

"No," Miles answered carefully, "in the king's name, of course." *God willing the Yorkist ranks might one day fall asunder.* He erred in looking up to ensure she understood the lesson. Her

moist lips were but a sweet breath away and for an instant there
was no defiance in her expression, but a grave thoughtfulness as
though she were our Lady considering a felon's prayer. The blas-
phemy shook him, together with the absurd fact that he had
never noticed that her pretty eyes were not silver-framed but
dark-lashed. He straightened up and stood staring down at her,
every sense aware how fragile she was, how easily broken.

He dared not offer his hand to help her rise but words he had
in plenty. "Lady, the animosity between you and me is not a
personal issue. I have no wish to see you destitute, believe me,
but I am high in the duke's favor and I do not wish to jeopardize
my future."

"Nor I mine," she answered stubbornly, rising again to her
feet.

"Then as you value your safety, hold your peace and do not
reveal what happened at Bramley. I am marrying Myfannwy."

"And . . . and if this Rhys asks you to set a day for your wedding, what is left for me—a free ride to England on your horse?"

"No," he answered and surprised both of them. "I cannot make
you my wife but I could easily make you my mistress."

Eleven

How the handle of the pitchfork managed to wham him hard in the belly before he could prevent it, Miles never fathomed. He was too busy with the pain while "Lady Haute" called for help, exclaiming he must have taken some poisoned food. If that was not bad enough, one of the grooms thrust a handful of charcoal into his mouth as an antidote. He half-choked before he could shove the fellow away. By the time he found some ale to rinse his mouth, his wife had fled, taking the child with her, and the trumpets were fanfaring the arrival of his Welsh betrothed and her guardian.

"Where in Hell have you been?" Harry mouthed, as Miles, in a fresh doublet, made his bow in the duke's solar. Rhys ap Thomas, accompanied by a superfluity of wet Black Raven banners and an excessive number of damp hangers-on, was already warming his hands before the hearth. Smirking, taller, and more clean-shaven than most of his retinue, the visitor gripped Miles's hand with vigor and drew forward his future bride, the demoiselle Myfannwy.

"*Y Cysgod?*" His name was spoken with sweet breath, and eyes, dark as sloes, evaluated him shrewdly. Her alluring smile showed tidy, unblemished teeth. Thank God, he thought in relief, and said something flattering in Welsh, his glance swift to note the parting of the girl's cloak, which permitted a glimpse of tempting cleavage framed by comfortingly brown braids. It was not just the alliance that was appealing.

It was an understatement to say that the Welsh, no doubt happy to be somewhere civilized with free ale on offer, enjoyed the banquet that followed. A parenthesis between his future wife and her guardian, Miles, too, indulged himself; Rhys's arrival had at least damped down any fires of reprisal for the hanging that

morning and the conversation was informative. Rhys took pains
to point out that Myfannwy's hips and dowry were both ample,
and that her husband would become the owner of considerable
flocks. Since Welsh wool was funding the spires on English
churches, he suggested Miles should please the Church in similar
fashion and earn himself a discount in Purgatory.

By twilight, the Welshmen were into songs that nobody could
understand unless they had been born west of Llangurig. The
duchess, not to be outdone, brought out her musical ammuni-
tion, including Lady Haute—perdition take her! Miles could still
taste the charcoal—who was beseeched to take her turn and afterwards surrounded by a little court of moist-eyed, scruffy sons
of Cymru.

"*Iesu Grist!*" exclaimed someone. "*A fynno iechyd, bid lawen,*"
and they launched into a rollicking song that involved cup bashing. Any translation would have been immodest.

Above the salt, as talk of politics and gossip grew stale, Myfannwy unwisely sought to explore between the milestones of her
future lord's past. Miles was courteously monosyllabic and glad
when she departed for the garderobe. Idle, he scanned the hall
and discovered his green-eyed witch seated near the dais in lively
dialogue with Emrys the harpist and another Welshman, who
had a hurdy-gurdy across his lap. A half dozen other young men,
including Ned's tutor, were gathered like fowls round a feed
trough. The schoolmaster had his gaze glued to the creamy curves
nestled between the teasing voile and the green velvet of Heloise's
bodice, while Rhys ap Thomas's secretary had positioned himself
behind her and was blatantly surveying the tempting adit between her breasts. Her questionable chaperone in this cluster of
idolaters was Bess, the girl's mouth a mournful, downturned crescent as she watched de la Bere fan Heloise's glowing cheeks with
his hat.

The Devil take Lady Haute! Those slavering wretches would
suppose her a bottle already unstoppered, worth swigging from.
Well, he must ensure no one broke the seal or he would never

be granted an annulment. Besides, if anyone had the right to initiate her, it was him. Displeasure pricked Miles further when Bess cowardly withdrew, leaving Heloise to the lecherous jackals. Tense as a highway brigand about to make an ambush, he watched for Heloise to leave the hall and then, promising Myfannwy to return, he excused himself from the high table.

His annoying quarry avoided the passage past the chapel so he was forced to double round and waylay her on the allure, the wooden gallery that led to the nursery. At least he startled her sufficiently to cross herself.

"I thought you must be a specter," she remarked, not waiting, and jerked to a halt as he stepped onto her purfiled train to tether her.

"You will wish I was when this little audience is at an end."

Clasping her forearms across her breast like bat's wings against the chill breeze goosefleshing her, Heloise addressed her words towards the wall. "Oh, surly, are we? I trust you are not making boot marks on the tail of my gown."

"Surly! Yes, and more. Much more." The lady's throat and neck gleamed white in the hazed moonlight, inviting worship, like a treasure he dared not touch.

"Oh, dear, was Lady Myfannwy such dreary company, then?" Heloise chided. "What did she want to talk about—sheep?"

"Sheep!" Miles removed his foot. "By all the saints, why should Myfannwy want to talk about sheep? We were discussing where our wedding—ah—I see your strategy, mistress vixen. You think to divert me from the matter of charcoal and sore ribs."

"Divert you, sir?" Free of the leather anchor, Heloise was able to swing round on him. "No! Pray spew out your anger like a gargoyle and then we may go to bed."

"Alone or are you expecting a friend?" he answered vehemently. Did she do it deliberately or was it his own fault that the word *bed* from her lips conjured up the sensuous image of her, bride-naked before him at Bramley? He had spoken of her becoming his mistress in jest but the thought roused him.

"Are you worried that I lack company? Only think, sir, if you and I were not concerned about an annulment, I could invite you in."

A murrain on the witch!

"Heloise"—Miles suppressed the urge to shake her—"after the way you behaved tonight, I wonder there is not a queue a mile long outside your door."

"Explain yourself, sir." Icy hauteur laced each word and, now that laughter no longer mellowed the air between them, he felt inexplicably bereft.

"Indeed, I shall, madam." He swept his sleeves behind him and paced from her, seeking words that would enforce his grave concern and achieve some revenge. "It is true that a married woman may behave with less modesty than an unmarried maiden but your attempts to behave with more worldliness fall rather short of the mark." He paused, thinking he had couched matters with finesse.

Her plain answer was a shock. "You mean I need more experience?"

"Jesu, madam, will you hold your tongue!" He put a hand to his forehead, distraught by her ability to thwart him. "You may be too innocent to be aware that every man in the hall was calculating whether you were fair game tonight. Do you understand what I am saying? I can scarcely make my meaning clearer."

"I think you are wrong, for there is no queue, sir." Her sleeve fluttered as she gestured to the lonely stone walls surrounding them. "Only you."

Was she playing games with him? He wished this encounter were lit by cressets so he might read her face. He clenched his jaw and tried again.

"I offer you warning as a friend. You tread a dangerous path with such behavior, leaving yourself open to . . . to seduction or worse." He strode away and turned, hands thrust on waist and legs astride. "I am telling you, mistress, if we are to dispense with this despicable marriage of ours, you must remain inviolated."

He was aware of her stillness, unable to tell in the darkness whether it was resentment that kept the words back.

"How very unjust," she answered with a sigh. "You may whore as you please and I must remain as unassailable as Pen-y-Fan."

"You mistake me, madam. I do not whore," he snarled, his anger up and snapping like a mastiff. He paced from her before he lost control completely and—and throttled her. Why did she have to provoke him so? He had not bruised her ears about this morning and he was trying to point out the dangers and—"And Pen-y-Fan is not unassailable," he muttered pedantically, adding ambiguously, "I know the way up."

With impeccable timing, she allowed the boast to fall awkwardly into the void between them before she remarked with deceptive sweetness, "Indeed, I hear you have explored most of the local hillsides. It is common gossip that the duke keeps whores in Llechfaen and Llanfaes. I suppose you do too. Even Bess thinks you are dangerous but worth consideration. How did Myfannwy take to you?" That drew a ripe oath. "There is no need to swear like that, sir. I am merely observing that—"

"Mistress, be silent!" Why was it that every time he tried to point out her errors to her, she held up a mirror to show him his faults? "Let me be plain, madam. While you are married to me, you will refrain from dalliance." At least she was keeping a meek, respectful silence at long last and Miles continued: "I am saying this for your own good. When Holy Church frees us from our oaths, you, lady, must have a reputation as pure as unsullied snow if you wish to find yourself a noble husband. People do not like to be made fools of and, believe me, the world will not look kindly on you for being a maiden and behaving like a . . ." *Pricktease* had been the word that came crudely to mind but that was too harsh a term for her vivacious spirits and too foul a word to be used before any lady of gentle upbringing.

"Like a mistress?" retorted Heloise helpfully and received a growl for an answer. Had she rendered him speechless at last? "How is it you never told me you were to be wed before this morning?" she asked, an edge of anger in her tone.

"Your father knew." Miles's tone was careless. Now that he had finally succeeded in annoying her, his amusement returned. "Jealous?"

"Oh, excessively. I shall warn your bride you may not keep your vows." Her voice dropped. "What do you intend to do with me, *Cysgod,* gag me for the duration?"

Oh, she had spirit. There was no denying that he might even miss her as a friend by the time he finally managed to catapult her from his life.

"By all the saints, lady, you and I are in agreement that our marriage should be annulled, are we not?" Why would she not look at him? "I have arranged for another letter to be delivered that will enable you to leave—*and leave you shall!* Must I be plainer? I want you out of here before I break your infuriating neck."

"Is Myfannwy what you want?"

It was her cat arching against his boot cuff out of the darkness that stanched a more honest answer. "Jesu, madam." He caught his breath. "It is not just a handfast." He slammed his hand against the wall and turned. Dafydd hissed. "The duke wants this alliance and I want her lands, do you hear me? I will compensate you with a house. . . . in Hereford . . . London . . . next to the pyramids in Egypt if it pleases me better, but utter one word against my betrothal and—" He glanced meaningfully past her at the bailey below. "Remember, I hanged a man this morning."

Heloise swallowed, retreating against the wooden planks. "I am not afraid of you."

"Well, you should be, sweetheart."

"Neither you nor your duke can go against the Church," she protested. "Our marr—"

He caught her chin. "Oh, but we can."

"How?" she exclaimed, jerking her face away. "Only the Pope can grant an annulment."

"An annulment, yes. But a bishop may bring a charge of heresy."

Her tone was freezing. "What are you saying, sir?"

"Just that I would not keep this cat if I were you."

His unwanted wife flinched as though Miles had struck her but it was the only way. Gathering up the creature, the girl turned away, hugging it to her heart, stroking its ears as she stared forlornly towards the keep, but even the cat played traitor, and sprang to the wooden boards between them.

"Going to turn me into a rat?" Miles snarled, hiding his self-loathing.

"Why should I? You are one already!"

"Christ's mercy! Must you reduce everything to feelings? This alliance is—"

"I . . . do not think it is sensible for us to continue this conversation any longer." She turned, drawing herself up as straight as a lady on a tomb. "Besides, Sir Miles, as you have so painstakingly pointed out in such delicate language, if you, sir, are seen talking to me here, it will unquestionably ruin my reputation beyond redempt—"

"I will see you in Hell!" he exclaimed with feeling and returned to the feast.

MILES SPENT THE FOLLOWING DAY BLISSFULLY HUNTING WITH the duke and his guests, but on his return Bess waylaid him. It seemed that Lady Haute planned to visit the town with the harpist. Damn her! So, before the fires were covered for the night and all the castle gates were bolted, Miles, clad in homespun and a black cloak that enveloped him from head to heels, unlatched the postern and stole forth behind his quarry.

In the April dusk Miles could almost map his way by the odors: the Honddu carrying the ordure of the castle to the Usk, the perfume of the violets thriving upon the bank, the cloying

scents used by the chandlers at North Gate, then other stinks
wafting from the town: the cooking smokes of sea coal and firewood, the uglier smell of boiling meat, fresh dung congealing
between the uneven cobblestones, rotting refuse mashed by cart
wheels, and, at Water Gate, the clean smell of planed wood from
the joiner's yard.

But there was also the earthy scent of rain and it was splashing
down by the time Miles reached Morgannok Street at the far end
of the town. The downpour reduced the sound of his footsteps
on the cobbles and let him follow closer. The old man set his
arm on Heloise Ballaster's and drew her into the courtyard of an
alehouse, but by the time Miles had traversed the puddled rear
of the tavern, they had vanished.

Godsakes, he cursed as he let himself out through the wattle
fence into a laneway, he should leave the rebellious wench to her
peril, save that he did not want some lout fumbling up the foolish innocent's skirts.

Finding an overhang for shelter, he halted. Above the rain, he
heard the river lapping close, but where, ye saints, was the plaguey music? What now? Perhaps St. Cecily was being charitable,
for the shower abated and a poignant cascade of music from Emrys's harp lured him along the sandstone wall that edged the
alley. At the third gate he tried the latch.

"*Pwy sy na?*" snorted a woman's voice.

"*Rhyddid i Cymryu,*" he murmured. "*Cerddoriaeth uned ni.*"

Satisfied, the woman led him through a passageway, dark as
Purgatory and stinking of stale urine and spilt ale, and down
stone steps into a hot cellar lit by naught but a blazing fire. It
was some sort of forge. The smoke stung his eyes before he was
able to make out a dozen or so people perched on sacks or crates.
All Welsh, he guessed. One fellow cradled a stretched hide with
jingles in its frame, another nursed a viola. Ruddy in the flickering flames, Emrys's thicket brows and flowing hair, riveleting
over his bared forearms, gave him the mien of the Welsh god
Govannon the weapon maker. The slender shadow beside him,

sensibly hooded, must be Heloise. Save for a man and woman conversing in whispers to his left, they were all listening to the singer, a huge man in his forties, sweaty-faced, black-maned, and fiercely bearded, with a belly that overstretched his belt, and an alepot in his hand.

Miles slid into the darkest corner but did not hesitate to intercept the leather bottle being passed around. The contents nearly ripped the inside from his throat.

Despite his quarryman's complexion, the singer's voice was wondrously rich. His huge rib cage, built for resonance, threw out so ardent a song of reprisal against the English that Miles, whose Welsh was keen enough to understand most of it, felt his blood run cold.

> "I will wield the blade of Cyffin,
> I will deal with my bare hands
> A hurt to that two-faced town yonder.
> From the town of Rhos at dawn,
> By nightfall to dark Chester.
> Let me kill, if my day arrives
> With Dafydd's sword, two thousand."

As the last verse ended to cheers and laughter, the only Englishman in their midst was rigid, anxious to leave. A rebellion? Christ!

"Pah, Lewis," taunted someone. "Why brawl over an English whore when there are plenty of pretty tits in Wales to fondle!" Miles reddened, both thankful that Heloise could not understand their crudity, and ashamed of his suspicions; there might be treason but this song was merely some personal feud.

The viola player was urging Emrys back into the firelight. God's rood, the old man was gifted! Just the first soul-wrenching, plaintive chords banished the bawdy laughter and the crackling of the logs upon the fire. The mountains and woods of Wales surged into Miles's consciousness. He could hear the rain in the

song lashing the leaves. Like a mythical hero, he strode beside
the singer down the slopes and stood beside the splashing
streams.

> "Not like the growling curse,
>   That makes the great tide
>   And brings the wintry cold.
>
> "Not like the scolding words,
>   That make miry torrents of the streams
>   And a full roar in the river's throat.
>
> "Oh, why is the day so raw and angry?
>   Speak gently and bid the sky
>   No more to glower,
>   Nor cast a veil across the moon."

Setting down his harp, Emrys cleared his throat, breaking the
spell that bound them to their memories. "I have a surprise," he
announced. "I brought with me a young woman from the castle."

"Surprise! Emrys, you old dotard," muttered someone. "Will
you get us hanged?"

"No, rest you, am I a block, an ass? I tell you she understands
not one word of our speech but she sings like an angel. You must
hear her.

"Uncover. Free your hair," he said in English, rising to take
his guest by the wrist. At least she was refusing. "Be yourself,
bach," Emrys was saying, setting back her hood with a bardlike
authority. "It matters not if you are wife or maid, lad or lady.
All are equal among my people, wel di."

As if she were under an enchantment, Heloise removed the
coif and shook her braids free like an elfin maid for all to see.
Silver hair tumbled over her plain russet kirtle like living metal
in the fire's light. Did she not understand the danger? At night
men are spellcast but in the day they see, they remember, differently.

"Sing, *arianlais,* as I taught you."

Her voice, husky at first, warmed to a beautiful clarity, the words powerful and wrenching, a trumpet to arms against her countrymen.

The lyrics were Welsh but did she understand? For she sang it so poignantly that Miles felt a sadness to choke, because he knew the words in his own tongue—the hatred and the hope:

> *"Powys, a land, liberal, lovely, fruitful,*
> *Generosity's sweet drinking horn of bright taverns,*
> *Oh, it was a pleasant orchard*
> *Before a youth, rich in wisdom, was slain by a blue sword.*
> *Now it is, alas, for widowhood,*
> *Hawk's land, without a nightingale of song."*

"More!" Slapping their thighs, the musicians were openhanded in praise. Even Heloise, cheeks pink as gillyflowers, understood. She shook her head and rose from the singer's stool, but she let them press a cup into her hand, and was both thirsty and exultant enough to gulp it down.

"Un arall? Iechyd da!" Laughing, they filled it again and the bard called Lewis heaved himself back and launched into a ribald drinking song. Others joined in—the man with the wooden flute and the young tabor player—but their eyes, like everyone else's, kept flickering back to the Englishwoman. The nervous sipping betrayed her naivete though she seemed at ease, smiling as they teased her in Welsh. Two of the men grew lewd in their remarks and Emrys, although his voice was calm so as not to panic their visitor, sat down beside her protectively, hissing rebukes.

Mercy, how long before the old man took her back? How much drink would they tip down her? She was whispering to Emrys, who beckoned one of the women over; she needed the latrine. At last! Miles slid off the palliasse by the wall and stealthily made his way to the door.

He heard the women's voices ahead in the yard. With luck

he might get her away now—but two of the Welsh had come
out to relieve themselves against the wall. The rain had cleared
and a moon, splendid as a pagan scimitar, was free of clouds.

As Miles stole out to hinder his wife, fierce arms grabbed him
and drew him kicking back to the cellar. Rough hands flung him
on his front, wrenching his right arm behind his back. Someone
seized a flaming faggot from the fire and thrust it towards his
head. Miles preferred to breathe in the dust than struggle for air
and be recognized.

"We have a spy, it seems." Someone thrust back his hood and
seized a fistful of hair, trying to make him show his face.

"Mistress!" Miles mimicked a servant's shriek, as he heard the
women returning.

The cold air of the passageway must have slapped Heloise's
senses clear, for she pushed in between his captors.

"Mistress," he wailed as pitifully as he could, squinting to see
Heloise's face. She was blinking at the sleek, greased hair plas-
tered back from his brow. Was there light enow? Was she sober
enough to know him in disguise? Well, if her fey mind was open
to messages, she had better receive this one or he was a dead
man.

Heloise wobbled; she put a hand to her mouth and then gave
a bubbly laugh. "You think . . . Oh, no, this is my servant," she
spluttered, taking the brand and tossing it back in the embers.
"You knave!" She waggled a finger close to his nose. "I told you
not to disclose yourself." Her drunken giggles were not subsiding.

"What's he a-doin' skulkin' around in the shadows outside?"
His captor gave another vicious jerk upon his arm.

"Let me go, masters," Miles wailed, his nose pressed hard
against the dirt. "Don't let 'em harm me, mistress."

"I thought I could trust you not to bring strangers into our
midst, Emrys," bawled Lewis, no longer indulgent. "And a *sais*
too."

"I never saw him afore." Suspicion larded the old man's English.

"No, no, of course you have not," Heloise answered cheerfully. "He is but late from Kent." Miles watched like a cyclops as Heloise patted the minstrel's sleeve. Evidently she had perceived the rivalry between the bards. "Master Emrys, I—I am sorry. No disrespect but I felt I needed a doughtier escort to see me back."

"Doughtier! Pah!" Lewis's guffaw of laughter was reassuring them. "You need a real man, *benyw!*" His hand patted his codpiece.

Miles's arm was freed. He moved it painfully forwards and stayed facedown. The humility irked him but it was safest.

"Get up, man." Heloise nudged him with her foot. "They mean you no harm." He lifted himself onto his hands and knees, blowing his cheeks out sulkily to give his lean face more breadth. His wife sat down again, spreading her skirts, and indicated that he should sit at her feet, so he snatched up his alecup and lumbered across to her, rubbing his face to mask his cheeks and remembering to keep his shoulders bent in servile fashion to hide his true height.

"Two songs more and then I must leave," she exclaimed merrily and raised her cup, toasting them all. "My servant will see me back, Emrys. You must stay and sing again. Make music until morning. Here, Tom." She tilted her cup and poured half its contents into Miles's.

His lower lip apucker, he took it sulkily, hoping one of the Welsh lads had not dosed it to make her more amenable. Inside he was thanking God that these musicians were all the worse for drinking. His millstone lady was tapping her foot to the music, and it was easy, sprawled as he was, to slide his hand around her ankle meaningfully. She smiled down at him, clapping her hands, and nodded, but she did not rise.

His fingers rose above the slender ankle, enjoying the smooth slope of her calf. It was wonderful what modesty that drew forth; as the piece ended, she stood up, trying her nursery Welsh in bidding them *"Nos da."* Emrys she bussed upon the cheek and then, sweetly blowing kisses to them all, disappeared up the stairs. With a mumble and a touch of forelock, Miles fled after her and, taking her by the elbow, hurried her across the shining puddles.

"I did not know you liked Welsh epics," she giggled when they reached the street.

"Tell me the one about the foolish English virgin. You should know it backwards."

Heloise tried to stamp her foot at him. Grammercy, she had not asked the rogue to hazard a beating! "That is not—"

"Christ Almighty!" She found herself swung into a doorway with his hand clamped over her mouth. "I risked my life coming after you tonight, madam."

"Why in heaven bother?" Heloise retorted in a fierce whisper as he loosened her. His hand had left her with a gravelly taste.

"Such gratitude. Because, lady simpleton, if you are ravished by a Welshman whoreson in the high street, I shall never be free of you and will have to suffer an egg smelling of leeks in my marital nest."

"Well, it would serve you right. Are you going to see me back or are we to huddle here like adulterers while you lecture me all night?"

"I thought I was a decent Christian man," he growled, grabbing her hand and hauling her along. "I reckon Job in the holy scriptures was better off."

"What's that to the point?"

"He mainly suffered boils. Why God has saddled me with such a shrew as you, I cannot fathom."

"Because you hang men and dislike children and kill innocent bees." That retort brought him up short. "And I . . . I rescued you just now, you ungrateful man!"

"Lady, be quiet! You are making enough noise to bring the watch from Bulith, let alone the next street."

"Well, you *are* ungrateful."

"Hush!"

"Huussssssssh!"

Miles cursed. His chance of taking her through the streets without discovery looked nigh impossible and if they were found together, he would be stuck in a marital rut with her forever. If he could sober her . . . He hauled her along a laneway towards the river and into a doorway built into the town wall.

"What is this?" She struggled to free her hand, stumbling in the darkness as he hauled her up a spiral stair into a watchtower.

"Somewhere to stare at Pen-y-Fan by moonlight while you regain your sobriety. Get down." A fierce hand forced her to crouch. "I want to make sure we have not been followed." He stooped beside her, listening intently, and then tensely edged upwards as though he expected a volley of arrows to come flying in if he stuck his head up. "I hope your magical powers run to alarum bells," he muttered.

Heloise muffled a giggle. "There is nothing here, sir, but the *tylwyth teg,* and us."

He ducked back down. "Faeries, that is all I need. We have enough problems already from the underworld—of Brecknock, that is. What is so amusing?"

"You, you are so gloriously serious."

"I think you mean sober, which is more than you are." He played sentry again. "Our luck is in, it seems." A hand, warm and dusty, located one of hers. "I should have learned by now that danger and you skip hand in hand and it always embroils me."

Upright, she untangled her feet and surveyed an enchanted world. Below them flowed the Usk, black as Lethe with the cleared moon broken in shards and glossed upon its waves. Gables and ridges, shingles and tiles all sleek with rain, glinted in silence like an altar painting. Torches burned at the castle but half-heartedly, as though the stones themselves were slumbering. But the wind was blowing from Pen-y-Fan; something was shifting.

Miles, scanning the gaps of cobble and dirt between the dwellings, was listing lethal possibilities. Murder? Bootcaps and fists applied strategically to rib and groin in reprisal for the hanging? A bloody means to stop the alliance with ap Thomas? Rape of the lily maiden at his side? Why in hell had he brought her up here?

"Best that we wait a little longer," he advised and, taking a corner of his damp cloak, wiped the forge dust from his face. They should leave now. What had begun in the orchard had to be withstood now but the ache was growing.

"There is no harm—yet." Her words were a soft sigh with the ripple of willow leaves. "I would know . . . and it is all right," she continued in a steady little voice. "I actually drank very little."

Ha, is the earth round? Shapeshifter!

"I am sorry that I put you at risk," she ventured softly, as if afraid to leave the abyss of silence between them unbridged. "It was kind of you to come after me."

"Kind?" You are my possession. "Lady, I have been at great pains to build up a reputation that will shake some respect out of the Welsh. God knows who is behind this little adventure of ours and it is not over yet. There is still some price to be paid." His grim tone warned against the perils involved in baiting him. God's mercy, but he was trying not to imagine the feel of her.

At his back, the bells of the abbey pealed in another saint's day.

"England is full of walls," she whispered, slithering her fingertips over the sandstone. "Castles, abbeys, towns, anchorite cells . . ."

Miles understood, or thought he did, but he had no answer; his thoughts were running widdershins, his sideways gaze lingering where it should not. He had seen her in so many forms, like a jewel toppled upon his palm, but now . . . God in Heaven why did she have to look so ethereal and lovely, and stand so damnably close that he could smell her fragrance?

"But music can steal through walls and conquer kingdoms,"

he observed. "That was sedition at work, my lady."

"Perhaps, sir, but their songs and voices were so beautiful. 'Speak gently and bid the sky no more to glower, nor cast a veil across the moon.' I shall not forget tonight."

His mind was reeling. He had tasted loneliness, the river pouring mercilessly through the arc of stones like sand through the glass of time.

"Nor I," he added wryly, drawing his cuff across his mouth. "I still have the taste of ashes in my mouth."

"Have you no heart, *Cysgod*?" she chided, laughing, turning to aim small fists playfully against his chest. "Is there no poetry in *you* tonight?"

"There is a great deal," Miles answered, with a Welsh lilt, "and it is mostly Anglo-Saxon and the theme is getting you back to the castle without having our throats cut. As for my heart"— he laughed—"I keep it where the Welsh can't steal it, see. I advise you to do the same, *cariad*." And then he added in his own voice, "Are you cold?"

"No, please," she protested, staying his hand from untying his cloak.

"At least I can keep the cruel wind from you." Hands, ungoverned by mind, spun her and drew her back against his shoulder. It took all his will to keep his hands armoring her shoulders and prevent them straying where his lips longed to touch; his imagination was divine sedition and utter torture.

A lady towered with her mortal lord, Heloise held her breath. Loath to cut herself free from the spell that was winding, she felt the hardness of Rushden's body like a stake against her back. Was this the passion that the saints denied themselves? This other fire kindled beneath her skirts? To confess her heresy would destroy her. Take him now, she could hear her father saying. Make him burn for you. Oh, if she were Dionysia, she would wind a halter of seduction around his neck and press her soft belly against his thighs. But for Heloise Ballaster, there would be no forgiveness in the morning; Rushden would call her passion wanton and her surrender cunning, because to become her lover he must become her husband. Oh, her inexperienced hands were shackled but she wanted to misbehave so desperately, to taste the words of love upon his breath.

What shall I do? her soul called out across the river to the ancient ones, the faeries that watched over her, and peace came with the rustling of the grasses. Look at the moon, whispered her inner being, is she not a veiled Diana staring out towards the planets, mourning Actaeon?

"Are you a changeling, Heloise?" The man's voice at last eased the silence, his words warm against her cheek. "Is that what you believe?" It was a step across the ice. A coil of woven words thrown out might help him reach her.

With a fragile happiness, she leaned back, surrendering to the moment.

"I see things ordinary—" She corrected herself: "*Others* never do." The answer was here, but this man would not know that, just by standing with her in this stone turret like a king, a spell was being cast.

"Are there voices in the bells?" Jeanne d'Arc?

"Not for me." She shuddered, sheathing her hands into her loose sleeves.

"You are trembling." Rushden slid his hands down to clasp hers beneath her breasts. "Not long now." Until . . .

"An owl, look!" she exclaimed delightedly as the grey wings skimmed soundlessly past their turret.

"The lady Bloedeuedd, perhaps," he said softly, his arms falling lower, hands splaying across her, melding her against his hardness. "Born of flowers, bewitched into an owl for being unfaithful." His voice was close, so seductively close. "What else do you see?"

"I—I saw . . . *foresaw* . . . a fire consuming the thatch beyond the church."

Rushden did not answer straightway. "Highly likely," he murmured. "Do you feel the fire as well as see it?" The fire, yes, she wanted to turn within his arms so badly. "And people, Heloise? The orchard . . ."

"I felt your mother's pain." Her breathing was growing swift.

"And us, Heloise?" So *y Cysgod* was hunting in the darkness for the future.

At least loosened, her silver hair could hide her face as she stared downwards, as if she were watching the torches ignite the wood beneath her. "No, not us. Something else is— I cannot tell." Wretchedly, she flung herself free. "For there is no pattern, you see, it is more like . . ." She was babbling but . . . "More like a glimpse of a page from someone else's story and then the book is closed. I do not hold the keys to the clasps either. Nor do I seek the lock. As you warned me yesterday, sir, I might be . . . burned for it."

His finger was gentle beneath her chin. "Then tell no one."

"I have told no one."

"Lady . . . you have just told me. . . . I am your greatest enemy."

"But I trust you." Her eyes were shimmering with more than moonlight.

"Well, do not." He lowered his head. "Expediency is the enemy of loyalty and all men are traitors when it comes to—"

"To what?" The question was a dreamy sigh; the answer . . . a shadow eclipsing Heaven. Oh, she wanted this more than anything in her whole life.

"This." His fingers tangled in her hair, holding her face to await his pleasure, tantalizing her until she could have screamed for him to kiss her with open lips—and open heart. She would not, dare not beg.

"Heloise!" He drew his lower lip along hers. She could have tempted Lucifer back to Heaven. His hands fastened possessively around her waist beneath her cloak and slid upwards, marveling at how wonderful she felt, her body sweet and delicate and close.

"No!" Frail manacles closed suddenly about his wrists. She

pulled away, leaving him aroused, unsatisfied. "Think of Myfannwy . . ."

"*Myfannwy!* When the moon is out you cannot see the stars."

"I do not want to be your mistress," she protested. "I do not
want to be bought a little house in Hereford and have the neighbors whispering, 'There goes Sir Miles Rushden's whore—when
he can spare the time.' "

Miles did what any quick-witted man would do, pushed beyond endurance, to hush a lovely woman. He kissed her properly.
It was his error. Heloise Ballaster tasted of mead—but such flowers, such divinity, that he felt like a god in tasting her. Within
the girdle of his fingers, her waist was delicate, and her hair
moonlight, celestial fire, about them both. As he deepened the
kiss with a tender hunger, it was as if a magic surrounded them
and some arcane power were touching a taper to pendant drops
of light on either side of a path to welcome him to another world.
Bewitched, he recognized himself inspired, renewed, as though
the shackles that bound him to the humdrum earth were severed
one by one.

"Heloise." He had never felt like this before.

As if she understood the raw hunger in his voice, her laughter
brushed his mouth and she drew back, her hair tiptoeing upon
the fingers splayed against her back.

Miles had committed sacrilege, yet at whose bidding? "I
should not have done that," he told her and hoped divine forgiveness was possible.

"No," she whispered, siren's fingers running across his lips.
"You should not have."

Miles felt dazed, lunatic. He took her face once more between
his palms and lowered his mouth to hers. His lips told her that
he wanted her surrender, that only in his conquest would she
find her truth.

Heloise slid her arms up round his neck and wreathed her
fingers into his hair. Her thighs were turning to fire as he kissed
her neck, her throat, his hands fondling and stroking with an

urgency. He was her destiny, her black, ruthless, desirable knight. The magic suddenly fled and the most profound feeling of evil made her struggle.

"No." She pushed at his chest, her heart beating frantically. "Let me go! You *must!*"

"Curse you, Heloise."

The iron bands of his arms freed her; sweat pearled upon his pale forehead.

She shrank against the wall, fighting against her soul's desire, wondering what power had dragged her from him, and struggled to reason.

"Yes, curse, Miles Rushden. But if I let you take what you do not want, tomorrow you will call me whore and witch."

"Come here!" Thirst for her serrated his angry voice.

"You did this of your own free will," she exclaimed and sped off down the steps like a fleeing princess. "You said so."

He hastened after her, grabbing at the cloak and gaining no purchase, but as he caught her to him on the last step, a nearby dog barked a fierce alarum. They froze, no longer melded in desire but waiting. He held his breath, his fingers tense in the furrows between her ribs, his heart beating behind her shoulder blade as she leaned against him. Oh, *this* was the evil. Not Rushden! Out of the darkness three men came at them with cudgels.

"Hide!" Rushden protectively flung her sideways out of the way of the attackers and quickly drew a dagger from his boot.

Cursing, Heloise landed indecorously amidst a pile of rubbish and scrambled round to face the enemy. Her husband had wrapped his cloak about his left arm as a buckler, but with no long steel to make the assailants keep their distance, he was hard pressed.

"*Dal y ferch!*" She instinctively knew the Welsh was meant for her. She must attract help at any cost. Swiftly clambering to her feet, Heloise sang forth her highest, most piercing note while her fingers fumbled in her purse for her only weapon.

"Christ Almighty!" exclaimed Rushden, laughing even though he was besieged on the first step. "It must be the figs!" As she drew breath, a choir of adjacent dogs took over, and tapers in the nearby dwellings suddenly flamed behind the shutters.

"*Diawl!*" One of the brigands charged at her.

"Come on!" she gasped and hurled the powder into his face.

"*Putain!*" A hand clutching his eyes, the large man staggered back. His sudden blindness gave her the chance to kick at his kneecap with all her strength. Wrenching his cudgel away, she whammed it behind the second man's knees, sending him sprawling onto Rushden's blade like a paid bill for spiking.

"Jesu, lady, I could hire you out when we next invade France!" Miles struggled to free the blade as the third man hurtled at him. Fleet of foot, he sprang aside. The vicious club smashed down against the steps. He slammed the side of his fist hard down on the fellow's neck, then with a hefty kick drove him crashing into the fence. But his assailant staggered back. Jerking free his cloak, Miles flung it in the other's face and leapt upon his enemy.

Of course, it might be Rushden she cudgeled if she interfered, thought Heloise, as the two men rolled across the stony ground.

"Be off, the pack o' yer!" bawled a woman and a bucket of pisswater hit the ground.

The rogue must have heard the thud of boots upon the cobbles.

"*Awn!*" he yelled, no longer struggling, and Rushden dragged him to his feet and hurled him at his staggering friend. The pair hurtled back against the wall. "*Dere 'mlaen!*" Grabbing the blinded man's belt, the third ruffian hauled him lumbering into the darkness.

"As if I have not enough trouble," growled Rushden. "There will be the Devil to pay for this night's work. The watch! Come on!"

"But . . ."

Godsakes, thought Miles, would she play physician? "Come!"

With a fierce arm about her waist, he sped her up the lane and into an alley just as the town watch arrived at the tower.

Her breath was ragged, her heart crying mercy, as they reached the end of Shepe Street. "Come on, mistress! If the watch catch us . . ."

"Yes, I know," she panted. "I will have to have your children." He recoiled as if her body were fire. "Go on without me," she gasped, glimpsing his shocked face, pale as a handsome wraith's, before she bent over, hands clasping her knees, her side burning as if she had been spiked by the Devil's trident.

"Easy, changeling." Strong hands steadied her shoulders and held her against him until the painful stitches had eased. "What was it you threw at the fellow, elfin dust?"

"Honest flour," she panted. "Did you think I would venture out unarmed?"

"My brave wench." His soft laughter heartened her. "I forget how skilled you are in combat." Once more he set his arm about her waist and, half-supporting her, drew her up towards the postern. She stooped and edged past, below the window, like a thief, while he kept the watchman talking. The clink of money echoed.

"May a man not visit his mistress without the whole castle knowing?" grumbled Rushden, his miserliness feigned. More jingled into the waiting palm. His curses were still audible until he caught up with Heloise in the bailey. "To bed with you, lady!"

"Upon my soul, I am truly sorry I endangered you," she whispered, running her hand along his sleeve before they parted.

"You endanger me all the time, Heloise," he answered cryptically and, like a nighthawk, vanished into the shadows.

Twelve

Weary, exultant, confused, and burned beyond saving, Heloise reached the first stair and froze as a hand touched her elbow.

"Ralph Bannastre, my lady, at your service. His grace requires your presence. Now!"

Heloise spun round to seek Rushden's help, but the courtyard was empty.

"May I not see him in the morning, sirrah?" No, she might not, he groused. And if she would make haste, he might take himself to his bed.

Grimy, hooded, her russet muddied with heaven-knows-what—self-stitched debris pearls and refuse spangles—she entered the duke's bedchamber with a prayer to St. Catherine on her lips. The duke, standing before the hearth, was a blur of kingfisher, his hair a sprawl of ruddy gold across the silken band edging his skin.

"Where have you been, Lady Haute?" He dismissed Ralph without a glance of thanks.

"S-singing, your grace."

"No leave was given you to go outside the castle."

"Your grace."

"But leave you shall have. You will depart tomorrow!"

"Very well, your grace."

"What?" he asked calmly, coming towards her. "No defense? No bargain?"

"Bargain, my lord?" He was too close.

"I could be persuaded to change my mind. After all, you have done a reasonable task of making my son behave." A jeweled forefinger hooked her chin. "What was this singing, then?"

"A Welsh bard. Lewis. I wanted to hear him, your grace, and . . ."

"Lewis Glyn Cothi?" As she nodded, he tipped back her hood and lifted a lock of her hair in astonishment. " 'Sufficient grey hairs.' By our Lady!"

"Sufficient, yes, your grace, but I assure you—"

"How very unusual." Cunning lit eyes empty of affection. "You have a choice, Lady Haute. If you wish to stay at Brecknock . . ." He gestured to his great bed, with its voluptuous, silken pillows. She blinked at him. Too much, unfair and unexpected. "You will, of course, cleanse yourself first," he was saying.

St. Catherine! Oh, she needed help to clear her weary head and talk this seducer away from her skirts! "I . . . I am a married woman, my lord."

"All the better, my lady. Your experience, I am sure, will do you credit."

"But I . . . I cannot deceive my husband." Nor could she divorce him if the duke seduced her.

Warm hands invaded her cloak, forcing down the russet gown to straining point. His lips trailed her neck. "Of course you can." He slid his hungry hands over her breasts.

"You are quite delectable, Lady Haute. Of course, if you prefer, you can leave Brecknock tomorrow with your marital fidelity still intact or perhaps"—a finger twisted in her hair—"I will send you to Bishop Langton."

She shuddered. Rushden had warned her. Holy Church had always lain beyond her door like a dog to be wakened. It only needed Buckingham to howl and centuries-old suspicions of both the unknown and the misunderstood would be picked up and hurled at her like jagged stones to hurt and kill. Perhaps the best way to deal with this was not to take him at his word.

"I do not think you would find me good company in your bed, my lord." He no longer seemed to care that the small hands which strove to prevent his rambling were still street-stained.

"Allow me to be the judge of that." Did he have to wriggle his tongue in her ear? Such unlicensed wantonness made her want to retch.

"I am sorry, my lord. I cannot lie with you. Sir Miles Rushden can tell you why." Rushden's name turned the key and the lock gave. Abruptly he released her.

"Sir Miles? What in God's name has he to do with— Are you telling me Rushden has enjoyed you?"

God curse these men! As if she were a pie to be sampled and shared around! She made no answer. Let the duke draw his own conclusions. Rushden would not forgive her but God damn her if she would lose her virginity to a creature who saw her merely as a plate to be licked. The duke took her wrists and rearranged them behind her back.

"So you are lying to me when you prattle of virtue. All this talk of husbands, yet you have already given your body to a lover."

"Speak to Rushden, my lord." *Help me!* she cried to the *tylwyth teg,* struggling fiercely as his mouth came down, half-suffocating her. "Ask him, my lord!"

"It seems I must." He let go of her and unlatched the door. "Pershall! Bestir yourself! Fetch Rushden!"

A sleepy mutter answered from the pallet beyond the door. "Saints preserve your grace! Is a woman not sufficient for you?"

MILES, A GYPON AND HOSE OVER HIS BARE FLESH AND A RICHER cloak flung about his shoulders, stared in surprise at an aggravated Heloise, tousled and delightfully unkempt, and then an invisible visor of indifference snapped down.

"She says she is your mistress."

Behind Harry's back, Heloise waved her fingers in denial. With a prayer to whichever saint had sympathy for white lies, Miles sucked in his cheeks and perused the lady with an interest calculated to goad her severely. "Not yet, my lord. Suffice it to say that I have made obvious my interest and the lady may reel me in any moment she pleases. You are rather late throwing in a line, I think, your grace."

"I consider your behavior inappropriate considering the delicacy of the negotiations with Rhys ap Thomas."

"Inappropriate or inconvenient, my lord?"

"Both." Harry evaded his searching gaze. "Lady Haute left the castle without permission."

Miles's smile was tepid. "With permission, my lord."

A red flush of annoyance exacerbated the duke's embarrassment. "You knew?"

"Yes, my lord, I granted her leave."

The pretend object of his admiration sensibly kept her head lowered as Harry looked suspiciously from his face to hers. But it was not over yet and to appease the duke, Miles circled her. "My lady, tell his grace your conclusions about Lewis."

"I—I consider him to be no danger. He sings words that might be considered seditious but I believe his passion is of a bodily nature, not political. Most of his songs seemed to be about women." She made no mention of Emrys nor that her Welsh was woeful.

With a sullen pout, the duke eventually unfolded his arms. "So, Lady Haute, you are reprieved for the time being, but I will hear a full report in the morning." Not a word of thanks, not a hint of an apology. Dismissed, the lady fled.

Harry unfortunately was not finished. "Why did you not inform me, Miles?"

"Lady Haute was in a half-mind not to place herself in danger." Any moment Harry would smell the lies.

"But she did and you let an English noblewoman go into that nest of vipers."

Oh, well, better he came clean. "I—I accompanied her, my lord."

Harry looked like a cannon with its fuse lit. "I see." Did he?

"It is best not discussed outside this chamber, my lord. Should the lady be invited again . . ."

"But you were set upon." No doubt the bruises on his jaw were ripening nicely.

"Yes. Welsh brigands, but I would wager a year's pay that the Vaughans were behind it. A payback for the drubbing I gave them. And we hanged one of their men for sheep stealing, remember."

"More complaints from the high sheriff tomorrow," the duke was grumbling. But it was not trouble with the Vaughans but the recent jab to his honor that made Harry as merry as a leper with a looking glass. "You could have told me, Miles. I have just made an utter fool of myself trying to seduce the woman."

"You have many others to choose from, my lord."

"So I have but . . . but the moonlight hair, so very intriguing. You knew?" Miles nodded. "Do you think she's silver everywhere else?" Personal annoyance had to be hid from dukes, especially this one.

Since he might dig himself a deeper hole with speaking, Miles gave a cold laugh.

"Do not assert rank, my lord of Buckingham." His grace was staring at the bed as if estimating its capacity. "No!" exclaimed Miles, following his thoughts. "If—*if* I decide to sample the lady's capabilities, I shall *not* be sharing her."

"No"—Harry's smile was ruthless—"you will not. Let us not delay matters any further. Tomorrow you shall wed Myfannwy."

GODSAKES, TWO WIVES! MILES WOKE UP HARD, THINKING OF Heloise. Last night had been an error, kissing her, lying to Harry. Well, he would wed Myfannwy, and tup her so much that by the time the church courts started hearing the case, she might be carrying a child and that would put the stamp on it. And he would not betray Myfannwy; Heloise must leave this very day and he must tell her so straightway and yet . . .

She was on her own, thank God!—twitching tapestries along the wall close by the duchess's apartments. He ignored this peculiar activity and the ache in his groin, and tried to imagine how blissful it would be without her. "What in Heaven's name were you doing going to the duke's bedchamber?" he rasped, dispensing with niceties.

She let go a dusty arras and rubbed at her nose like a rabbit washing its whiskers, not looking at him but up and down the passageway. "His man Ralph Bannastre was lying in wait while you were shinning it to your bed in lily-livered fashion. You might have warned me. Have you seen Ned? He was not with his tutor."

"I got you out of the scrape." With a jingle of spurs, he kept pace with her.

"Yes, thank Heaven, I could have been violated otherwise and then not even a score of Holy Fathers could have severed us. Where is that child?" She was opening doors to all the chambers along the passageway and, frustrated, halted. "Your duke nearly had me naked to the waist. A few minutes more and I would have told him who my husband was out of perfect desperation. Sir, if you want that annulment, protect me better." She turned and marched back the way she had come. "Women have the right to bestow their bodies where they please. Any man who thinks otherwise is . . ."

"Heloise." He grabbed her by the elbow. She was blushing, averting her face, the fury of activity a mask. "Changeling, all men are heretics in that respect."

"I—I have to find Ned."

"Be still! Will you look at me, woman! He wants you, Heloise. It seems that half the castle does." Something, surrendered in his voice, made her obey at last. Tears glistened like dew upon her lashes. All eternity was telling him to kiss away her misery. "Harry takes what he desires, Heloise. So do I. You have to leave today for *all* our sakes. This morning. I shall arrange an escort."

Hazel eyes awash with tears implored his mercy. "Oh, I know my sand is through your hourglass," she whispered sadly. "The . . . the real Lady Haute may arrive at any hour. I gave myself a week, no more, to win your heart."

His heart?

"*Boo!*" A small figure in a demon's mask sprang out in front of them from behind the arras.

"Oh, Hell!" exclaimed Miles and let her go.

"MY LADY?" BRIAN THE ARCHER ENTERED THE NURSERY. Heloise's bags, ready for slinging across the packhorse, stood waiting for him to shoulder. He frowned at her cat lolling in a patch of sunlight. "It is time. They are all in the chapel so the way is clear." He nodded at Rushden's two men-at-arms who had been posted outside her door.

Heloise glanced from Daffyd curled before the hearth to the ribboned letter she had left for Bess to read to Ned. "I have been happy here," she murmured, pulling the door closed. The soldiers fell in behind her.

"You have been good for the child, my lady."

She had no choice but to let them escort her down the staircase. She faltered at the music from the chapel. Rushden was in there saying his vows to poor Myfannwy. Not at the church door this time, she thought numbly. He had made sure of that.

Across the bailey, a saddled Cloud fidgeted, but Martin was standing with the porter and two guards. They seemed to be arguing with a tall scarecrow fellow, a scholar, judging by his dark clothes.

"Oh, my lady," the porter called out in relief when he saw her, and came puffing over with the others following. "This fellow reckons he has come from Westminster with an urgent message. I dare not interrupt the service. Will you speak with the fellow?"

Oily black hair unpleasantly rambled over the humbled hunch of the messenger's shoulders but the bearded face was sharp with murky intelligence.

"Thomas Nandik, madam. I come from Lord Hastings, madam." The voice—scholarly with an Essex dialect—was insistent.

"From Westminster?" she said in disbelief, noting that his

chewed fingernails played upon the rolled brim of a hat so thread-bare she could see the rushes inside.

"Aye." Dark eyes, red with fatigue but burning with purpose, fixed her and suddenly every instinct told her this was vital. She glanced towards the chapel and bit her lip.

"Very well. Come on!" Grabbing his arm, she ran as though her life depended on it.

"No, Lady Haute!" Brian bawled, racing after her. "I have— *oooff!*" He toppled headfirst to the ground as Martin grabbed his ankle.

"Quickly!" Heloise flung open the door of the chapel and bundled the stranger in. There was no time for holy water.

"What in—" Gasps from those nearest the door disturbed the priest; the Latin halted.

"My lord of Buckingham!" Heloise exclaimed, marching towards the altar.

Rushden, standing with the Welsh girl's hand in his, turned. His face went white.

"Christ in Heaven!" Buckingham pushed past his duchess to face the interruption, scarlet with fury.

The scholar would have babbled his message to Rushden, save Heloise had him by the elbow still. "*That* is the duke!"

Fumbling, he drew a letter from his breast and knelt.

"Three days ago . . . the king . . . God rest his soul . . . is dead."

Thirteen

"No lusty comets at his highness's passing. You would think we should have seen some portent," mused Miles, a widower still, passing Harry the calendar, as the duke's close councilors swiftly reassembled in Harry's chamber. Rhys ap Thomas was with them (it would have been difficult to deny him) and Myfannwy, unwed and lips quivering, was being soothed by Cat and the woman they thought was Lady Haute. The marriage could wait.

"Ha! Why bother with a dead king when we may concern ourselves with the new one?" retorted the duke.

"Lord Hastings writes that the queen is sending two thousand men to fetch her son from Ludlow." Miles read the letter through again. "We ought to swell the retinue." It was difficult to stay calm. At last, his dream of high office might come true. Hastings was asking for *Harry's* help against the queen.

"Should you not see which way the winds of power blow?" ap Thomas suggested. "I am told, see, that Gloucester has little liking for the queen and her kinsmen."

"Exactly," the duke chuckled, "there could be rich pickings." Yes, thought Miles, and if the queen and Gloucester could be encouraged to destroy each other, the House of Lancaster might rise again and Harry claim the throne.

"Here, Miles." With a scatter of sand across his broad scrawl, the duke folded and sealed his letter. "I am sending a pledge of support to my cousin Gloucester," he informed the others, swiftly grinding his signet into the soft wax. "Pershall shall ride with you, Miles, in case of mishap, and take this too." He tugged off a smaller ring. "Convince Gloucester of my loyalty. Convince him that he is in mortal danger if the Woodvilles seize the kingdom.

Tell him to bring an army—where is that map again? Tell him I shall meet him at . . . at Northampton."

CROSSING THE BAILEY WAS DANGEROUS WITH HORSES BEING led out and couriers mounting, and Miles, fastening his sword belt across his riding doublet, nearly collided with Heloise. She had Ned in her arms, watching the preparations but no doubt lying in wait for him. Well, he was not rid of her yet but . . .

"Is it so certain the king is dead?" she exclaimed, hastening after him. "What did the letter say?"

"Infection of the lungs. From fishing, I believe. And now we have a child for king!"

"Huzzah!" Ned flung his arms up.

"Exactly," muttered Miles, with feeling. "Enjoy the reprieve, madam." He caught the reins of the post-horse from his groom, sprang into the saddle, and slid his feet into the leather messenger guards. "I am for Yorkshire to my lord of Gloucester." He could have said more but there was no privacy.

"Sir—" Heloise longed to beg him to bear her love to Dionysia and Lady Margery but there were greater matters for him to deal with. "Go safely," she said, a wife's concern tender in her voice.

"I pray so! We may well be on the verge of war. God keep you, my little lord, and you, too, my lady! Stand aside!" And he spurred the post-horse through the gate.

AT MIDDLEHAM IN WENSLEYDALE, MILES, WITH A THREE-DAY beard untidying his chin and his eyes gritty from weariness, knelt before the Duke of Gloucester. His grace, somber in mourning, his sorrow for his much-loved brother writ large upon his face, read Harry's letter with stern concentration; perhaps the promise of alliance was unlooked-for; the two dukes had always been polite to one another but never close.

"My lord suggests you bring as many men as you can hastily

array, your grace, and meet with him at Northampton to escort
the Prince of Wales to London."

The ivory complexion of Duke Richard creased, displeased.
"Holy Paul! I trust my cousin of Buckingham is not suggesting
I arrive with an *army* at my back to escort a twelve-year-old boy.
That will seem a trifle aggressive!"

Miles was almost too tired to argue. "My lord, Lord Hastings
wrote to his grace that the queen is sending two thousand Woodville retainers to escort the prince."

"And so he wrote to me." Golden-brown eyes, longer-lashed
and warmer than Harry's, examined him.

"My lord, his grace of Buckingham believes that the queen
intends to crown the prince with all speed and make herself the
power in this land. He fears for your future and his own if she
prevails." He held his breath as Gloucester arched an eyebrow at
his henchmen.

"Most considerate of your duke, Sir Miles," said Frances, Lord
Lovell, folding his arms. "But how do we know this is not some
enticement to lure his grace of Gloucester into danger? After all,
Buckingham is brother-in-law to the queen."

Miles turned his dusty face again to the duke and stood up
at his bidding. "I think you know my lord's mind where the
queen is concerned, your grace. He has no love for her or any of
her kin. He is willing to support you as Lord Protector of England in whatever path you take."

"Harry's message is timely, thanks to you, for we were about
to leave early tomorrow." Gloucester's coppery red-brown head
bent consideringly over the letter again before he looked up at
Miles. "However, Sir Miles, it seems to me that making good
speed is better than delaying to gather a larger force, and I trust
we go to welcome a king, not to make war. But, given these
uncertain times, your master's warning is accepted right gladly.
I shall send a fresh messenger posthaste to tell him so. Ride with
us south tomorrow, Sir Miles, if it pleases you."

Like a chance to spend eternity in Hell! Miles bowed his willingness, but all he wanted was anywhere horizontal where he might sleep and sleep.

"SIR MILES RUSHDEN?" A NOBLE LADY INTERCEPTED HIM AS HE followed the steward across the great hall. Maybe she thought him befuddled, for he was scarcely able to confront the wide blue gaze, and he disliked the sense that he was being weighed in her balance.

"I am Margery, Lady Huddleston, sir, half-sister to the duchess. Her grace craves forgiveness for her curiosity but she believes she may be acquainted with your wife and desires news of her."

His tired mind was not up to careful phrases nor did his clouded sight focus on the female blur of yellow hair and gauzy veil hovering behind her. "Madam, I crave her grace's pardon. I have no wife. I am . . . betrothed to a Welsh demoiselle."

The lady frowned, drew breath to make some comment, then changed her mind. "There must be some mistake, then. Good night to you, sir," she replied coldly and drew the younger girl with her.

For some reason he was too tired to fathom, his answer had not pleased Lady Huddleston. Nor, when it came to the truth, did it entirely please him.

NORTHAMPTON, WHICH STANK OF TANNED LEATHER ON A still day, boasted smithies, horse dealers, wheelwrights, and alehouses of sufficient standard to please the fussy traveler, as well as shoes for kings. For a Tuesday afternoon and such a modest town, decided Miles as he rode in through North Gate in Gloucester's retinue, there was an excessive amount of horse dung being cleaned up from the road. Evidence of the new king's arrival? If so, why were there only townsfolk to greet them?

Yes, gasped the mayor, panting as he headed the crowd of welcome on the steps of the Queen Eleanor Cross, the prince had passed through Northampton with Lord Rivers, and, yes, their

retinue had filled the entire main street before departing for Stony
Stratford, some fourteen miles ahead.

So the Woodvilles had not bothered to wait for Gloucester as
promised. Fourteen miles! Miles groaned at the thought but
Duke Richard, too, was weary. He sent a messenger to Stony
Stratford to advise of his arrival and, to Miles, muttered that he
hoped Buckingham was still of the same mind; then he dug
himself in at the cleanest inn.

And where was Harry? worried Miles, downing a jack of ale
outside Gloucester's lodging. Surely Harry had not broken his
word and gone on to Stony Stratford with the prince? The aldermen, hanging around Gloucester's hostelry like dogs waiting
for a she-dog in heat, were not much help. There had been so
many pennons earlier, they told Miles apologetically.

His fellow travelers, Gloucester's men, had suddenly developed short leashes on their tempers. It had been three days' hard
riding since Nottingham and before that, the long, pressured
journey down from York with the road constantly beneath their
smarting eyes. And it was not just saddlesores that made them
terse; two thousand men loyal to the queen lay but an hour's
hard riding south and Buckingham and his retinue were inexplicably missing. Godsakes, thought Miles, more of this and he
might end up manacled in the prison by the gate by nightfall.

It was not until after the town bells chimed two that a
horseman in the Stafford livery was sighted and Miles with relief
led Ralph Bannastre in to kneel at Gloucester's boots. *At last!*
His grace of Buckingham would be in Northampton by sunset.
If Gloucester huffed a sigh of relief, it was not audible. Oh,
Christ, he does not trust us yet, thought Miles.

When Harry finally blessed Northampton with his coming,
Miles had reason to be proud. It was not just the silken knots
and collared swans aflutter on the sarsynett banners and the company of some three hundred men in scarlet and black. It was
because, astoundingly, and with a surge of ingenuity, Harry had
Ned across his saddle before him. He presented the epitome of

a friendly lord bringing his little son to meet the young king—certainly not with any treacherous thought of raising a sword against anyone, no, not at all! It was as good as rolling belly up.

With a flourish of sleeves and manly hugs, the two dukes greeted one another. The White Boar men whistled with relief. Miles was the one who tensed, pleasure and displeasure curdling, as the child's governess located him like a foraging bee.

Heloise, her saddle calluses hidden beneath a dusty riding kirtle, accosted her astonished, haggard husband at the rear of the crowded outer chamber with a blend of sparkle and caution. "I give you good day, sir." Her curtsy was knee-deep; his armored bow was less than deferential. "The duke has brought Traveller for you and Myfannwy is all forgiveness and sends her greetings."

"Good God, madam," he answered honestly, "I thought I had seen the last of you."

"I can see you missed me." Her dry answer reached out to nettle him. "It was Ned's insistence. Your duke thought it seemed like a good idea."

"I cannot think why." Rushden's mouth held firm but his strained gaze was reasonably forgiving as he allowed her to isolate him. "Or maybe I can," he murmured, the steel in his eyes turning molten as he examined her for fingermarks and creasing. "Do reassure me that Harry has been too preoccupied"—his gaze lingered on her breasts—"to press you into other duties." A double-layered concern, no doubt.

"Oh, you still hold the key," she retorted, and caught her breath, the hot blood flushing her skin, "but—but I quit Brecknock by the skin of my teeth. After you left, I sent Martin to Hay so he might alert me when the real Lady Haute arrived there, you see. She had and he did, so it was fortunate that Ned threw a splendid tantrum."

"I see," lied Rushden, glancing round to make sure that they were still out of earshot. "Well, this is no place for you, believe me."

"Why, what are you up to, sir?" she asked. "Improving Buck-

ingham's fortunes?" The wicked serpents on his breast glinted at
her murderously.

"It is not a woman's matter." He rubbed a hand across his
weary forehead.

"Is it not the queen's?" she retorted; and risked adding, "Half
of England is made up of women. Why should we not be interested in who rules us?" A loud jingle of harness outside distracted
him. She would have asked for news of Middleham but the buzz
around them had changed its timbre.

"Godsakes, changeling, not now," he muttered as the White
Boar men's hands hovered at their sword hilts. Jesu!

"Sir!" She was scared now, seeing the alert soldier in Rushden
take control. His mouth thinned and he scanned the Stafford
men, making swift contact with each.

"For your own safety, Lady Haute," he said grimly, as de la
Bere brought Ned to her, "just play at nursemaids and keep the
boy from harm. The Woodvilles have double the men and the
situation is delicate." Then he tensed like a drawn bow as a tall
lord, fair and handsome despite his harvest years, clad in a brocade doublet worthy of an emperor, entered, looking utterly incongruous—an iridescent beetle surrounded by armored ants—
and proud of it.

"Who on earth is that?" she whispered, tiptoeing behind him
to see better.

"Lord Rivers! He must have come back from Stony Stratford
to kiss hands or else . . . Bring Ned and be wary!" Urgently taking her by the forearm, Rushden pushed through the throng to
Buckingham's side.

A Woodville! The queen and Duchess Catherine's brother!
Heloise sensed Buckingham's hackles rising beneath his broad
collar as the newcomer with an urbane laugh stretched out his
arms to the two dukes, just like a clever tumbler who had just
landed on his feet. They did not applaud. An emerald of roseleaf
proportion flashed on the cool hand that clasped Buckingham's
fingers and sea green eyes smiled cleverly into Gloucester's with

a hard brilliance. For an instant Heloise glimpsed misapprehension brush like a bat's wings swiftly across the latter's face. Was he wondering if Rivers and his brother-in-law, Buckingham, were dissembling allies out to disarm him with a main course of words and a dessert of daggers? Were they? But Buckingham set his heel upon any fuses by summoning Ned. The child made a bow to his maternal uncle, clearly disliking the scrutiny he was receiving.

The eldest Woodville sprawled himself across the chair they offered him, his grin lazy and apologetic. "Yes, yes, I know I arranged that we were to meet you both in Northampton, my lords, but there simply would not have been room for all our retinues, so we are just up the road at Stony Stratford. The prince and my other nephew, Grey, send you their greetings and are looking forward to meeting with you both tomorrow *et cetera*." That done, Rivers flashed a shiny smile at Buckingham. "I hope Northampton does not hold too many ghosts for you, Harry?"

Buckingham for an instant missed the ball. Heloise did too, until she remembered Sir William explaining that Ned's great-grandfather had been slain in a battle at Hardingstone Fields outside the town, fighting against the Yorkists. Was Rivers being tactless? The unexpected verbal scratch after the handshake of courtesy drew its own ambiguous response:

"No ghost that will bother me, Rivers. Loyalty to one's king is nothing to be ashamed of, as you know well."

Interesting, thought Heloise. Parry and thrust! She knew that Lord Rivers had supported the House of Lancaster until his sister became the Yorkist queen.

"Shall we dine?" said Gloucester diplomatically and there were uncertain glances and tactful hesitations among the retinues. Who would be dining with these great lords? Rushden, summoned by Buckingham's nod, gave Heloise a reassuring glance.

"You are better out of this." He tweaked Ned's nose. It surprised all three of them. "Remember what I said," he admonished her.

"Oh, I keep a commonplace book of your utterances, Sir Miles. Come, Lord Stafford, let us leave these grown men to their games."

AFTER SUPPER, LISTENING TO THE SPARKLING CONFIDENCE OF Rivers, which put the less learned Buckingham and his quieter cousin in the shade, Miles wondered how without the numbers they could seize the initiative from this smooth courtier. He read the answer in Harry's face, the hate nailed down like a coffin lid. Gloucester, in contrast, still mourned, his chin resting on his hand, watching the swirling depths of his wine as he moved the cup back and forth, making wet circles on the wood. Fatigue hovered in the dusky shadows about his eyes and his chestnut hair looked lank in the candlelight.

"I heard a good story the other day," Rivers was saying. "There was a man who heard that his wife had drowned in the nearby river. He set out to search for her body. 'Why are you walking upstream?' asked his neighbors. 'Surely you know that the body will be carried downstream by the current?' The man answered, 'Of course I know that, but when my wife was alive, she always acted contrary to my wishes. That is why I am looking upstream. Even though she's dead, she probably is doing the opposite of what she should.' "

"What are the arrangements for the morning?" asked Harry, letting the laughter lapse, and instantly every man present held his breath for Rivers's answer.

"I suggest the three of us shall ride together to Stony Stratford. I have told them to expect us around noon if that suits you, my lords?"

"And how is the prince?"

"The king," corrected Rivers loftily as if he were issuing an official proclamation, "has a nagging tooth and is not accustomed to so much traveling, but is looking forward to seeing his mother and the rest of his family again. One does wish the weather was better. I do not like the look of the sky tonight."

"Poor little prince," Harry laughed. "Three uncles bearing down on him."

"There must be a word for it. I really ought to be able to think of something." Rivers snapped his fingers. "Ah, I have it, a triangle of uncles." With that he rose and bowed to Gloucester. "Would you be offended if I leave you now? I simply must go to bed. What with traveling and the king's grace so full of questions—only to be expected, I daresay, but one feels one must answer them—it does wear one out."

Gloucester pushed back his chair to escort him out; Miles's duke did not rise.

"Good night, Harry," Rivers said pointedly before he ducked beneath the lintel. Buckingham raised his winecup in valediction.

"What o'clock is it?" asked Gloucester, returning to the room.

"Almost nine," replied Sir Richard Ratcliffe, rising unbidden to refill his master's cup, but the duke spread a hand over the rim.

"Rivers has left me with a gift. Let us see what it is."

Lord Lovell slid a leather-wrapped parcel from its traveling box out onto the board. Miles stood up with the others and went to look over his lord's shoulder. A printed book—still a rarity—manufactured by Caxton under the Red Pale in the precincts of Westminster Palace. Lovell undid the fastenings and opened the embossed leather cover. Rivers's personal translation of *The Dictes and Sayings of Philosophers*.

"Generous," sighed Gloucester wearily and Miles could see that although he valued the book there was pain in the acceptance of it.

"A very learned man, your grace," Miles remarked, narrowing his eyes urgently at Harry. There had to be some strategy for the morrow and his duke needed to be part of it, not a passive witness.

Harry brought the grit to the surface. "There is a matter I should like to discuss with you, cousin, but perhaps it should wait until morning."

Gloucester was gazing into the tired embers, his foot resting upon the andirons of the hearth. "I have no inclination to go to bed yet. I would not sleep anyway." Perceptively, he dismissed all of his henchmen save Lord Lovell, and glanced questioningly at his cousin. Harry nodded to Miles and Knyvett to remain.

And so at last.

Harry's fingers brushed against the pigskin book box as if it might help him find the phrases. "Cousin, I did not come laden with costly books, but only—only words of another nature: promises." He timed the pause and added a caveat, "But I need to discover what you believe of me. You may have always thought that I was one of the Woodville faction. I never have been." A pensive finger stroked the grained oak. "When I was a boy at Westminster they never lost an opportunity to humiliate me."

"You do not have to go through this." Gloucester glanced at Miles, who had set a comforting hand upon his lord's shoulder.

"No, cousin, there are things that have to be said now." Harry's blue eyes rose, seeking absolution. "You have not seen me since your brother Clarence's trial. I want you to know that although I had to pass judgment on him, it was not my wish to deal out such a verdict. The Woodvilles wanted him dead."

The skin of Gloucester's smile was taut as he moved back to the board and emptied the jug into Harry's goblet. It was some moments before he spoke. "It was the king's doing as much as the queen's." He took a sip from the goblet and watched his kinsman thoughtfully over the rim.

"There is more. Your brother never gave me the opportunity to serve him. I want you to know that I am prepared to work tirelessly on your behalf if you will give me the chance." Harry put it so well, a blend of humility and plea that twisted compassion into Gloucester's lips.

"Yes, you deserved better, Harry. I do not think my brother treated you fairly."

"I want my rights, cousin. I have waited long enough."

"You might achieve more by offering the kiss of peace to your wife's family."

Harry rose, finally taking the risk of dwarfing the shorter man. "You know the tale about my marriage. I was ten years old when I spoke out against them and not one of the Woodvilles ever forgave me for it."

"Even Rivers?"

"Even him," Harry exclaimed bitterly. "You saw how condescending he was to me."

Gloucester rubbed a hand across his chin, where a dark shadow of stubble was beginning, and at last came to the business between them. "By Holy Paul, he took a risk riding back to make merry with us. He must be feeling confident. Why *is* he feeling so confident?"

"He wants to rule England with the queen," Harry replied curtly.

"Must you be right, cousin? He is more brilliant than the others. There is a quality about him. . . ." Miles saw that Gloucester was probing.

"Oh, come, cousin." Miles's duke sidestepped the snare. "Let us not delude ourselves. He is as grasping as the rest. Why, he is virtually master of Wales."

"That hurts?" asked Gloucester unkindly.

It was then Harry forgot all the lessons, all the advice that Miles and Knyvett had crammed into him, for he slammed his cup down and swung full face upon Richard of Gloucester. "Listen, I do not know how much convincing you need, but in my opinion unless you act the soldier tomorrow, you and I shall be caught in a snare like a pair of helpless rabbits. The times are hurly-burly. You are going to have to fight for survival, cousin. If the queen crowns the prince within the month, you will not make old bones and neither will your son."

Miles saw mischief flicker in his grace of Gloucester's eyes and Harry let out a sigh, realizing belatedly that the other duke had already thought it all out.

"I am tired," Richard Plantagenet said, rubbing the heels of his hands against his high forehead. "Yes, of course, I have to act soon, but it must be just. I must not appear the aggressor or I shall lose the support of the Royal Council. Do not look so disappointed, all of you. You must understand that to be ratified and remain as lord protector, I need men like Suffolk and Howard behind me too. You will see. It is not so easy." He paced to the window and glanced through the shutters. "I have to have a good reason to arrest Rivers."

At last Miles was at the throat of history, listening to the lord protector discussing arresting the queen's brother in such a matter-of-fact way. Oh, excellent! And at last Harry had found a strong ally and all Miles's own plans to edge his lord into the council chamber at Westminster were coming to fruition.

Harry's tail was wagging. "Arrest him? What, tonight, while he has so few men with him?" and then he blanched, along with the rest, as they heard the sound of hooves in the yard outside.

"God ha' mercy," exclaimed Lovell, his right hand going to the handle of his sword. Only Gloucester, peering out the chink in the window boards, was calm.

"Perhaps I have my reason," he said grimly, moving across to open the door. His henchman, Ratcliffe, thrust back the curtain and a weary horseman followed him in. "Cousin, this is Sir Richard Huddleston, banneret, husband to my lady's sister." He bade the knight abandon courtesies and sit. Lovell passed him a cup of ale. The newcomer drank thirstily and wiped his thin lips with the back of his hand.

"It is as you thought, my lord. The young king's men are all packed up for an early start with orders to leave at daybreak. Word is they plan to have the boy crowned straightway in London and prevent you becoming Lord Protector."

"And numbers, Richard?" asked Gloucester. That was the crux.

"Sir Richard Grey has brought a large force from London. Far greater than ours but by how much we could not tell in the darkness."

Miles turned exultantly to his lord. "Now the wind blows cold."

Gloucester thrust his fist against his palm and swung round on Ratcliffe. "Dick, set a cordon about Lord Rivers's inn and make sure it is done quietly. I do not want him to suspect anything tonight. No one is to leave. At any sign of movement within there, wake me, whatever the hour. Are you happy to leave this to me, Harry?" Buckingham nodded and Miles knew a sense of relief. If matters went awry, Buckingham's men might wriggle out from beneath the mêlée with their political virginity intact. "So be it." Pleased, Gloucester turned to Lovell. "Post guards on every road and footpath out of Northampton. Not one of Rivers's men must have a chance to warn Grey." His hand fell on the seated man's shoulder. "Richard Huddleston, to bed with you!" Then he gave his hand to Harry, Miles, and Knyvett in turn. "Good night to you all. We need to rise early to be at Stony Stratford before light."

The walk back to their inn and the sharp smell of danger in the smoky air cleared Miles's head of wine. Harry was seething with excitement; if the street had not been as quiet as a tomb, he might have whooped.

"We still need to be careful." Miles tried to poker the enthusiasm.

Knyvett grunted assent, adding, "You know what I would do, Harry. Take Ned with you tomorrow. That way if things go amiss at Stony Stratford, you have some cover of goodwill if Grey orders your arrest. Let Gloucester take the blame."

"That is good advice. Wake Lady Haute now, and warn her."

"Pah, not I!" Knyvett answered. "Had too much plaguey wine to tiptoe. Don't want to wake the town, do I? Might alert old Rivers."

Which was how Miles found himself creeping upstairs like an

unfaithful husband. Benet was snoring as loud as a hog across the doorway. A poor watchdog! Miles leaned across without waking him and lifted the latch quietly.

Heloise lay fast asleep with the boy curled at her back, their heads silver and gold upon the pillow. No sadness rose in Miles as he stood lonely in the darkness, only the thought that should Heloise have a son, he might one day lie against her back just so like a squirrel kitten. And if their marriage had been otherwise, that son would be his. Gently, Miles stroked a fingertip lightly across her cheek and watched a slender arm free itself from the bedclothes. The glint of light on her eyes told him she had wakened.

He crouched, his fingers hushing her lips. "There is no panic. I have a message from his grace." She glanced over her shoulder crossly to see if he had woken Ned. "Heloise, listen. You are to have the boy ready to leave at two hours before dawn. Try to keep him as quiet as possible. We do not want the entire town to hear his tantrums. Sir William will come for you."

"If he must." With an oath, she carefully hoisted herself onto one elbow, brushing her hair back behind her ear, her face close enough to kiss. If he had hoped to see a silken shoulder bared, he was relieved by the undershift; there were enough decisions being made for one night. "Oh, I am so weary of traveling. Keeping him contented is no jest." It was awkward to draw the covers up across Ned's tiny chest but she managed.

"Weary! But, changeling, there is a Northampton coven meeting before lauds. If you are interested, we can share a bonfire. They are initiating the new cauldron."

"And you have been ladling from it already, I think. What o'clock is it now, sir?"

"Midnight." The lady cursed him.

"Ah, but I could entertain you until you rise. The bed is warmed and all the lice have already found you and . . ."

"Enter—" And then she realized he was jesting. "Away with

you! Away before you lose your virtue, sir. If I said yes, you would—"

"Run a mile? In the dark? Perhaps my virtue might be worth the sacrifice. You look extremely desirable."

"Go to!" she chided softly, glancing at Ned again.

"Whatever happens tomorrow, Heloise, take care of the child. Stay with him."

"You are being ambiguous, sir. What danger will there be?"

"You have had no dreams then, lady? I am right glad of that." He wanted to peel back the sheet and look at her in the starlight—there might be no tomorrow. Only the child's presence kept him sane. "If Rivers should take us all prisoner tomorrow, best not tell anyone of our handfasting. The Woodvilles are greedy enough to attainder me and take Bramley into their own hands on such a pretext. And if any misfortune happens to me, and well it might, I . . . upon my soul, changeling, I want you to know I am sorry for the suffering your father and I have put you through, and I have written to my sire, urging him to let you take Bramley for a second dowry without dispute. It will help you find a husband by honest means."

"You *have* had too much wine." Warm fingers touched his forehead. "Thank you."

His hand rose to waist her fragile wrist and held it back. "I am not jesting." Then he raised her hand to his lips. "God keep you, lady."

Fourteen

"Your grace! Sir Miles! Sir William!" Pershall shook the inn bed that held the three of them. "His grace of Gloucester's man is below." Memory burst over Miles like a bucket of cold water and he staggered from the bed, doused his face from the ewer, and hurried downstairs, thankful he had gone to bed fully clothed.

It was the banneret Huddleston, bringer of news from the night before, booted, spurred, and impatient. "Rivers has tried to leave. His grace requests my lord of Buckingham attend him. I trust that is not a problem?"

So it was to be a song in unison after all.

Miles was in attendance on both dukes when they visited Rivers. The earl was caged at his inn, pacing in his dressing robe, his hair retousled to lend him innocence. The air hung stale save for the expensive musk and sweat emanating from him.

"My lords," he exclaimed, "what can you mean by this? My servants have just roused me in panic saying the place is surrounded by your men and none of us are allowed to set foot outside the door."

"Yes," said Gloucester.

Rivers opened his mouth, fishlike, and shut it again. There was an uncomfortable silence while Gloucester's brooding countenance waited for the man to damn himself.

"So you do not trust me. I do not believe it! I ride back fourteen poxy miles out of love and brotherhood and this is my thanks. What has happened since last night, Gloucester? Have Buckingham and his crony here been spewing poison about me into your ears?" Miles's blood chilled beneath Rivers's stare, and the single candle sputtered at the spittle from the man's vindictive breath. "I should wear good armor on my back if I were you, my lord protector!"

Miles swiftly moved around the trestle to defend Harry, but Gloucester slammed the table and rasped out: "You were in full riding gear earlier and you gave orders to your men last night to quit Northampton before we were astir. Deny it and there are sufficient witnesses to make a liar of you."

Calmer, Rivers shrugged. "I am sorry that it has come to this and that you have misinterpreted my good intentions. I always considered you a just man, Dickon."

"You shall have your justice." Gloucester turned to the men-at-arms thronging the open doorway. "Hold him fast here until you receive further orders!"

"You would not dare!" hissed Rivers, making play of his superior height, the perfect face marred with a sneer. "I have a letter here that your brother wrote to me a full month before he died. Read it! I have full powers to escort the prince to London with as many men as I choose."

Gloucester took the paper he held out and scanned it at the candle flame. "It says here 'if need be.' There is no need!" He handed it to Harry, who thrust it into the consuming flame. "Come, cousin, we have to meet the king." He strode out.

With a grin at Miles, Harry bestowed a fulsome smile upon his very articulate brother-in-law standing there in the last of his glory, ridiculous among the scoured, coarse trestles. "Adieu, Anthony. You see I am not the village idiot you always thought me."

Rivers made no reply, no cutting or foolhardy jest, but just stared, expressionless, at Harry. Then finally he looked at Miles and his face unfroze. "Is this your doing? Did you prod this snail out of his shell?" he sneered. "Harry here"—he reached out to cuff the duke as though he were a servant—"young Harry always needed a nursemaid."

The duke ducked back, his hand going to his sword, but Miles grabbed his arm. "Leave him, your grace!"

"See, Rushden, he is spineless." The mocking face was bitter, showing age at last. "We all knew that at Westminster. Spineless."

UPON HIS DESTRIER, HIS MANTLE'S MASSIVE COLLAR RAISED against the chill, Gloucester looked like a man about to take his rightful place as lord protector. It was as well, thought Miles, as they mounted up to quit the town before dawn; the worst danger lay ahead at Stony Stratford.

Spurring down the line with a lighted torch to ensure that Ned was with the Stafford retinue, he found Heloise mounted beside Knyvett, her cheeks still creased with sleepiness and the boy a thumb-sucking, sleepy curl in front of her.

"You have done well, Lady Haute." Easing Traveller back, he signaled to Harry, and the entourage set off down Bridge Street to cross the Nene River.

Done well! Heloise growled silently as he left her. What in God's name was this about? She could smell their fear. Where was Lord Rivers? Why would no one riding close give her a proper answer? God's mercy, why this journey on such a churned-up road before daylight in the drizzle?

They made poor progress. Ned grew peevish as the sky lightened, distracting Heloise so bitterly with his complaints that she hardly noted the causeway and the bridge leading the weary procession into Stony Stratford. It was the smoky air and yeasty aroma of fresh bread clawing at her empty belly that alerted her. The White Horse, she thought, lifting her drooping shoulders, an inn she had sometimes breakfasted at on provisions trips when her mother was alive. But now?

"Jesu mercy!" Grim and tight-lipped, Sir William grabbed Cloud's reins, keeping Heloise and the boy tightly within the duke's bodyguard.

"Amen," she agreed in appalled astonishment, for ahead of them, the entire high street from one end of the town to the other was perilously filled with foot soldiers. The mutter of "Lord

Rivers" mistakenly ran ahead of them, and the Woodville men standing in half-armor, with their scallop badges the only gleam about them, looked up bewildered as the Gloucester and Stafford heralds forced their horses through.

"What's happening?" shrilled Ned, sensing the tension in Heloise's tightening arms as her horse was drawn forward with the rest. She calmed the child but all around them the ordinary people's minds were emanating terror. It was close to panic in the horsemen protecting her. If the Woodville foot soldiers pulled them from their saddles . . . Ned should not be here. It was wrong to use a child.

The muttering grew. Urgently the townsfolk began pushing their way out, away from the soldiers. Faces crammed the upper open windows of the merchants' houses—women's faces, lined by fear. Heloise anxiously craned to see where the prince might be. The Swan with Two Necks would have been her wager, but they rode in silence past it. The lack of cheering had become terrifying.

In Horse Market, beneath the lily and leopard standards and the damp pennons drooping with sunnes, white lions, and falcons perched in fetterlocks, the prince was already on his horse. Whoever they had been waiting for, it was not the dukes, for consternation panicked the faces of the men about the twelve-year-old. A blond man in his twenties—Heloise guessed he must be Sir Richard Grey, the queen's son by her first marriage—froze as he recognized Gloucester, his complexion turning yellow and sour like expiring milk. Had the young man been of greater rank or more experienced, he might have ordered his escort to sever the two dukes from their retinues. Instead he hesitated and it was a tall, portly bishop in a broad-brimmed hat who kneed his horse forward to blithely offer greeting. The prince's other officers followed the bid for peace, but they looked as guilty as a queue of felons lined up for hanging.

Beyond them Heloise glimpsed a second bishop, whose horse's rein was fisted by a servant. An old, diminutive bishop, round-shouldered from too much study, whose expression looked cramped as if both his mind and body ached. For an instant the narrow eyes beneath the furrowed brow intercepted hers and then he seemed to catch an inkling of the confrontation about to ensue. A sense of hope flooded to her across the metal-plated shoulders that sat between them, as if the man's soul were stirring after a winter of sleep.

Then Rushden was at Heloise's stirrup, lifting Ned from her. "You are to make your bow to our new king, my lord. Come, madam!" She hastily dismounted, tidying her veil. The crowd parted for them as he carried the child through.

With fair hair and a long build, the royal stripling in his mourning of blue doublet and matching cote sat upon his white horse, fair as a faery prince. She tried to send him a message of peace as he studied his uncles' bent heads in confusion. His grace of Gloucester rose from his obeisance, brushing off a straw that was clinging to his mourning hose. Buckingham, with a brief scowl at the offending cobbles, lowered himself dutifully.

"Where is my uncle Rivers?" repeated the boy.

"Your highness, we shall explain if you will but step back inside your inn with us. See, here is Lord Stafford come to greet your grace."

Buckingham reached out a hand to his son and so did Gloucester. With impeccable dignity, Ned took both dukes' hands and stepped forward until he looked straight up into the chill blue eyes of Edward V. He showed no fear of any of the horses and Heloise said a silent prayer of thanks that the lesson had been well learned. His father lifted him to kiss the reluctant royal hand held out to him.

"Now I have done this, can we please have breakfast?" The five-year-old's voice begat a rumble of laughter from the newcomers, but the prince's men stood like statues, waiting for the blond man's orders.

"No haste, is there?" Buckingham asked the prince affably, straddling his son on his waist with difficulty since he played at father so rarely. "My lord of Gloucester and I have not yet break-fasted nor, I will be sworn, have you, your highness. What say you we return to the lodgings you have just left and talk while breakfast is being cooked?"

Edward V had little choice but to dismount. It was then that Gloucester threw his arms about him, clearly close to tears. The boy accepted his sympathy and, with an uncle at either elbow and his tiny cousin at his heels, he returned to the inn he had quit hours earlier. The press of people following them was so great that Heloise was almost cut off from her charge, but Rush-den and Sir William flanked her.

"Where is Lord Rivers?" she asked her husband.

Under arrest, he mouthed at her. Jesu! There could have been a bloody battle then and there; the dukes had cleverly avoided a public quarrel that would have sent panic circling out from Stony Stratford across England.

Inside the warm, fetid atmosphere of the inn, Heloise could still sense the mortal fear pulsing in the minds of the prince's retinue, but one stocky man was distracted from his dilemma as he noted her standing with her hands protectively upon Ned's shoulders. His brow creased beneath his black hat and he pushed his way across.

"You are not my aunt Haute."

Within the instant, Rushden stepped between them, his hand against the man's shoulder. "You have more pressing matters to concern you, Haute." His other hand, behind his back, signaled Heloise to retreat swiftly.

Moments later, he located her in refuge behind Knyvett. "Dear me," he remarked behind his gloved fingers, "you have a poor memory for your relatives. There are a pair of them in this very room."

"You might have warned me, but thank you for helping me just then."

"Lady, I am warning you. The Hautes are cousins to the Woodvilles." But he seemed too exhilarated by the currents of danger and excitement that eddied around them to share her fresh anxiety. Dear God, they were like hunting dogs that had tasted a kill, these Stafford and Gloucester men.

Against the inappropriate backdrop of a wall that was daubed with Adam and Eve sprinting before cherubims armed with flaming swords, their leader, hands clasped behind his back, was telling his royal nephew how saddened he was over King Edward's death. The entire room hushed to listen to Gloucester's eloquence. The careful phrases were well couched but one could have been pardoned for wondering if Duke Richard had missed his vocation as a bishop or a schoolmaster. The sermonlike flow of words recalling his loyalty to his brother was listened to in respectful silence but then the floodgates of his dammed-up grievances burst and out poured a righteous indictment of the Woodvilles, of how they had encouraged the late king to whore and glut when he should have been coddling his belly and administering the realm.

The prince's half-brother, his cousins, and his retainers, with everything to lose, at last began to interrupt. But Grey had lost his only opportunity. Now as the beleaguered young man opened his mouth to refute his guilt, it was Buckingham who tersely bid him hold his tongue while Gloucester, more passionate than Heloise had ever imagined possible, reached a predictable peroration: "Arrest them!" His voice was hoarse as he stabbed a jeweled finger towards the escort leaders.

"No!" Grey flung himself on his knees before the prince, grabbing him above his spurs. "Brother, save me, for the love of God! Stop them! Stop them! This is treason!"

"Why is that man on his knees?" Ned tugged at Heloise's girdle tassels.

"Treason!" exclaimed Buckingham righteously, grabbing the torch of fury from Gloucester's exhausted breath. Ebony taffeta rustled assertively as he gestured like a player towards the street. "This—this *army*—can have no other purpose but evil towards my lord of Gloucester."

"These men are here to honor me, perhaps, Uncle Bucking-ham." But sarcasm and the icy Woodville gaze were merely blunt weapons in the hands of a twelve-year-old. "As for treason," the prince added, his gaze falling with concern upon his desperate half-brother, "I am sure her grace my mother and Uncle Riv—"

"The ruling of this land is not women's business," Buckingham exclaimed indignantly. "Your father left no such authority to your mother. Your so-called friends have deluded you, your grace. Up!" He wriggled a shiny bootcap menacingly at Grey.

"Nephew," said Gloucester gently, his virtuous anger fled. "Did they not tell you I am to be lord protector until you come of age?" The boy's mouth quivered. "Do you think that after fighting for your father and holding the north for him over these many years, I should do you harm? I am only carrying out my brother's will, God rest his soul. Shall you be content with your father's wishes or not?"

Respect shone in the boy's eyes. "Yes, of course I am content with the government my father wanted but—"

"Then, Lord Grey," Gloucester cut in with a quiet courtesy that was more natural to him than anger, "would you and your com-panions be kind enough to submit yourself to custody until further inquiries have been made?" There was no choice for Grey or for Haute and the others, who were escorted out.

Edward V sniffed: "I am sure you are wrong, Uncle Richard."

"I sincerely hope so, your highness," answered Gloucester. "It was Lord Hastings who warned your uncle Buckingham and my-self of the danger." That drove away any argument ripe upon the boy's lips.

"Come on, lad, let's have some breakfast." A man unused to children's company, Buckingham came in too heavy-handed. "Lady Haute, bring Lord Stafford. He has drawn a picture for you, your highness."

The prince, as tall as his uncle Gloucester, sent a scornful glance at Ned and then he glared at Heloise as though she were a clod of dung upon the instep of his shoe. "Pray remove him, mistress whoever-you-are."

"Her name is Lady Haute," corrected little Ned stoutly.

The cold young gaze fixed upon the wooden arch that crested the ceiling. "Mind your manners, Lord Stafford," he declared, "you are not duke yet. Come, Uncle Gloucester!" Gloucester pulled a face at Buckingham and the two men followed their unanointed sovereign up the staircase.

Ouch! Rushden grimaced, returning Heloise's lift of eyebrow. If they listened at the new king's breast, would they hear a heartbeat?

"I do not like him. He is a very rude boy," exclaimed Ned, fists coiled. "And it was my best picture!"

"Kings are allowed to be bad-humored, especially if they are in mourning." Heloise crouched down to look him in the face, tickled him in the ribs, and whispered, "And I think your manners are far superior."

She sat him beside her on the settle beneath the window and produced from her purse a length of knotted string, which she wound around her fingers and then pulled free as if by magic. Ned was too little to copy her but it took his mind off the insults.

With a sudden burst of nervous conversation, the two dukes' retainers mingled better now that they had enjoyed a common enemy and come through unscathed.

"Mistress." Sir Richard Huddleston bowed above her, sat down unasked beside the boy, and, taking the string, showed the child a simpler trick. "Now go and show Sir William." The child scampered off. "It seems to me Lady Haute has lost weight and shed at least thirty years since last I saw her."

Heloise smiled and momentarily set a finger to her lips. "Ask your friends not to give me away, please. I pray you, how is madam your wife?"

"Mistress, a realm is at stake and we are dealing with the housekeeping." He observed that her husband was glancing suspiciously in their direction. "To be brief, his grace of Gloucester asks if you could let us know anything untoward. New alliances. Whether any of them"—he glanced towards Rushden, Knyvett, and the other Stafford knights—"are ever closeted in secret talks. In return, my lord protector will do his best to convince Holy Church your marriage must be annulled, and we shall find you a different husband." The child ran back to her and clambered onto her knee. "Think about it, my lady."

Rushden homed upon her like an arrow after Huddleston left her. It would be pleasing if he was jealous.

"What did that man want, madam?" he demanded coldly, though his hand tugged Ned's hat playfully enough to tease him.

"Renewing acquaintance. He brought me word from Dionysia. She is at Middleham."

"You never told me that." He cast a glance about the room and regarded Heloise speculatively. "How many more of Gloucester's people here do you know? It could be useful. Why are you glaring at me, madam?"

"Because I now know what it feels like to be a tenez ball," muttered Heloise.

"Boing, boing!" shrieked Ned and had to be removed.

IT WAS TEDIOUS WAITING. THERE WAS LITTLE BREAKFAST TO GO round and while the dukes placated the prince upstairs, Heloise tried to keep Ned content. She was halfway through telling "St. Brendan and the Whale" to Ned when Rushden joined them.

"When do we leave for London, sir?" cried Ned, grabbing the knight's hand and swinging his full weight upon it.

"When Lord Hastings sends us word it is safe to do so." The little boy was seized with both hands, swung in a circle, and then turned upside down for good measure.

Heloise waited until the pair of them had come to a standstill. "We are staying *here?*"

"No, we are going back to Northampton with the prince. There are far more beds there and it is something to do. Better than hanging round here the rest of the day with that petulant whelp." He grimaced at the ceiling.

"For shame," she chided, well aware that deafness was not one of Ned's attributes. "His highness is young, uncertain."

"My lady"—Rushden lowered his voice—"he looked at you as though you were scum." Annoyance tightened his voice as though the insult had been to him.

"Kings can do that, sir," she warned him, well pleased at his concern.

His face told her he would see about that.

THEY WERE ALL GROWING HEARTILY SICK OF THE ROAD BE-tween Northampton and Stony Stratford but the wind had blown the rain away and the air had become blowsy, seductive with the hum of insects and perfume of the meadow flowers.

Rushden, riding back down the column, saluted Heloise indifferently but on his return he reined in between Sir William's horse and Cloud to tip Ned's hat askew.

If only she might reach out gloved fingers to tidy Rushden's wind-ruffled hair, thought Heloise, melting with pride. Astride Traveller, his serpent badge gleaming against a black velvet shoulder, her husband looked as though he had just galloped out of a legend. There was dependability in this man, she thought, remembering his protection of her, but ruthless self-interest too. You could load his shoulders and his spirit would not break, but there were sunless parts of his soul that chilled her heart. Unsatiated ambition lurked like a wolf—wild, untamable in him and Buckingham. And she disliked Buckingham. You cannot change Rushden, her common sense decreed; the treacherous stirring of her body each time he came near her had to be controlled, but the Heloise of the cockatrice and Potters Field did not lack courage.

"You look cheerful, sir," she teased, reaching out a gloved hand to fondle Traveller.

The morning's bloodless victory had pleased Rushden; his eyes were like quicksilver against his tanned face. "The country of French romances, this," he exclaimed, pointing a crop towards the woods horizoning the pastures to the west, his smile roguish. Heloise's body stirred treacherously, remembering the pleasure of his hands caressing her.

"If Elizabeth Woodville had not waylaid King Edward while he was hunting in that very forest, we might not have had this morning's confrontation," Heloise answered.

"The problem was that he married her," muttered Sir William beneath his breath. "Two things to be avoided in a wife, greed and cunning. Shirt off your back in no time."

"I assure you, Sir William, I have not had my husband's shirt off his back," Heloise murmured silkily, rearranging Ned before she sent a flirtatious glance sideways.

"My dear Lady Haute," interrupted Rushden, "perhaps you have not tried."

ONCE MORE IN NORTHAMPTON, HELOISE EVADED FOUR O'CLOCK supper, preferring to sit on a bench outside the inn and mend a tear in Ned's second-best cote. Martin stood by to guard her against any froward soldiers. She watched as a platter was taken across the road to Lord Rivers's inn. It was returned untouched and then went forth again, this time to the house where they were holding Lord Grey. The platter was returned empty.

While she sat watching the world pass, the fat bishop, Alcock, the President of the Royal Council at Ludlow, rode in from Stony Stratford too, and there again in his company was the mysterious churchman, garbed like a bishop but with no retinue of his own, drooping in his saddle. Heloise felt the old cleric's mind groping, struggling to free itself. Eyes, beneath drooping lids, met hers. Help me, he seemed to be saying, bleak with despair.

"Find out the old man's name," she bade Martin. He returned, cheerful with success.

"Robert Stillington, Bishop of Bath and Wells. Seems that

the late king, God rest 'is soul, ordered 'im to be kept in custody. Isn't Bramley within 'is diocese, my lady?"

"Oh yes," murmured Heloise frowning, "indeed it is."

AT GLOUCESTER'S INN, MILES, NOW THAT THE DANGER WAS temporarily in abeyance, felt like celebrating. A breach in the Woodville-Yorkist wall after all these years of waiting! The Rushdens would be powerful again as they had been under Henry VI.

"Now you, sir."

Miles tried to concentrate as Ned—permitted grudgingly into the prince's presence—pushed the walnut halves back along the table. Obediently Miles slid them in a figure of eight, covering them with his palms. "Which one now, little lord?"

"There! There!"

The child's excitement drew a royal scowl. "Can you not play outside, cousin!"

Miles took Ned back to Heloise and returned to wait on a bored Harry. Gloucester had finished signing his dispatches to London and was suggesting the prince might wish to reward some of his household back at Ludlow. But there was no manual for being a lord protector.

"It might be advisable for you to practice your new signature before you sign the order. A wobbly script denotes indecisiveness and the people want a strong king."

Parchment and quill were set before the prince. The boy wrote *Edwardus,* hesitated, then added *Quintus.* His handwriting, Miles noted, was anxious and the script sprawled, large and untidy, barely legible.

Harry was getting fidgety, clearly frayed with listening to the schoolmaster oozing out of Gloucester. "It is said you can read a man's character from his writing," he remarked, examining the raw royal signature with a feigned interest.

"Indeed?" replied Edward haughtily. "I have never heard that before."

Miles watched Harry keep a snuffer on his temper. The prince was a Woodville to the thick skin of his heels. Did the brat not notice he was turning Uncle Harry into an implacable enemy?

"You write something then, Uncle Richard." Dipping the shaft into the inkwell, the prince handed the quill over.

Gloucester smiled round at the amused audience, was pensive for a moment, and then in small neat writing scratched out *Loyaulte me lie.* "Loyalty binds me."

"Yes, I know what it means. I did not quite waste my time at Ludlow."

"But it means more than that, sire," replied Gloucester gently. He wet the point again and wrote *R. Gloucestre* underneath. "I took the motto for my own when your father made me Duke of Gloucester and now I am pledging my loyalty to you." He bracketed the motto to his signature in eternal synonimity.

"Now, you, Uncle Buckingham." The prince pushed the paper towards Harry challengingly, as if to say: Outgloucester Gloucester if you can!

Harry wrote *Souvente me souvene* and beneath it *Harre Bokingham.* The writing stretched across the page, making up in breadth what it lacked in height, a sure contrast to Gloucester's careful Italian script.

"So, I must 'Remember you often.' Your writing is most clear, Uncle Richard, and tidy like your person, whereas Uncle Buckingham is much more extravagant in his writing, person, and dress." He glanced along the table for agreement and stopped at Miles.

"Very true, your highness," he agreed, grinning at Harry.

"Well, it's not hard, is it?" the brat retorted, making enemies thick and fast. If it had been permitted, Miles would have happily left the table. Fortunately Harry had endured a bellyful of singing descant to Gloucester's avuncular melody.

"Grant me your gracious leave, sire," he murmured, and excused himself and his officers.

Free of subservience, Harry was as ebullient as a duke might manage as he and Miles rounded the corner to their inn ahead of the rest.

"The Woodville summer is over, over at last! Christ, Miles, thrice today I thought you and I would be hauled through the Tower of London's water gate."

"Whoa, London may play the whore with us."

"But, Miles," purred Buckingham, "Lord Hastings is so used to handling whores."

The pair of them slapped palms. Safe from the windows of Gloucester's lodging, Harry might have even performed cartwheels had Miles encouraged him.

"I cannot believe it. Rivers and Grey under arrest and the king in our hands. By God, I should like to hear the queen's scream when the news reaches her. This will ripple up her fur like an ill wind." Startled, he crossed himself as a thin wraith uncoiled itself from the doorstep.

"Who's there?" Miles drew out his sword.

"My lords, good evening to you." Thomas Nandik, who, having delivered the news of the king's death to Buckingham, had subsequently suckered himself to the duke's retinue like a leech, bowed obsequiously. He would have groveled on request. "Your grace, do you need letters written or is there some other way I may serve you?"

Buckingham shrugged. "Attend me, Nandik. You may talk to us while we disrobe."

Miles disliked the fellow but the scarecrow turned out to be good company. More wine on top of his evening's drinking made him leak scandalous tales of student romps and the peccadilloes of learned Cambridge masters.

At a late hour it was Sir William who remembered it was the Devil's Eve and the conversation shifted to Satan's works. Nandik boasted he was a scholar in astrology.

"Can you cast a horoscope for me now?" Harry sounded far too eager.

"I do not think this is wise, your grace." Miles looked to Sir

William for backing but the older man was almost snoring.

"I have already done so, your grace, in an idle moment. You understand I am no expert at the art." An idle moment! Sweet Christ!

Miles leaned forward uneasily. "You are too modest, Nandik."

The man ignored the warning under the civility. "Anyone who has studied arts at Cambridge is fully competent."

The duke grinned at Miles. "So what did mine reveal, Nandik, or dare you not say?"

The man's dark eyes glimmered wickedly. "It promised great wealth and titles."

Laughing, the duke quaffed down more cider. "The title I already have, but great office I desire." Thank God, thought Miles, the mattock had turned the turf of common sense, or had it? Harry was happily drunk.

Nandik was not. "Your grace, to forecast so for any man might be taken as flattery, but for you, now . . ." He did not need to finish.

"For me, now, any man might make that prediction."

Miles let his breath go and Harry, the familiar, predictable Harry, smiled across at him. Nandik was still the outsider.

The duke was pensive as de la Bere saw the fellow out. "Is there truth in prophecy?" he asked. "Do you think that Satan has crawled from Hell to listen to our idle words?"

Miles swallowed, feeling his skin gooseflesh beneath his shirt.

"Prophecy?" He remembered the angry hum of the bees and Heloise's warning. "I have met a woman whose premonitions are always right." Somehow mentioning Heloise banished the acrid taste of Nandik's presence. "Surely you will not put any faith in that groveling wretch, my lord. If you asked him to lick your shoes free of dung, he would do it."

"And would you?"

The question hurt.

"No, my lord duke, I should make sure you never sullied them in the first place."

Fifteen

Heloise was awakened next day by Ned prancing barefoot shrieking, "It's May Day!" All Hallows' Church across the market square was only pealing six o'clock but she could hear the squeals; young men with hunting horns were hallooing the girls of Northampton to fetch in the birch and hawthorn boughs with them.

The town celebrated self-consciously, unused to a young, leggy king in their midst. Today's archery contests and dancing were definitely a relief after the sword and buckler rattling of yesterday, although when the exuberantly merry Men of the Green Wood had finished trying to lift the women's skirts with their quarterstaves and Maid Marion's bosoms had ended round her shoulder blades, Northampton went home red-faced to dinner.

Bidden to take Ned across to dine with the great lords, Heloise shook a scatter of almond petals from her veil onto the cobbles outside Gloucester's inn and looked up to find Rushden and de la Bere grinning at her. Rushden adroitly delegated de la Bere to take charge of Ned and in the confusion of the entourages sorting out where they were to eat, it was easy for him to discreetly detain her.

"Well, changeling, has the royal temper improved?"

"Barely. The Northampton maidens insisted on garlanding him with daisy chains, much to his disgust. Evidently, all my gender are to be avoided as if we carry the pestilence. Were you like that?"

"Of course," he laughed. "I made up for it later. He will too, given his family tree so—" A horseman riding past the inn momentarily distracted him but, relieved that the fellow was merely on local business, Rushden looked down at her wickedly.

" 'Northampton, full of love, beneath the girdel but not above,' "
he quoted. "So were your skirts teased by Little John's weapon?"

Heloise was determined not to blush. "With half a dozen
Welsh pikemen for protection? Sadly, no, but does being severely
ogled by Maid Marion count?"

"Ah, it is the pikes you have to watch." With a grin, he
rubbed a hand across his chin. It reminded her.

"Sir, Prince Edward is still complaining that his jaw aches."

"Then it will be wonderful if the toothache carries him off.
Once the crown comes down on that scowling brow, I will be
saying prayers."

She hid a smile. "Oh, hush, that is treason. You must not
speak so."

"Be grateful I trust you." Astonishment shone in his silver
gaze as if he had surprised himself and then the portcullis of
controlled cheeriness slammed down again. But the untethered
remark gave her hope. He was growing used to her, like a comfortable shoe. The confidences, the deliberate seeking of her company, were becoming regular and welcome. Besides, she could
return his trust in equal measure:

"Sir." She waited for the hawk gaze to fix again upon her.
"I . . . I fear there is something more to the prince's pain than
just toothache."

"Heloise!" This time he gripped her by the elbow and pro-
pelled her with unmannerly haste into the shadow of the laneway
that flanked the inn. "You had better elaborate."

"I do not mean poison." She watched his face lose its rigidity.

"Is this one of your premonitions?"

"No." She patted the air as if trying to keep matters lidded.
"Sometimes I can sense when a body is aching." A teasing expression lit Rushden's eyes. "I will clout you, sir, if you look at
me like that. I thought you were the one being serious. No, it
is just that I can feel a kind of echo of someone's illness, sometimes before they are even aware of it themselves. I could sense

the torment of that churchman in Bishop Alcock's entourage, for instance."

"Stillington?"

"Yes, him. It was as though his mind was longing to wrench free of the lassitude of his body." Rushden did not seem appalled that she could perceive such things. "I am glad you do not cross yourself, sir," she said, much relieved, "for it is not witchcraft, but a gift I cannot help."

"I am learning not to belittle your instincts, believe me. So, is there some infusion you can give his sulkiness to mend him?"

"I spoke with his physician, Dr. Argentine, who seems quite sensible. He has advised the prince to rinse his mouth with sage water and given him powdered cloves seethed in rose water to rub on his gums."

"Then the brat's breath will be sweeter than his temper." Rushden pulled a face at her reproving look.

"And the apothecary here has made up some henbane ointment for his highness to rub on the outside of his jaw."

"Pah, I reckon you could concoct something better."

"Oh, no, I want no part of this, sir," she answered the suggestion gravely. "If we are still in some danger from the queen, as you seem to think, then it would be easy for her to accuse us of sorcery and with my strange hair and being a woman, I should be the first to be accused and very likely be the scapegoat for the rest of you."

Rushden frowned and made no answer, narrowing his gaze down the high street, as if he were willing a messenger to arrive.

"What will happen if the queen does hold London and sends an army against us, sir? You have only a few hundred men here."

"Do not worry! We hold the prince. If an army does head our way, we will straightway dispatch you and Ned to safety. We shall know the worst soon anyway when Lord Hastings sends us word." But she saw the pearls of moisture on his forehead and knew it was not the sun that was the cause.

*   *   *

By three o'clock that afternoon, the awaited messenger had arrived—no covert necromancer this time but a fox-eyed lawyer, Sir William Catesby, suave though dusty, bearing Lord Hastings's assurance that London was rolled out like a welcoming cloth for the lord protector's foot. Such cheerful news had Miles humming contentedly as he walked back with de la Bere from Mayor Lynde's house at the top of the Horse Market. They had been part of the delegation reassuring his worship that no blood was to puddle Northampton streets.

He slackened his stride, frowning, as he recognized Heloise and Ned outside the gate of the Grey Friars, deep in conversation with Gloucester's brother-in-law, while Benet and several pikemen fidgeted at a polite distance. Sir Richard Huddleston, seeing Miles bearing down, took his leave.

"We have just been for a walk to the castle." Heloise, trying to keep her tisshew veil well behaved in the breeze, noticed Rushden's sour expression. "You are looking vexed, sir. I understood the news was good."

Miles made no reply. A dusty street with an audience of Welsh soldiers was not the time to demand why Huddleston was showing such interest in her.

It was de la Bere who answered: "London has shown no support for the queen." He stooped to Ned's level. "Want to come and fight a duel with me, lordling?"

"Yes, yes," shrilled Ned, drawing a wooden sword from his belt.

"Take the escort, then," muttered Miles. "I shall see Lady Haute back."

Heloise was delighted to find herself left alone with Rushden. "Are you sure there will be no battle?" she asked, anxious for the truth.

"Of course, be easy. All the queen's men are scattered leaderless 'twixt here and London and half the treasury is at sea with her brother Sir Edward Woodville. The foolish woman has no retainers left to hand nor ready money to raise a new army, so she has taken refuge in Westminster sanctuary with her children."

Hardly foolish if all the royal mint was in Woodville hands, thought Heloise. Sir Richard Huddleston had just been telling her that while the queen had cunningly distracted Lord Hastings in argument, her kinsmen had been tearing down a wall at the sanctuary and stuffing in as much gold plate as they could. It sounded as though Lord Hastings could not control a coney warren let alone London, and Gloucester would be short of funds to run the realm as lord protector.

"Surely the queen will try to seize back power once her son is crowned?"

"We shall cross that bridge in time." Rushden's tone was chilling and a hard smile serifed his mouth.

"You are reveling in all this," she protested, glimpsing the darker side in him.

"Oh yes. I intend to make Harry so powerful that lands and offices will come my way with a grateful handshake. I have been waiting a long while."

"I wish this was all over."

"Which family war are we talking about?" he teased, offering her his arm. "The feud over England or the one over Bramley?"

"Both," she blurted out, resting her gloved hand upon his wrist. He drew her around a puddle, sidestepping the verbal issue too by keeping to the drier ground of politics.

"Do not be anxious. Gloucester is going to keep Rivers and Grey as hostages to ensure the queen makes no more mischief. Haute, too. Sending them all north."

"Haute, hmm." Heloise's thoughts were busy with the future. "If I come to London, there will be other people who will know I am not Lady Haute."

"Shall I keep you, then?" Rushden's thumb tickled her palm. "Mayhap I should turn heathen and house a whole pantry of wives and concubines. Wednesday and Saturday nights for you, Tuesdays and Thursdays for Myfannwy and—"

"Oh yes, and Hell will freeze over." She tugged her hand free and waited for a cart to rumble past before they crossed the street. "I am weary of the lies, sir. I wish our annulment would arrive."

Miles studied her profile speculatively. "When your father broke the tidings that he had taken me captive to wed you, how did you truly feel?"

"Now, you ask! Backed into a corner with a sheer ten-foot wall behind and a couple of bulls hoofing the ground at me."

"And I was one of them?"

"I mean it metaphorically," she added with a sideways glint of apology to mollify him.

"Thank you," Miles answered dryly.

"Admit it, you were threatening. Especially as you promised to take your belt to me at Potters Field."

"Dear me, did I make such a threat? And if I were hoofing the ground at you now?" He paused as they reached the other side, turning her down the cross street in the direction of the Drapery.

"Are you?" The query was lightly tossed at him like a ball. Miles chose to let it fall and watched her playfulness waiver and rally.

"Try and answer the question." He reached down and plucked away a clinging stem of goosegrass that Ned must have hurled at her skirts in mischief.

"You mean if I knew you as well as I know you now but back at Bramley."

"You voice it so clearly." He fingered the sticky fronds— sweethearts, some called it—and tossed them aside.

"Yes, I would feel threatened."

"You *still* find me threatening?" It seemed to him that God should have made woman from man's brains instead of his ribs and then he blanched at the thought. "Do you?"

She turned, pausing by a churchyard wall. "Oh yes," she purred with sufficient enthusiasm to goad him. Any maid looking less threatened was hard to imagine. For a long moment he studied her with the growing suspicion that he had lost the reins of the conversation. "Given the hypothesis, would you consent?"

Because she did not reply straightway, he was unsure if confusion clouded her understanding, but she drew a long breath finally, picking a yellow-tongued heartsease sprig from its stony crevice. "I seem to remember I did consent."

Languidly watching the progress of his bootcap as it investigated a patch of weeds, he asked, "Supposing the annulment is not forthcoming?"

The lady's fur was ruffled now. "But how can it not be forthcoming, we have not—" She swallowed.

He smiled quizzically but inside he was inexplicably pleased that she had not lost her ability to blush.

"—been intimate," she finished, biting her lower lip and glancing away as if to veil her thoughts and then her eyes went round as cartwheels and she swung round in panic as if she were seeking a lane or doorway to swallow her. "Dear God," she whispered. "There is my father! *Ohh!*"

She staunched a squeak as Rushden's strong arms lifted and tossed her over the churchyard wall. Then he vaulted it effortlessly and landed beside her, grinning with merriment like a mischievous page hiding from a steward.

"That was a close shave. Bruised, changeling?" he asked the tangle of gown and veil.

"No, only my dignity," she gasped, her cone headdress askew and her skirts indecorously at midcalf. "Oh, Miles." She clapped her fingers to her lips to stifle her laughter as the hooves of her father's party clip-clopped past within a few paces of them.

Rushden looked astounded, as though daylight had exposed some hidden truth. Heloise had not meant to say his baptismal name, never allowed herself to think of him that way but . . . His laughter had died and he was looking at her as though she had suddenly slid a dagger beneath his ribs.

Miles forgot Heloise could use magic; he was just staring at a young woman who was lying on the long grass in disarray and laughing with all the abandon of a miller's daughter. Did she know how adorable she was? He should have helped her to her feet and straightened the squat velvet steeple over her glistening braids. Instead he wanted to halt time itself. All the loveliness of her belonged to him. She was at his fingertips, a breath away, not to be given to another man's keeping. His fingers reached out and touched her slender wrist, tracing the pulse beneath the silken skin before he pushed her gently back against the grass.

Heloise held her breath as he leaned upon his elbow, his face above her. This was a Miles Rushden with armor abandoned. The desire in his darkened eyes excited her and the lawful mastery he held over her alchemized Heloise's whole being to molten fire. His mouth came down on her lips, questioning and yet unable to take denial.

Soft and trusting, the girl raised her arms up shyly to scarf his neck, curving her body against him. Miles knew he wanted her now beyond all reason. His right hand rose to fondle her firm little breast and encountered the sheath of velvet. Ruthlessly his hand slid up beneath the shoulder of her gown and down beneath her collar to fondle and coax forth that delicious—

"Ahem! . . . I said, *ahem!*"

The earth stabilized itself again. Two sandaled feet in darned stockings, lapped by the dusty hem of a black houppelande, were waiting for him to abandon the chase of love.

"Who in hell are you?" Miles growled, not bothering to turn his head.

The shadow on the wall before him fidgeted. "Oh, no one in particular, merely the priest of the parish. I have an aversion to people fornicating between the graves."

With a stifled oath, Miles rolled off Heloise and glared up at the man who had both spoilt his pleasure and restored him to his senses.

"We were not fornicating. We are married," he drawled.

"A likely story! You should be ashamed of yourself, young man. We do not want your lewd court habits here. Northampton

is a respectable town." Hands tapping on forearms, he clucked
in disgust. "Befouling St. Catherine's! In broad daylight too! Be
off with you!"

Color high, but vastly amused, Miles climbed to his feet and
helped Heloise up. Godsakes, she was shaking with laughter.

"Good sir, I assure you we are married." Desperately trying
not to splutter, Heloise stanched her bittersweet hilarity—Rushden finally admitting the truth! He was squeezing her hand,
drawing her close behind him so she might hide her face. They
had offended the fellow enough already.

"Married! Aye, no doubt," retorted the priest. "To others. I
pity them. Get you gone!"

He dogged their heels as they zigzagged between the graves
to the pathway and latched the graveyard gate noisily behind
them, leaning upon it lest they should have second thoughts.

They walked with dignity round the closest corner to reel
against the daubed wall of a merchant's house, surrendering to
an emotion less perilous than lust.

"Court habits!" giggled Heloise, mopping the corners of her
eyes and patting his chest playfully. "I wish *I* might take *y Cysgod*
to task so thoroughly. Is the priest still there?" She dared a glance
around the corner. "Lord, yes. Like a mastiff."

Miles hauled her back to safety. "Behave!" he admonished
affectionately. "Shame on you, Heloise, that contraption looks as
though it has been struck by lightning. Come, let me help you."

Fearful as ever of her silver hair being seen, his erring wife
glanced about her before she let him remove it and repin the
strap that went beneath her chin to hold the cone firm. To his
amusement, she stood still like a small girl until he was done.
"The veil will need stiffening again." He gave up trying to dis-
cipline the abused gauze and untangled a snagged clover burr
instead. "I am afraid you look as though you have been tumbled,
changeling."

"I believe I nearly was," she said huskily and flirtatiously
peeped up to see if her remark had found a vein.

"Am afraid so." He tugged emphatically at the front and back edges of his doublet and risked a wicked smile. "I beg your pardon."

These last few weeks she had taken every care not to encourage him lest he think himself seduced. Now she was left with little choice but to be gracious still, as if he had been the only one out of control.

"If word of this should spread . . ." Yea, like ripples until it splashed her father.

His smile was rueful yet wondrously shameful. "I know, we are undone. Cheer up! I will wager that the cleric will not gossip. We shall merely be part of next week's sermon against worldliness and sinful lust."

"It was lust, wasn't it?" It was more a statement but it should have been a greater question and Heloise, confused by herself and him, was not sure what answer she wanted.

"Yes, but technically not sinful."

Her glance rose, embarrassed, to discover the man she was handbound to studying her face, and still in surprisingly good humor, but it was necessary to be pragmatic. She had imagined her father still at Bramley but he must be back at their Northamptonshire home.

"My father—"

"—will expect a reckoning. A sale or the merchandise returned unopened." His gaze fell admiringly upon her neckline but she was determined on being serious.

"Returned? God forbid! Oh, Heavens, what if he is here to make mischief for you!" She stared up unhappily at the jut of oaken joist above their heads. "H-he will order me to . . . to be examined."

Miles cursed. Her delicate body probed by a midwife's grimy fingers behind a curtain while some lewd cleric eavesdropped to see if he, Miles Rushden, had used her and, yes, he almost had— until God intervened.

Anguished eyes beseeched him; fingers twisted, tormented,

against her embossed leather belt. "I vowed I would never let him bully and beat me ever again." Irresistible tears sparkled on iridescent lashes. "Could you speak to Buckingham for me, tell him the truth and ask if he will permit me to remain as Ned's governess? Please."

"You dream, changeling." Miles tucked a wild wisp of hair behind her ear and wondered how long they dared delay. Two housewives passed, twitching their frieze-skirts and glaring as though he and Heloise were ribalds. Was there nowhere they could speak without the world's condemnation? "And I doubt that Harry would give your father audience. He knows about the feud over Bramley."

"Father may speak to Gloucester, though, and my lord duke has already offered to find me another husband," she muttered. "Sir Richard Huddleston told me so just now."

"Huddleston! Christ, Heloise, did you confide in him?" His fingers bit into her shoulders. "And, Godsakes, what plaguey concern is it to Gloucester?"

"Because I was in his household, you see."

Miles let her go and furiously slapped the wall. "Christ Almighty, woman, why on earth did you not tell me this before?"

She hung her head. "It was not your business." The euphoria of the churchyard had evaporated. *Y Cysgod* was back in command of himself.

"Everything about you has become my business. There is only one thing for it," he muttered, straightening his hat, his expression resolute. "I need to see Gloucester, God willing, before your father does."

"What will you say?" She hurried after him, setting an anxious hand upon his sleeve, but he would not tarry.

"I do not know. I am hoping for divine inspiration. Go back to your inn, and bar yourself in your bedchamber lest your father come for you. Plead indisposition or whatever womanly excuse you can until you hear from me."

"But I should come with you, sir," she gasped.

"No. This is better dealt with without any women's interference."

"Oh, come, how dare you say so! It is my life and liberty."

"And mine!" he muttered. "Go to your inn!"

Heloise, almost tripping, swore. Men were a curse. Damnation to the lot of them! "I hope the Devil reserves a row of toasting forks especially for you."

"I have felt the prongs already, Heloise," he tossed back grimly. "Trust me."

"SIR MILES!" HE WAS ALMOST WITHIN A STONE'S THROW OF Gloucester's inn when Ralph Bannastre, sweaty with exertion, halted him, gasping. "Oh, sir, his grace of Buckingham is asking for you."

"I cannot come now." Miles scowled, anxiously scanning the throng of petitioners outside Gloucester's lodging to see if Sir Dudley was among them. "Make some excuse, man, tell him you could not find me. Ralph"—he set the servant aside—"get out of my way!"

"But, sir," Ralph insisted, hurrying after him, "he's in a right pother."

"So am I! What is so poxy important?"

"Something to do with the prisoner Haute, sir."

"Oh, Christ!" That brought him up short. Which damned duke should he deal with first? And now, that cursed meddler, Huddleston, was striding purposefully his way with two pikemen in White Boar surcoats at his heels. A pox on it! The last thing he needed was to be rounded up like a missing bull and led into the sale yard.

"Get out of here, Ralph! *You could not find me!*" He crossed the street towards the hunting party.

"Sir Miles." Gloucester's velvet-voiced trouble solver blocked his way.

"Sir Richard," he echoed the dry courtesy.

"What a much-sought man you are." An embroidered unicorn

stitched in silver thread glinted upon Huddleston's glove as he gestured to the guards to fall in behind Miles. "You can guess what this is about."

"Kissing among the graves?" Miles retorted flippantly, striding alongside Huddleston. Some score of faces were already gawking. He was not going to march in behind like a traitor brought for questioning. "Can we dispense with the pikemen?"

"But they like to feel useful." The crowd parted. "I heard it was fornication *on* a grave."

"Wait a minute." Miles grabbed his pouched shoulder before they reached the doorway. "Are you telling me this *is* about this afternoon?"

His escort's smile was cryptic as he languidly pushed aside Miles's hand. "I think it is about a lifetime." Letting that sink in, he cleared the way through the cordon of Gloucester's bodyguards. "I would be circumspect, if I were you. Your lady does not lack for friends."

Circumspect! Miles could do with two curtain walls and a ten-foot moat to protect him, for Sir Dudley Ballaster was sitting at the trestle on Gloucester's right hand, with a tankard at his elbow and a smirk a mile wide.

"Be thankful they are both sitting down," Huddleston murmured cryptically and with a soft laugh turned to latch the door.

"Rushden." Gloucester leaned back, rubbing jeweled fingers across his chin, his expression sea calm.

"My lord." Miles removed his hat, wondering if a two-knee genuflection might be interpreted as guilt. He was beginning to sweat beneath his leather doublet.

"Is this the man, Father?" The duke's chaplain, Dr. Dokett, led forward the priest of St. Catherine's.

"Indeed, it is. See, his hose is grass-stained." They all stared pointedly at Miles's calves and Gloucester, sucking in his cheeks, gestured for the witness to be removed.

"You have been busy, Rushden." The duke's fingers found a quill to play with. At his side, Ballaster set a hand upon his belt and leaned back like a man who already owned half England. It was not a pleasing sight; neither was the church court smile glued to the chaplain's visage.

Miles waited. He knew the timings and the twists of interrogations, the deliberate control, the sudden smash of anger.

"I am hearing complaints about you from all sides. They boil away to one matter. Whether you are betrothed to a Welsh heiress or married to an English one. What do *you* say?"

Fixing his attention on Gloucester like a mariner on the polestar, Miles shook his head. "Your grace, until I hear from his holiness in Rome my hands are tied."

The Ballaster fist unwound at the edge of Miles's vision and its owner perused his fingernails. "But other parts of you are not, man." Sir Dudley's crudity was calculated. "Same old story, eh, boy?"

"I find myself between Scylla and Charybdis, your grace. My lord of Buckingham—"

"Scylla? Charybdis?" Ballaster sneered. "Forget the learning. Which of 'em do you want?"

"My lord of Buckingham," repeated Miles doggedly, "has been at pains to negotiate an alliance with Rhys ap Thomas over the last year." Good, the brief flicker of Gloucester's eyelids implied interest and my lord protector needed Harry's goodwill at the moment. Harry still had the numbers in Northampton; if he suddenly changed allegiance and let loose the Woodvilles on his terms, Gloucester would be on his knees.

"Upping the stakes, are we?" Ballaster missed little.

Gloucester cleared his throat and tossed aside the quill. "It is important that we reach a satisfactory solution for all parties, especially Mistress Ballaster. If an annulment is granted, I will undertake to find her a husband who will cherish her *particular* virtues." *He knew.* Gloucester plaguey well knew about her premonitions.

"May I speak, your grace?" asked the chaplain. "In my humble judgment, this is hardly a civil dispute. Seeing as the alleged

marriage took place within the diocese of Bath and Wells, it is
a matter for Bishop Stillington and it would be good to have his
counsel; but unfortunately his lordship, God keep him, is not in
his right mind, so—"

"No, he's not, and I'm not waiting for the slimy Italians to
interfere either," ground out Ballaster.

"—perhaps we should send to Lampeter for Bishop Langton,"
persisted the chaplain, adding swiftly, "There is also the question
of heresy."

"Heresy!" Both of Ballaster's fists hit the table.

"Or something more sinister," the churchman added. "I am
trying to keep a lid upon this pot."

"Confound you, Dokett, whose side are you on?" Aggrieved,
Ballaster looked to the duke.

The churchman had his teeth into the bone. "*Let* me finish,
Sir Dudley. Your daughters are immodest mischief-makers and
your eldest—"

"May I say something, your grace," demanded Miles, "before
this digresses into utter ridicule?" He had a sense that Gloucester
was listening with godlike amusement. "Yes, sir priest, Heloise
is different but there is much virtue in her. God's truth, your
grace, if I had not been forced at swordpoint to marry her, I
would—" Words failed him. "It is just that . . ." he faltered,
"that there is no enmity between us. We just wish to be severed,
that is all. And Heloise is as I first found her, Sir Dudley—
unviolated."

"Ha!"

"Your grace, this matter is but little compared to the troubles
confronting the realm. I pray you, adjourn this matter until we
hear from Rome." Why did Gloucester not answer?

It was Ballaster who dealt the coup de grâce: "I am willing
to loan my lord protector here a considerable sum if you take my
Heloise."

The cunning whoreson! So that was it! Coercion of a subtler

kind. Because the Woodvilles had stolen the treasury, Gloucester would need coin in hand to keep London licking his toecaps like a friendly cur. No wonder the duke was silent.

Miles leaned forward, grasping the board. "Ballaster, you can offer me Jerusalem and all of Christendom but I will not be bought." Nor his allegiance either! "My family have been barons since the time of Edward Longshanks and the blood of de Burgh and de Clare flows in our veins."

But Heloise's father had brought thumbscrews too. "I think you are missing the point. Aren't you a bloody Lancastrian, Rushden? This could be misconstrued."

Miles could have hit him. "My loyalty is to Buckingham and his to you, your grace," he exclaimed to Gloucester but the duke's head was bowed.

"And do you imagine Buckingham will thank you, Rushden?" Saliva flew from Ballaster's lips. "My God, he can have a loan as well! God's truth, man, do you people want England or don't you?"

"I . . ." Miles took a step back, glancing towards the chaplain for support.

"And another thing," Ballaster left the bench and advanced towards him. "You want some other man to tup Heloise, eh? Like her, don't you?"

"I am . . . betrothed to Myfannwy." The humiliation endured at Bramley came flooding back.

"But is it what you really want?" Loathsome red-veined eyes bored into him.

"I . . . I am marrying Myfannwy and . . ." Miles retreated. Oh, God, he did not want to lose Heloise but he could not stomach her bully of a father. "I will not be bought!" he shouted and, shoving Huddleston aside, he wrenched the door open and stormed out . . . to find himself face-to-face with Rhys ap Thomas.

"You bloody liar!" roared the Welshman. A mighty fist drove

at him. Miles ducked and heard the thwack of bone on bone and
a sickening echo. Sweet Jesu!

Turning, he found Duke Richard's horror reflected his. Between them, slowly sliding down the blooded doorjamb, was
Dudley Ballaster.

Sixteen

Would Rushden acknowledge her? Heloise paced impatiently. There had been such a wondrous alchemy at work this afternoon—desire, yes, but affection too. She wanted this marriage more than anything in her whole life. Oh, a curse on the priest for his intervention! Please, she begged the faeries, *please*.

The rattle of armored heels and rough knocking on the door cruelly jolted her. "Mistress Ballaster? Open up! The lord protector's orders."

She never expected what awaited her, her father's corpse beneath the fine scarlet cloak he took such pride in. What use was his riches or his blustering now? And the inn was full of faces floating in and out of her vision like wraiths: Rushden's pale as ivory and Rhys ap Thomas's drained and bloodless. Stunned, she had no voice as Sir Richard Huddleston, with a brotherly arm about her, led her past them through a doorway, and his grace of Gloucester came round the table of the inner room and drew her to a settle by the fire.

"You will forgive me if I come to the point," he was saying. "Heloise?" His voice was soft with kindness. "You must listen, my dear."

"Your grace." Guilty of wishing her sire dead an hour before, she forced herself to pay attention, looking up into Gloucester's concerned face.

"I have sent a messenger to your stepmother and arranged for you to leave straightway. You should be with your family by nightfall."

"Your grace, you are very kind." She sighed. "At least I do not have to take him as far as Bramley."

"No, there's that." He sighed and turned back to the hearth.

"I deeply regret your father's death for many reasons, Heloise. He was a good friend to the House of York, and the blow that killed him was . . . was not intentional. We all of us pray to die in a state of grace in our beds with our families about us and I am sorry that this was denied him." He paused and glanced round at her pensively, twisting the ring on his little finger. "You must not be concerned about your future. In short, I have decided that you and your sisters are to become my wards." Wondrous news. "I see you are pleased. I am glad." Clasping his broad furred collar in advocate fashion, he continued, brisker now: "As to this business of your marriage, Heloise. I have yet to hear your feelings in this matter."

"Your grace."

"I suggest two things, however, lass. Will you hear me?"

"Of c-course," she stammered.

"Good." He straightened, pleased. "Firstly, if your marriage has not been consummated, I suggest you permit me to find you another husband, *but* before you give me a decision, give yourself time to consider. A month at the least. Is that good sense?" He waited for her nod. "I am glad you think so, because I have to tell you that Sir Miles stated this afternoon that he has every intention of fulfilling his betrothal vow to Rhys ap Thomas's ward."

"But he—Jesu!" Dazedly she stared at him as her dreams disintegrated; the pearl brooch on his black brim shimmered in an unsubstantial world. "If my father had not interfered . . ." The words, wrenched out, held no healing, for her heart was bitter.

"Oh, little lass." Richard of Gloucester stooped before her and clasped her hands. "Never say you have grown fond of the fellow. Holy Paul, I can find you a fine Yorkist with a bloodline back to the Conqueror or a handsome, prosperous London merchant if it pleases you better. In the meantime, I should like you to remain with your family until I send for you. Perhaps when my lady duchess comes south, you may return to us, little cockatrice, hmm?" He tilted her chin up.

"Yes . . . if you please, my lord. Thank you for your care." He smiled and withdrew his hand. "But . . ." her voice trembled, "it . . . it is hard when someone whom you believe is a f-friend betrays you."

He drew breath to answer and then thought better of it. "There is someone who desires to see you before you leave." Heloise's heart leapt, hoping it was Rushden. She deserved that at least but it was Ned who hurtled in.

"My lady." Little arms flung themselves about her, pinioning her with butterfly gentleness against the settleback. "Please do not leave me."

De la Bere stood behind him. "I have brought him to say farewell."

"SIR!"

Miles, sitting on a bench alone in the inner courtyard of his inn, raised his unhappy head from his hands at the sudden shaking on his shoulder. Seeing Ned at his elbow, impish eyes redrimmed, he bit back a terse dismissal. Behind the child at a distance, de la Bere coughed and seated himself with his back turned.

"I have just come from saying f-farewell to Lady Haute," the boy gulped, swallowing back his tears. "M-my lord father says I am to go back to Brecknock without her and I am not to gainsay him but I've not been wicked." The small lower lip quivered rebelliously. "B-but it has to be my fault. She looked so unhappy and she was crying." He searched Miles's face uncertainly for help.

"It was not your fault, little lord," Miles answered wearily, trying to hide his own misery. "Lady Haute's father has just been killed." He kindly drew Ned before him and took the little hands in his.

"M-my father says that I am never to see her again." The little boy stared solemnly, his blue eyes glazed with further tears. "I love her, Sir Miles." Jesu, Miles felt as though his heart would break. "Can you not make my lord father change his mind?"

"Me?" He rubbed a calloused thumb over the child's fist, his voice husky with humility.

"You like her too, don't you, Sir Miles?"

"Yes," swallowed Miles. "I like her very much but I . . ." He shut his eyes, trying to stanch the pain, the hollowness. "I cannot help you, Ned. I am sorry." Little hands jerked away. Opening his eyes, he found the thwarted child ugly with anger.

"You and my father want her but you won't let *me* have her."

Oh, God, how much had Ned eavesdropped? But what did it matter anymore? Harry knew it all now. Unhappily, he let the child run from him. But Ned stopped and turned, examining something in his hand.

"I forgot," he said nastily. "Lady Haute said I was to give you this."

Something metal hit Miles's cheekbone and spun into the dirt—the garnet ring that had adorned Heloise's marriage finger.

"MAKE CHEER, MAN." HARRY, HIS GOOD TEMPER RESTORED now that he had Miles back on his gauntlet like a tethered hawk, leaned from his saddle and clapped him on the shoulder as they rode out of Northampton next morning in the prince's retinue. "You made the right decision. You do not want to be in Gloucester's pocket. A shame ap Thomas fell foul of him but no matter, he will come round in a day or so. 'Sides, there may be richer pickings ahead." Oh, Harry was damnably forgiving *now,* a right Job's comforter!

Miles thumbed the garnet ring beneath his glove. *Trust me!* Ha! What a jest that had been. How Heloise must despise him! Oh, he should have made his peace with her, but Gloucester and Harry—God curse them—had cleverly ensured he was tied down answering the Northampton coroner's questions while they parceled Heloise and her coffined father back to her family. Then there had been the chaplain, playing message boy, informing him he was to have no more truck with Gloucester's new ward. The lord protector, curse him, had been swift as lightning in snatching control of Ballaster's wide resources. Guardian indeed! Itching to cream off a lucrative interest to make up for losing the loan, no doubt, and Miles would wager his soul that Gloucester had no intention of ever letting Ballaster's vast resources disappear into the Rushden ledger. No, Heloise would be sold off to someone "reliable," some fawning Yorkist who licked Gloucester's boots. Christ forbid! He could not bear the thought of another man even touching her.

"Stop chewing the cud, Miles," muttered Knyvett as they rode knee to knee. "Would you jeopardize a prosperous future for the sake of a wench? Harry has forgiven you, so make the best of things."

But Heloise's soft hazel eyes haunted him throughout the journey. Each hay meadow they passed made him daydream of tumbling her. The bluebell wood they rode through conjured possibilities of delightful dalliance. He could only sigh with relief when the royal procession arrived at St. Albans.

The great monastery there had been forewarned, and the abbot's house—all insects chased out with pennyroyal, scrubbing brushes, and ardent prayers—was at the disposal of the noblest of guests while the lesser beings cluttered the adjoining guest house and overflowed cheerfully into the town. Richard of Gloucester was happily playing uncle and the prince had been gratified—publicly by the address from the townsfolk and privately by a large bowl of luscious cherries all to himself. Only Harry and Miles needed placating.

"This journey is becoming a pilgrimage through my family's defeats," the duke groused, rising from the visitors' prie-dieu, tossing his dressing gown to Pershall, and mounting the steps to the abbot's second-best bed.

"And mine!" muttered Miles, who had pulled the long straw over whether he or Latimer should sleep on the trundle bed in the alcove by the garderobe, shifted morosely to the bed's middle. "I hope no one starts a fire," he jibed, scowling at Harry's red hair looped in linen twists. "If anyone sees you looking like that, they will never let you within a mile of Westminster."

"Wait, your grace. One of 'em has come out." Pershall, like a diligent nurse, retrieved the damp scrap from the oxhide rug and wound it back in place.

Harry was still grumbling as he thumped the pillow: "First Northampton, and then today dear Uncle Gloucester had to take the brat across the St. Albans battlefields. The precocious whelp was smirking at me. Asked me where my grandsire had been slain. And there is Barnet still to come tomorrow, a Yorkist victory conspicuous for my absence."

"Since you were only sixteen at the time, my lord, surely . . ." Miles broke off wearily.

"That is not the point, is it?" The duke plucked at the abbot's insignia embroidered on the bedcurtain. "Gloucester was leading the vanguard at eighteen. He will know every poxy molehill on the field and be able to fill in all the gore and glory to his heart's delight. By supper there will be a martial halo around his head and the whelp will be snuffling out of his hand like a lap dog."

"Can we not get some sleep?" suggested Latimer from the corner, but the duke continued in a fierce whisper: "I am out in the cold, Miles, and I do not like it one jot. Every time the brat looks at me in that arch way of his, I can see his mother in him. Nudge Knyvett, for God's sake!"

Miles elbowed Sir William, who was already snoring like a sty of porkers, onto his side, while Harry spat on his fingers and pinched the candle flame.

"I guess we had better pray that the queen is too cowardly to leave the sanctuary." Miles extracted a spike of lavender that had snagged beneath the pillow and javelined it across Sir William. It fell short of Latimer. "Gloucester is in your debt, my lord. He will protect you."

"Oh yes, my wondrous lord protector," sneered Harry. "The trouble is I want him dependent on me, not the other way round. Once we reach London, he will have Hastings and Howard and all his other friends flocking to polish his bootcaps. I shall be as redundant as a flea on a corpse."

"I am sure your loyalty will be rewarded threefold, but if you could keep his grace somewhat anxious . . . Suggest he should summon more followers from York." Buckingham made a face at him and jerked the curtain across to keep out the moonlight from the shutter slats. "By the by," Miles added, his politic mind beginning to turn once more, "my w—" No, best not mention Heloise. "Someone," he said carefully, "pointed out to me that Bishop Stillington was traveling with Bishop Alcock's retinue like a prisoner."

"Yes, I noted that too. Mind, the poor wretch looked as though he was *in dementia*. It explains why I hadn't heard of him since he fell foul of King Edward when Clarence was put to death."

"Have you ever wondered why King Edward punished Stillington, my lord?"

"Yes, *and* why he executed his own brother," added Harry, loosening the laces of his nightshirt. "You are right, it is curious—why should Alcock, the queen's man, be still guarding Stillington? Pity the bishop's brain is addled. You think it worth making inquiries in London?"

"Certes, I do."

"If Stillington had his wits, he would be the bishop dealing with your annulment, would he not?" Binding insult to injury, Harry continued: "Could Mistress Ballaster have put the evil eye on him?" It was tempting to grab the Plantagenet pigtails and hold a fist under the Stafford chin. "You know it adds up, does it not? Hag's hair, potions, cat, and young Bess said she had a strange look at times as though she was seeing things. Bewitched us both if you ask me. Gloucester's chaplain wants her examined on her Articles of Faith. Miles? *Miles?*"

GOD'S TRUTH, THE SMELL OF POWER WAS A HEALING VAPOR! Shading his eyes against the hurtful brightness of the morning,

Miles drew rein on the hill and felt the Rushden serpent in him stir. Ahead lay the selfish city of London—the unpredictable powder keg of the kingdom. A calligraphy of walls, spires, and towers on the horizon with the tall letter of Paul's against the hazy sky, higher than anything else man-made in the entire realm. He glanced at his duke and saw his own emotions mirrored. Mentally they slapped palms and prayed that the long years of waiting were at an end.

"What in God's name is that?" Harry's face, of a sudden white as whale's tooth beneath the black beaver hat and the imported ostrich feathers, froze as the drumming reached them from the wooded valley.

"It seems as though we are about to be either welcomed or attacked," murmured Miles, then bowed as Gloucester rode up with his nephew and henchmen. Beneath a smile, the Rushden blood was running cold; what if the queen had managed to best Lord Hastings after all?

Edward V looked across at Harry, his cornflower eyes feline beneath the blue Burgundian cap and creamy plumes. "You think it might be my lady mother riding to welcome me, Uncle Buckingham?"

"Won't that be a blessed miracle if it is," Harry replied but his knuckles were tight upon the reins as the Stafford and Gloucester heralds rode down the hill to investigate.

Deo gracias! Relief flooded through Miles when the scarlet velvet and black cap of the estate of the Lord Mayor of London emerged from the trees with a caterpillar following of aldermen in scarlet and city worthies in mourning violet with sprigs of rosemary pinned on their shoulders.

LONDON, THE FLOWER OF CITIES! FLOWER, NO! MILES SMELT the city's odor long before they reached sight of it again at Aldersgate: not just the smoke issuing from the thousands of chimneys but the stinking ditches that surrounded the city, oozing

the filth and the detritus into the innocent streams. Hunger was
fraying his temper as they traversed the drawbridge into the city
but the press of people was a heady antidote. The battlements
were iced with citizens cheering so loudly that he could hardly
hear the city bells ringing out their welcome. Many of the earls,
arrived for the coronation, were waiting on caparisoned steeds
with their glittering standards and retinues. Miles recognized
Suffolk, Lincoln, Kent, each bowing low as the prince passed
before they swung their horses in behind the dukes. Golden
chains of office gleaming, jewels flashing in their hats, they made
a glistening sable train for the royal fledgling.

The procession followed a circuitous, poetry-hindered progress
along Cheapside and then back along Watling to the reception
at the Bishop of London's palace, and in every street liveried
guildsmen and apprentices ran alongside tossing up their caps.
Chains of flowers hung betwixt the gables, pennons decorated the
rooftops, bright cloths cascaded from every window, and maidens,
blushing blossom pink, tossed garlands. The prince was wreathed
in early roses, white, of course, for York, his shoulders besnowed
with blossom. As he waved, the wind played out his sleeves, blue
and gold like a kingfisher's wing, and the crowd roared its loyalty.

Sweet Christ, the boy would be a saint not to have his head
turned. There were huzzahs also for Gloucester but few for Buckingham. Harry was not well known *yet*—but he would be, vowed
Miles, trying to see him as the crowds would: handsome and
striking with the red-gold hair (no longer curling) bright against
his sable collar. Would they be offended by the knops of gold
that belied the mourning or the nosegay held closely to the ducal
nostrils at Paul's churchyard, where the excess of reeking armpits
was strongest? Miles sympathized, trying to hold his breath as
the odor of the charnel house added a bass note to the already
sweaty air. But better this than a few damp Brecknock aldermen
and a scatter of rounded-up Welshmen.

He brushed a scatter of petals from Traveller's mane—Heloise
would be amused to hear how—

Suddenly the glory and his pleasure diminished. It took two
to tell a story.

Seventeen

"I never care if I set eyes on it again but here's to Wales!" exclaimed Harry, bashing cups with Miles and Knyvett. Three damnably long weeks since they arrived in London and Miles was weary from carousing and being careful with anyone who mattered. It had been edging curfew tonight when they arrived back at Harry's London house, the Manor of the Red Rose in Suffolk Lane, but they had really something to celebrate.

"Justiciar of North and South Wales! Thank you, Gloucester! I could almost wish Lord Rivers at liberty so I could gloat." Harry gestured Pershall to remove his boots. "Dame Fortune at last is playing godmother but if that royal brat tries to make me appear a Philistine one more time, I shall turn rebel. 'Oh, have you not read the *Institutes of the Emperor Justinian*, Uncle Buckingham?' I could kill him."

"Still early days," consoled Knyvett.

"Pah, if Gloucester lets the child be crowned next month, the boy will immediately invite his mother out of sanctuary and she will have our heads. And another thing, Gloucester will not be able to hold Rivers and Grey hostage much longer. The royal councilors are already muttering about conciliation and, ooh, we have to please them. What do you say, Master Sagacity?"

"Perhaps we have not gone far enough," suggested Miles and let that droplet swirl in their minds.

Buckingham swaggered to the window, hands on waist, and swung round. "I want my Bohun inheritance which King Edward withheld from me," he declared through clenched teeth. "The devil of it is that it can only be given by a king, a friendly one, and it is not within the power of a lord protector to make the grant." He glanced at Miles. "Now if Gloucester were to wear the crown, he would hand it over gladly but this Woodville whelp will not."

"Just so," Miles agreed, twisting the garnet ring. "Leave the matter with me, my lord."

"Ah, now I think on't, you will be relieved to know that your erstwhile wife has been brought down to my aunt of York's household. Dr. Dokett tells me the deceitful creature is consumed by guilt for her father's death and is thinking of taking the veil. Gloucester is not pleased but if that is what the woman has decided, it should speed the matter of your severance."

No wonder he had received no answer from Northamptonshire. The bewitching bane of his existence was but a short boat ride along to Paul's Wharf. Becoming a nun? The trouble was it might just be true.

A SCRAWLED, OVERDUE NOTE AND AN UNEXPECTED WHITE rose of peace were delivered to Baynards Castle, but the plethora of prayers and penances in her grace of York's household had left Heloise as implacable as a caged-up lioness. It was true that Gloucester's mother, the Duchess of York, had been compassionate but Heloise, younger than her grace's companions by some thirty years, felt she might scream if she had to endure another pious reading from Walter Hilton's *Scale of Perfection* or St. Bridget's *Celestial Revelations.* She loathed the hushed conversations over meager helpings, the snoring naps, and the inflexible regime of devotions. Stirred by Dr. Dokett, they were trying to net her soul. A silk chemise in exchange for a hair shirt? As for self-scourging—No with an illuminated capital! But her joints ached from hours of kneeling and it was a wonder that her rosary beads had not been worn down to a nothingness. Miles Rushden could go hang. How could she have ever considered him as a permanent husband at Northampton? She must have been moon-mad. Three weeks it had taken the knave to remember her existence. Well, Myfannwy was welcome to him. She could decorate him with leeks and daffodillies and bed him in a sheep byre.

*   *   *

"MISTRESS BALLASTER SENT A MESSAGE AS YOU COULD HAVE IT back, sir, put it somewhere personal like, and she hoped it still had thorns on it when you did so." The offending blossom, withered and pitiful—except for the thorns—was thrust into Miles's hands and his servant fled from the hall before he had his backside boot-marked. With a dagger-sharp look at de la Bere, who was bent double with laughter, Miles unfolded the letter and saw his writing was much water stained.

"It has not rained these last two days, has it?" he asked, frowning.

"No, what of it?"

"I am going to Baynards, Dick!"

"But you cannot," spluttered de la Bere, mopping his eyes with his sleeve. "Have to escort his grace to dine with Lord Hastings at Beaumount's Inn."

"To Hell with that, I have feasted enough." Heloise needed him.

"I AM AFRAID YOU CANNOT SEE MISTRESS BALLASTER, SIRRAH. The young woman is not to receive any male visitors."

"And why is that, pray?" Miles asked the elderly lady-in-waiting who had received him like an abbess in the duchess's audience chamber after keeping him waiting. If he had understood the geography of this sprawling palace, he would have hunted Heloise out already.

"Those are her husband's orders, sirrah."

"I *am* her husband." But he was dressed like a notary, mostly to entertain Heloise and partly to test his disguise upon her, since he intended it to be his means of gaining access to Bishop Stillington.

The censorial gaze swept over him. "No, I think not, young man. Now go and do not make a further nuisance of yourself."

"I am her husband," Miles answered, smiling through clenched teeth. "Pray order her down immediately!"

The widow clasped her hands across her waist. "I will not be party to infidelity nor am I easily cozened. Her husband is a knight in the service of his grace of Buckingham. You, sir, are evidently a common notary—and a rapscallion. Be off or I shall have you removed!"

Miles set down the wooden box he was carrying and removed the clear-paned glasses from his nose. "Perhaps you would like to go and ask my wife what manner complexion her husband has? Give her this, please." He drew off the turquoise ring he always wore. "I shall await her in the garden." The woman stood immoveable. "Now, if you please!" And he advanced upon her with an authority that did not match his clothing.

Waiting beyond the trellised arches and the neat, lozenged beds of herbs, he had time to study Heloise above his spectacles as she walked towards him. Waifs begging outside the castle gate looked heartier. Dear God, the wench must have taken some foolish vow of abstinence—a fragile flower that could be borne down with a breath.

If they were ill-treating her . . .

"Pray leave us, madam!" he ordered her chaperone curtly.

The nuisance of a woman shook her head. "Certainly not. We know her unfortunate circumstances. Her reputation is in our care."

Amusement and the utter joy that Rushden had sought her out fizzed Heloise to life as she gazed in astonishment at the eyes without humility behind the twin glasses and observed the absurdly serious hat and the dull, long gown of broadcloth. Then she nodded gravely as though he were a notary of her acquaintance, and waited to unleash her temper.

"We shall go and sit on the exedra," she told her elderly keeper. "You may observe us from here." The stone bench to which she led her visitor was framed by columbines and periwinkles. It was tempting to ask him as they bruised the lavender with their passing why he was dressed so strangely and carrying such a curious box, but there were other matters to be dealt with first. Spreading her skirts, she sat down and, knowing that he longed for her to comment, perversely waited with demure indifference.

"What in Heaven's name have you done to yourself?" he growled, doubly angered by the lack of privacy. "Surely you have not let these hens talk you into taking some foolish vow of chastity? How long have you been here?"

"Too long," Heloise muttered, endeavoring to keep her fists on her lap. "And they have certainly tried. Perhaps you should tell Dr. Dokett that *you* will become a monk instead! That should solve the problem just as well. They have vacancies at the Crutched Friars. 'Trust me,' you said, you lying cur! Well, your stratagem has failed. I am not in the least penitent!"

"Well, that is a relief," he answered lightly. The metal tip of his dagger's leather scabbard scraped the stone as he made himself comfortable beside her. "Jesu, what have these fools done to you? And there was I thinking you happy." His grey eyes were kind and concerned. "Devil take it, Heloise, why did you not send to me?" She bit her lip, determined not to cry. His letter had contained news and no endearments. "And what is this nonsense that it is my order you are to receive no male visitors?"

"Dr. Dokett has told Father William and the rest of the household that my sinful behavior brought about my father's death and that I am a featherheaded woman whose body tempts men, and therefore I must ask God's forgiveness and stay out of sight."

"A murrain on these interfering old crabs!" He scowled at their voyeuse. "Look at her watching. Anyone would think you were St. Edward's crown and I was trying to thieve you."

"I am not supposed to tempt you," Heloise reiterated, tears hidden like water beneath the ice. He belonged to Myfannwy now. Oh, but he looked so utterly adorable behind his glasses.

"You do not have to be with me to tempt me, changeling." He smiled, stroking an ink-stained forefinger over the scrolls carved into the edging of the seat. "I am sorry about what happened at Northampton."

"Please, I have tried to put it from my mind." Afraid of the painful feelings tumbling inside her like well-paid acrobats, she huskily resorted to something that was not about next week or next year. "So why bone frames and broadcloth, sir?"

"To test the guise upon you. Would you believe me a notary?"

She glanced derisively at his garments. "Does a leopard change his spots?"

"Oh." He took off his hat and ran an annoyed hand through his lustrous black hair. "What then? You see, you were right about Bishop Stillington. I have to find a means of getting him out of the Bishop of Worcester's house."

Heloise tried to stay sane. "*You* do? Why you?"

"Part of my duties. Besides, I want to find out why he is being held."

And maybe a grateful Bishop Stillington would speed the annulment, she added as a postscript. "I believe a brawnier guise might suit you, sir." She sent him a glance that might have swiftly breached a lesser man's walls.

"You could be right. Hmm. I do know that some of Bishop Alcock's lay servants drink at the Strand Tavern. I suppose that if my purse is generous and my willingness to lose at dice fortuitous, they might welcome my company. If I sleek my hair down . . ." The cogs were still turning in one direction and it was not hers. "It might take a couple of days or more to gain their confidence but, yes, there is merit in your suggestion."

"My dragon is fidgeting," she warned, hoping to raise his hackles, and read the mischief stirring above the lenses. "Here is your turkisse back."

Distractedly, Miles slid the ring into place. "Do you just *look* half-starved, changeling, or is there a hungry demon perishing in there? What if . . ." He wickedly took her hand prisoner, and watched the older woman's neck crane. "I can meet you with fanfares at the main gate or we could stir these watchdogs up. What if you were to wear good shoes and your plainest gown and steal out the water gate tomorrow?"

"For what purpose, sir? To ride in at Bishop Stillington's window on my broomstick? Or am I to stand below with a blanket while you shin up a rope and smash your way in through the shutters with your boot heels?"

Miles flicked her cheek. "Sourpuss! No, a hearty meal and a dose of frivolity." He would come back tomorrow in more seemly clothes and speak with the duchess. Heloise was no sinful creature to be starved into holiness. This misunderstanding had to be remedied. "Here comes the guard dog now. Receive your hand back. I will come by water boat. What o'clock?"

"Five." She rose to curtsy. "The duchess takes her supper then."

"And this is for you." He lifted the crate into her surprised arms.

WITH EXCITEMENT SHINING IN HER EYES, HELOISE WAITED SINfully next day at the top of the castle broad stairs that led grandly down to the Thames. She felt like a princess waiting to be rescued from a dragon. The mullioned windows of Baynards glowered down at her truancy but the wavelets licking at the walls of the palace were whispering of adventure as the Thames oarsman brought the boat alongside. It was an exquisite evening and she longed to hug the gentle air to her like a soft mantle.

"I have never been in one of these," she exclaimed as Rushden steadied her beside him in the little cog. "And thank you for the psaltery. It was a wondrously kind gift. I shall make great use of it, I promise you. I have already driven the household demented with my practicing."

His eyes gleamed good-humoredly. "So long as you never send it back with an order to shatter it over my unworthy head."

"Oh no, it is far too valuable." Heloise shook her head solemnly and wondered why he was laughing as he set his arm protectively behind her.

"And did any of your watchdogs try to stop you leaving?" he asked.

"No." That was a wonder. Even the porter at the water gate had kept a still tongue. Maybe her quelling look had silenced him. "I would have let no one stop me."

"Good. Now forget Baynards." Above the odor of the southern muddy shoreline and the stinks of fish and pitch, the pleasing musk Rushden was wearing stirred her senses. She wanted desperately to reach up and kiss his cheek in gratitude but shyness reined her back. Freshly shaved and clad as became a knight, he was once more a man of authority.

As they were rowed from Vintry ward past Queenhythe, Rushden told her about the prince's entry into London. Beyond the warehouses, she could see the pennons fluttering above the houses of the great lords. "Some of these wharves belong to noblemen. See the gold lions, that is my lord of Suffolk's barge."

"Shall your father be coming to see the coronation?"

"Yes, but he will delay setting out to give my mother more time to recover. Did I ever tell you that your prediction at Bramley was true? She fell from her horse and broke a rib. Now no more soothsaying, hmm?" He flicked her cheek.

"God willing." What was Rushden at? Was he courting her for Saturdays in London when he was tired of begetting lambs in Wales? But she was so hungry and so deliriously happy that if he offered her a mutton pie and a cup of ale, she would kiss the ground he walked on. "Can you see Crosby Place from the river?" It was where Gloucester lodged.

"Heavens, no. It is in Bishopsgate, close to the north wall of the city."

"And the Tower of London?"

"No, that is east of the bridge downriver. Another day, changeling."

Because it was too dangerous to pass the narrow channels beneath London Bridge, they disembarked at Dowgate. "We will go down to Eastcheape, but up there in Suffolk Lane, Heloise, lies the Manor of the Red Rose where I lodge—see that high, square tower with the crenellations, across from St. Laurence's?"

"Where is your duke tonight?"

"Feasting with Lord Hastings close to Baynards." No wonder the disguise! "You see, I have also taken leave when I should not."

The revelation that she could distract Rushden from feasting with the lord chamberlain made Heloise cheerier than an apprentice on holiday. Her gaze was everywhere as her husband guided her through the labyrinth of streets but his hand in the small of her back gave her the greatest pleasure, as if this was a courting. And the food! He bought a double share of beef ribs and a little pannier of lip-red cherries, and found her a seat beneath a pear tree in the garden at the Garland Tavern. Except for the wasps and a drunken, long-haired pardoner who tried to flirt outrageously with both her *and* Rushden, she thought it Paradise . . . until her particular Adam wanted her to bite the apple.

He stretched out his legs, his gaze idling upon her. "Why is it that when you hide behind a mask, you are quite incorrigible, but today our conversation limps like a lying beggar? Do you realize you have had me pointing out each tower and turret as though I were some hireling. *Por favor,* my lady."

The unexpected assault threw her. "Mask?" She slid a cherry between her lips.

"Visor, then." He counted off his fingers. "The knight, the beekeeper, the governess, the singer." And the cockatrice, she added in silently. "Trust yourself, Heloise."

"Why does it matter what I am, sir," she flared. "It is what the world thinks."

"Not with me. Do I scare you without a sheath of metal between us?"

"I did not realize I was behaving badly."

"I wish you were." He snapped his fingers at the tap boy to refill their leather tankards. "A common fellow takes the wench he is courting to a tavern to make her drink and make her pliant."

The way he said the word so languidly, watching her, sent a sensual shiver streaking down her lower spine.

"How *can* I be pliant?" she reminded him. He was making her feel voluptuous, moist by just looking at her.

"I am not sure." He was watching her lick the gravy from her fingers. "Would you want to be?"

"Perhaps," she said recklessly. "I wish that Bramley had never happened, that we could begin again. I like you"—she looked down at the cherries in her lap—"too much for my own good."

"Bramley." He smiled a rogue's smile and aimed a cherry at her cleavage. "There were aspects of Bramley I have not forg—" His shoulders went rigid as if she were Abraham about to sacrifice him on a stone like Isaac. Oh, a plague on whatever had interrupted him!

Fellow patrons might have thought when he leaned forward that his finger bestowed a kiss instead of cautious silence on her lips. "Go, dabble your fingers in the water butt." He joined her there a moment later. "I have paid. Let us go." With a hand upon her back, he swiftly pushed aside the wicket gate and led her rapidly up the lane towards St. Leonard's.

"I glimpsed one of Alcock's men," he explained and, seeing the fellow had not left the inn, slowed to a more appeasing pace.

Not her fault then. "You heard something at the Strand Inn?"

He must have thought her interest sincere. "Aye, talk aplenty. I have been there twice. Mind out!" He shielded her from the mucky wheels of a passing donkey cart. "Stillington is ailing of a sudden, some seizure which I do not like the sound of one whit. I shall speak to Harry about it tonight."

"Did you hear those basket weavers talking just now, saying that my guardian will make himself king?"

"The gossip is inevitable until the prince is crowned." No elaboration there. "Are you content to walk awhile? Not footsore yet?"

"No, I am enjoying myself." Heloise tucked her arm through his and they walked on companionably up the rise, sharing the cherries. Valerian flowered lavishly along the stone wall and the perfume of pinks stole from a garden. A brace of evening rats skittered across their path and one of St. Anthony's pigs watched them morosely from the central gutter where it had discovered a dead kite.

"You know, we are not out of the woods yet as far as the Woodvilles are concerned." At Grasse Churchyard, he paused, less on edge. "They sell herbs here by day," he murmured, shielding his eyes with his hands as he looked back to make sure that no enemy had followed them.

Heloise, her fey instinct for danger unstirred, stooped to rescue a forgotten sprig of rosemary and tucked it into one of the silver loops that fastened his doublet. "Rosemary alerts the senses. You fear your Strand friends may have found you out?"

"No, just taking care." He studied the rooftops as though they were enemy battlements. Above their heads a flock of jackdaws wheeled noisily. "It is three weeks to St. John's eve. Enough time for the queen to rally her friends."

"Which means?" she prompted, as they turned towards Dowgate once more.

"Midsummer madness, changeling. Bonfires in the streets, free tables of viands and ale, and every door garnished with St.-John's-wort and white lilies. You should see Thames Street. They cast ropes between the gables to hang wrought-iron candelas. Half the city watch, the aldermen and the old soldiers, all clad in armor or else scarlet—white fustian if they were archers—march from Paul's Gate to Aldgate and back through Fenchurch Street. The guilds supply the cressets. You shall marvel, I promise. The procession is almost a mile long and a fine sight to behold, for the street is like a river of light and there are pageants and morris dancers aplenty."

"I could dispense with the morris dancers," commented Heloise tartly. "So the queen's retainers might be in armor and no one will suspect them and everyone will be watching the procession."

"Exactly. It is the day after the coronation, perfect to dispatch an unwanted duke or two."

"A pity there is no such a feast day this week, else you and your men could disguise yourself as revelers and invade the Bishop of Worcester's. What you need is a cockatrice."

She was abruptly lifted and spun above the cobbles. "Such brilliance, my little owl of wisdom!" he exclaimed, kissing her on the mouth.

There should not have been air beneath her feet as they returned to the stairs at Old Swan, not far from London Bridge, but there was. Rushden whistled up a boat and bade the oarsman row them as far as the Temple so she might behold more of the city. Heloise leaned against his arm, enthralled and happy. The encircling sun was drawn beneath the horizon, leaving the clouds in a glorious rosy wake across the sky, and the river was no longer silver beneath their little craft, but a great bale of shimmering cloth of gold flung across the broad valley.

"Oh," she exclaimed with a sigh. "I wish I could save this moment forever and take it out whenever I feel sad." But soon it would be curfew; glittering cressets were already lit along the long waterfront of Baynards and shortly the boat must turn and the evening would end. "Thank you, sir." For once, she dared to be froward and chastely leaned up and kissed the pitted cheek that Dionysia had so disdained.

"That is a paltry thanks, lady. I want more than that." His kiss slid a dagger into her self-resolve. What magic and mysteries did a woman need to please a man? she wondered, despising her innocence; she kissed him back rebelliously with all her heart, flattered when his right hand slid from her waist to clasp her silk-sheathed breast. Oh, if Lancelot had caressed the tip of Guinivere's breast so cunningly, no wonder that queen had broken her vows, weak and dazed with desire. Kingdoms had been lost for love and now Heloise understood why.

"This is heresy," she whispered, her fingers tangling in his hair and drawing his head back so she might fathom him. He might want her now but it was not enough.

"Why?" The words were breath against her cheek as he took possession of her lips again.

"Baynards!" announced the boatman and unkindly let the rocking timbers slap against the steps to jolt his passengers apart.

Rushden boldly squired her in past the duchess's guards. There were no scoldings, no raised eyebrows at her high color. Wafers and fruit had been left beside her pillow. Wonderful! She crossed her arms across her breast and threw back her head in sheer happiness, only to come back to reality with a bump. Her eyes opened again. What were Rushden's motives in being so kind? Guilt or . . . ? Was it not madness to encourage him when all she might be left with was a broken heart? Opening the window, she sought out the boat that might be carrying him away. I'll not be Miles Rushden's mistress, she told the faeries and St. Catherine. He must not come again.

But next day Miles arrived respectably at Baynards' front gate, and kissed hands charmingly with her grace of York before he requested his lady's company.

"Where are we going? To sign our annulment?" Heloise goaded, trying not to care, as he lifted her onto Cloud's saddle.

"Nothing so exhilarating. Merely to collect a wagon, bribe our way into the interlude cupboard of the royal wardrobe, don our disguises, and create misrule. And pinned to a feather cushion, owlet, is already a ribbon with your name writ large."

SNIFFING AT THE DOORWAYS, SCRATCHING ITS UNDERBELLY and lifting its leg to piss upon random doorsteps, a cockatrice danced its way along the Strand, accompanied by an individually selected entourage of twenty of Buckingham's more imaginative men-at-arms costumed as roosters, gryphons, and yales. In the procession's midst was a curtained cart containing a feather bed, and upon the driving board, a beleaguered carter had been joined by a crowing gryphon whose minions whooped and perched upon the vehicle like maddened apes, hurling firecrackers at the apprentices. By the time the raucous procession trooped over the bridge, the noise of its coming had emptied the Strand Inn of customers and collected such a crowd that Miles, shaking with laughter in his feathers and fustian, was sorry they had not thought to pass an upturned hat for donations; he might have broken even with the bribe to the deputy keeper of the royal wardrobe for loan of the costumes.

At the Bishop of Chester's portal, the cockatrice laid a large egg and skipped happily past a row of tenements to snuffle at the backside of the embarrassed guard at Bishop Alcock's residence. The apprentices cheered the monster on to more impertinence and the housewives shrieked with laughter. Its cavorting and the accompanying explosives sucked out Alcock's household like poison from a wound.

"Clear off or we shall summon the watch," bawled the bishop's officials, struggling to be heard above the pandemonium, helpless as the cockatrice scratched its head perturbed before it danced up the steps, followed closely by its masked friends, who draped their arms round the necks of the officials. Only the extremely observant in the crowd would have seen a gryphon jab an elbow into the guard's gut as it flapped its eagle wing and force him inside with a hand grasping his collar.

The onlookers waited, breath hushed, for the watch to arrive for fisticuffs. The cart, dull entertainment now it was bereft of firecrackers, slunk into a laneway forgotten, but two yales rushed out of Alcock's door with firkins of ale to woo the crowd, who in consideration blocked the main street in each direction.

Inside, it took Miles precious time to find the locked door that hid Stillington. He set a mask upon the bishop's unconscious head and his attendant gryphons wrapped the sick man in curtaining ripped from Bishop Alcock's bed then carried him tenderly like a battered comrade out to the wagon.

Breaking the city limit for empty carts, the vehicle hurtled down Fleet Street then south to Knightrider Street to avoid the watch. Along Eastcheap a zealous sergeant of the sheriff pursued it, forcing it recklessly to a halt, but inside there was only a wretched woman writhing with the early pangs of childbirth, on her way to her mother's house and the waiting hands of a midwife.

By the time the western sun was silhouetting the central turrets of the Tower of London, Bishop Stillington was tenderly bestowed at Baynards Castle; Heloise, no longer in labor, was shaking down the cushion from beneath her skirts; and Miles and his companions arrived home, soberly clad, to find Harry yawning while Bishop Alcock discussed the Dominican Heinrich Kramer's draft treatise on witchcraft with Archbishop Bourchier and Dr. Dokett.

At Baynards Castle that night, Heloise kept vigil by the bishop's bedside while below, in the chapel, her grace of York and her household knelt to pray that God would look in mercy upon his servant, Stillington, and grant him salvation and the healing virtue of heavenly grace. The prayers were needed. Rushden was right; it looked as if the bishop was being slowly poisoned.

"Is there nothing more we can do for Stillington but pray?" Buckingham demanded of Miles after his ecclesiastical guests had gone home well tippled.

"My lord, I would stake my life that he was being poisoned. I have left it to her grace of York and her physicians to do all they can. We could have tried purging him with bryony but since he has lost consciousness, we might have ended up choking him. And if it is deadly nightshade, we cannot risk belladonna or mandrake as an antidote. Believe me, we are like blind men in this. It could be anything—poppy, foxglove, toadstools, even hemlock. If the sleep leaves him, we may purge him then. This business is in God's hands now."

While her grace's physician snored in the antechamber and Father William, the Baynards priest, intoned prayers on one side

of the bed, Heloise sat resolutely upon the other, stroking her
fingers along veins that ran across the mottled back of Stillington's frail right hand like hedge roots, willing him to live. She
questioningly touched the soft skin where he had once held a
quill. The swelling that usually betrayed a scholarly man had
almost gone and no ink stain discolored his fingers. Through the
night, she sat silently urging him to fight, and slowly as the sky
grew pearly grey beyond the wooden shutters, she felt the light
in him begin to grow. The faint pulse was still there. Her
thoughts whispered to the old man that he was not alone, that
she understood the struggle within him—the temptation to be
rid of the world and its troubles—to surrender and eke out Purgatory until his soul's doomsday.

Father William withdrew, and Heloise sang softly with such
sweet sadness that tears made rivulets upon her skin and seeped
beneath her gown. As blades of gold pierced the shutters, gentle
arms assisted her away. Rushden was in the bishop's bedchamber
with the duchess and the physician when she returned to find
that blessed color at last suffused the sick man's countenance.

"Well, your grace," her husband was saying, "it is Sunday,
the first of June, and here we have a rusty bishop." He offered
Heloise a smile that warmed her heart. "With your permission,
my lady, may I open the casement and let the bells in to stir
him?" At the Duchess of York's nod, he set back the shutters.
"Listen, my lord bishop!" he exclaimed as the sunshine's bene-
dictory light fell upon Stillington's tired face. "There is Paul's
peal of bells, and the chimes close by are from St. Laurence's on
Poultney and that distant cascade must be Allhallows."

"No." Fragile as breath to stir a crinkled fallen leaf, the faint
Yorkshire voice was edged with pride. "No . . . St. Martin . . . le
Grand."

Eighteen

Bishop Stillington was as weak as a rabbit kitten from whatever foul dose had been given him but his heartbeat slowly strengthened. By Monday he was returning to the brawnier Yorkshire dialect of his childhood and stealing birds' eggs at Nether Acaster, but slowly, as he whetted his mind on reminiscences, his intellect sharpened. Why would anyone wish to poison him?

"Were you the shepherdess that sang me back into the earthly fold?" he asked Heloise. "Methinks I was carried by gryphons from my prison but I suppose it was a dream."

"Actually . . ." began Heloise. Out tumbled the events from Stony Stratford to the cockatrice. Then, emboldened by the bishop's dry chortle, she confessed the swordpoint marriage within his diocese and that the chief gryphon was her reluctant bridegroom. Stillington soaked in her tale without a comment but when Rushden came to visit, the old man studied him with new-grown suspicion, as though he might sprout feathers again.

"Well, my lord bishop," drawled Harry, joining Miles next day at the bishop's bedside. They were alone—Heloise was keeping well clear of Buckingham. "I daresay you are feeling more secure about your future now, seeing that the Woodvilles are finished."

The former chancellor, propped upon the pillow and bolster, hands limp upon the coverlet, stared at him as though he were an insubstantial mirage over a summer ocean.

"Who rules this realm is of little consequence to me." He did not move his coiffed head but spoke it like a litany.

"Your pardon, Bishop, but that is not the answer I want." Harry met Miles's ironic glance. "Dear me, *Cysgod,* I thought you told me he was sane." They watched the bishop's watery blue gaze rise to evaluate the last lawful heir of the House of Lancaster. Perhaps he did not respect the murrey satin doublet with silver thread acorns and the beading of pearls, for he looked away as though Harry bored him.

"Did you know he was once lord chancellor?" whispered the duke in mock confidence across the coverlet. "I never thought he would become so mouselike."

Stillington folded his lips tighter, staring stubbornly at the coverlet. "Have I unwittingly committed some offense against you, Buckingham? You have my thanks for dragging me back from my body's doomsday. Is that not enough?"

"We have helped you, my lord bishop," Miles threw in his pennyworth. "We should now like you to help us."

Harry leaned forward. "We have the queen muzzled but, of course, there is not the slightest doubt that if she regains her authority she will have you killed, Bishop—thoroughly this time. *Why?* What is it you know?"

The old man glowered. "I was friend to Clarence. Will that suffice? You headed the peers that sat in judgment on him. You heard the testimonies."

"But they proved so insufficient that King Edward *ordered* us to condemn him. *Why*, Stillington?" Within the generosity of the night robe's sleeves, the bishop's hands were agitated. Harry leaned forward. "What was the secret that Clarence died for?"

The grey head drooped. *Keep at him,* Miles gestured. The arguments were his but the performance had to be Harry's.

The duke's tone softened: "Gloucester is a good man, righteous, compassionate. You helped him when he was a youth. He needs your help more than ever now. Will you advise him if I bring him here? Tell him what he needs to know?"

It was whistling in the wind. Miles held his breath as Stillington ran a tongue nervously over cracked lips like a waiting reptile. Harry fidgeted.

The wrinkled Adam's apple moved finally. "A pretty speech, your grace. Someday you may grow famous for your silver tongue.

Tell me, is this altruism in you, my lord of Buckingham, or is it the Bohun inheritance that you desire? The lord protector cannot give you manors for your friends when he has insufficient to reward his own." God's truth, the old man was shrewd. He guessed that Harry wanted to play the kingmaker. The ancient gaze crawled over Miles's face like a foul spider but his question was for Buckingham. "Or is this merely revenge?"

"Why deny it?" Harry stormed to the foot of the bed. "The Woodvilles are parasites, Bishop, crawling to riches through the bedclothes." Miles frowned at Harry. Perhaps they should come back later—let the arguments mature—but the duke strode back to the bedside. "I think about the future, Stillington, the Woodville future. Our new king will be even more a pawn than his father was. Elizabeth Woodville will rule England and when her poison is once more congealing in your belly, it will be my turn to kneel down at the block, and Gloucester's, and our sons' after us, not to mention Clarence's boy." The bedchamber was silent. "Well, Bishop?" Harry rasped. "I need an answer."

"I shall pray for guidance, my lord duke," the ecclesiastic replied perversely. "It is God's matter."

"It is England's matter, I believe," said Miles to them both, making an end of the conversation as he unlatched the door and bowed.

"So do I get an accolade for 'silver tongue,' my friend?" Harry flung his arm about Miles's shoulder as they landed ebulliently on the bottom stair.

"You deserve the Holy Roman Empire." Miles grinned as their horses were brought to them across the courtyard. "I doubted whether there was actually any secret at all, but there is, there plaguey well is."

"You were right. He was worth the expense."

"I think, my lord, you should stir Gloucester into the Stillington brew. Shall you go to Crosby Place straightway before the council meeting starts and apprise his grace?"

"Yes, but do you not intend to accompany me?"

"Not yet, my lord, I crave leave to transact some business of my own." A caravel named Heloise and it was high tide.

HELOISE HAD NOT MEANT TO DROWSE AND THE DREAM MUST have lasted but a few moments—a dream of a lord clad in black dragged struggling from a mighty keep by soldiers. They threw him to the ground and his sleeves crawled like spider's legs as he fell forward and then a bell struck thirteen times.

St. Mary Magdalene's in Old Fish Street was tolling a funeral bell as she awoke shivering. For an instant she was uncertain where she was, for the anguish of the prisoner in her dream was still with her. The scavenging kites flying westwards over Baynards drew her gaze; their cries had been in her dream too.

"Heloise, are you ill?" Rushden stepped out from beneath the mulberry tree.

With a swift denial, she rose, disliking the edge of misgiving in his expression. How long had he stood observing her? She shook her head, warming beneath the male discerning eyes that were observing her black gown and the stiff reversed front of her cap, in silver taffeta that helped disguise her hairline.

He smiled slowly in the maddening way he sometimes had. "I wondered if you might like to come and see Crosby Place."

Gloucester's London hive? Heloise brightened. "As a reward for stuffing cushions up my girdle, sir?"

"Something like that." The hand held out to her assumed her obedience; she did not mind.

"You realize," she pointed out, "that all this associating with me is verging on the scandalous."

"Yes," he agreed, ushering her towards the stable. "Suffice it to say that tail-pulling of the noble-and-flattered has some appeal."

"I suppose you will not bother to explain that."

"Absolutely not." And his brigand's smile tightened the band already round her heart.

*   *   *

THE BELLS FOR TEN O'CLOCK AT CROSBY PLACE IN BISHOPSGATE
had not yet struck and Miles had plentiful time to escort Heloise
up to the minstrel gallery to watch the royal council assemble
below. A chair of estate dominated the long trestle that had been
set up down the length of the hall with benches on either side.

"Oh, this is wonderful," exclaimed Heloise, tapping her fingers on the rail, her doelike eyes wide with admiration.

"A gracious dwelling, is it not?" He was heartened that she
beamed at him like an excited child, sharing his pleasure in the
lovely symmetry. Unlike other lords, Gloucester kept no house
of his own in London nor did he choose to lodge at Westminster
Palace or Baynards Castle; he always rented Crosby Place.

The house was built on three sides of a courtyard—a great
hall and private apartments facing the chapel, kitchen, and buttery. At the back lay a large garden, protected by a high, cren-
ellated wall. For Miles, the beauty of the dwelling was stolen by
the magnificent five-sided oriel window, set in a framework of
wondrous stone tracery, built into the great hall's southern wall.
He watched with pleasure the sunlight surging in through the
lozenged glass to play warmly on the black and white Purbeck
tiles and the matching clustered councilors. Above the window's
soaring bay, a boss embellished with a crest and helm embroiled
the stone ribs that fanned across the arches of the windows into
a soft-edged stone sun. Opposite the oriel window was a large
wall fireplace. There was a central stone hearth, too, for standing
braziers in wintertime. Beams rose with perfect grace to meet
each other lovingly beneath gold-leafed bosses. Nor was the hall
bereft of hangings fit for a great lord's pleasure: a French hunting
tapestry, its colors glowing against the whitewashed masonry,
brightened the parlor wall behind the chair of estate. The sheer
perfection of it all started him thinking what changes could be
made at Bramley.

"A pity Bramley is so lofty," remarked Heloise disconcertingly. "This hall is spacious and yet intimate."

"Different purpose and newer, too," he answered, disturbed

that she might actually have read his mind. "Built in the sixties on wool money. Word is that Crosby never actually lived here. Mayhap he overstretched himself. A Lucchese banker, Antonio Bonvice, owns it now."

"It is perfect." Heloise sparkled, bringing her palms together in sheer exuberance.

Why did she have to be so lovely? It took all Miles's strength of will to wrench his gaze from her moist parted lips. He should not be standing with her in the common gaze. She was arousing too much attention and she was arousing him. He cursed, wanting to steal his seductive madonna-in-mourning away to a bedchamber and peel the black damascened silk away inch by inch. He forced himself to stare instead at the lords, spiritual and temporal, amassing below, gratified that there were plenty of lesser nobility like himself diluting the assembly.

"Others like yourself, sir?" Hell take her! She must be reading his mind. He frowned at Heloise's profile and then let out his breath with a self-conscious grin. If the lady was actually tapping into his head, then she should have been blushing, but there were only healthy smudges of rose along her cheekbones.

"Yes, ability riding on the backs of lordly mediocrity for the most part, though I admit some of them were born with brains as well as titles."

"Just as well they are talking too loudly to hear you." She laughed. "Are there any Woodvilles?" He shook his head. With two in sanctuary, three in prison, one at sea, and Dorset, who had been tracked by dogs out on Moorfields, now in hiding, the queen had no glib defenders on the council. He did a swift calculation of how many councilors might still support the queen.

"Counting heads for the dukes?" Heloise's soft chiding broke through his reverie.

"Mistress, will you stop—" He broke off. Lord Hastings had entered the hall and, glancing up at the gallery, recognized Miles.

"Dear God, who is he?" Heloise's sunshine pleasure vanished. "That man nodding to you?"

"Ogling you, morelike, madam. The famous Lord Hastings. You might say he was to King Edward what I am to Buckingham." Another *cysgod.*

Heloise stared wide-eyed at the great lord who had summoned the two dukes into alliance against the queen. "D-does he always wear sleeves like that?" The lower ends of the lord chamberlain's mourning sleeves had been slashed from heel to midcalf level into equal strips, each edged with gold embroidery.

Miles tried to make light of her change of humor. "Italian, I should not wonder. Stand here for much longer and you will see him goose a passing maidservant. Keep a league from him, changeling, or he will charm your underlinen off you."

Heloise gripped the rail to steady herself. Lord Hastings had been the beleaguered victim in her dream! Mercy Jesu! Was she meant to warn or prevent . . . She watched the late king's friend move affably through the hall bestowing greetings until he drew level with Buckingham, who had just come in to take his seat to the right of the chair. The air vibrated with mutual jealousy.

"Do those two know one another well?" she asked.

"Harry and Hastings? Well enow. From what I have gathered, Hastings was one of the few who took pity on Harry when he was a page boy in the queen's household."

And haughty Buckingham might have wanted help but he would have loathed pity. A man who did not like sharing, thought Heloise, wishing now that Rushden had not brought her here. The interplay beneath the gallery was dangerous and the man at her side was reveling in it as though it were a chess game.

"And which bishop is that?" she asked sharply. A broad episcopal hat and dewlapped chin perimetered the shrewd face that perused them for a moment, before the man turned his head to observe Hastings and Buckingham with a thoughtful intensity.

"Morton, Bishop of Ely. He gave up his Lancastrian allegiance in seventy-one and became one of King Edward's councilors."

Unease tensed Heloise's body. "I do not care for him." Like a sentry under fire, she jerked out of the bishop's range of sight and retreated against a solid door between the tapestries. As if gasping for air, she leaned back, eyes closed.

"What did you see?" Against his own will, Miles was beginning to acknowledge her damnable abilities.

"No. Dear God, I—" Eyelids lifting, she swallowed uncomfortably at him watching her. "I can feel their thoughts."

Miles's interest quickened even though the hairs of his head prickled at such evil. He had not been meant to play the confidant, but some presentiment had overwhelmed her cautiousness. "Tell me." The words came hoarsely as he watched the glassiness of her gaze return to normal.

"Feelings. All scrambled." Her hand slid up defensively to her throat as if shielding her heart.

"Are you telling me that you can stare at Morton and reach *his* thoughts?" he whispered fiercely, his fingers curling round her cuff.

"No, no. Their emotions. Greed, envy, fear."

"Can you look at each?"

"To forewarn you?" Contempt turned down her lips and her answer was vehement. "Not for all the gold in Christendom!" Then fear shimmered, misting her eyes. "Your pardon. I should not have spoken so."

Horrified at her sudden terror of him and at the ancient fear deep within his own being, Miles grabbed her chin, compelling her to look at him. His rational mind rebelled against the superstition urging him to recoil from her. "And I? What am I feeling?"

Delicate lashes, with a patina of rainbow, fluttered down in panic. "Do not burn me," she pleaded, color seeping back into her pansy face.

So she knew how much he dreaded her otherworldliness. "It is you who make me burn, changeling." His kindness was a visor, hiding the rapid prayers within, and, confused by his own emotions, he walked across to the rail, leaving her uncomforted.

"So it is true." The door gave way behind her and Heloise,

righting herself, looked up horrified into John Dokett's satisfied face.

"Miles," she called out in panic, and Rushden turned.

"Dr. Dokett?" He frowned.

"Sir Miles." The priest inclined his head in greeting and, with a tight smile at his prey, disappeared down the stairs.

"Heloise?"

She was shaking. "He—he overheard what I said."

"So?" Rushden made no move to comfort her. "You are Gloucester's ward."

"It is not enough. He—oh, Christ, he wants to put me to the torture, I know it."

"And you just accused me of that too. Be rational. Is this the courageous knight of Potters Field, hmm?" She nodded, trying to be brave. "That is better."

Below, the benches scraped to the table. Gloucester had arrived. The guards' pikes clanked into vigilance outside the lower entrances. "Time to go." He put an arm about her shoulders and led her towards the stairs.

In the lower passageway, Heloise turned. "You do not attend the duke?" she asked huskily, in an attempt to restore normality between them, but his eyes narrowed.

Miles knew she had not intended to rile him. He had his own means of ensuring the decisions beyond the defended doors; today's arguments had already been raised last night like targets for Harry to practice upon and the right words sat in the quiver waiting to be loosed. But no, he was not permitted in the council chamber—not yet, unless he chose to play at secretary.

"I—I should like to inquire whether my sister will be coming to London with her grace."

"Of course, an excellent notion."

To cheer her and safeguard his own sanity, he left Heloise talking with Gloucester's steward, and made his way alone to the garden in search of solitude. His reluctant wife's uncanny ability to show his thoughts back to him like a watery reflection disturbed him. If his mind could not stay free of her, might she not enslave him in time, invade his brain inch by inch until he knew not whether it was his thoughts or hers impelling him? What if Dokett hauled her before the church courts?

Air warm and languorous with the perfume of honeysuckle and lavender soothed him as he traversed the cloistered gallery that ran below the duke's apartments, and stepped down into a haven that was momentarily free of power-broking or, mercifully, Heloise's unsettling presence. Beyond a stone wall, too high for enterprising thieves, the slate roof of St. Helen's was bright with sunlight and he heard the sweet voices of the black nuns creating hills and vales of music for God's pleasure. And this part of the garden was an earthly delight, designed for dalliance and planted with flowers to perfume the air and seduce the senses. Miles passed a fluted birdbath and strode beyond a flower bed brimming with lilies of the valley to the heart of the garden, a small, fashionable mede bright with white daisies and yellow cowslips, enclosed by a low oak lath trellis heavy with white roses. Crab apple blossom dappled the path and in the southern corner a grapevine twined into a canopy above a raised turf seat. Miles did not linger. The gravel path beckoned him beneath an arch, past spiked broom and hawthorn and a flower bed ready for planting, where someone had left a lady's waterpot, before he came to the farthest corner hidden by a laurel hedge. There, casting his sleeves back, he sat beneath the honeysuckle, most loath to bend his mind to strategies. A ladybird in Stafford colors landed on his shirt cuff and he watched it idly, listening to the plainsong, and a blackbird's descant, until the new sound of dibbing from the other side of the laurel hedge invaded his privacy.

Investigating, Miles paled. It was not a gardener but a gentlewoman and he had a sense of time reversing like a cart. Heloise's sister knelt, a cloth tucked protectively over her mourning gown, planting seedlings. Sensing herself observed, she raised flirtatious eyes but, recognizing him, her amiability fled and she sprang to her feet, the dibber raised threateningly.

"You!" she snarled, springing up menacingly. "What have you done with my sister? By my soul, if you have done her harm, I will rend your face further, you vile man." The girl's hair blazed gloriously but he felt no warmth for her.

"Calm yourself! Denise, is it?"

"Dionysia! If you have murdered her . . ."

"Not yet," he answered coldly. "Despite temptation. What are you doing here?"

"Oh, trying to allay the tedium," she retorted shrewishly but her ruffled feathers settled somewhat. "Part of the distaff force under Lady Percy, sent ahead by her grace of Gloucester to womanize this male demesne. We are expecting her within the week. Now perhaps you will answer *me!* Where is my sister?" It gave him pleasure to walk away. The weapon was lowered but she chased after him. "Is she at Brecknock still? Answer me, you fiend!"

Not looking at her, he paused at the nearest doorway, praying for a corner untroubled by harpies, and nonchalantly stroked a gloved finger along the ribbed stone arching the door. "Middleham has not taught you better manners, Dionysia, but I shall see if it pleases her to come and speak to you."

OH, IT DID! DELIGHT BROUGHT OUT THE SUNSHINE IN HELOise's face as she almost skipped down the stairs to find her sister. Pleased, their go-between leaned out of the casement to watch the reunion.

"Ah, Miles." He turned, annoyed to find Harry holding out a paper to him. "My notes of what the council discussed this morning. Let me have your comments by noon." The duke halted by the door. "Oh, by the way, Dokett still thinks it possible to arraign the Ballaster girl on witchcraft before the annulment arrives." Caution lowered his voice. "Can't ruffle Gloucester's feathers yet but we should soon have her out of your hair for good. I will leave you to it."

Stowing the note angrily into the breast of his doublet, Miles left the chamber a few minutes later and sent a page with a message to his groom. High tide.

DOKETT WAS KNEELING IN THE DUKE'S PRIVATE CHAPEL—praying for his employers' dead kinsmen was part of his duties—and he was alone. "Are you here for confession?" he asked officiously as the door closed, not opening his eyes.

"Yes, yours!" In an instant, Miles had the quaking bigot flat-palmed against the wall.

"R-Rushden?" Dokett scowled at the eight inches of determined steel pressing into his throat. "Are you insane? I am the lord protector's chaplain. How dare you—*oooff.*"

The air whooshed out of him as he was bounced against a different wall. "I do not care if you are chaplain to St. Peter and St. Paul," Miles told him with much satisfaction. "Slander Heloise Ballaster's honor or her faith one more time, and you will not see sunrise."

"Oh, I understand you, yes." The priest pushed his arm away undaunted, rearranging his chasuble fastidiously. "I can read Satan in your eyes, I hear him in your voice. Holy Church destroys heretics and witches, and those who shelter them. I heard her confession to you just now."

"You think I jest." Miles strode to the altar and slammed his hand down upon the open Gospels, his gaze holding the priest's eyes. "Did I not make myself clear? Bring charges against her and I swear in the name of Christ that I will have you killed."

"My lord protector *and* his grace of Canterbury will hear of this, Rushden. This land is not going to be godless anymore, do you hear me! Blasphemers like you will not go unpunished." Dokett's body might be rigid against the wooden panel, but he was watching Miles with all the ferocity of a cornered boar. "I am not afraid of you." He ran for the door.

Miles hurled the dagger. The priest screamed in pain as it landed with a quivering hiss, snaring his hair beneath its blade. "*Now* do you believe me?"

Pinned to the door like a proclamation, Dokett's skin was bleached of blood. His eyes goggled, empty now of courage. "I believe you, yes." The priest held his breath as Miles wrenched the dagger loose, and then bolted as though all the demons in Hell were after him.

Gloved applause wiped the satisfaction from Miles. "You have ruined the woodwork," drawled Sir Richard Huddleston. He was sitting on the colonnade wall outside, his arms folded.

"How long have you been there?"

"Long enough. His grace of Gloucester can be quite blind to people's faults sometimes, but we all have our weaknesses." The lazy gaze seemed to say: *And now I perceive yours.* "You were rather precipitate. Dokett is on his way out. A month maybe." He sauntered across and ran a gloved finger over the damage and turned. "The Loathly Lady . . . She asked Sir Gawaine the question, What do women most desire?"

"Yes," answered Miles uncertainly, "I know the ballad."

"Well, there you have it. Good day, Sir Miles."

IT WOULD BE HARD TO DISCERN WHO WAS MORE SURPRISED, decided Heloise, as she confronted her aproned sibling. Returning Dionysia's fragrant hug, she wondered with feminine perversity where her sister had acquired such expensive perfume.

"You look like a skeleton, Heloise, but then you must have been desperate until Father—God rest his soul, though it's unlikely—offered that loan to Gloucester before he died. You see, I know all about Northampton. The White Boar men are such sillies, too easily bled for gossip. Matillis and I had a wager as to whether you could seduce Rushden but I suppose everything is settled between you now, since you have the lion's share of the inheritance—not that I begrudge you anything. Certes, you may have your churlish husband to yourself and good riddance, say I! Why, I do not believe there is a gracious bone in his body. I heard Matillis had a girl-child. Fortunate for us, thank God!" A wonder she was not gasping for breath.

"Matillis!" echoed Heloise, her thoughts running the other way like panicked thieves. Loan? Lion's share? Was that what people thought?

"Tell me about our father's funeral. Did Sir Hubert stay sober?" It was a sure wager that she would interrupt Heloise's account but, astonishingly, she listened. "Our father will be trying Satan's patience now," she said when Heloise was finished. "But enow, what of the living? Has Rushden got you with child yet?"

"Dionysia!" Would a scathing glare be sufficient?

It was. Her sister gave a playful shrug and knelt back down. "So tell me this then"—she separated a seedling from its fellows—"are the Welshmen hideous? Is it true they wear leeks in their hats? What is the duke like? I should so love to meet him. I hear he has a garden at Thornbury."

How could Heloise have forgotten that Dionysia's mind was planed in one direction? "Why are you so anxious to meet his grace of Buckingham?"

"Because his grace may have some plants at Brecknock or Thornbury which might please her grace of Gloucester. Goodness, what other reason could I have?" Heloise recognized the worldly purr in Dionysia's tone. "Now there is a handsome fellow coming towards us. I wonder what he is worth."

"That *is* my lord of Buckingham," answered Heloise in a fierce whisper.

"Saints be praised! Introduce me!" But the duke's shade already fell across them. It was obligatory to curtsy.

"Good day to you, my lady," he said to Heloise. It was a waste to answer, his interest was already captivated by the golden hair tumbling across the voluptuous satin curves of her sister. "What are you planting, demoiselle?"

"Marigolds, sir, and I had best get on with it."

No novice at this art, Dionysia knelt, offering him an over-generous view of her deep cleavage and, with a coy smile, stroked a seedling's roots. Heloise helplessly looked on as the man fluttered like a hapless moth that could not see the web.

"If you were not clearly somebody in authority, I should ask your help." The teasing allure stunned and held him like sticky threads.

"Important, no." Unbelievably the duke went down on his haunches and tucked a plantling snugly into its hole.

"You have the right hands for a gardener." Admiration oozed through every feminine syllable.

"Are you the creator of all this?"

"I wish I was, sir." Her sister dimpled and sat back on her heels. "I have not seen you here before. You do not talk like a northerner." Dionysia's dab of Yorkshire dialect making fun of the White Boar men delighted Buckingham.

"If I spoke like where I live, mistress, I should be encouraging you to plant leeks, see, *fy mgeneth.*" The Welsh lilt was perfect.

"Ha, one of Buckingham's retinue, yes?"

He took the trowel from her and Dionysia protested: "You will get your hose dirty and your lord would not like that." The impertinence! Dear God, Heloise thought, folding her arms, one day her sister would charm the Devil to let her out of Hell.

"No, mistress, his grace would not." The hour bell sounded and he rose, dusting the soil off his knees. "I wish I had time to stay longer, demoiselle. Believe me, this garden is a little haven."

"Only when the sun is shining, as it is now." Dionysia's smile flattered him before she lowered her gaze in sultry fashion. The troweling began again. He was dismissed.

His embarrassed gaze recalled Heloise's presence and he touched his hat to her. They heard his boots crunch upon the path, hesitate, and then they were alone again. Dionysia looked up, sucked in her cheeks, and gave a familiar, irritating, knowing smirk.

"Didie! That was blatant! How could you?"

"We all have our ambitions, sister. If you think I am content to wed some boring braggart who thinks of naught but hunting, and expects me to whelp babes year after year . . ."

"You would prefer to be a courtesan? Oh, Jesu, Didie, not Buckingham, please, no."

"Yes, Buckingham, and do not try and stop me, either, Heloise, prattling your foolish warnings like a Cassandra."

It would be like telling the sun not to rise, sighed Heloise. Useless, then, to warn her that women were no better than food or drink to the man.

"And here is your pitted millstone bowling towards us, sister. Does he hang heavy upon your neck?"

The loan! It was too late to ask Dionysia what she had meant and now Rushden would barrow her back to Baynards until the next time he felt like taking her down from the shelf to be revalued—or discarded. Pitted millstone! she thought angrily as Rushden came towards her, reveling in the power in her husband's mien and lordly bearing. How dared Dionysia be so insolent? Pique, no doubt, because Rushden had not dirtied his knees slavishly with all the rest.

"Heloise?" Her husband's silver eyes smiled down into hers, the question a command to leave. She would miss these squirings and jaunts, his hand in the small of her back, the freedom in his company, the friend looking out for her safety.

"I shall see you soon, I expect, sister," she exclaimed, setting her hand in Rushden's with a sunshine smile. When she looked round, she discovered Dionysia had gone.

Rushden was leading her not to the outer courtyard but past the hedge that lay beyond the mede to a bench within a honey-suckled arbor. She wondered painfully what he might have to say. Had he spoken with Stillington about the annulment?

Miles was thinking how Heloise's ethereal quality reduced her sister to a mere spangled creature. The princess-elegance of her damask, the covered curves, firm and young, pleased him more than the displayed flesh, the opulent breasts.

"This garden is one of London's treasures." Miles made himself comfortable on the wooden seat, and set an ankle across his knee, appraising his wife as though she were a concubine sent for selection. He patted the seat and she sat down, wriggling her toes out from beneath her hem, suddenly shy and maidenly.

"I have spoken with Stillington, just as you have."

So this was the reckoning, thought Heloise. A cock robin and his more reserved mistress landed hopefully in front of her.

"How do you see . . ." No, not *see*. With Heloise, Miles must make it doubly clear. "How do you desire your future, Heloise?"

Tossing her veil back, she answered uneasily: "Wishing is one thing—" Her unspoken words were bitten back as he shifted to face her. She was terrified of Dokett but she did not dare raise her fears again. How could a man as self-assured as Rushden come close to understanding?

"Tell me."

As if uncomfortable at his closeness, she stood up abruptly. Miles watched her step into the dappled shade, and waited as she searched for words to light her future.

"How can I answer you?" Heloise replied. "After the annulment, unless I chose to shut myself away from this world within a holy order, another husband will be found for me. And . . . and he will want to blow the candle out at night so he cannot see my hair and he will take care not to wake beside me lest he hear my dreams in the morning." Slender arms rose to cradle her heart; her hands fled to the taffeta refuge of her sleeves. What was the use of this? She had no more say in her destiny than Traveller. "I do not think of myself as a beast to be sold at market, and yet it is so, save that marriage bargaining is more discreet and done out of the common hearing. If women—" She faltered.

Her answer devastated Miles, bombarded the battlements he had built two years ago. He could not let Heloise go. No! Not to some cur who would not protect her nor to the torture either. He no longer minded her silver hair. He liked it, liked her being different. He not only wanted to savor the candlelight shining in her eyes, he wanted to wake beside her and feel her hair like gossamer across his pillow, touching his cheek.

"Go on," he prompted huskily. *"If women . . ."*

Heloise, seeing the midnight head tilted, his mouth stern, was astonished that he was still listening. "What use to continue, sir? Must I be meek to be a woman? I fear you mock me by even asking me to dare to dream." As if she expected him to argue, she hesitated, then, emboldened by his silence, continued wryly, "Even if the queen was esteemed as much as my lord of Gloucester, you still would not accept her as regent, would you, because of her gender? It would be setting a perilous precedent." He nodded, and as if she feared her time was run out, she shook her head with a little shrug. "Even a queen has no say in her future. Anyway," she whispered and sank down defeated upon the bench, her head back, "there is my answer."

"That is no answer, changeling. I thought for once that I had asked the right question."

"Asking does not change things."

"Then it would be a waste of breath to argue with you, Heloise." He sat forward, leaning his elbows on his knees. "Besides, changing the way the world thinks may take centuries and we have but a little lifetime." As if to underscore his thoughts, the bells began to ring the new hour in. He stood and, staring at the honeysuckle with its adoring bees, redirected his life. This woman, of all the women he had made love to, needed his name and protection against a hostile world. She had not gone to Brecknock to force him to acknowledge her, she had fled to him out of desperation. Nor had she demanded aught save friendship. Maybe that was all she wanted. "You do have a choice, Heloise."

Aware of her stillness, her breath held as if she feared more words from him might snatch back the gift, Miles waited a few heartbeats and then could no longer resist turning for her reply. She was gazing at him as if he had just rid her of a crutch. Gentler now, her eyes were cleared of the brief glaze of tears, but her chin rose questioningly.

"Are you saying that I can choose whether to stay wed to you, that it is for *me* to decide?" Incredulity rendered her as sweet faced as a surprised kitten.

"Upon my very soul."

Heloise bit her lip. Was this out of contrariness or charity? Oh, he thought himself magnanimous, did he? A choice? When she was frightened to her very soul that pious Gloucester would not save her from Dokett's determination to break her?

If I wrap a silver bell about your neck, sir cat, and send you forth, there may come another cat in your place.

Rushden was waiting, fingers plucking at his tight cuff, the dark lashes moving patiently. His tarnished face pleased her; the black hair and steel eyes that had almost stolen her courage on the tourney field now robbed her of breath. Did she have a choice? Her destiny lay with him. The dream of him at Yuletide had told her so and yet here was no gentle husband. When he was in good humor her heart danced with happiness, but there were dark rivers running in him that she wondered if she had courage to cross. Was it the Ballaster wealth that was making Myfannwy weigh too light now in his balance?

She would not make it easy; aloud she answered, "If it content you, sir, I had lief our marriage stand."

His chin rose with his usual touch of arrogance, or conquest, maybe, but if he was astonished or pleased, he gave no sign. She made no curtsy on her part to tenderize the decision, no obeisance of thanks, but took her own cue from his iron control.

"My hand upon the bargain then." He set his heel to the ground. His expression kindled to a sagacious smile, losing its edge of laziness.

No words of love then. With fingers that trembled as they touched, Heloise placed her hand in his. He raised it, firmly held, to his lips and she read the satisfaction in his eyes and a growing heat. What had she done? Was this wise? "Ohhhhh!"

Strong arms whirled her up into the air and spun her round. Laughing up at her, Miles Rushden snatched her soul. This *was* right. It might be for the wrong reasons but it was meant. He had chosen her! He had actually chosen her!

Held so, she beamed down at him with love, all her fears stashed away at last like a forgotten coffer.

"You should have had trinkets and poems, and a nosegay on your pillow."

"But I have a psaltery." Her fists crushed the velvet gathers of his sleeves. "Oh!" A rosebriar snagged the airborne damask, and her husband—yes, husband—harnessed, slid her slowly down his stomacher, his body hardening as he held her.

"Hungry?" he asked, smiling like a successful night thief, and kissed her with such tenderness that she could have wept with joy.

"Oh, always," she whispered, opening her lips to him and cuddling him tightly lest he turn to vapor and vanish from her arms. "Only the household officers at Baynards may breakfast."

"Yes, you feel . . ." His hands gave ardent testimony. "Bird frail to me. But that shall be remedied right fast." His hand slid across her belly with proprietary freedom. "A babe beneath your girdle, hmm."

Heloise gasped, catapulted from maid to wife. He was laughing at her blushes as he stooped to free her from the rosebush. Then he stilled—voices, Buckingham's. *No,* she pleaded, *no, not now.*

"Quickly." Her lord's hand took hers. "Can you run, changeling?"

Yes! Oh yes! They sped along the path, hurtled behind a hawthorn where he kissed her again before he peered out along the path. "This way! Now!" Along the waist-high trellis they slunk low like assassins, out into the stable yard where the stable boys held Traveller and Cloud waiting side by side like faery steeds. Rushden lifted Heloise onto the sidesaddle and swiftly paid off their grooms with ale money.

He took the leading rein of Cloud along Threadneedle Street, for his lady seemed quite unable to take charge, utterly and wondrously bewildered that she had surrendered herself to his good lordship.

Busy Cheapside, loud with the shouts of apprentices and strolling vendors, made conversation, like Heaven, an impossibility. Heloise had taken back Cloud's reins, letting the mare drink from a trough at West Cheap before they battled through the throng. Miles was exuberant as any bridegroom untroubled by guests and family, but the lady suddenly was brewing with something he could not fathom.

"Where are we going?" she asked uneasily as they turned southeast towards Queenhithe. Did she fear he might immure her somewhere other than Baynards?

"To feast, lady knight. Mayhap hen in pastry will put you in good cheer."

"And then what?" she asked, cynicism weighing every syllable.

"And then I think there should be no turning back."

Nineteen

 Heloise nearly toppled from the saddle in shock. "You mean b-bed me?"

She had not meant to speak her thoughts aloud. Her lawful owner cast her a smoldering sidelong glance that told her it was exactly what he meant. In fact he looked tempted to tumble her in the nearest garden. His answer, however, was disconcertingly nonchalant: "Well, it is the final way of settling things."

Heloise had trouble swallowing, let alone finding an answer. "I—I suppose it is," she said huskily, growing hot and cold at the prospect of being expected to perform a wife's duty at long last. She was glad of his silence, suspicious that he was amused at hers.

Inn servants were grabbing at their stirrups, squabbling for their patronage. She was proud of Rushden's wisdom in selecting a hostelry where the servants were neither sneering nor slack. They were made comfortable at a board so clean that even the most careful housewife would have approved it, and the best mead was set before Heloise as though she were a princess. Soon there were more platters than words between them, and while trying not to devour the lady that might salve his growing appetite, Miles ate little.

"Steady," he warned with husbandly concern. "Be not so ravenous, my Lady Rushden, they will not take your platter away."

"I do not know where my next meal is coming from," she answered truthfully.

"Yes, you do. You think I am still playing games with you?" His hand covered hers reassuringly upon the table, and he called for more mead to fill her goblet. "Why are you suddenly so afraid, changeling? It was your choice to accept the cup, but do not see me as the spider at the bottom."

"It is not that." Foolishly Heloise felt like crying but forced back the tears, dismayed and happy in the same breath, desiring the comfort of his arms and yet knowing he was still fathoms deep for her. How could she tell him she wanted him to honor the marriage because he loved her?

"Then be thankful." He gave her a long, slow smile.

"I am not sure yet." It was said with the heat staining her cheeks, but she looked more like a wild creature about to bolt if he touched her.

"Whether to be thankful?" Miles did not mind her honesty; rather he preferred it that way and it was timely, for he too had truths that needed to be stirred and set before her. "I warn you, do not expect too much from me." His seriousness evaporated as he saw astonishment blossom in her eyes. "No, sweet shrew, I do not mean that," he said, laughing, and then grew solemn again, and watched God's gift of merriment still in her, too, as she waited. "There are things to be said."

Heloise held her breath, silent as a bird in a hedgerow sensing the storm approach. She guessed what he was going to say, but not the bruising manner of it, for the phrases tumbled past her rehearsed and far too fast; emotionless, though the hurt was there. "I think you should know that I have been married before. I was twenty. My first wife, Sioned, was sixteen. It was, of course, arranged by our families, but we were very happy together. Then, two years ago, there was a visitation of the pestilence in Dorset. Phillip, my little son, was taken. He . . . oh, Christ, Heloise!" Pain choked his voice. "He—he was only three years old. And . . . and Sioned died next day."

So that was it. His love had been spent and there was nothing in his purse for her. Heloise leaned away slowly, as if his sorrow was a tide washing her back upon a lonely shore, and searched the air about his head for a futile reply to such a joyless confession. "Do you mean she is still with you? I do not sense that." Then, realizing her dreadful mistake in telling him so, she dared not look across at him, aware he had curled his right hand into a tight fist upon the table lest he cross himself.

"Christ be merciful," he whispered, his grey eyes hostile. "Never tell me that you can see the dead."

"No, no," Heloise lied swiftly, and searched for words that he would not stumble from, "but I have an . . . an awareness . . . of people's sorrow. Is she still with you?"

His answer was a quiet sigh. "No." Strong fingers rose to shield his anguished face. "I blame myself. Perhaps if I had been with her . . ."

Heloise, remembering the terrible vision of his suffering, reached out a comforting hand to touch his wrist. Rushden's skin was warm, dependable, beneath her fingertips. "But is it not vanity for you to take responsibility for a decision that was God's alone?" It was risky counsel; he might hate her for that insult.

"Perhaps." Miles drew back, letting his hands slide down to his lips with a deep sigh. He was almost afraid to treasure Heloise, afraid that God would curse him a second time. As if she had read his mind with damnable insight, she said:

"But Lady Myfannwy. You agreed to her."

The shrug was apologetic. "Wide hips," he answered and then regretted his crassness. "Oh, be fair, Heloise, if love arises between a married pair, it is after the wedding, rarely before. With Myfannwy, it would have been a trencher marriage, without piquancy. You cannot say that our friendship lacks that." Friendship! So he did not want to become afflicted with love. "There is something else you should understand."

"Your duty to the duke."

"Of course, duty—and friendship," he admitted, glad she had the wit to perceive it. "My family have served the Staffords through good and bad times. You must realize, I have been waiting years for the planets to fall into line and, yes, I mean to ride to the stars on Harry's back, madam, and I warn you of that now."

A warning certainly, thought Heloise. So she was merely

fourth in line, after Sioned, his son, and Buckingham. Or did Traveller have precedence over her as well?

"And if your friend stumbles, and brings you down?"

"It will be still worth the risk." An unwelcome line marred his smile. "What, are you already imagining yourself the widow of an attainted traitor?"

"Yes, I have to consider that." If his cutting honesty could draw blood, so could hers.

"Heloise," Miles cautioned her, his chivalry wearing thin. The bench scraped harshly on the flagstones as he rose. "I am not a green youth." But he could see that she spoke out of present fear, that the bright courage which he so admired had almost deserted her. "Do you want a husband or not, changeling? They come in all shapes and sizes. This one has several endorsements attached to the parchment and you have read them now." He stretched out a hand for hers. "This is not a decision that either of us have made lightly. Nor should it be so." Her hand trembled and he clasped it firmly. "Believe me, we should make this irrevocable." He was going to lay his skills of lovemaking at her feet like a gift. This was not going to be a fumbling meeting of flesh but a slow dance of pleasure. Awakening his sorceress to a magic that was as old as Paradise would require patience and tenderness.

Heloise felt like a woodland creature watching the hunter inch his way towards her. *Make it irrevocable.* When no words of love had been spoken? *Irrevocable.* The word was sinister. Instinctively her fingers struggled for freedom. "I am not sure any longer." They should have done this with Gloucester's blessing, not behind his back.

Across the board between them, Rushden's jaw slackened. "But you said this was your wish also. Be grateful, madam, in God's name! You have a husband who desires you. Come!" His hold tightened, urging her to her feet. His intense gaze was unrelenting—waiting, predatory.

It dawned upon her addled mind like a mystic revelation that he was half-turned towards the stairs, that a bedchamber was spoken for. That the necessary act of consummation was not to be tonight but now! Now in the daylight.

Outwitted at last, Heloise was into deep water, her magic useless. His mind was made up. He wanted her. The thought that he would intimately enter her body ripened her, made her womb quiver in readiness, and she shivered at the incredible sensations that were throbbing through her body and forcing her powers of reasoning into abeyance.

This was a different Miles Rushden. A bridegroom. Doublet half open, shirt neck loosened, this was the stranger that she had known at Bramley and feared: his black hair wild, his mouth mocking and determined, a man of power and consequence who had her breathless and trembling. But this must be a marriage of equals. He needed to learn that now, else he never would.

"No!" She stared down at the crumbs scattering the grainy wood, biting her lip, frightened of her rebelliousness, but she was not a horse to be led into the stable and mounted. "I went to Brecknock because I had nowhere else to go and . . ."

"Go on." He seemed to be circling like a hawk.

Heloise's fears bred fast. St. Catherine protect her and grant her body's defenses could safely prove she was a virgin! She was afraid of tyranny—of finally becoming this man's property like her mother and Matillis had been her father's. "If you think I am going to lie down for you obligingly, the moment you snap your fingers and whistle, then . . ."

"Oh, but you shall." Strong arms came from behind her to clasp her elbows and raise her. Her heart fluttered like a frantic moth as she felt his body hard against her, his breath stirring her veil. "And believe me, I shall do more than whistle, lady."

His little witch was shaking as Miles drew her up the stairs, his arm about her waist. This was the last thing he had expected; his level-headed Heloise behaving like a skittish bride. The bedchamber did not help but where else could he have taken her?

At least it was clean and spacious. Apart from a screen that hid a corner of the sunlit, whitewashed room, the bed, huge enough to sleep half a dozen travelers, took up the entire space. Heloise gasped audibly. Miles gently pushed her over the threshold and kicked the door to behind him lest the inn servants carried the gossip over the entire city. It was not ideal, he admitted with wry amusement at his predicament, but give a mare time to balk at a fence and she will not take it.

"I assumed you would not want another wedding feast and a public unrobing." He lifted off his silver collar lest the intermeshing rings bruise her, unlooped the last pearl buttons of his doublet, and shrugged his gathered shirtsleeves loose. Drawing her gently towards him, he kissed her. The lady began to thaw.

"I promise you I can be deft as any servant," he murmured against her mouth and then cursed inwardly as he tried to ease free the inner wire of her headdress so he might uncoil Heloise's moonlight hair from beneath her cap. It was she who finished the task, which did not appease her uncertain temper. Miles had not tamed his little rebel yet.

"What if I had wanted an annulment, sir?" she protested as his hands fell to mold the curves that had tantalized him all through their repast. He eased away the triangle of black satin that covered her from cleavage to her slender, high waist. She was as exquisite as he had remembered her from Bramley. The sable, sloping collar of her overgown erotically half-concealed her coral-tipped breasts and he pushed back the fabric, feasting his gaze, delighting in the knowledge that this wondrous pleasure garden belonged to him, to wander where he willed. "An annulment?" he answered dazedly. "It is too late for that, believe me." She was his shapeshifter, the she-knight who had fought him. He needed her to know that she was his. His fingers slid to where touching had been denied him and watched with the satisfaction of a skilled journeyman as her lips parted in pleasure more than protest. "So you like that."

"Well enough."

"You shrewcat, you do." Yes, she did.

He unfastened her platelet belt, ignoring the hands that shyly sought to prevent him. Her outer robe was swiftly lifted.

"Sir, I wish you would wait until darkness and spare my modesty." Heloise's voice was muffled within the damask's depths. She emerged tousled and defiant, but this was a very determined bridegroom she was dealing with and there was a wicked, sensual glitter in his admiring gaze.

"And spoil my pleasure?" Outrageous man, he was making her feel as though she were naked already. She retreated, clutching the gown in front of her until the back of her thighs met the bed.

"Well, what of my pleasure, sir?"

The gown was twitched from her hands and flung aside. "You will find, my delight, that I have sufficient experience to please both of us. I thought you wanted this, *cariad.*" The intensity of his clouded gaze was working a magic that she could not resist. Yes, she wanted him very much, Heloise decided. "Turn, my armored angel." She felt the hardness of him through her thin underskirt. Relentless fingers were freeing her of the chemise, peeling the tight sleeves from her wrists.

"You are perfection, you know that? Beautiful beyond most men's imaginings." His words were soft breath caressing her cheek. Her body willingly arched against his shoulder as skillful hands slid slowly down her in persuasive adoration. An unassuaged hunger flooded Heloise's body between breast and thigh.

Miles lifted aside the veil of her hair and kissed her shoulder. Why had he been a fool to delay tasting her delights? "Admit you have kept me hungering for you, my sorceress, ever since you lured me to your orchard, punishing me night after night."

"Can you not understand"—she gestured helplessly, wriggling around to face him—"what I want from you?"

"You think too much, my darling." Rushden tipped her face up. His eyes were darker than she had ever seen them, ruthless as an enemy's. If she kept her arms defiantly at her sides, thought Heloise, regretting her inexperience in bedchamber jousting, perhaps he would listen, but she had no defense from his lips. His mouth came firmly down on hers, demanding and taking, while his hands wandered, testing, teasing, lighting fires that burned and melted. "Why do you not trust me to be gentle with you?" he asked, setting his hands beneath her arms and lifting her onto the bed.

"Because . . . Oh!" She needed more than adoration, more than the worship of his lips.

With strong hands upon her forearms, he rolled sideways. Heloise found herself straddling him, his aroused body hard beneath her lawn underskirt, her hands splaying the proud symmetry of shining skin and curling hair where his shirt had fallen away.

Further knavery suffused his handsome face as she blushed above his appreciative gaze. His hands, curved in support beneath her elbows, shook her teasingly. "Lady Rushden, you do understand what we are supposed to do in order to consummate this marriage?"

The question distracted her from her mental battle. Heloise moistened her lips consideringly with sudden confidence—she rather liked having him beneath her—and received a curl of lip from him. So he thought her an ignoramus, did he? Well, she had seen stallions mounting mares. She knew he would have to approach her from the back so he was definitely not dangerous or threatening at the moment. In fact it was delicious to have him at her mercy and she wriggled herself into a more comfortable position, disregarding his deep, ecstatic growl. And one of them had to retain common sense.

"I—I think whatever is necessary, sir," she declared, exploratively drawing a finger down through the silky pelt of his breast, "we should do it twice to be sure. So that there is absolutely no confusion afterwards."

"God ha' mercy!" He bucked, laughing heartily. Thrown off balance, Heloise tumbled forward onto her forearms across his chest, almost drowning him in her hair.

"Do you think you can manage to call me Miles?" he asked, tenderness and desire deepening his smile.

"Hmm." She tilted her head and mischievously twisted a black lock of his hair about her finger, then she traced the line of his lips; but the passion in his eyes belied his calm.

"Heloise," he said hoarsely, "I hope I have not tethered my future to a tease. I would very much appreciate it if you kissed me."

"Like this, *Miles*?"

"Promising," he murmured against her mouth and, with a swift thrust, had her on her back again. She was sweetly parting her lips to him, threading her fingers through his hair. "Do you know what you do to me, Heloise?" His voice was a soft, ragged whisper. "One by one, all my rational thoughts have succumbed to a delicious, divine aching that only you can satisfy." His experienced hand reached beneath her skirt and drew down her stockings. The lady's breath grew swifter still as his fingers worked their magic between her thighs. He relished her astonishment, enjoyed watching the dark centers of her eyes widen with yearning. "The *tylwyth teg*," he lied as he efficiently dispensed with her undergown, "believe that a bride who is a changeling must be bedded in the afternoon lest she disappear by twilight. That is why we could not wait until tonight."

"That cannot be true," she protested.

"Having slept in several faery rings, I can assure you it is common gossip in such circles."

With a ripple of laughter, Heloise clouted him, and then she realized that he had utterly demolished her shyness and blushed all over.

A faery maiden with silver hair. Her modesty pleased Miles, reassured him that it was not witchcraft that had him hot for her. Once she learned that lovemaking was not sinful, she would know how to touch him also. He swung his feet to the ground and loosened the laces of his gypon—that would be her task another time—and pushed it down with his hose and under-drawers so he might step free.

Upon his soul, what mischief now? Looking round he saw that Heloise had rolled away from him onto all fours and crouched like a wildcat, her enchantress's hair cascading down her shoulders. Her firm pointed breasts were driving him to madness.

"Why is it that you suddenly find my merchant blood acceptable? Is it because I have the lion's share of his estate?"

With an effort, he tried to stay sane. "No," he exclaimed. Battling his shirt, he flung it from him. "I find *you* acceptable."

The virgin in her was too disconcerted at his sudden nakedness to argue more. As she glanced swiftly away, her sweet body blushing, he sprang onto the bed and snared her wrists.

"So what is it to be, madam? Do you want a marriage between us or not?"

What was he doing wrong? He was only human, for God's sake. He had hoped to light a fire of passion in her that would burn all her doubts, but the fey in her was still embattled, still fighting to keep control. Or was it that she wanted him as a friend but not a lover? Perhaps he was wrong to think that she could be attracted to him.

"Heloise. Is it my appearance?" His voice gentled and he knelt, holding her up so that she faced him, her balance dependent on his strength. "Changeling, look at me." Her gaze fell upon his pitted face. "Heloise Ballaster, will you have me as your lord and husband and plight me your troth?" Slowly she nodded. But he needed more. "Truly, lady? For if you find me repugnant, by the saints, you must tell me now and we shall pretend this never happened."

"How could you think so?" Her fingertips smoothed his cheekbone with great tenderness. "I swear I would not wish you otherwise in any way."

"Then God's blessing on us." He drew her right hand close and kissed it. Then he drew the ring she had returned from his hand and set it upon her finger. "For I hereby take you as my wife, for better and for worse, to have and to hold until the end of my life." The tension left her face. As she calmed, he steadied her shoulders within the frames of his hands, thankful that God had shown him the right way, grateful that the offering of words had cleansed away the falseness of their winter ceremony.

"Amen," she whispered and lifted her other palm to his cheek.

"So, Lady Rushden?" He waited.

Her soft laughter filled the kissing distance between them and chased away the demons. "So, my newly married lord, whistle!"

Twenty

There was something akin to treason about being un-clothed, Heloise decided. The May sun was filling the room with soporific warmth as they lay across the middle of the huge bed face to face, but outside the window, a hungry thrush beat a snail against a branch. Miles Rushden, arms folded, studied her as she lay with her chin upon her crossed wrists. With consideration and intelligence, with sensitivity of touch and patience, he had led her into a realm beyond her imagining.

"This is wondrously sinful." She drew a nameless map with her nail upon the sheet and could not resist teasing: "Buckingham may be running amok."

"He will when he hears of this." Rushden ran his finger along her swollen lips, amused at her growing confidence.

"Yes, I know." Blushing, she lowered her head so that her hair veiled her.

He pulled aside the silvery curtain. "The first time is hardest of all. There is much to accommodate."

Her lips quivered, her impish glance interbred with ruefulness. "Yes."

"She-devil!"

"And what now? Am I to be returned to Baynards' gatehouse like a borrowed horse, bruised and ridden?"

"Crumpled certainly. Perhaps that might be best, unless you would like to share a bed with me *and* de la Bere."

"I thought you were going to suggest dear Harry for a moment. Perhaps we can invite him, too." She rolled over, gleeful at teasing him, and then, feeling his lusty gaze, swiftly rolled back to hide her womanly parts.

Had Cleopatra looked so when Caesar rolled her from the carpet? Miles laughed and generously dragged his gaze away from the beautiful valleys and rises that now belonged to him. It was tempting to make love to her yet again but he remembered his first wife had suffered the soreness that affects new brides. Wiser now, more controlled, more understanding, he would not make the same mistake with Heloise.

"I should like Bishop Stillington's blessing and we must inform her grace of York."

"It shall be done."

"And now you may tell me about the loan." The sudden question winded him, as she had known it would. Heloise watched him roll from the bed, his back a surly breadth of angered manliness.

His shirt briefly muffled an answer. "There are hundreds of loans being arranged this day in London. Which one are we talking about?" He tugged on his black hose and stood up to fasten his points.

"The loan my father promised to someone in Northampton."

Under control, he studied her across his shoulder. "There was none made to me, I promise you."

"No, to Gloucester, I believe. My sister spoke of it."

"Your sister is a brazen, interfering piece." He disappeared beneath the level of the bed and her much-creased gown, followed by her sorry headdress, hurtled up. She gasped as he bowled her over backwards on the coverlet, shackling her wrists beside her head. "My sword is not for sale, nightingale." His lower lip roughed hers.

> A beauty white as whalles bone,
> A pearl shod in goodly gold,
> A turtle dove my herte desires
> The joy of hir . . .

"Forget the past." The manacles broke and he gathered her to him. "Lady knight, the only loan I took out was you."

*   *   *

HER NEW LORD TOOK HER TO THE RED ROSE FOR SUPPER AND announcements. Buckingham, to Heloise's relief, was dining at Lord Howard's. Miles, merry with ale after their repast in the hall, led her up into the duke's solar and flung open the casement to let in the western sun. The seven o'clock bells rang out across the city.

"You know Gloucester better than I," he murmured, taking a piece of clean parchment from a shelf. "I should like to write to him out of courtesy and tell him that he has one ward less. Is that a wise notion? Or do your instincts suggest he will clap me in the Tower?"

Heloise beamed. "He has more important matters than us."

"You think so?" He looked up from sharpening a quill, disarming her with a wicked grin. "And now, Lady Rushden, you need entertainment." He seated her upon the settle that backed the hearth in summer fashion, lifted a gilded book onto the small table before her, and unlocked the clasps.

Running her fingers across Buckingham's broad signature below the handsome illuminated title, *De Propietatibus Rerum,* Heloise felt not the duke's delight in such a treasure but his envy of the dead author, Bartholomew. Perturbed, she turned the pages distractedly, preferring to watch her husband as he at last leaned forward to write in swift, decisive strokes.

"There," he said eventually, jabbing a Rushden serpent into the sealing wax. "Signed and sealed, like us."

"Buckingham will not be pleased." She was not referring to her perusal of Harry's book.

"Nor will I if he says aught to distress you." Miles wandered across to the window, where he made himself comfortable, his back against the casement and a boot upon the sill, and stared unseeing across the thatched roofs; straw turning to gold beneath the rose-soused, blowsy clouds. "Today may have changed the course of the river," he murmured, wondering if Stillington had divulged his secret to Gloucester, "and there may be a babe to grow beneath your girdle, mistress mine."

"You would be pleased? Truly?"

His grin was roguish. "Why should I not? I can see you like a little fluffed-up wren, all belly." Before she could land a fist on him, he had her by the elbows, lifting her off the tips of her toes. "Faith! Not much heavier than thistledown." Laughing, he held her back from his shins. "Are there no bones in you?"

"I cannot possibly hold a conversation with you suspending me in midair."

"That is because between the elements of earth and air I have the greater power than yours, lady sorceress. And between the sheets."

"His grace may come in at any minute." Heloise's nerves were jangling like folly bells—this was the duke's demesne and they were traitors.

"Let him." Miles slid her down the length of him back to the floor and his strong fingers stroked down her arms and fastened her fists behind her back. His mouth teased hers before he freed her. "We never shared a trothcup, you and I." Selecting a key from his belt, he unlocked the catch of Harry's ambry and let down its door to make a shelf. "Choose what you will."

The muster of lidded goblets, brought up from Brecknock, twinkled at her in the fading light: bloodred Venetian glasses, a Russian pewter with a bear entwined about its stem, an ancient horn set in a pattern of golden hounds, a silver fluted cup of Persian craftsmanship, and a dozen more. Recklessly, to test him, she pointed to a jeweled mazer. Without a comment, he set aside the lid with its golden pinnacle and picked up the wine flagon from the small table. Like a high priest, he poured sufficient in, studying her solemnly over it as if he had not yet fathomed her. The amber liquid quivered against its encircled reflection as he set his hands over hers, forcing her fingers to find comfort in the gilded valleys between the cabochoned gems.

"Still having doubts, Heloise? Until death sever us?"

"No, I am sure," she answered huskily and felt the great cup lifted for her to taste. The touch of lips to wine at this instant was now a commitment, a sacrament between them. She urged it towards him. He drank, watching her with intensity over the rim of gold, and then set the mazer back upon the board and drew her across the moat of air once more into the bailey of his arms.

"It will take more time," he warned, setting his forefinger beneath her chin and tilting her heart-shaped face like a mirror.

"I know it." Better to sup with Miles Rushden than any other, though words of love should have garnished the repast. She surrendered this time as his lips, tasting of mead, came down to claim her and shyly crept her hands up the velvet of his doublet to knot behind his neck, and feel his hair tickling her wrists.

"Why, Heloise." The silver look was roguish. "How very compliant you are."

"I am only humoring you," she teased.

"By God, what goes on here?" Harry, glinting with gold thread, too ruddy with wine, came through the doorway and halted, swaying somewhat with drink slopping his soul. Heloise broke away, straightening her skirts.

The duke was not looking at her. "Miles?"

Miles's common sense lurched. Within the loyal speechwriter, drinking companion, and official sycophant—no, that office had fallen upon Nandik—something rebelled. The resentment in Harry's face, the duke's blatant irritation at seeing him with Heloise in his arms, jarred. He might revolve around the Buckingham sun but he had acquired a moon of his own now.

"Have you met my wife, Heloise Ballaster?" It was brittle, cruel, not how he had planned to break the tidings. Beside him, his freshly bedded wife sank into a curtsy.

Not a ducal muscle twitched in the handsome face. It was not politic to see in the third most powerful man in England a stunned fish out of its element, but for that moment Miles did not care a jot. *My wife.* It sounded right, righter than ever before.

"If you say so." Harry dumped a leather bottle upon the table and, pulling off his cream gloves, dropped them beside the cup.

That did not escape him either. Heloise rose from her obeisance but he ignored her. "I may be in my right wits come dawn, Rushden, but you, unfortunately, will still be a married man. Here!" The words were bitter as he pushed the mazer at him. "Take it as a wedding gift."

Miles held his gaze, tears suddenly threatening to unman him. This was not how it should be. Harry had deserved better of him. "I do not want to do that."

"Nevertheless, it is yours. Take it! Tomorrow you will perhaps explain why you disappeared without leave." He stood back curtly so their way to the door was free.

Miles bowed. "Come, madam."

But Heloise lingered. "The demoiselle at Crosby Place," she began. "I think you should know that—"

Buckingham stretched and yawned. "Do they all have addled wits where your wife comes from or is it an effect of making crossbows?"

"She was not a gardener but—" Heloise continued stubbornly.

"We shall cross that bridge if need be, madam," cut in Miles. Outside the door he stopped and looked at her sad face, his heart troubled. "I am sorry." Sincere, yes, but she understood that she was an interloper.

"He needs you. Make your peace."

"Then wait for me in the solar. I shall see you back to Baynards before curfew." Closing the door behind him, Miles leaned against it. This was not how it should be.

Harry was sitting at his small table, biting his thumb. "Go away and enjoy her!"

"I can explain if you will listen."

"I do not feel like listening." With a sneer, he knuckled the goblet and the flagon aside as though both stank of pestilence.

His feelings visored, Miles picked up the leather bottle, broke the seal, and took a swig. "Not bad. Your taste has surprisingly improved since you acquired Wales." The jest failed but he shoved the bottle at Harry's chest. With a defiant sniff, the duke drank, wiping his mouth with his wrist. "What ails you, *your grace?* You have thriving sons and Gloucester has given you a principality to scrape your boots on—more power than you know what to do with, for God's sake—so what have I done wrong?"

The corners of the ducal mouth were down like a dog's that had been denied a bone. "You hid the truth away from me at Brecknock, God damn you, letting her loose on my son, and now you have done it again, deceived me."

"Why should you complain? Ned adores her and he has learned how to say please and thank you at long last."

Fingernails nakired the table menacingly. "Do not goad me, Miles."

"Why not? I was wed to her at swordpoint. It simplifies matters if I keep her and I am sure you will find someone else suitable for Myfannwy."

"Christ, Miles. You knew that alliance was important." Harry violently struck the mazer from the table.

"Then you wish me to find good lordship elsewhere?" A violence hung upon each word.

"All right, I apologize," Harry snarled, blinking sullenly at the paneled ceiling. "Go and tumble the Ballaster girl. But do not forget she is a filly from Gloucester's stable and may have deeper loyalties branded into her hide."

Miles swore, flung the bottle down, and stormed towards the door. "So be it, my lord." God ha' mercy, why did Harry have to shove him down a staircase of insults? Heloise was Lady Rushden now and deserved some respect.

"No! *Miles!*" The duke recanted and struggled to his feet, his expression maudlin. "By our sweet Christ, I was looking forward to chewing today's cud and enjoying a drink with you but no matter." He slumped back down at the table. "You should have left me to die on Pen-y-Fan, Miles."

So it was not just the drink afflicting him. Miles let go the latch. "I thought you had the salacious Nandik to light your candles now."

"Pah!" Harry winced and, glancing sideways, cheered a little, his voice strengthening. "Why did you not tell me you had changed your mind about Mistress Ballaster? I deserved that of you at least."

It was an effort to find the real truth in his own maze of logic. "Because she needs my protection against fools like Dokett. And do not tell me I am bewitched!"

Harry swallowed, plucking at his gloves. "Are you lunatic with lust then? Or debilitated by love? I do not know how that feels. Tell me!" Plantagenet's fingers manacled Miles's sleeve and were stonily unpeeled. "What, no answer, damn your soul! No better than wine, women are," Harry sneered venomously. "Bodies bought with baubles. I am envious, can you not see that? I wish to Heaven I had a woman I cared for."

Miles did not have one jot of patience tonight to lard Harry's self-esteem. "I will bid you good night. Tomorrow—"

"A piss upon tomorrow!"

"So Stillington has divulged nothing?"

"No, Devil take it! Gloucester did not even visit him."

Miles's smile was tight. "And if I attend the prince's court, smell out the gossip, and invite Catesby to dine?"

"Oh yes, most excellent." Harry rallied. "That will needle Hastings no end."

"And in return . . . you will apologize to my wife."

The duke pulled a sour face. "Lord, if I must." He rose and held out his arms to Miles. "*Pax vobiscum.* But promise me you will not go panting after her like a dog on heat the whole time, not now when we have our shoulders to the wheel."

"I know my duty."

"I just hope that your witch knows hers."

HOW DID ONE ENTERTAIN A BISHOP? HELOISE WAS TRYING HER best the next day. *Piers the Plowman* was not to her taste—too much labored wisdom, but one could not read a French romance or a list of herbal remedies to a bishop.

> *Then there ran a rout of rats, as it were,*
> *And small mice with them, more than a thousand,*
> *And they came to hold council for their common profit;*
> *For a cat of a court came whenever he liked*
> *And pounced on them easily and caught them at will.*

God's rood, she had put Stillington to sleep. With a sigh, she rose from her footstool at the bishop's feet and tucked a fur around the old man, knowing he was prone to aching joints. June had turned fickle, the early sun had left the chamber, and a dull day stretched tediously ahead.

Playing nursemaid to a creaky bishop was not her notion of being a married woman. She needed her own demesne to bustle in and a husband who did not spread himself like liver paste, but at least she was fully a *de jure* wife and in a state of grace. After hearing Heloise's confession when she arrived back last night, Stillington had agreed that since the marriage was now consummated, Miles's betrothal with Myfannwy was void. This morning he had kindly consigned his decision to parchment—signed, witnessed by her grace of York and Father William, and endorsed by sealing wax. They also spooned prayers over her head about obedience, fertility, and other conjugal virtues. Thinking of which, she wondered whether Miles would find time today to spirit her off to another hired four-poster like a toy to take to bed.

A fanfare sounded down below in the courtyard. Heloise opened the window then ducked in swiftly, for it was Gloucester come with his entourage. God forbid he had come to chastise her. No, he must be calling on his mother, or maybe Stillington. With housewifely care, she quickly twitched the bed coverlet straight and turned to the bishop's chair to gently pat him awake.

And then her mind began to weave a cruel tapestry of Gloucester prostrate upon a bed weeping into his shirtsleeves like a lost child. Heloise recoiled with a gasp, trying to slam the shutter on the sight, only to look on helplessly as the duke raised his head, his expression the most haunted she had ever glimpsed on any man.

"My child, are you ill?" The bishop, awake now, was squeezing her hand.

"I . . ." Her mind still spinning like St. Catherine's wheel, she swallowed. "I—I think the lord protector is come to visit her grace."

"No." Stillington was alert now, smiling like a *crocodilus* with its mind on dinner. "*I* sent for him."

The sudden display of vanity was repulsive, like glimpsing a filthy shirt beneath a glistening cope. She should have guessed his tired exterior still nested a cunning brain—he had once been chancellor of England.

"D-did you, my lord bishop?"

"Yes, to offer him an apple from the Tree of Knowledge." The old man's smile was leavened unpleasantly by power.

"I—I want no part of this," Heloise protested, her instinct screaming withdrawal. The rapport with this wafer cleric, begun in Northampton, made her an accessory.

"My clever child, it is too late. His foot is already on the stair."

Gloucester was laughing as he followed his dark-robed mother into the antechamber to the sickroom. "Ah, Heloise, good morning to you, I have been hearing it was a cockatrice that abducted our worthy bishop."

"And yales and gryphons," exclaimed the Duchess of York, folding her hands upon her pectoral cross. "Not to mention Lord Rushden's son."

"Well, I am waiting." The duke folded his arms.

Waiting? Heloise, still dazed from the contrast between her imagining and the real Gloucester, rose from her curtsy and threw a puzzled glance at the bishop's door before realization dawned.

"Oh," she exclaimed, her cheeks starting to burn. "I . . . regret to say—"

"Regret already?" The fur-edged sleeves she was staring at shifted.

"No, I . . ." Why was Rushden not here to share the blame? "My most noble lord," she exclaimed, sinking to her knees. "It seemed the right thing to do."

"A politic answer," threw in the duchess dryly, "and there was tenacious Dr. Dokett hoping to make a nun of her."

"Mother, hush," muttered Gloucester, unknotting his arms to raise his badly behaved ward to her feet. "You would have been well advised to ask my permission, Heloise. Let us hope it was not just your fortune that Sir Miles was courting."

"It was *my* decision, my lord."

"Was it?" he exchanged a meaningful glance with his parent. "The only thing that acquits you and Rushden is that it is one less problem that needs resolving. Thank your husband for *tardily* informing me. How did my cousin Buckingham take the tidings or is he still in the dark?"

"Like an ill-tasting medicine, my lord."

"Indeed. So Harry's shadow can detach himself at times. Well, show me to the bishop, my lady Rushden. Mother?"

"No, I shall be downstairs, my darling. Shall you stay for dinner?"

He shook his head and turned to find Heloise stubbornly blocking his way.

"Please," she whispered, "do not go in, your grace."

"Why, is he contagious?"

"No, but . . ." With all her power, Heloise willed Richard of Gloucester to think again. He did, bronze lashes blinking, the cheerfulness sheathed, but curiosity can be as great a vice as all the other deadly sins. His gloved hand pressed her arm in reassurance. *Whatever this is, I can manage it,* his light brown eyes told her, *I need to know.* And he went in alone.

But he was like a beaten servant when he emerged, his straight shoulders slumped and his face— Dear God! Her vision! What secret had the bishop told him?

*   *   *

At Crosby Place that afternoon, Miles was restless, itching like beggar's scabs to know the outcome of his scheming with Harry. Something had happened; not only had Gloucester forsworn dinner on his return from Baynards, but he had spent an hour in swordplay, slashing at Huddleston, his combat partner, in the hopes of spending some of the pent-up misery that was so obvious in his face. Now instead of attending his inner council, his grace curtly dismissed everyone and disappeared into his sanctum, slamming the door.

It was left to Huddleston, sweaty from the swordplay, to fend off questions from Gloucester's other henchmen. "By Christ's blessed mercy, I do not know what gadfly has bitten him," he growled, mopping his brow, glancing down in irritation at Lord Lovell, who was making a tabor of the table where the morning's correspondence lay unanswered. "A cursed pity my lady duchess is not yet arrived to ferret out the cause."

"God's nails, what's the pother?" exclaimed Lord Howard, hugging his naval dispatches to his chest as he stood up. "He only went to a bishop's sickbed."

Huddleston, loosening his swordbelt, turned suspiciously towards Harry, and Miles, flanking the duke, found his face also reconnoitered. "Is there something about Stillington we should know, my lord of Buckingham? I hear you, too, have visited."

Knyvett cleared his throat. "Tell them, your grace; mayhap it is relevant."

Harry was as good as any holy day mummer. "It may be nothing, my lords, a sick man's ravings." His shoulders rose apologetically. "But Stillington believes the queen was trying to poison him."

"Who? *Gloucester?*" barked Lord Howard.

"No, Stillington. And that is all I can tell you. The bishop beseeched right desperately to speak with Gloucester and I merely played the messenger. They are old friends, the bishop

tells me. So"——he took up his gloves——"I shall leave you with
that conundrum and be off to Baynards."

Gloucester's good men and true were at a loss. They had been
heading happily towards the coronation like courtiers on a royal
barge; now the morrow seemed as hazardous as shooting London
Bridge.

Harry ran down the steps to the courtyard. "I think the hammer has struck the right anvil at last," he exclaimed to Miles and
Knyvett, stealthily veeing his two fingers in an Agincourt salute.
"We may yet have Gloucester as our king. That to the Woodvilles and their prince! Now get you to the Tower of London
both of you, talk to our agents there, and invite Catesby to supper
tonight. I have some unfinished business before I go to Baynards—I saw a rose I thought might do well at Thornbury."

"He seems to have developed a sudden enthusiasm for loiter-
ing in gardens," muttered Miles as they rode out of earshot.

"Always had an interest in plants." Sir William stroked an
earlobe thoughtfully. "Used to sit in the gardens at Westminster
and draw 'em when he was younger, until Lord Rivers made an
ass of him over it. Are you listening to me or not?"

"Definitely not. I was thinking we might take Heloise to see
the lions."

"What, add an extra innocence to our visit, eh? I warrant you
would prefer an afternoon's dalliance in bed, young Miles. A hit,
eh? You should see your face, lad. Poppy scarlet, you are. Let us
go and fetch her, then."

"IN THE DUMPS, ARE YOU, HELOISE? WILL YOU NOT CONFIDE
in me?" Miles chided lightly, as he waited with her in the courtyard at Baynards while her mare was saddled. Heloise felt as
tetchy as Cloud when her girth band was too tightly buckled.
"Are you displeased because there is no place for us at the Red
Rose yet?"

She cut to the core. "What is amiss with his grace of Gloucester, Miles? What has Stillington told him?" and watched the swift flicker in her husband's eyes doused.

"How should I know?" There was care in the indifferent answer. "Now, be cheerful. I thought you would be joyous to see the lions at the Tower this afternoon. I had more amorous plans for the two of us but . . ." He glanced round briefly as Knyvett came down the steps to join them.

"Poor lions. Why should I want to gloat at their imprisonment?" she threw back.

"Lady mine, I have business with the young king's council. Be content that I would see you entertained." Before she could step back, her chin was taken and his kiss—which told her he would enjoy her later—left her breathless. "That is better," he said, reluctantly releasing her.

WATCHING TWO BORED LIONS BEING PRODDED TO GROWL AND swipe each other at the smelly Lion Tower was hardly entertainment, so, pleading the need to find the latrine, Heloise blithely slipped her leash and left Martin and Miles's men-at-arms, to wander up the laneway towards William the Conqueror's great keep. God's truth, the Tower of London was a town within a city, antlike with activity, especially with the coming crowning. The yard before the White Tower was dusty and strewn with shavings where workmen were building extra lodging for the youths that were to be dubbed Knights of the Bath on the eve of the ceremony; and sprawling along the shelter of the inner bailey wall was the gabled, half-timbered house where the Prince of Wales was housed, as was customary before a coronation, with lords and prelates in attendance.

A furrier winked at Heloise as she watched him unload sables and ermine from his cart, and a tailor and his assistants staggered past her from a side door laden with bales of crimson brocade and cloth of gold. Fascinated, she lingered and then she noticed Sir William. He might be bantering with the sentries but his attention was elsewhere—on her husband.

She recognized his companion—Catesby, Lord Hastings's retainer. A wonder they could hold a conversation with the hammering and sawing around them, and there was something unpleasantly familiar about where Miles was standing in the shadows between some scaffolding and the outside wooden stairs that led up to the first floor of the White Tower.

"Mind out, woman!" yelled a voice.

"Godsakes!" She flung herself against the nearest wall as Lord Hastings and other lords on horseback galloped past her as though the Devil were chasing their souls. Hastings reined in outside the royal lodging, dismounted angrily, and then he beheld Catesby and Rushden. His riding crop moved against his thigh like a twitching cat tail as he closed in on them. Catesby disappeared beneath the stairs and Miles turned and saw who approached him. The nearby workmen set down their lathes. Miles bowed and gave some answer. Hastings grew more rigid and, for an instant, Heloise thought he might slash out but instead he grabbed her husband by the lapels of his cote. One of the other noblemen, Lord Stanley, and Sir William instantly intervened. The marvel of it was that *y Cysgod* calmly straightened his clothing, undaunted. What in God's name was going on?

"My lady." She realized Martin was at her elbow.

"Did you see that?"

"Aye. Your pardon, but he's a dark horse, your husband. Best come afore 'e sees you gawking at him." She let him urge her back down the lane.

"I wish I knew what was going on, Martin."

"Aye, so does the rest o' London. Buckingham's been offerin' higher wages to any that would serve 'im. Maybe 'is lordship there 'as lost a few."

But it was more than that.

"I saw Lord Hastings ride past in such sweat," she observed to Rushden when he collected her later at the West Bulwark.

"How observant you are, changeling," he replied coolly, lifting her onto Cloud's back. "I believe that Gloucester refused to see him this afternoon."

"Refused to see Lord Hastings! But he is the second greatest lord in the kingdom."

The corners of Rushden's mouth twitched into a smile and he stole a caressing hand beneath her skirt. "Not anymore."

MILES SAW HER BACK TO BAYNARDS, WONDERING WHY SHE did not wish to sup with him at the Red Rose. Trusting her, he supposed it might be her approaching monthly flux that was putting her out of sorts. Well, if he was making a poor job of being a bridegroom, he would amend matters later in a world that was no longer threatened by the Woodvilles and their allies. Besides, Catesby had agreed to dine with Harry and there was a fair chance they might persuade him to change masters. Much as Miles longed to be with Heloise, this was important. It was part of his plan to make Harry as powerful as Warwick the King- maker had been and if Hastings opposed that, so much the worse for him. Jesu, the Yorkists were lucky that Harry did not rally their enemies against them.

The Red Rose feted Catesby that evening. Ravenous with am- bition, Lord Hastings's friend accepted their morsels of flattery like a starving cur on a December night.

"I gather Lord Hastings is bedding Mistress Shore and that she often visits the queen at Westminster sanctuary," Miles re- marked eventually, and watched Catesby's hand freeze with a winecup halfway to his lips. "The lady seems ubiquitous."

Given half the chance, the old king's mistress would have wriggled into Gloucester's bed, too, like a homing salmon. But this sudden triangular traffic was dangerous; an alliance between the queen and Hastings might be in the wind.

"Mistress Shore is busy, yes." Their guest looked from one man to the other and set the vessel carefully down again.

"You have a chance to come in with us at cockcrow," Miles

murmured, "not when the hurly-burly is over. The old moon or the new?"

They were interrupted by the arrival of the fish course.

"So, Catesby," the duke murmured after a whole perch had been set upon his platter, "shall you warn Lord Hastings to be careful of the company he keeps?"

Catesby stared at his plate. The fish eye stared back blindly. "He knows it is foolish, but"—he raised his head and his fox-miened face was hard—"he cannot help himself."

"A pity." Miles showed no sympathy. Having scraped off all the good flesh on one side of his fish, he pulled the backbone out; it was surprising how many small bones came away with it.

He was whistling confidently as he returned from relieving himself before they served the subtleties, when Pershall waylaid him with another matter.

"Sir, you know Master Bannastre has fetched the pretty widow his grace has been bedding this last week?" Miles nodded; at least the woman was clean and wholesome. "Well, sir, some other wench has wormed her way in and there's two of 'em to deal with. I have taken the liberty of putting one of 'em in his grace's bedchamber. Will it please you to ask my lord duke if he wants one at a time, neither, or both at once?"

Glad that he was free of such dilemmas, Miles whispered the tidings to Harry and resumed his place upon the dais. The guests, garrulous with fine wines, departed an hour later and Miles, whose duty it was to supervise Harry's unrobing that night, accompanied him up the stairs.

A veiled woman, impossible to recognize in the light of the scant candles that had kept her company through her vigil, rose as they entered the antechamber. The fragrance was familiar though as yet he could put no name to it.

Pershall caught Miles's eye and jerked his head at the bed-chamber, easing open the door for him to glimpse a winsome, raven-haired beauty reclined upon the pillows, languidly filing her nails.

"Whatever are you doing here, mistress?" Harry was saying behind his back. "I do not even know your name. Your reputation—"

The stranger did not need unveil herself for as Miles turned back, he saw a plant with its roots bound in a canvas bag upon the small table and knew.

"I . . . I came before curfew." Tremulous breath fanned the delicate gauze before Dionysia shyly drew it up. "Your pardon, my gracious lord, I did not intend to stay but your servants let me in and said you would not be long."

"My people shall see you safely home but . . . but will you sup before you go? There are . . . well . . . viands aplenty." Harry ignored Miles's icy hostility and Pershall's facial contortions for attention; his gaze was only for his fair guest—like a man besotted.

She nodded with a quiver of lip. "I have a great hunger on me. . . ." The lovely eyes confirmed the ambiguity. "But I cannot delay you, you must have . . ." She waved her hands with charming helplessness. Had she smelt the other woman's perfume?

Harry, curse him, did not even wriggle in the web Dionysia was spinning, but two might play at cocooning; the duke's white teeth glinted in a predatory smile that promised earthly treasures and pleasurable experiences.

"This is an iris, is it not?" he murmured, lifting the plant closer to the candlelight.

Dionysia moved to his elbow and stroked the swordlike leaves. "A golden flower. It will unfurl its petals for you by tomorrow."

Behind her back, Pershall threw his eyes heavenwards in incredulity before he coughed. "Will viands be sufficient, your grace, or shall I bring refreshment for the flower as well?" Then he bowed to Dionysia. "May I show you where the garderobe is, my lady?"

"Aye, do so," ordered Harry, thrusting the door open so that it was impossible for her to refuse.

Miles's anger broke the instant she was gone. "That woman is—"

"Quick, Miles, get the other whore out! Pay her off."

"But she is—"

"As you love me, *do it!*" Harry fiercely thrust him towards the bedchamber and disappeared downstairs. Fuming, Miles paid off the disappointed widow and delivered her to Bannastre for unloading at her house in Thames Street.

Pershall was sitting on the bottom stair on his return. "Order a cell at Bedlam, sir. His grace has been bitten by a rabid bitch."

"I have to stop this!"

Pershall did not shift. "I would not go back up, Sir Miles. He has an appetite on him and it is not for the strawberries."

"She is Gloucester's ward and—the Devil take her!—my wife's sister."

Pershall grimaced, shaking his fingers as though the air had burnt him.

"Exactly," snarled Miles.

"To cut to the hilt, sir, love can creep up on us, like. Might not be such a bad thing."

Love! It was not on the agenda. "He is in love with power, Pershall. Let that suffice."

A woman's laughter rippled down the staircase and Miles turned away cursing. God damn her! Dionysia had won this round.

NEXT MORNING WAS AS SHINY AS A GEMSTONE AS HELOISE climbed the Baynards battlements after prime. The river lay like a pane of grisailled glass; the sky before her a smoky blue broken by a fleet of swans beating their wings up to Richmond. Westwards, a purplish brown haze hovered above the polished spires, and Paul's steeple pointed an indicatory finger towards Heaven like a warning but no one beneath it was listening. The wharves nearest to Baynards were spiky with derricks, the air buffeted with ribald curses as wharvesmen and crews unloaded upriver

produce: hay bales for the stables of the city's inns; cheeses like
village footballs, their rinds comforted by cloths; and sacks of
flour, peak-eared from handling.

For Heloise it was a relief to observe the rooftops like a soaring
goshawk and not have her unwilling mind overladen with the
intrigue that insinuated between Westminster and the Tower,
but the horrid protuberances spiking London Bridge's city gate
like monstrous decaying seedpods horrified her. What new adorn-
ments might be hoisted? Miles Rushden's head? Despite the heat,
she shuddered and closed her mind against a fearful future. The
battle for England was not over yet.

"It seems you did not wish to be found, Heloise!" Like a raptor
that might steer its way by night, Rushden had discovered her
roost. His mood, by the look of his stormy brow, matched hers.

"Well done, sir." The chill belied the applause. "I needed
peace to think," she added, hiding her pleasure in being his,
delighting in the glazy sheen of the black leather knee boots, the
cascade of outer sleeve, and the lacing of his shirt that begged
untying. Tendrils of damp hair lapped Miles's freshly shaven jaw
and the musk he used reached her across the still air. She saw
the corners of her lord's mouth curl down at her tepid welcome.
If he had considered gentle tail-pulling, he changed his mind.
"In future, changeling, will you please leave word of where I may
discover you. I do not have time for these games."

"I noticed." It was necessary to cold-shoulder him and show
more interest in a passing barge.

"I thought you indisposed."

"No."

"I am not sure I understand."

"I . . . I want to be honest with you."

"Ah." His jaw clenched and he waited.

"Whatever it is you are doing, sir, I do not like it." She
glanced sideways.

Her newly wedded lord swore beneath his breath. "It seems
to be what I am *not* doing, madam." Wondrous manly, he paced

away from her, his long cote fluttering above the knightly spurs. "Why is it that now I am tethered to you for eternity, Heloise, you are become so perverse? How may I please you?" Ice edged each word.

"By sharing."

"My bed?"

"No, your trust."

"I see." He perched himself between the crenellations. "Well, I am not sure I know enough to tell you, save to say I am rattling the die as best I can." A black-gloved hand fingered the enamelled sword hilt warily. "Is there another question?"

"Oh, a cupboardful, sir. To be frank, why are you baiting Lord Hastings?"

"I am not." His expression was distant and then the mercurial gaze returned to her as though she entertained him. "Mind, I think he is in my way."

"Miles," she pleaded, "I want a husband not a severed head."

The cutting amusement softened to kindness as he held out a hand for hers. "You knew I was ambitious, *cariad.* I have never made a secret of it." Heloise ignored the gesture, but she wanted so much to believe in him, wanted Rushden to hold her and kiss away her demons. To take his hand was to forgive the future.

He stood. "So skittish, still," he murmured, looking down at her like a victorious captain. "I think you feast on danger, changeling. A pair of boots and you will wade in beside me." The steel eyes had grown devilish. "Give me the kiss of peace."

"I will give you the slap of war," seethed Heloise, retreating.

"Then do so, sweetheart, but I will tax you first."

The bastion tower was no ally as she took a step back and felt the stone wall merciless against her back. His arms became her prison.

Satan take him! She fought to free herself, trying to keep her anger blazing, yet to be held was divine penance.

"Why will you not accept my good lordship, Heloise, and trust my judgment in such matters?" With a slow smile, he pulled her against him. "Be content that you have a husband who appreciates all you offer." He tilted her face towards him. The familiar stirring his touch aroused warred with her reason. Her mind protested at this feudal passion without love. His lips seduced the sensitive skin below her ear and provocatively trailed lower until she arched towards him, desperate for him to touch her breasts.

Her husband's laughter was soft. "Ah, so you have an appetite for this, but no dalliance now, my lascivious enchantress. The duchess likes to keep her ramparts pure. Besides, we have an audience." A couple of boatmen and their passengers were whooping at them.

The rebuff hurt her. Did he not feel the same passion? How could he be so controlled? Oh, every time she thought to capture the real man, he eluded her grasp. He was the shapeshifter, not she: he was the master of the game, and she was trying so hard to understand the rules.

"Now I have need of your help, Heloise," he was saying. "It would please me if you would take your annoying sister to task. She wants to become Harry's reigning mistress."

How had he found that out?

"Dear God, Miles, that must be avoided at all costs," she exclaimed, stowing her anger away briefly. "She is unwed and . . ."

"Unplucked? Hardly. When did it last rain . . ." He stared out towards Southwark, his mouth a furrow of displeasure. "She came to the Manor of the Red Rose last night armed with a fleur-de-lis."

"What!"

"They talked about more than gardening and he has sent out for some pansies."

"Pansies!"

"How else do you reward a night of pleasure? Valerian for the nerves? I can see I should have presented you with something flowery. Speak with her, please."

"You find this amusing."

"No, I find it irritating. Best Gloucester does not learn of it, hmm? Your sister has told Crosby Place she is staying here with you. Let that suffice. Give this bonfire a few days and, with God's good grace, it may burn itself out, despite your sister's ambitions. Men are fickle creatures." Was he a fickle creature too?

"In God's name, sir, she is only seventeen. Can you not speak with the duke?"

"Divert him. Not this time. The seduction was unhappily mutual."

"What is it that binds you to that man?" she demanded, her misgivings finally welling to the springhead. "Richard of Gloucester would give you good lordship."

"It seems to me that your wondrous Gloucester is too well served already. As for Harry—notched and directed, he flies true." Her expression must have been stony for he carried her hands to his lips. "Are you jealous, *cariad?*"

"Sir." It was an effort to sound businesslike. "I would be a proper wife to you. Now that the bishop is mended, I serve no purpose here."

"My father has a London house but—"

"Then . . . then could I not go there?" she cut in. "Oh, to be sure, I can help here with these noble ladies' charities but I am used to running my father's household or looking after Ned. Miles, please."

"I am sorry, we cannot use the house. Harry has taken your sister there."

"Dear God, you let him use it as a stew!"

"Peace!" His fingers fastened about her wrist. "I am sorry that you lack attention. After the coronation I vow we will leave London and I shall take you to Dorset to meet my family and reconcile myself with yours. Here." He tipped his leather purse and offered her a rose noble. "Take Martin for escort and go purchasing this afternoon. Buy a new headdress to replace the one I ruined."

Heloise kept her hands by her sides. "You think trinkets will mollify me? Your duke crosses himself every time he sees me and you use me as though I am some doll to play with when you remember to open the nursery chest."

The indifference that snapped across his face nearly disarmed her. "I do not seek to *buy* your goodwill, madam, I expect it." His hand stroked down her cheek. "Truth is a many-sided gem, Heloise. It takes time to appreciate all its facets."

And what was that supposed to mean? she thought angrily as he turned on his heel and walked arrogantly away. The bells of the city sounded but eight o'clock and already she missed the rasp of words between them. The day yawned ahead, hours and hours.

"Saddle Cloud," she bade Martin, and went to confide in her pious hostess before she packed. She was going to her guardian— running away.

FINDING SOMEWHERE TO LICK HER WOUNDS WAS NOT EASY. By the time she reached Bishopsgate, Crosby Place had inconveniently barred its doors against the world. Together with the King of France's embassy, thirteen petitioners, five irritated aldermen, puzzled messengers from various noblemen including Lord Hastings—she recognized the sable maunches—and a ribbon peddler who was too slow witted to take a denial, she, too, was turned away. It seemed that Duchess Anne was come with her ladies down the spine of England to be with her lord and Crosby Place was not receiving visitors.

At the rear postern, the story was the same: "Return tomorrow, my masters." Which was all very well for those who had no grievances with their husbands and a choice of beds for the night. The day was hot, the streets were reeking, and Heloise could feel perspiration dampening her collar and the cotton wadding that protected her gown beneath her arms. It was needful to bribe the back porter with the rose noble to ensure he carried Heloise's unicorn brooch to its giver. Time limped; but at last Lady Margery Huddleston came down and salvaged her from the stinking street.

Margery's delighted welcome and the merciful coolness of the house's interior restored Heloise's spirits—as though she had touched a sanctuary doorknocker.

"I had thought you a queen at the Red Rose by now, or has your ubiquitous sister already deposed you? Lady Percy tells me she is trying to snare a duke in her talons."

"She is welcome to Duke Harry," answered Heloise, blushing for her sister's sins. "For my part, Margery, I have come in search of enlightenment."

"But I think you may be the one to provide it," answered Margery wryly. "And what of your man of shadows? Will he not miss you?"

Heloise sighed. "That is why I am here. Blessed are the unobtainable. I only hope he will."

Twenty-one

Crosby Place lazed in the afternoon heat, the lords and ladies lying low as if the least movement would overexert them.

"So," murmured Margery, "I am anxious to hear of your adventures." She sent a yawning page to fetch them cordial and, lending Heloise a fan, led her out to the shady colonnade. "Let us sit here for a while, then I shall bespeak you a bed for tonight." Wondering guiltily what Miles was doing, Heloise leaned against one of the pillars that cloistered the garden. The air was drowsy with the hum of insects.

Margery, fanning herself with a cluster of plumes furled into a silver stick, that bespoke Tripoli or Alexandria, waited until the page had served them, and then she swung her feet up onto the wall and recomposed her skirts discreetly. "So tell me all that has happened to you."

Heloise did her best to be concise but by the time she faltered to a finish, she could hear the servants setting up the trestles for supper.

"Let us walk in the garden," murmured Margery. "That is quite a tale, Heloise. I am not surprised that you feel yourself neglected now, but all the men are edgy. Someone is setting chestnuts to cook and they are shooting out all over London, particularly around here." She waved her fan towards the great hall. "It could be Margaret Beaufort, Tudor's mother, but I rather suspect it may be your husband."

"Chestnuts?" The heat must be addling her brain.

"*Rumors:* my lord protector is going to seize the crown—Hastings has changed his cote and is making an alliance with the queen—our late sovereign lord King Edward was unlawfully begotten so his children have no right to the crown."

"Certes, Rushden is ambitious, but . . ."

"Word is that he moves Buckingham like a chesspiece."

Heloise's stupor vanished. "He has the duke's good lordship, yes. Their friendship runs deep, but rumors, no, I do not believe . . ."

"He rescued Stillington."

"Ah yes, Stillington." Heloise lifted her chin, anxious for enlightenment. "My lord of Gloucester was right merry when he came to visit Stillington but I saw his face as he left and, upon my soul, he looked like Atlas, as though he carried the troubles of Christendom upon his shoulders. Surely if the royal council approves of all that he has done, how can anything Stillington said rile him?"

The fan paused. "Oh, yes, Heloise, yes, it all comes back to Stillington."

"Margery, I feel like a blindfolded player. If this concerns Rushden, for pity's sake, tell me."

Margery glanced around before she lowered her voice. "If I share this with you, will you swear on the rood that you will not divulge it further?"

Heloise clasped the small gold cross about her neck. "By Christ's blessed body, I assure you I shall not."

"It is very simple. Stillington swears that King Edward's sons are bastards and may not inherit the crown."

"Christ forfend!" It was as if the realm of England shook beneath her. "How is this so?"

"King Edward"—a wry smile touched Margery's lips—"fell hopelessly in love with a beautiful widow and because she would not surrender to him without a wedding ring, he married her secretly. Does that sound familiar?"

"Yes, Elizabeth Woodville. But . . . are you saying that their marriage was not lawful?"

"Yes, and I will tell you why. The beautiful widow I am talking about was *earlier,* before King Edward ever set eyes on Elizabeth Woodville. You see, the king made two secret marriages. The trothplighting with Elizabeth at Grafton Regis was done properly before a priest and plenty of witnesses but it was unlawful because his first wife was still living. Her name was Eleanor."

"And is this Eleanor still alive?"

"No, God rest her soul. She took holy orders and died some fifteen years ago."

"But were there witnesses to the first marriage?"

"None living save one, the priest who married them." Margery raised an eyebrow.

"Stillington!" Heloise's fingers rose to her lips in amazement. "Oh, but surely the queen knew. The prince is only twelve. Providing the king and queen went through a second marriage after Eleanor's death, that still makes King Edward's sons legitimate."

Margery's blue eyes misted. "I do not believe they did. King Edward could be careless sometimes, always trusting that fortune would bless him. Like the time he underestimated my father and was forced to quit his throne and flee to Burgundy. And I am sure this secret marriage is why Clarence . . ." She spoke the name with a sigh—he too had been her brother-in-law. "Why Clarence was executed and Stillington was imprisoned. Clarence knew. You see, Heloise, the queen was certain that if King Edward died unexpectedly, Clarence would claim the throne. Perhaps that is why she has tried to seize power and have the prince crowned and anointed straightway. Gloucester is the rightful king."

"And now Gloucester knows the truth?"

"Yes, now he does, Heloise, and the dilemma is half-killing him."

"What do you think he should do, then?"

"There are many of us who would like to see him king." Margery stood up, smoothing her skirts. "We need a strong leader, otherwise Scotland and France will soon be slavering for war. I have met King Louis and, believe me, that vile dissembler would like nothing better than to see England weak so he can conquer Burgundy. I labored hard to prevent that.

"Heavens, you have lived in Gloucester's household, Heloise. You know we could have none better to rule us. There are so many excellent changes to the laws he is itching to propose."

Yes, Heloise remembered. Like allowing a prisoner bail before his trial if he could find friends to stand surety for him, and preventing a suspect's goods from being seized the moment he was arrested.

"Our laws should be written in straightforward English so every one of us can understand them," Margery was saying. It was one of Gloucester's personal crusades that he had aired at Middleham.

"I doubt the lawyers will ever allow that." Heloise's tone was dry, but she had always supported the duke's views. Especially his belief that nobody should dispose of land unless they had a true title to it; and remembering the feud that had thrown her into Rushden's unwilling arms, she sighed. Margery might have hopes of a rainbow world but it would be hard to achieve and one had to be practical. Even if Gloucester's lawful claim to the throne were proven and he were allowed to become king, there would be malcontents in plenty. If he did not reward his northern followers with offices, they would be angered; so, to please them, he would have to turn the current officers, mostly southerners, out of their positions, which would cause perilous unrest. And there were still Lancastrian lords abroad and secret sympathizers at home who hated the Yorkists and would readily scourge him as a tyrant. She hoped Rushden was not among them.

"Poor Gloucester," Margery murmured, "caught between the rock of loyalty to his brother's children and the hard place of his own common sense." Suddenly everything began to make sense. Miles and Buckingham wanted to make Gloucester king.

"I can think of a very jagged rock," exclaimed Heloise. "Lord Hastings is hardly likely to stand by and clap his hands at his beloved king's children being set aside."

"Throw rose petals? No, I doubt he would, and this adds to Gloucester's dilemma."

"Does Buckingham know of Stillington's revelation?" If the duke did, then Miles had been keeping the matter secret too.

Margery shook her head. "Not yet. Gloucester wanted to talk over the matter with my sister and some of us first. I suspect he intends to confide in Buckingham when the duke comes to sup tomorrow night." Another morsel of information which Miles had not shared. "That is why Crosby Place has shut its doors for a little space, not because of my lady sister's arrival but to take counsel.

"Ah, that is the warning bell for supper. Their graces will not be eating in the hall today so you need not make your obeisance until tomorrow."

When the duke and duchess emerged for mass next day, Heloise saw with relief that Gloucester's aura was brightening again. As Heloise knelt before them, she sensed the assertive waves of love and strength that the duchess willed her lord, and saw it in the intertwining of their fingers. They made her welcome in a distrait but kindly manner, assuming she had come with Rushden's blessing to make ready for the feast.

"You need apparel for tonight." Margery led her back to the women's bedchamber where she shook out a gown of peony silk. The two months' sorrowing for King Edward was over and Heloise, still in her black damask, felt like a dark moth among the duchess's women in their bright apparel.

"But I am in mourning for my father," she pointed out.

"Then I shall spill my platter down your mourning robe at dinner, and if you wear this veil of gossamer tisshew, the matter is settled. Try it on."

She felt envious hearing about the blue velvet bordered with crimson satin that they were to wear in the procession from the Tower and the crimson velvet and white damask to be made up for the crowning but it was amusing to listen to the gossip. Some tittle-tattle was censored, she suspected. Although my ladies Parr, Tempest, and Percy discreetly spoke no ill of Dionysia, Heloise guessed their reservations; her sister had never curtsied to the household rule book. She was indisposed at Baynards, she told them, hating the lie.

As if the world had gone from humdrum to dazzling color, Crosby Place by four o'clock glinted, shimmered, and perspired. Gloucester, in murrey samite with panels of golden stags flanking the shining buttons of his doublet, had forsaken raven mourning and looked less pallid but the duchess's complexion was effaced; the mauve daisies with their gold-thread hearts ought to have flattered her. Heloise, remembering her vision at Middleham, felt the Devil run an icy finger down her backbone.

Margery, misreading her expression, pressed Heloise's arm reassuringly. "Rushden cannot haul you out."

"The trouble is he may not want to."

The hour crawled between bells as red-cheeked earls, with sweat crawling pore by pore, dampening their silks, shook Gloucester's gloved hand. His household flanked him like a brotherhood. Up in the gallery, the arms of pages wearied as they flapped huge linen tablecloths to turn the air and prevent the viol strings from breaking. The cloying heat promised to stifle everyone's appetites, and their host's edginess made his guests' tongues cleave to the roofs of their mouths. The sauces would be wasted on the fesaunts and fenneled sturgeon; beggars would feast tonight.

The fanfare announcing the arrival of the Stafford entourage was the last to sound.

"Deliberate, I imagine," mused Margery, as Buckingham entered. "He might make the part of Potiphar's wife if he applied himself. Has he sold his Welsh flocks, do you think?" She was not the only one wide-eyed at Buckingham's magnificence. The duke who complained of poverty at Brecknock must have borrowed sacks of money to clothe his skin. Flamboyant was not quite the word, nor was ostentatious, but they were not far short. His doublet was low belted, flounced with ermine, and just long enough to render his groin respectable. Tugs of a gold silk shirt

rose Italianate through the creamy slits of his upper sleeves and
shone beneath the laces that trellised his doublet. The beaver hat
with its broad curled-up brim was ornamented by a fist-sized
brooch of pearl and sapphire. If angels had come to dine in mor-
tals' fashions, they could not have surpassed him except . . . Except, decided Heloise, a shade maliciously, he was putting on
weight.

Not so her husband. At the duke's elbow, Miles's finery might
be subdued, certainly less exuberant, but his taste was sinless in
comparison. The silver, pleated doublet and slate silk stomacher
were harnessed at his waist by a platelet belt and the shining
collar of his lineage sat proudly on his shoulders. The dark hair
that she could imagine now beneath her fingertips was newly cut
beneath his low-crowned hat, and tidied behind his ears so that
nothing of his scarred face was hidden as he looked about him,
noting who was present. Save for Lord Hastings and the prince's
household lords who were feting the French embassy at the
Tower, most of the peers were here.

"*Y Cysgod,*" Margery mused at her elbow. "Shadow in name,
but in nature . . . ?"

"You are well informed, my lady," Heloise remarked sharply.

"As I told you once before, Gloucester has friends, even in
Wales."

INVISIBILITY WAS NOT ONE OF HELOISE'S FEY SKILLS BUT THERE
were broadly girthed lords to hide her from her husband. She
need not have worried; Miles Rushden was preoccupied. He was
moving through the throng with Buckingham, busy with greetings, a firm hand given now and then conveying more—or less.
It was not until dinner when the noble ladies, their veils shifting
like wind-tossed flowers, were sitting in rank upon the left of
the hall that Miles Rushden met her gaze across the spitted larks
and rollettes of venison. He was no longer smiling. Nor did he
deign to seek her out some two hours later when the acrobats
had been tidied away, the trestles propped below the tapestries,

and the two dukes had withdrawn alone into the great chamber behind the dais.

As the shawms and viols struck up in the English manner, Heloise, who had only bothered with the strawberries, tried to display a lighthearted, independent spirit. She wanted Miles to care who squired her and where their gaze fell. Veiled, she might dance, though she dared not attempt the boisterous Florentine dance with its countless improvisations, for the borrowed bodice was tight across her breasts. The sets formed and Sir Richard Huddleston led Margery on his right and Heloise on his left. They progressed with brawles and flowerdelice, now in arches, now dipping beneath, and Heloise at last came almost breast to breast with the man to whom she was supposed to owe obedience. For this evening, she was a princess, reckless with desire for what she did not have.

"Sir Miles, how very kind of you to lend us Lady Rushden," Margery murmured, with a quelling eyebrow upon her own lord, as she held Heloise's hands to make an arch.

"My horse is available too," Miles offered witheringly as his shoulder brushed beneath Heloise's arm. The dance compelled him on.

"I have met friendlier wolves," hissed Margery. "Do all Buckingham's men growl so?"

"Only when they are hungry," observed Huddleston. "Will lands appease him, Heloise, or does he want the crown?"

"W-who?"

Green eyes questioned her naivete. "Rushden."

"I—I do not understand."

"But we should like to." Huddleston reverenced each of his partners as the music ended. "Friend Buckingham wears his kingly ancestry on his escutcheon—does he wear the mantle of Lancaster too? Or has that been sent for laundering to Henry Tudor? You will have to do better than this, young Heloise, if you want to dance at Westminster."

Heloise blinked at him. Had she indeed missed the undertones of this particular tune? Then it dawned on her that they were afraid. Afraid that good dog Buckingham might turn and maul their master—at her husband's bidding.

Lips parted, she turned her head to find Miles, wishing he might take her leading rein and reassure her that she had not married a devil, but a circle of Gloucester's knights withheld him from her. Did the Huddlestons truly believe that Buckingham was but a glove upon Miles Rushden's hand?

"Is dancing at Westminster to be the zenith of my wheel of fortune, Sir Richard?" Scathing serrated her question.

"Lady Rushden, it is better than the base torrents of the millrace. We can all drown. Excuse me, mesdames." He strode across to Duchess Anne. "Are the dukes still arguing in there?" she heard him ask.

And it was then that Buckingham emerged, his forehead spangled with sweat. Miles instantly broke free and joined his lord, and Heloise, watching the light-fast understanding that flashed between them, sadly knew herself an outsider still.

HARRY'S EYES SHONE LIKE A MAN WHO HAD HEARD THE VOICE of God as he disdained the throng and urgently drew Miles aside to tell him Stillington's secret.

"Christ Almighty, the prince a bastard!" Miles's mouth gaped adit-wide. "This is what we always dreamt of. You could be high constable within the week." But ill news followed: Gloucester—a true Libran man to his toenails—after hours of weighing matters had resolved finally to crown his nephew.

"Christ Almighty, Miles." Harry's mutter was low and furious. "The crown is there for the taking. 'What will Lord Hastings say?' he kept moaning and he is scared his brother will come back and haunt him. The dolt was in tears just now, shouting at me to get out. Jesu, as well I did, I was right close to shaking him, the fool!" To be within a spade's edge of the crock of gold!

"But that is a good sign, my lord, you are wearing him rag-

ged. You warned him that it will not just be his head that falls
beneath a Woodville axe, but his son's too?"

"Oh, I said that, Miles, yes, and that he had best have his
friends close by and armed come St. John's Eve. I used every
plaguey argument. You may buy me a striped hood for my saint's
day. I can become a lawyer if the Woodvilles leave my head
alone."

"You have to keep at him, my lord. The duchess has just gone
in to him but mayhap she is on your side." It was guesswork but
a fair assumption that Warwick the Kingmaker's daughter might
share her father's dream.

"But my quiver's empty, Miles."

"Remind him that Queen Margaret used poison to rid herself
of good Duke Humphrey. A different queen, but another Uncle
Gloucester." Miles watched understanding dimple Harry's
cheeks.

"Ha! A wondrous precedent." Like an athlete ready to perform
again, the duke wriggled his neck. A wonder he did not spit
upon his palms. "Pray hard, Miles, else we shall all be in the
Tower dungeons after the coronation banquet."

Frustrated that he could only guide not row their eggshell
boat, Miles watched Harry reenter the inner sanctum. His entire
future depended on Harry's eloquence!

"Miles."

His lady stood before him—exquisite, more beautiful than he
had ever seen her, as if in covering herself she offered secrets.
Brocade sleeves, lined with lily pink taffeta, tumbled back from
bands of crimson stitched with pearls as she raised a slender arm
tightly sheathed in silk. An arrow point of silk edged the delicate
wrist he raised to his lips. Her eyes were fawn-wild. No, fey-
bright, or was that an illusion? Oh, Heloise! He felt the heat of
desire struggle against the need to keep his mind clear of her
sorcery.

"No baying hounds after me?" she asked, with a lift of brow.

"You are mine, changeling." Her hand was gallantly turned

but he intended the sensual kiss upon her palm to pass the sentries and set fires anew within her citadel. "I will whistle when I need you." The words were barbed. The rosy silk trembled, her little breasts, tight and full, lifted in breathy anger.

"And I shall not hear you."

"Of course you shall, but since we circle different planets, it shall be by my clock, not yours!" His voice was stern with challenge; she had yet to learn his measure.

"Lady Rushden!" Knyvett moved in like a diplomat and Miles turned on his heel, leaving his wife, he hoped, besieged and hungry.

Heloise needed to drag Rushden from the hall and quarrel properly but greater matters weighed in the balance; like a household listening for the squeal of a newborn heir, the entire throng were turned towards the inner door. When Buckingham finally emerged like a successful butterfly scrambling from its casing, speculation ran rife.

"This is the stuff of chronicles." Margery joined Heloise. "So Buckingham has swayed our duke. How very eloquent of him. I hate to be a dampener to their hopes but . . ." She studied the men over her shoulder. "But, Heloise, what happens if *he* stops listening to good advice or, worse still, hears a different voice?"

"Who, Gloucester, Margery?"

"No, Heloise, Buckingham."

THE AIR IN THE WOMEN'S BEDCHAMBER AT CROSBY PLACE WAS as thick as a rich man's blanket. If she had been alone in the huge bed, Heloise might have wept, but she was packed with the other ladies like a salted stockfish—a hot, salted stockfish hammered into a crate—and fears like wakeful demons were pincering her. Did her infuriating lord not realize she longed for him to imperiously fetch her back to the Red Rose and take her into his bed to be seduced with apologies and tenderness? Had she lost the battle already and was there nothing worth winning but an empty heart, at the high cost of breaking her own?

As the London roosters began their dawn duties calling their hens to order, she fell asleep only to dream again of Lord Hastings struggling against the soldiers. This time she recognized the wooden stairs of the great keep; this time the captain of the men-at-arms raised his helm and laughed. It was Miles.

FOR SEVERAL DAYS HELOISE FURIOUSLY LINGERED AT CROSBY Place and Miles Rushden let her simmer. Around her, the northern noblemen were tight-lipped, their lord tense and anxious. Something dire was building like a tempest. On Friday, the thirteenth of June, the duke's household attended mass at St. Paul's and the dean lashed out from the pulpit with a bitter sermon on St. Peter's denial and Judas's vile treason, before Gloucester rode off with his henchmen to kiss hands with the prince and meet his council at the Tower.

Friday the thirteenth! The fearful feeling within Heloise grew until it was impossible to sit and embroider with the duchess's ladies. She fled to the arbor and sat beneath the drizzling unhappy sky. She heard the shouts as far as Leadenhall and the hooves and clank of men-at-arms returning.

"Heloise." She had known Miles would come, his soul turned to the outside for a brief space.

"What is it that you want, sir?" But she knew. Absolution, that priceless, intangible commodity that let princes slumber well at night.

He was in half-armor—a studded tunic of black and scarlet leather belted across a metal hauberk. His hair was sleeked with rain but his cheeks were unhealthily devoid of blood as if he had had a glimpse of Hell.

"So have you dragged Lord Hastings from the White Tower?" Miles crossed himself, appalled. "How did you know that?"

"I dreamt it." A truth meant to hurt. "Are you pleased, Miles? Contented now?"

He swore, wiping a hand across his mouth, and turned his face away. "I want you to come back with me to the Red Rose."

The high tone was there, no supplication to soften it for her pleasure.

"Why? So you can take refuge?"

"In your arms, Heloise? Yes, curse it!" He flung himself down beside her, leaning forward, his fingers to his temples as if his mind ached with pain. "We had evidence."

"I am sure you did. You and your master would have made sure, otherwise."

"No!" The anguish in his voice set a delaying hand upon her revenge. "It was not like that. I—I thought Hastings would cool his heels in the Tower for a few months and come to terms. No, do not turn away!

"Catesby gave us evidence against Hastings, Stanley, and Bishop Morton. Gloucester did not believe it at first and then he accused Hastings of conspiring with the queen, using Mistress Shore, his mistress, as a messenger. Hastings was so angry that he drew his dagger upon him. It was in the meeting chamber on the upper floor at the White Tower and I was outside the door with Lord Howard's son and some of the guards when we heard a bench crash and we rushed in. Harry, Howard, and Suffolk were struggling to overpower Hastings, and Lord Stanley was on his hands and knees beneath the trestle. We hauled Hastings out."

"You were there waiting for it to happen."

"I was there in case something went amiss. Hastings knew we had a case against him. Christ Almighty, Heloise, he was guilty as Hell. So were the other two."

"*Was?*" Dragged from the White Tower?

"Yes. *Was!* There were sufficient lords to try them! There was evidence. You only had to look at Stanley—every jowl was quivering, the man was close to soiling himself, he was so scared.

"Harry ordered the guards to take Hastings down to the yard. Someone fetched the priest from St. John's chapel to shrive him and then"—he swallowed—"then one of the sergeants found a carpenter's block. It was too awkward to lift so the fellow kicked

it along . . ." He winced. "Oh, Heloise, it was all scoured and
crisscrossed like a chop's cooking board, but Harry gave the order, wanted it done before Gloucester came down. Blessed Christ
pardon me! Tell me I had no choice." Miles cast his arms about
her, burrowing his face in her lap like a tiny boy. "There was so
much blood, so much blood. I never . . . Oh, God forgive me, I
did not know a man could bleed so."

Although she stroked the crow-wing hair, she was appalled
by the power in him. Was there some bloodlust in these men
which made them stain this precious peace? Was it Miles who
had moved the pawns in place to ensure this outcome?

"Be pleased, sir," she said scathingly. "Is not your way open
now, as you determined?"

"I do not wonder that you berate me." His eyes, stormy-hued
against their reddened rims, begged her forgiveness. "Come back
to me, please, tonight."

"What of Lord Stanley and Bishop Morton? Are they dead
too?"

"No, madam," he replied, angered by her manner. "We are
not butchers. One killing was enough. Morton and Stanley are
in prison."

"And I suppose you will all descend upon Hastings's manors
like carrion."

"No! No act of attainder. His family are not to blame."

That was a surprise, thought Heloise harshly. Such pickings
would have provided rewards for the two dukes' land-hungry
followers.

"Well, I expect Henry Tudor will be very pleased to hear
today's news when it finally reaches Brittany, for it seems to me
that you have just levered aside one of the cornerstones that holds
the House of York in place."

Miles stared at her with scorn, but she could see he was smarting. "You would be wise to keep that observation to yourself. I
shall send an escort for you, madam, since you are still unfortunately my responsibility." Drawing on his gloves, he declared

icily, "You will pardon me if I remove my unacceptable person hence. I have work to do. Harry has offered to give employment to any of Hastings's men who seek it."

Her damp skirts clung as she rose. "And is he going to sell a couple of his doublets on a Cornhill stall to pay them? Or shall you turn heathen and marry a half score of wealthy merchants' daughters in order to finance him?" Had he possessed a warlock's magic art, his expression would have conjured her to stone for such rash impertinence, but a new voice ahemmed through the freezing air between them.

"Sir Miles. His grace of Gloucester desires you attend him. Likewise his grace of Buckingham."

Miles gave a curt nod to the esquire and swung round on Heloise. "You were waiting for a whistle. Did you hear me, lady mine? Make ready!"

"A whistle. I am sorry, no. It was a pat on the head I wanted." Her head tilted towards the hall. "You are the one being whistled, I think."

Hard as it was to watch his face frost over and her harsh words drive cold iron down his spine, the hour was not yet come to play the pardoner's part.

"A pat, I see." Bitter amusement twisted his mouth.

"I want you, Miles, more than I have words to tell you, but not like this."

"And who is to learn the lesson? You or I?"

"Whichever one of us is wiser, sir."

"Then you will not obey me, madam?"

She inclined her head in dismissal. He swore through fine, clenched teeth and left her, sad and drenched, among the roses.

But Miles did not leave Crosby Place. In a defiant show of unity to convince the Londoners that a riot was unnecessary, Buckingham, his retinue, and the lord mayor stayed to sup. Heloise pleaded indisposition and stayed out of sight in the women's bedchamber. Not even Margery could spur new heart into her.

It was Duchess Anne who took her aside before mass next morning.

"Heloise, dearest, I think you should know that his grace of Buckingham's company was attacked on the way back to Dowgate last night. The duke was unharmed but several of his retainers were killed."

"My husband?"

Twenty-two

"I am glad you are back, my lady. It was a nasty business last night." De la Bere, a bandage round his forehead, lumbered up the Manor of the Red Rose's spiral stairs behind Heloise's hastening feet. "Poor old Brian, gone to his Maker." He nearly collided with Heloise as she turned.

"The archer, Brian, dead?" She crossed herself, her eyes watering. Dear God, this was a deadly game they were playing now.

"Aye, and several other good fellows who raced up from the back. We took the brunt of it at the front, or rather Miles did."

"Defending his grace?"

"Yes and no," de la Bere panted. "Happened so fast but it was as if . . . as if they tried to close Miles off from the rest of us. Three of 'em tried to drag him from the saddle and one of the knaves cut Traveller's girth. Miles's foot was caught in the stirrup and he fell badly. It should not have happened, my lady. And what is more, the lousy watch were tardy coming to our aid. Swear those ribalds would have heard the brawl as far as Paul's. Adder deaf they were. Ha! And no doubt richer, come this morning. Need more men to safeguard us in this city, Lady Rushden, no doubt about it. I am right glad that my lord lord protector has sent to York for reinforcements. Through here, please." She stepped into a chamber, furnished with no more than a folding chair and a small table stacked with ready-cut parchment, several stubby candles, and a couple of pipe roll cases. He overtook her and unlatched the door beyond. "Your pardon for the untidiness," he muttered, snatching a saddlepack out of her way.

"Jesu mercy!" Heloise clapped her hand to her lips as she entered. It was the ewer of bloody water standing upon the bedsteps that appalled her.

"Sorry!" whispered de la Bere, dumping it outside the door. With a finger to his lips, he drew aside the bedcurtain.

At first she thought someone had set a coif upon Miles's head but as her eyes adapted to the shuttered dimness, she saw it was a wad of linen tethered by a bandage beneath his chin. His entire face showed bruising and a fist must have driven up beneath his lower jaw, for his top lip was cut and badly swollen. Why had there been no portent? She, of all people, should have been able to warn him. Gently, she took up his hand. At least his pulse was regular. There was no fever yet, thanks be to God.

"It is a good sleep," murmured de la Bere.

"Where is the blood from?" Her calm was undermined by despair.

"Reckon that in the mêlée he must have caught his head on one of the iron candelabrum set up for St. John's Eve. A glancing blow, see, across there. The duke's leech has cleansed and stitched it. Swears he will be as good as new and even his mother will not see the embroidery. At least the whoresons missed his lungs, by Christ's mercy. And Dr. Argentine came over from the Tower at the duke's summons. Fellow is supposed to be a magician at bone-setting. Said to tell you it was a clean break." De la Bere demonstrated on his own leg. "Here, just above the right ankle-bone. Reckons you are not to worry, so long as you keep Miles off his feet. No need to tell *you* that." But he urgently drew her back into the outer chamber and pushed the door to. "I do not know what is amiss between the pair of you, my lady, but surely you will stay. Miles was asking for you, needs you, and, believe me, we want him hale again. Only one of us able to bridle Harry. Was that a nod? That's the spirit. I will have a palliasse put up for you in here and shift my gear."

He followed her back into the bedchamber and opened the upper lights. "May I leave you, then, to bark at visitors?"

"Yes, right fiercely." The housewife in her gazed in astonishment at the clothing strewn across the floorboards. A variety of muddy male boots in differing sizes obstacled the surround of

the bed whilst the corner of the room looked like a collapsed
armorer's stall with bits and pieces in a hurly-burly mess. Sword
belts added menacing interest to the wallpegs and a laundry pannier, awaiting collection, overflowed on the chest at the foot of
the bed.

"Mostly my gear, sorry. Didn't like to disturb him."

He left her picking up Miles's bloodstained finery. She ran
her fingers pensively across a vicious tear before she laid the cote
aside and stooped to retrieve the Trinity chain. No end of be-
longings had been kicked beneath the bed and a platoon of papers
sprawled out from a satchel as if they were trying to escape. She
pushed them back in and secured the strap. A scrunched-up doc-
ument had ventured further than the rest, and, softly unwrin-
kling it, she carried it to the shutters.

Chinks of light showed her Latin numbered phrases! Some
sort of notes—no, arguments! Arguments for making Gloucester
king, written in her husband's hand! *You shall need to pause here.
Estimate how this is received. If not, omit VIII and go to IX.* Upon
her soul, these were instructions for a speech! She bit her lip and
stared at her sleeping husband anew. *They tried to cut him off from
the rest of us,* de la Bere had said.

God have mercy! Margery was right. Miles Rushden was playing at kingmaking. Had the attack last night been made in op-
portunist vengeance by Hastings's friends? Or did someone
intend it as a deadly warning to Buckingham's men if they continued to support Gloucester? Jesu! If ever the queen regained
her power, these notes were sure evidence of treason. Wearily
Heloise put the paper in her purse. She would burn it later. It
was frightening how little she knew the man who lay there in
such rare silence. With sadness, she carried Miles's hand to her
cheek.

"Changeling?" It was a weak, half-growl half-purr, but he
seemed pleased to see her, or at least one eye and half his mouth
was. "I—I have not the strength to pat you yet."

"Oh, Miles." Tears threatened but it was needful to be practical. "Shall I see the extent of what they have done to you?"

Let in, the morning light was not flattering as Heloise coaxed Miles's bandage up. The edge of the stitching was clean but a fresh dressing would soon be needed. Fresh moonwort or adder's tongue would no longer be available, the summer heat would have withered them, but powdered root of dragonwort or shepherd's scrip ointment from an apothecary might serve. And a daily dose of crushed Solomon's seal infused in wine would speed the healing and mend the bruising. She must ask for a crucible and trivet. "So you foiled the Devil last night."

"I will not woo my appearance in a mirror yet." His fingers fumbled to trace the rough edge of the wound but she swiftly barred further exploration. "Argentine was a good fellow to tumble out so late for me, and Harry's physician—sober to his fingertips, thank God."

"The scars will not show, they say. Lie back. Do you know who attacked you?"

He coughed and pointed to the leather bottle. She helped him take a swig.

"T-too many—oh, Jesu, leave it!—enemies now."

"Stay calm. Let me see the other damage."

"Spare my modesty! Ouuucch!"

The furrows in her forehead diminished for she had sufficient sensitivity in her fingertips to know that the leg bone had been broken cleanly and excellently reset against the wooden splente. Her wrist was clasped as she straightened.

"Did . . . did I have to go through this, changeling, to make you come back to heel?"

"Of course." She kissed the purpled brow. Perhaps, after all, this was an answer to her prayers—God's way of keeping Miles alive.

"You are so . . . so beautiful, Heloise. Do not run away anymore." He lifted a hand to knuckle her cheek and she took it within the casing of her fingers, so close to weeping for sheer joy that he was still alive. "Your visions, my fey. . . ." He swallowed and stared towards the morning sky. "I am just a mortal and I forgot that. I have been trying to play God, Heloise, and He doesn't like it. But I meant it for the best. I swear to you I acted within the law. I—"

"We will talk another time, when you are strong enough to argue."

"No, now. *Why,* changeling? Why did you fly from me?"

She let go of his hand evasively. "Because you are a man of secrets. Because I believed, like a dullard, that you married me for other reasons."

"I did. You have divine breasts." The chuckle was painful. Serve him right!

"For your face?" Briskly, she examined the jar of ointment left by the physician with a professional sniff. "I believe I can do better. Is there an apothecary close by?"

"Several streets away. Pershall knows it. He will go for you if you smile."

"I had rather see to it myself, sir. They may not have what I need. I will confer with your physician first."

"If you go slapping some . . . some mash of fermented toad tongues and ground-up newt turds on my sores, I shall not be answerable for my actions."

"For you, sir, an infusion of arsenic in nettles strained through cheesecloth." But it was a poor jest. "I will send up your manservant to guard your virtue."

"Then go if you must. Wear your pattens and take Martin to squire you, but hurry back, and in God's name, *take care.*"

It needed a north polestar to help her locate her groom; she should have used intuition instead of asking; the Red Rose servants all were at half-mast and the labyrinth of passages and boltholes would have thrilled the Minotaur.

With a borrowed basket on her arm, feeling useful and housewifely, Heloise finally set off along the cobbled thoroughfare hoping to circumvent the Flemings' quarter. Not that she distrusted foreigners; it was more that they would be unable to assist her if she lost her way. Martin trustingly trotted behind her but, like any countrywoman, his mistress was soon flummoxed by the lack of signposts and close to admitting that the common belief that women had little sense of direction might be true. One instant there might be a nobleman's house with a porter standing duty but turn the next corner and there was a narrow, beggarly street, beset with sinister alleyways and tightly shuttered casements. Gutters oozing their fermenting contents to pleasure the soles of passersby dismayed her further and Heloise heartily wished she had worn her pattens as Miles had advised.

They retraced their steps to the Red Rose and ventured east, ill at ease, but the Hanse shopkeepers nodded in friendly fashion. It was shameful to ask directions and the unfathomable river of words dismayed her, but she and Martin ended up with a flaxen-headed lad guiding them for a groat.

He chattered easily, insisting they observe the famous "London Stone" as they passed along Walbrook Street. Even if the stone had been there since the days of King Ethelstane (as the boy explained), Heloise was not impressed. Save for its iron casing, it looked more like the "pay on the nail" stones found in most marketplaces, and surely it was most inconveniently placed, too— close to the gutter, and a hazard to passing carts.

Their young guide led them on to a narrow tenement hard by Oxford Place, and when they showed reluctance to leave the main thoroughfare, he pointed out the apothecary's pestle and mortar painted on a hanging sign.

The shop's innards gave lie to its weathered, humble exterior and Heloise's soul sang at the powdery odors and the bundles of drying herbs tasseling the beams and tickling her headdress. No dust velveted the orderly shelves and the variety of earthen-colored jars, labeled in spidery Latin, looked as clean and cheerful as a stall of monks on Easter Sunday.

The apprentice prattled as he weighed out the ingredients: was it not strange the coronation had been canceled a second time? And why? he asked, tapping his nose. Gloucester wanted his nephew's crown. And what was more, these brawls between the retainers of great lords were bad for business: honest customers stayed home.

Heloise concealed her concern as she placed the tiny twisted bundles into her basket. London, it seemed, was as jumpy as a dog with fleas. So was Martin and he prevailed upon her to return to Suffolk Lane by a different route—along the broader Candlewick Street. Even there, the passersby glanced warily at any men-at-arms.

Would Miles be safer at his father's London house? Was it like one of these? she wondered, staring up at the carved joists of the merchant drapers' houses. Then Martin of a sudden plucked at her sleeve.

Across the street, her veiled sister was speaking to Sir Richard Huddleston. The pair were standing beside a shop board showing no interest in either scarlet flannel or the Italian cotton underdrawers. Was it a chance meeting?

Cautioning Martin, Heloise slowed her step. Huddleston's gap-toothed groom, waiting a few paces away with his master's horse, was ogling the women shoppers. It was easy for Heloise to let a spotty apprentice pluck her sleeve and garrulously lure her to test his stall's best worsted. Dionysia's conversation looked earnest, certainly not one of dalliance, but it was ending. Huddleston bowed and swung himself into the saddle. Once he was out of sight, Heloise caught up with her furtive sister.

"A murrain!" snapped Dionysia and then calmed. "I suppose even veils are useless against one's family. Stop looking so outraged. We were talking about the skirmish last night, and, no, I was not flirting, I would not dare covet *him,* and he was on his way to Cold Harbrough. Mayhap I shall go back to the Red Rose with you." She coiled her arm through her sister's. "At least you shall lend me respectability, for now you are come there, I may come thither also. God's rood, I have done with slinking in and out of Harry's dwellings like an alley she-cat just to save old Gloucester's blushes." It was tempting for Heloise to scold her but better to be a crutch than a whip. "And, sister dear, you shall be the first to know that Duke Harry declares he has quite fallen in love with me. I did not intend it but I really am growing wondrous fond of him. Look at this!" She spread her fingers to display a voluptuous sapphire.

"Didie! We shall have every cutpurse in London after us."

"With you for protection, sister! Harry has told me of your exploits in Brecknock. How you threw flour at some loathsome footpad and broke his knees. Very impressive. I did not know you had such courage." So Miles had told the duke some details of their adventures that night. That pleased her. "And talking of kneecaps, how is your ill-humored husband then?"

"Tender."

"Ha! Then I had best wait awhile before I make a dutiful call. Heloise, tell me, what is it like to be in love? Is it obligatory to blow hot and cold like August weather?"

"Now how would I know?"

"Because I can see where Cupid's bolts have shot great holes in you. You are in love, Heloise Ballaster, and any ass can see that."

EXCEPT MILES, WHO WAS CERTAINLY NOT AN ASS. MORE LIKE a ship dry-berthed for careening, which should have given Heloise plentiful opportunity to establish a monopoly of his time and a chance to understand him better. But, no, not a whit of it: the man's bedchamber was as busy as the sweet water conduit at West Cheap with queues pumping him for this and that.

At times stretched like a spider's windblown web, she was nurse, alchemist, secretary, and jongleuse through the days that followed, but not lover (he was not recovered sufficiently, though his eyes lied). She was frequently dispensable; whenever Buckingham's council shifted to Miles's bedside, the duke chivvied her from the bedchamber like a disgraced lapdog. Then her patient hit on the notion of sending her forth like a worker bee on his behalf to bring back gossip pollened from Crosby Place and other parts. In particular, he wished to know what was going on at Westminster.

With Martin and her maidservant for escort, Heloise took a boat upriver. The courts of justice were in session in the Westminster Great Hall so she joined the queue of pilgrims to St. Peter's great abbey and lit a candle at St. Edward's marble shrine. Like the other commoners clustering at the tomb of Henry V, victor of Agincourt, she longed to stroke his gilded armor, as if his fame might seep in through her fingertips, but a priest with a leather switch stood guard, daring any visitor to be so bold. At least the poet Chaucer's modest grave in the abbey cloister might be touched and a prayer spoken for his cheerful spirit.

It was the new curiosity at Westminster that was drawing the greatest crowd. Cordoned by kettle-helmeted White Boar halberdiers in azure and murrey jackets, the abbey sanctuary contained the beleaguered queen. Modest lodging for a great lady used to a palace! Standing on tiptoe, Heloise stared up at the stern embrasures, hoping for a glimpse of King Edward's youngest son or one of the princesses. Poor children, hedged in by weaponry, how they must yearn for freedom to frolic.

The captain of the guard was examining warrants. A man in physician's garb was waved through and so were two brawny laundresses laden with pressed sheets. Was this slapshod security deliberate, to encourage recklessness and conspiracy? Goodness, she chided herself for thinking so suspiciously.

"Lady Rushden, this is unexpected." Thomas Nandik, the Cambridge student, materialized at Heloise's elbow as she led her servants down to the King's Bridge Wharf. Clean shaven though little less swarthy, and with vertical scarlet satin ribbons ribbing his black broadcloth doublet, the scholar still wore a hungry visage like a dog waiting for scraps. "Perhaps I may escort you back to Dowgate?"

"Thank you, I—I have other errands yet, Master Nandik."

"No matter." His long loping stride kept pace with her swift steps.

She halted. "No truly, Master Nandik, I hardly think you will be interested in Rennes linen and Paris thread."

"On the contrary, my lady." The earthy eyes understood the excuse, knew she disliked him, but the wretch insisted on waving up a boat for them and helping her aboard. "I think we should get to know each other better, my lady. I would do much to earn your favor."

"I am not sure why." She shifted in the stern to avoid his thigh.

"Can you not read my mind?" His meaning was perilously plain. A perdition on the creature! If only Martin and her maidservant were not facing the other way.

"Do not belittle the power you have over others," the scholar murmured, blatantly setting his hand upon her knee.

"Go your way." His hand edged round her waist, making a stealthy foray for her breast. Biting her lip angrily, she halted that adventure, but the odious creature bent now so that his breath prickled her neck.

"I needs must come swiftly to the precious nub of the matter though I would rather have couched this more circumspectly. I know you have a special gift, my lady, and I envy you. Despite all my charts and texts, even if I were to spend the rest of my life studying the magic arts, I will never master the forces that are already at your command. Oh, madam, if Rushden has not yet broken your maidenhead, the two of us can unleash a force on Midsummer Eve that will make us rich beyond our dreams."

"Are you insane?" Have carnal knowledge of this creature in the midst of some sordid pentangle! His lewd glance made her blushing flesh crawl further. "I have no inkling what you are babbling about, Master Nandik. Now unhand me and, not that it is any of your business, I am a wife in every sense of the word and glad to be so."

"More's the pity, then. I should have warned you earlier to keep yourself unsullied." The earthy gaze was sour now. "Like taking a life, the breaking of a virgin's hymen releases a power that can be driven against one's enemies."

Miles, when she later told him privily, did not know whether to roar with laughter or risk his leg and hobble down to punch the villain.

"It is not amusing," Heloise repeated with a shudder and in compensation was coaxed up to nestle in the crook of his arm.

"No, it is not," he agreed. "Do you feel safer now?"

"With you tethered to a lump of wood? Oh yes, safe as . . . as a lamb baaing defiance at a full-grown wolf." She had been going to say as safe as the treasury had been in Lord Hastings's hands, but that bone was best avoided.

Miles chuckled. "To think that I might have driven an arcane power released by your— Mercy! You cannot strike a sick man."

"Watch me!"

"Hmm, what a beggar the fellow is! Can you not use your gift to drive some fear into our necromancer's mind so he will hoof it back to Cambridge?"

"Certainly not." The encounter with Nandik had taught her something: she must never use her gift for evil—to control others.

"Perhaps you should test your powers a little. Could you, for instance, make me sneeze? Try!"

"Sneeze?" She giggled and sobered. No, her gift was not to be squandered, but she was happy to pretend. "Is it working?"

"No," he purred, staring back. "I am having an entirely different reaction somewhere else. Bar the door, if you please!"

Heloise's eyes widened. "You cannot possibly—"

"Hmm, difficult, I grant you, but not impossible. Nothing else is fractured. It may require some resourcefulness on your part."

She pensively slid the bar down into the slots and swung round. "I am not sure I am in that humor," she murmured to torment him, but his lazy smile was already willing her towards him. "But perhaps . . . yes, I think I am going to enjoy this."

"So am I." His voice was a low masculine purr. "Unclothe yourself, delight of my heart!"

Despite his imperiousness, it was she who had him totally at her mercy. She withdrew her feet from her little leather slippers and set her right foot upon the bedsteps and with slow grace eased up her satined hem to uncover her garter, which she tardily untied and cast at him before she rolled down her wool stocking with a fine and tantalizing care.

"Is it the pain in your leg that keeps making you groan?" she asked wickedly, and seductively removed her other garter.

"You witch!" It was a gasp now. Slowly she removed her headdress and shook her silver hair to swing about her waist. Then she slid her inner sleeves down, unleashed her tasseled belt, and let it snake around her skirt with a slither to the floor, and finally she eased her gown inch by inch upwards.

"Ha! I make a better job of this," he scoffed, laughing as she was forced to seek his help.

Strong hands lifted her gown free. "It rather spoils your game but I have you fast now."

"I may cause you pain."

"It will be sublime agony, I assure you," he exclaimed huskily, dragging off her chemise. "Wait—what are you doing? Heloise!"

"What you did to me. Do you not like this . . . or . . . this?"

Heaven could not better this—or that—he decided, closing his eyes in divine delectation. A few months ago he did not give a fig for life—but now, with his sorceress stirring his blood to an ecstatic heat with her fingertips, he was learning other values afresh. "You have been waiting for a time like this to torture me, I think."

"Oh yes," she growled, moving up to tease her lips across his mouth while her fingers worked their feverish magic elsewhere.

"I will die, you wanton. Mercy, I surrender! Heloise, if you do not get atop me now, I vow I will strangle you." Iron hands nested her elbows as he hauled her into place, and slowly fitted himself into her with a low cry of pleasure that ancient Pan might have envied.

For an instant, astonishment suffused her fawn's gaze and then the centers of her eyes grew dark and wide and she rode him, driving him to such exquisite heights that he stayed her, and then it was his turn to play the sorcerer, enforce his own magic upon her, and carry her with him soaring as the world shattered about them into iridescent shards.

Heloise collapsed across him with a soft huff of breath, her hair flooding about his neck and breast. Loving arms wrapped her close, as he chanted softly:

> *"As moonlight dancing on the sea waves,*
> *So is my fey mistress beauteous;*
> *As a dew necklace spun on a morning web*
> *So my lady's eyes shimmer with starlight.*
> *Fortunate am I beyond all others,*
> *That I can wind her silver hair*
> *On the distaff of my fingers."*

"That is very beautiful," she whispered, snuggling against his breast, and he felt her tears like warm rain. "Definitely not Lewis Glyn Cothi."

"No, an Englishman." He was out of practice in versemaking but it was not bad for a rusty lover. "An excellent guess, though. The Welsh have written more about loving for their ale money than laments for their lovely, bully chieftains." Why was she crying?

Could he ever give her his heart? Heloise wondered. How pleasing it would be to find a litter of scrunched-up love speeches, tossed from his pillow: *Note IV: if this does not win her, omit VI and VII and proceed to VIII, tell her that you love her and pause here to press a kiss between her breasts. Remember to sigh loudly.*

"What is amusing you, my adorable wife?" Her lips were folded into a mischievous seam. "Secrets, hmm? Then while I recover my enfeebled power from your seductive craft, tell me what you observed today."

Predictably the sanctuary interested him most, especially the laundresses. "Hmm, so there is plenty of opportunity for conspiracy."

"You still believe that the queen is a force to be reckoned with?"

"I know it. But so long as she has the other little prince, the lord protector cannot take the throne."

"But if the princes are bastards."

"No matter. We have the proof that she was dealing with Hastings and I will wager she will smuggle her younger son out into hiding any day now as a rallying point for our enemies. There is a royal council meeting this morning and it is vital they drive their full weight against her and demand the boy, else you will be visiting me in the Tower. Curse this plaguey injury!"

"Has the queen not suffered enough?"

"What!" His eyes glittered. "Do you not want to be a countess?"

"Miles, it is not a game." Perhaps it was time for truths. "I found the speech you had written for Harry." The enigmatic gaze shifted from her face. "You have this all planned. We are like a giant chessboard to you." She watched him evade her accusation, pound the pillow and bolster as if they were scapegoats for the limits on his soaring ambition while he found words to satiate her.

"No, Heloise, not planned. I am merely seizing every opportunity. I warned you I intended to restore my family's honor. You cannot win the game if you do not toss the dice and, believe me, if you play for high stakes, you cannot afford to lose."

"But you risk attainder and a traitor's death if aught goes amiss. Supposing Parliament refuses to accept Stillington's testimony, you know the Woodvilles will take revenge. Your family will surely suffer." *And so will I. What about us, Miles?*

"Take my hand and make the climb. You have the courage."

"I? Jesu, I see how you move Buckingham like a pawn and if he is a duke, then in God's name, what am I to you, how expendable?"

A bruising question. He swallowed, then reached out to wind threads of her hair onto his finger—yes, like a distaff. "You were an inconvenience. Jesu, when your father's ruffians hauled me to the altar, it was risible. There was I with my lofty ambitions being handfasted to a merchant's daughter but now, *cariad . . .*"

"Now I am worth money to you, not just Bramley."

"You are my mirror, sweetheart. You show me my soul." He drew a caressing finger down her curves. "What is it you want from me, madam wife?"

"I do not know how much you are prepared to give."

"What, every secret, Heloise? There will be nothing to gloat over with a miser's satisfaction in the bedchamber at the end of the day."

"Miles!"

"Yes, Heloise, I play with people. That is why I want a fool like Nandik off the board. But you, my darling witch, I keep in my pocket like a talisman to be stroked. Remember that and be content."

Be content? When she loathed his dangerous lust for power? He was watching her now, his grey eyes wary as if he feared her condemnation. The intelligent mouth that she had begun to love quirked apologetically beneath her scrutiny. His gaze was asking for her acceptance and her trust. The suspicion and dislike of their swordpoint wedding night had been utterly vanquished.

"Oh, Miles." Heloise reached out a hand to touch his cheek and he turned his head and kissed her palm. *She* had become Miles Rushden's talisman, despite her feyness? The warmth of being accepted suffused her with a glorious blessing. If he could welcome her into his future, then he deserved the same of her. For now, she must set aside her fears and rejoice in this wondrous absolution. Loyalty was not to be given lightly but she offered that fealty now in mind—and body, her eyes and lips a mirror of the passion and desire in his. "My lord."

A knocking upon the arched door made her jump, cursing at the interruption, but her husband's thumb and finger anchored her and, laughing, he drew her, now sweetly desperate for his arms about her, down for a kiss of peace.

RUMPLED, DIMPLED, AND ONLY STILL PARTIALLY ENLIGHTENED, Heloise let her sister in on Monday morning to annoy her husband.

"I am visiting the invalid," Dionysia declared provocatively, swishing her skirts as she cornered the oaken bedpost. "Did you know I have moved in, Sir Miles?" Her fingers tiptoed up the shining wood. "I mean, well, since my darling eldest sister sleeps beneath this roof, it makes it respectable for me to dwell here too."

"Respectable." Weighed by her husband, the epithet grew furry. "Is she capable of being discreet?" he asked Heloise. "For I, being disagreeably tethered here, unquestionably comply with Gloucester's standards for a faithful husband. But if his northern grace discovers Harry is busy betraying marital vows and molesting virgins in his leisure time, he may believe him capable of other betrayals. Not that you were a virgin, Denise," he added acidly.

"Miles!" Heloise agreed with his sentiments, but a reproof was surely her demesne.

"Poor man. Your injuries must really be hurting." Dionysia delivered her sister a pitying flash of lashes before she flounced closer to the bed. "Is it not in your plans that Harry should fall in love, new brother?"

Miles did not answer immediately. No soft pad of humor lay beneath the message now. "Are you familiar with the prophet Jeremiah and the words 'the abomination of desolation,' Dionysia?" he asked her wearily. Could this frothy girl, tinseled with golden hair, steer Harry to safe anchorage when the heavens loured? "No? Then let me tell you that I am reminded of that phrase whenever the black moods come upon his grace. Fumblings and tumblings will not keep them at bay, mistress. At such times he detests himself and the whole of Christendom."

"Pah, it is affection he needs. He told me how there was never anyone in his childhood to love, how all his kinsmen were slain in battle, and that his grandmother sold the wardship of him."

"That is true." Harry's brother had died while still a page. As for the duke's mother, because she had married her third husband out of love, a knight with less land than he had ability, she had seen little of her son.

"Then let me help, brother-in-law. I can give Harry love."

Miles leaned upon his elbow, unmoved by the appeal in the kitten eyes. "If you speak true, so be it, but I am warning you, Dionysia, that if he ever weighs you in his balance and finds you wanting, he will make you pay."

"Pooh, a fine friend you are, to be sure, for you do naught but disparage him."

"Go away," he muttered. "You wear me out."

Heloise closed the door behind her. "Is that why you will never leave the duke, for fear of his vengeance if you do?"

"I saved his life, Heloise, up on Pen-y-Fan, and in return he gave me his friendship and I have guided him since. I will not abuse that trust."

"Even if it imperils your life?"

"Even then. With Harry's support, Gloucester will safeguard England better than any Woodvilles. Is that so wrong? Now hush, changeling, we have company."

An exuberant duke burst in with Sir William panting behind him. The older man closed the door and leaned against it. "We managed it, Miles. All is done!"

"No wonder you look so smirky, my lord duke."

Harry, pleased with himself and pretty as a popinjay, raised a brow at Heloise's presence but Miles kept his arm about her waist. "So spit it out, my gracious lord."

"The queen has surrendered the other boy. We obtained a royal command from Prince Edward that his little brother should join him, so the royal council went by barge to Westminster. Gloucester and I waited in the star chamber at the palace while Canterbury and Howard went over to the sanctuary with the abbot and requested the boy. It took two hours of arguing but she gave in eventually and we gave the little lad a right royal reception at the palace—mind, there is precious left to sit on, let alone eat off—and then the archbishop escorted the child to the royal lodging at the Tower."

"That is most excellent. No force was used, I trust?"

"Well, we did surround the sanctuary."

"Harry!" Miles had not meant to use the familiarism he kept for his thoughts. The duke looked surprised but recovered swiftly.

"That is what forced her hand, not old Bourchier's bletherings. She knew we could have broken the door down and grabbed the boy as soon as blink an eye."

"At least it has been done with the assent of the prince and the council."

"Sounds immodest, but I can claim the credit for that. 'I have heard of sanctuary men—thieves, murderers—but not sanctuary children,' I scoffed at them. 'This child is in no danger from the law, and I think if the little fellow was asked to make the decision he would tell you that he would rather not be cooped up like a chicken. And so, if Prince Richard has not asked for sanctuary, it is not breaking the law to remove him.' They all agreed. It was wondrous pleasing."

Watching the two men laughing together, Heloise wondered again why a clever man like Miles wasted his time with Buckingham when he might work for Gloucester, but she was at last beginning to understand; Miles was the steel in Buckingham's backbone. He was manipulating his duke in order to give England the stability it needed. In fact he was doing Gloucester far greater service than any of the White Boar men. Did my lord protector realize how much he owed to Miles's sensible counsel? Did Buckingham?

THE DUKE BREEZED BACK TO MILES'S BEDCHAMBER LATER THAT night with Knyvett and de la Bere, armed with leather bottles and Spanish apples, skylark high in love and a-thirst with power. Drunk already on civic wine, Harry gleefully boasted that he had persuaded Ralph Shaa, the lord mayor's famous preacher brother, to amend his Sunday sermon at Paul's Cross and hint that King Edward's children were bastards. Such high-handedness bothered Miles. Nor was he pleased when the duke bussed Heloise on the mouth and set her outside the chamber like washing for collection in the morning.

Nandik, hallooed from a straw mattress in the hall, arrived to pour soupy ale down his scraggy throat, and when Harry unstoppered a bottle with his teeth and spat the bung clear across the bed, Miles knew it was going to be a long night.

"Now is the time, Nandik." The ducal swagger had grown wobbly. "I want you to cast the lord protector's horoscope. Just for amusement, lad." A lift of jeweled hands endorsed the feeble claim that no harm was meant.

"For Sweet Christ's sake, my lord," protested Miles, wishing they would all go.

"No, your grace," Nandik replied resolutely. " 'Tis akin to witchcraft, not to mention treason. You might as well ask me to cast the young king's too and put my head fully in a noose."

"Aye, that too."

"Harry lad!" This time it was Knyvett sobering fast.

"Nay, my lord duke." Nandik adamantly shook his unkempt head. "My innards ripped out and my balls pulled off while all you may get is a few lousy weeks in the Tower and a dose of penance, *your grace.* No, I thank you!"

Harry wanted obedience. "Between the four of us, man, and then you may destroy it all. I will pay you well."

"My gracious lord, you have been generous enough but . . ."

"Forcing the price up?" Miles took a fruit from the pewter dish upon the coverlet and dug his thumbnail beneath the marigold peel.

Nandik ignored him. "I can promise little accuracy or even truth."

Harry had the bit between his teeth. "Gloucester's future, Nandik. His horoscope before morning."

Nandik's eyes fell before Miles's condemnatory gaze and then he lifted his head with the same crafty mien as when he broke the news at Brecknock. "I have already done so. My lord, he will be king."

Twenty-three

"What took you, changeling?" exclaimed Miles, relief destroying his tense expression. "You did buy a seat in the stands, did you not?" Pleased he had been concerned for her, Heloise leaned over to kiss him and waited as he struggled to unbutton the knop of her Sunday cloak. "Ugh! I thought witches hated water."

"You deserve a clout, sir! Your leg may be mending but your manners are not. There is a limit to wifely duty." She had just spent two hours at St. Paul's Cross. "I was never one for sermons, and I have not changed my mind."

"Not enthralling?" Disappointment edged his voice.

"About as inspiring as watery gruel—'These bastard slips shall not take root.'"

"Oh." Distaste wrinkled the Rushden nose.

"Yes. Not a good idea of your noble friend's."

"Tell me the worst."

"Friar Shaa was obviously supposed to show that the princes were bastards and that Gloucester was the most English of the Yorkists."

"He was born in Fotheringay," her husband offered pedantically.

"Yes, as opposed to Rouen or Dublin like his brothers. Anyway, my lord protector was so late arriving that the part where Shaa was to flourish an arm at the duke and declare that he was English and the image of his Plantagenet father made no impact. So what does the friar do but stop in midsentence and wait while Gloucester and his retainers settle themselves, and then he repeats a quarter of the sermon at galloping speed so that he can do this grand gesture again. Believe me, the reasoning fell as flat as any pancake missing the frypan. The intelligent were not impressed, the stupid were even more confused, and Gloucester was crimson with embarrassment." She grinned mischievously. "Do you want something to hit?"

"Yes, preferably Harry's jaw." Miles carried her hand to his lips. "Thank you for putting up with it and with me."

Her muddy pattens clattered to the floor as she perched herself on the bed beside him and frowned at her toes pensively. "There is some sinister mischief at work. This 'being English' business is fanning the shameful rumor that her grace of York slept with a Flemish archer to beget King Edward, and I can assure you, Miles—having lived in her household—that it is a wonder that she slept with anything save beads and a missal, or begat all those children."

Miles nodded, his mind's cogs and wheels turning. "And where is Gloucester now?"

"Gone home to his mother's to lick his wounds, and she will need soothing too, I imagine. Both dukes need their ears boxed, if you ask me." There had been gratification in Buckingham's face as if he had been pleased to see his cousin discomforted.

"Well, Harry shall do better at the Guildhall on Tuesday, I promise you, Heloise, for I have rehearsed him hard, and he is to address Parliament on Wednesday. With luck, we shall have a new king by Thursday night."

But what of tomorrow—St. John's Eve, when the Londoners caroused around their bonfires? Were the Woodville retainers planning an uprising? There had been no more glimpses of the future, but Heloise welcomed the reassuring warmth of Miles's hand.

"What if Buckingham gets a taste for it, Miles?"

"Kingmaking, *cariad?*"

"The power and the glory. It is heady fare."

"For a lad from Brecknock? Never fear, I shall nail his feet to the floor."

Heloise bit back an unwifely retort. The ship was in full sail now. She only hoped that Gloucester would survive the voyage.

*   *   *

NEXT EVENING LONDON WAS ABLAZE WITH BONFIRES AS A *crocodilus* of armed men clanked its way through the carousing streets. Gloucester and his duchess stood on the stone balcony of Tamersilde, a royal pavilion flanking St. Mary Bow in West Cheap, watching the torchlight procession with Lord Mayor Shaa and Juliana, his wife. Heloise, invited too, and tense to her knucklebones, was carrying a whetted dagger in her sleeve, praying that there would be no rising; fearful a vision of Miles strung up on a scaffold for the executioner's knife might come to her.

Around her, she could feel the others' fear. Gloucester's henchmen sweated in breastplates hidden beneath high-necked doublets tailored for a winter feast. Only Buckingham wore his shirt untethered at the neck, and the heady glitter in his eyes outshone the splendor of his golden knots and Venice buttons.

"There is nothing amiss," murmured Huddleston, materializing from the back stairs to join his wife and Heloise. "Perhaps you should advise Anne to smile, Margery. From the street, she looks more like a lady in travail than a happy duchess."

Margery nodded and glided across to tug her sister's veil but Heloise lingered.

"Sir Richard, a word with you, pray. Did you set Dionysia to spy on Buckingham?" Her smile was honest, hiding the claws of the conversation.

Sir Richard Huddleston raised an eyebrow. "It was she who made the bargain. Does it bother you?"

"I am his grace of Gloucester's loyal servant, I assure you, but Buckingham, so my husband informs me, shares the Plantagenet distaste for treachery. Could you not retire her from your service straightway? If this is discovered, the duke . . . well, might be unforgiving."

"I thank you for the warning, Heloise. I have told her so but your sister chose this path and her services do not come cheap. Ah, Margery, my mousekin, and my lord and lady." He bowed his head to his duke and duchess.

"It is not like being in the north," murmured Duchess Anne. "How glad I shall be when tonight is over."

"Ah but this," exclaimed Buckingham, insinuating himself between the Gloucesters, an arm about either of their slight shoulders, "is only the beginning."

"NEVER PAUSED TO SPIT," EXCLAIMED SIR WILLIAM, REPORTING back to Miles next evening on Buckingham's kingmaking speech at the Guildhall. He accepted a tankard of ale from Heloise. "Excellent performance, though I heard one guildsman mutter, 'Who does he think he is, the angel Gabriel?' and a few of 'em had their mouths hanging open like holes for nesting gulls. Well done!" He thumped Miles's shoulder and handed him a celebratory drink. "You would have been proud of him, lad. What perverse fortune, eh, that you should be missing all the huzzahs."

"Tomorrow is the key," cautioned Miles, clinking the pewter tankards. "Providing Harry can persuade Parliament to petition Gloucester to take the crown, all will be lawful."

"Aye, it'll need to be." Knyvett tugged his earlobe. "Someone's peppering the rumors and it isn't us. Old loyalties are crawling out from beneath the stones."

THERE SEEMED TO BE LITTLE LEFT OF THE OLD DAUB-AND-wattle Buckingham showing through the newly surfaced exterior, decided Heloise; all his phrases began to sound rehearsed. He breezed in after supper to visit Miles and finalize next day's speech, but when Heloise was allowed in afterwards, her husband's jaw was a little more tilted, his tight-lipped frustration at his immobility more apparent. If he was unable to keep a watchful eye on his lord, Heloise was feeling the same about Dionysia.

She ran her to earth in the ducal bedchamber next morning after the duke had gone to make his speech to Parliament.

"Didie, I need to talk with you," she announced, dismissing

her sister's maid and making sure the antechamber was clear of servants.

"Would you like to check the chests and ambries too?" snapped her sister, snatching up the hairbrush the maid had relinquished. "I have an amorous goldsmith hidden beneath the mattress and that is not a nightingale within that cage but an agent for my lord of Gloucester. Has the invalid turned you out for an airing?"

Heloise counted for six heartbeats to still her temper and then persevered. "Agent, strange you should say that. I was thinking of the yellow-haired spy who reports all she hears." Dionysia made no comment and she added, "Be Buckingham's mistress if you must, but for your own safety, be loyal to him."

Dionysia's attention diverted to a well-snagged tress. "So you fathomed me."

"Didie, listen to me!" Heloise put her hand down over the matted bristles. "If Buckingham suspects you of coaxing his confidences . . ."

"If, if. What can he do to me?" The hand mirror rose; the cherry lips were drawstringed to a pout. A long-nailed forefinger explored whether the whitehead's hard center might be exuded. "Only until the coronation, Heloise, that is the arrangement." The mirror tilted so the silver surface snared her sister's face.

"I insist you go back to Crosby Place. Your spying puts both of us at risk."

Dionysia laid the mirror on its face and ran a finger beneath the emerald collar that encircled her throat. "See this? Harry trusts me. He *needs* me. Deep inside he is uncertain, unloved. I want to prove to him that he undervalues himself."

"Pigs might fly! Buckingham has not undervalued himself since Gloucester made him ruler of Wales a month since. He probably kisses his shaving mirror when his valet holds it up to him."

"I want to have a child by him, Heloise."

"Grow up, Didie. You are talking such utter nonsense."

"Am I? I want to be loved by the most powerful man in England and Gloucester is a pious bore, so it has to be Buckingham and that pleases me well."

"Well, it does not please me. I really fear for you."

"Oh, Heloise!" She struck a pose like a Yuletide mummer, her hand a question mark upon her brow. " 'Oh woe, alack, I see a great black crow cast its wings across you, Dionysia, oh yes and there will be plagues of locusts in the Cotswolds.' "

"And there very well might," snapped Heloise, "and I hope they all land on you. What if I should receive a warning? What would you say then?"

"Darling Cassandra, I love you but I do not believe in your predictions. Does anyone? 'Changeling,' " she mocked Miles's affectionate tone. "Ask *him* if he believes one word of it. Please, do not look so put out, Heloise, I am not saying you are a charlatan like Nandik—Harry keeps him like a pet ape for amusement—but I do not believe in your faeries. It is wealth that makes our dreams come true."

Heloise closed the door of the bedchamber and leaned against it, eyes closed. An amused cough alerted her; Pershall, the duke's servant, was sitting in the window seat.

"I . . . I was quarreling with my sister."

"Were you, my lady?" His pebble brown eyes gave her absolution. "Upon my oath, I did not eavesdrop. In this house, one learns to be as discreet as a cat watching a birdtable."

"Pershall, you must keep him safe."

"Who, my lady?"

"The duke, Pershall. If he falls, we shall all land in a heap."

The weathered wrinkles tightened. "Aye, I know."

BY THURSDAY NIGHT, THE KINGMAKING HAD BEEN COMPLETED. Harry on bended knee had eloquently offered the crown to his cousin at Baynards Castle, and Gloucester, flanked by his wife and mother on the barbican, had looked down at the plump worm of nobles and worthies coiling into the cobbled triangle with godlike suspicion but of course he had accepted. At least the coup had been bloodless, Miles congratulated himself, if one discounted the demise of Hastings and the distant executions of the hostages Rivers and Grey.

As the bells of the city pealed in the reign of King Richard, it was Harry who decreed a repeat of the final moments of victory for his frustrated speechwriter.

Bolstered by muscadelle and pillows, Miles lay back with Heloise embellishing his outstretched arm like a serif, while upon his other side, Dionysia Ballaster sat detached, with catlike independence, her study entirely centered upon her lover.

Harry, hatless, took up his stance below Knyvett, who was poised sternly on the oaken chest like an unearthed Roman statue. De la Bere and Latimer provided the crowd.

' "My lords, gentlemen, friends all,' " Knyvett declared, trying to sound like Gloucester, " 'you do me greater honor than any man may dream of, and yet the task you wish on me is . . .' "

"Onerous," prompted de la Bere.

" '—onerous. I pray you do not ask this of me for even if Prince Edward is England's unlawful king, he is still my brother's child. I cannot agree to take my nephew's crown'—or words to that effect," Knyvett added. "Can I get down now?"

"No, William, we have not finished yet." Harry turned to Miles. "Basically, I said that if he would not accept the crown, we should have to send for someone else and that there was another right willing across the water."

"Tudor!" exclaimed Miles. That had not been in the speech notes.

"Aye, it lit the powder. Oh, he went rigid."

"So what did he answer?"

Latimer threw a cushion to prompt Knyvett, who knotted his hands before him and declared: " 'If it is truly your desire, then I shall accept, but *be sure* all of you that you want me for your king, for without your love, such kingship as I may offer you rests but as on eggshells. I have no wish to be king.' There was a jeer then. Just one. Someone jeer!" Latimer obliged.

Heloise shifted uneasily beneath Miles's arm. His wife's hidden disapproval echoed his own misgivings at the irreverence. England needed a man like Gloucester, a man who cared about justice and consultation. Why the mockery? *In vino veritas?*

" 'Then I must obey God's will and yours,' " Sir William declaimed solemnly. " 'I swear before almighty God that I shall do my best to bring peace and justice to this troubled land.' " The room was silent. Somewhere in the laneway a dog barked.

"God save King Richard." Harry's soft words caressed the unexpected quiet. He shot Miles a swift ironic smile before he turned to help Knyvett back to the floorboards. "I think we may dispense with the hat-tossing, huzzahs, and applause at this point."

"I certainly received the drift."

Heloise felt the arm about her stiffen and raised her head, questioning. *It shall not be the axe for me yet a while,* his expression swiftly told her, but his eyes were as brilliant as lodesterres as he studied Buckingham. For an instant, the two men stared at one another and then Miles disengaged his arm from entanglement and, palms up, offered the silent wreaths that were expected.

Buckingham gave him a mighty hug, buffeting his shoulder. "We are safe, Miles! We did it! You clever whoreson, this is all your doing."

Tears ran down the panes of Miles's soul.

Gulping back his own emotion, Buckingham withdrew his moist cheeks so that his expression might embrace them all. "We plaguey did it!" The bed at that point descended into a rout of limbs until Miles yelped loudly and his apologetic friends sprang off like a volley of cannonfire.

"YOU HAVE AN UNEXPECTED VISITOR," HELOISE ANNOUNCED next day, swiftly kicking a forgotten stocking under the bed as Sir Richard Huddleston entered.

"Is it someone's saint's day?" asked Miles dryly.

"Sir!" rebuked his wife.

"Not unless you are a culinary devotee of St. Martha." His guest's glance took in the abandoned trivet, the tray of phials and herbs, and the half-played chess game. "We can cook you an omelette to the chanting of prayers if Lady Rushden can purvey some eggs." He sat himself uninvited on the bed and tossed his riding crop and gloves aside.

"I hear your hearty northerners have arrived," Miles remarked smoothly, his fingers stroking a captured pawn. "My lord of Northumberland too. How very embarrassing, now the hurly-burly is over."

"Yes," agreed Huddleston, clearly aware that he was being baited. "They are to be sworn in as special constables for Coronation Day. We have ordered hat badges so they will have something to take home with them other than London curses. I am the bearer of thanks from our new king, by the way, master speechwriter. A gift of fresh quills might have been appropriate but let us hope there is no need. Something more permanent might be arranged in due course—*when the hurly-burly is over*." Here he bestowed a light smile upon Heloise, who was resisting the temptation to bang their heads together.

"The king's grace desires you both to attend at the abbey on Sunday week," he added. "I am afraid that even if we dress you in colors to match everyone else, Rushden, your palliasse will untidy the procession. Now if we had another horizontal knight to keep things tidy . . ." He finished the sentence with a shrug.

Miles took up the challenge. "We could stab the Marquis of Dorset if we could find him, carry him in to balance appearances, and hold the funeral at the same time as the corona—"

"His highness's thoughtfulness is most appreciated," cut in Heloise swiftly, "but I am not certain that—"

"Perhaps a cart the night before," suggested Miles, quelling her. "We can tidy away the bedpans before people in ermine start arriving."

"I will clear matters with his grace of Buckingham." Their visitor retrieved his movables and rose. "One last thing. Are the tavern rumors all from you?"

"No."

"That is what I thought but . . ." Huddleston had no intention of finishing the sentence before he left.

"Well," exclaimed Heloise as she returned from escorting their visitor down the stairs. "I missed half of that, or were you growling at one another beneath the level of female understanding?"

Miles's forehead was like a ploughman's strip. "There were no growls."

"I hate to say it but this going to the abbey is foolish. You could spoil the mending."

"You think they want me permanently crippled? There's a thought."

Bestowing icy looks upon him was to cast water on an impervious surface. Her drake, having had a bout of feather ruffling, looked fit to curse. "Make sure you know where *your* interest lies, madam wife," he muttered.

"And what is that supposed to mean?" Fists on her hips. One could not pummel one's horizontal husband.

"I thought you could read minds."

"Not when they are as obtuse as yours!"

"Miles!" bellowed an impatient voice from the stairs. "Curse it, lad! Do you have to have your bedchamber half . . . way to Heaven!" Red-faced and panting, a large man lingered, stoppering the doorway until he was poked forward. "What is this I hear that you have gone and married a cursed Ballaster wench?" There was no mistaking to whom her husband owed his ebony hair and aristocratic beak.

"Would you like to curtsy, Heloise," suggested Miles suavely. "It might help."

Pushed off the coverlet, Heloise blinked up at the intimidating man she had nearly encountered at Potters Field. "Lord Rushden." The sudden huskiness of her voice was lost in a rustle of skirts as she sank obediently.

"You must admit it settles the matter of Bramley, Phillip." The lady who spoke materialized from behind Lord Rushden, and Heloise's gaze met the sea grey eyes of Miles's mother. She raised Heloise up and kissed her on either cheek. "It *is* the right one," she murmured, but such a cryptic remark confused Lord Rushden. He stared puzzled at Heloise's right cheek and then understanding came and he reached out and pinched it anyway in a friendly manner.

"Wear your armor to bed, do you?"

"Not anymore," answered Heloise cheerfully. "The lance-rest was a nu—" She turned pink as a billowy sunset as Miles's fist thumped the bed and he curled sideways laughing. It was not what she had meant.

"It is all right." A large paw shook her shoulder. "She will do, lad. She will do!"

MILES ABJURED THE CORONATION. VIEWING NOTHING BUT sweaty ankles from his mattress would be too obnoxious. He was safer stewing in Dowgate, decided Heloise, who was herself crushed in the overscented throng at Westminster beside her mother-in-law, for the July sun was not cooking the abbey; it was steaming it. Paste-stiff veils were growing limp upon their wires, and ermine and gris trimmings began to heat their wearers' tempers before the fanfares shimmered through the holy, perfumed air. Drawing Miles's mother with her, she edged through to the edge of the nave. On tiptoe she could just glimpse the scarlet platform beneath an embroidered canopy and St. Edward's chair swathed with silk imperial.

The procession of the cross and the anthem *Ecco milto angelum meum* hushed the congregation. The lords spiritual, from cathedrals and abbeys all over the realm, passed by, their heavy brocades fumed with frankincense. Two by two came the young Knights of the Bath, all freshly dubbed and washed the night before, hesitantly led by Clarence's son. Heloise was curious to see the young boy who was barred from the throne by his late father's treason; no wonder he was forgotten, for the lad's face was moonish like poor Benet's.

To the chanting of the Twentieth Psalm, *Domine in virtute*, came the high nobles of England, bearing the ceremonial weapons and jeweled regalia which somehow had been retrieved from the queen's pilferings. Howard, the freshly minted Duke of Norfolk, carried within his hands St. Edward's crown, its golden buttresses shining as it passed beneath the shafts of sunlight. The great lords did not falter in their steps but the ceremonial cushions shook a little. Only Lord Stanley, freed from the Tower to encourage reconciliation, had difficulty in timing his stride to match the rest.

Richard of Gloucester was magnificent in his crimson, miniver, and gold but his face reminded Heloise of a devout priest about to be ordained as though it was not the crowning but the anointing with the holy oil that meant so much to him. Four barons held the tasseled cloth of estate above his head and two bishops flanked him: Durham and, as was customary, Bath and Wells. Stillington, mitered, splendid in fine wool and glistening tartaryne, met his nurse's study. The crow's-feet eyes bestowed a conspiratorial blessing, the dried lips a smile. Heloise knuckled the telltale tears away. She was proud of Gloucester, her duke, and happy for England.

Careful, but perhaps tempted to tread upon the king's long train of Roman purple, Buckingham, in blue cloth shot with gold and wrought with pearl droplets, followed bearing the white wand of office. He had insisted on being made High Steward of England for the occasion. The black velvet lining the mulberry train whispered at his heels, dusting the tiles before the earls bearing the queen's crown and scepter.

Queen Anne also walked beneath a canopy tasseled at each corner by a golden bell. She looked frail under the heavy robes, her forehead strained below the pearl and gems, and her milky skin outfaced by the rose red that had never suited her. Corn-hued hair, so rarely visible, caped her to the thighs. She turned her head as Heloise willed her attention. The smile came from the new queen's heart but pain like a torturer's iron band fastened inside Heloise's ribs. *Oh, your grace, God keep you!*

Jesu forfend! Heloise recoiled, instinctively suspicious of the stranger who bore Queen Anne's train. Behind an enigmatic smile, the heavy-lidded eyes were making an inventory of who was there and who was not. The shrewd gaze paused on Miles's mother and the jeweled coronet dipped in acquaintance.

"Who is she?" Heloise gasped, her mind buffeted by a will-power more formidable than anything she had encountered in her life.

"Margaret Beaufort, Countess of Richmond." Henry Tudor's mother! As if sensing that Heloise carried the wrong allegiance, the countess tightened her gloved hands upon the purple velvet, her gaze passing on. But with all the fey power that she could muster, Heloise slit through the mind behind the high-boned cheeks like a surgeon and laid it open. What she discovered was a putrescent envy of immense proportions; in Margaret Beaufort's mind, it was her son's face beneath the crown.

She scarcely noticed other noblewomen passing by until Lady Margery Huddleston sent her a beaming smile and the world righted itself again. And there was Miles's father too, among the lesser barons, giving her a broad wink as he passed.

The Latin anthems soared upon the organ's winging sound, for King Richard's love of music was great indeed. Only those clustered round the throne might witness the anointing, the oath to England sworn for the first time in English, the final lowering of the crown, and assess Buckingham's expression as the shouts rang forth.

> *"Verus rex, Rex Ricardus!*
> *Rectus rex, Rex Ricardus!*
> *Iustus, juridicus et legitimus rex, rex Ricardus!*

Cui omnes nos subjicio volumus.
Suaeque humillime iugem, admittere guernationis!"

God's will was manifest but Heloise felt uncomfortable as she
watched the duke follow his new sovereign down the nave. No
longer cousins nor peers but king and subject. And how would
Miles's Harry feel about that?

THUNDER ROLLED AND SHOOK THE CITY AS HELOISE, WAFTING
incense fumes, regaled Miles with her account before the others
trooped back, sloshing with claret and malvesey. She had de-
canted some hackled peacock, great carp in foile, and close tart
indorred for him to savor and he was grateful, but he lay awake
beside her in the early hours, desperate for flight like a tethered
hawk, grieving that he had had the journey but not the arrival.

His new wife, as if wakened by his mind's call, slid her hands
over the breastplate of dark hair and pressed her body questioningly against him. Encouraged, she used her new learning to
please and his yearning flesh hardened hungrily within her hand.

"By the saints, I could not have endured this without you,
changeling."

"Harry could have hired you a trio of Winchester geese to ease
your problem."

"You," his lips told her hair, "are not supposed to know of
such creatures. Nor of the Hereford whores or—"

A woman's scream split the silence like a lightning strike and
a howl of anguish followed.

"Christ!"

His lady would have grabbed her robe and followed the sound
but Miles's fingers fastened round her wrist. "No! Leave it to
Knyvett!"

"It is—"

"Your sister. Yes, I know. Wait! Wait!" Bridling a wildcat
might have been simpler but he held on grimly to Heloise as
Dionysia's voice rose in argument. They heard the sound of

heavier feet hurrying up the stairs and Sir William's rumbling tone, then a smack of bone and a woman's keening wail, sad and lost.

"No!" Miles muttered through clenched teeth. "It is not your quarrel!"

"She is my sister!"

"You will stay here, madam!" In kindness he forced her back against the pillow, his hands upon her wrists like iron staples. "Let her learn to manage the darkness in him."

"She loves him."

"Love!" he scoffed. "Dionysia? Do you need spectacles, *cariad?*" It was a risk to loosen her in such a humor. Starlit hair hid her face from him as she sullenly rubbed her wrists, legs sideways beneath her like a mermaid tail.

"You would not know love if it buffeted you between the eyes," she hissed. "You buried your heart six foot deep two years hence."

Astounded at the lash of words, he gazed at her and then said quietly, "Give me a crutch and a spade and I will go and look for it."

"You have to dig for it?" Indignation fired the words at him like hostile crossbolts as she sprang off the bed. Thank God she lacked the beehives.

He swallowed, devastated that he had somehow unleashed a Fury. "I have given you the protection of my name, Heloise; I have given you the loyalty of my body and—"

She tossed a scathing look at his injured leg. "Ha, that has yet to be tested."

"You shrew," he exclaimed, "I married you because—"

"Because it amused you to annoy both dukes and because I was suddenly wealthy and you did not have my father to disgrace you. Oh, answer me, is not that the truth?"

"Yes."

"Ohhhh!" The candlestick was seized. He ducked. Jesu, he was becoming good at ducking.

"Perhaps you should know, madam," he threw back as haughtily as he could from the horizontal, "that I saved you from persecution."

"That was self-interest and you know it—naught but drunken Welsh poe—"

"No, Dokett."

"Dokett! Gloucester would not have let—"

"You are mistaken. Dokett was all ready to speak with Canterbury. He wanted you pincered, sweetheart." Ah, that silenced her. His tone shed the sarcasm. "I will have your gratitude, madam, and you may keep your rebukes scabbarded in future. It seems to me there is much you have to learn."

"I! Well, thank you, sir, for your charity and condescension. There is more to a marriage than being your concubine and nursemaid but I doubt you are capable of learning something so simple, you arrogant dolt!"

"Dolt!" No one had ever—

"I—I am going back to . . . to Bramley until you—"

"*Heloise.*"

He nearly fell with the pain as he stumbled after her but she caught him in time and heaved him back against the bed. With no words left to lean upon, he let her help him back into the prison of sheets.

"Heloise, you are not going anywhere, *please.*" His hand opened upon the coverlet, palm uppermost in peace. "I married you because I wanted you alive. Beside me."

She left the chamber. He heard her moving things in the outer room and closed his eyes tightly, trying not to imagine how empty the world would be without her.

"Here." Metal touched the side of his hand. "It will ease the pain." Relieved, he dragged himself up against the bolster and took the cup.

"Thank you." He thanked God too as his slender wife climbed back beside him.

*   *   *

DIONYSIA HAD VANISHED WHEN HELOISE SOUGHT HER OUT next morning. The servants shrugged, disclaiming knowledge, and Buckingham and his retinue had gone to mass with the king at Westminster.

Miles did not share her sisterly concern. "I warned you she expected too much. I'll wager she has bolted back to Crosby Place. Probably pulling up irises in a huff."

"You are not going to like what I have to say, sir."

Miles suppressed a husbandly groan. He did not remember Sioned being this difficult.

"I believe Dionysia was just a whipping boy last night. Hurting her was the only way your friend Harry could vent his jealousy."

"What in God's name are you saying?"

"I am saying, Miles, that he covets the crown." The words spattered between them like foul droplets contaminating the air.

Her lord's expression was as chill as Purbeck marble. "Christ Almighty, Heloise, as you value your life, hold your tongue!" The ensuing silence was bitter even though she sensed the man's anger cool. "Come here." He held out his hands.

"It is true—" But his mouth came down on hers, stanching the truth. "It is true," she repeated, wrenching her face away. "He cannot live with himself. He has to prove he is better than anyone and now it will be King Richard who must be taught that lesson."

Miles turned his face away, breathing hard. Heloise sprang off the bed and sought refuge at the window, her fingers clenched against her breastbone.

Please help my sister, her heart cried out, but no sparkle of wings caught the moon's cold light. Instead, Nandik's face floated through her mind like a reflection rippling upon dirty water. Was it he who had set the mischief threading through Buckingham's mind like a fungus? She could feel the evil insinuating itself like a monstrous fog.

*   *   *

In desperation she set out for Crosby Place but the household had moved to Westminster Palace and it was past noon when Heloise managed to steal Margery away from the new queen's presence and beg her help.

"Sweet Heaven, Heloise, your sister could be anywhere, on her way back to your family perhaps?"

"No, I do not believe so. Buckingham has found out she has been informing on him. I am certain of it. Ask Sir Richard to find her, please, Margery. I know she is in peril."

"Of course, of course, we can start with Buckingham's closest manors, but it will take many days. Since your husband knows of the quarrel, could he not broach the matter directly with his duke?"

If he was speaking to her! She found him playing chess with Knyvett when she returned. Both men were looking grave.

"Is there news? Can *you* tell me where my sister is, Sir William?" she pleaded, drawing off her gloves. "What happened last night?"

"A bad business." Knyvett shook his silvering head. "I hit Harry last night because I thought him in the wrong, but it seems your sister was a paid informer." Oh, Jesu!

"Who says so?" she asked with sisterly disbelief.

"Nandik."

"*Nandik!*"

"Aye, apparently Harry set him secretly to mind her. See that she came to no harm. Nandik saw her meet each day with one of the king's henchmen."

"But, naturally she is acquainted with king's men, Sir William. She was at Middleham. Oh, for pity's sake, where there is a will to do evil, anything will serve. I beg you both, ask his grace what is become of her."

The older knight pulled a wry face at Miles. "Harry will not be speaking to me the rest of the day. If you want my advice, my lady, keep away from him. Certes, I shall." Then his expression chilled. "I hope your sister's duplicity was news to you, madam."

"Of course my wife knows nothing of this," Miles answered for her. "So where *is* Dionysia now?"

Knyvett's lower lip curled. "Pranced off in a womanly sulk? When Harry's temper has cooled, we may learn something. I will see you later, Miles."

"Dear God!" Heloise whirled round on her husband. "Could you not ask the duke outright?"

"Let this rest! His grace will tell me when he is ready."

"Dionysia is afraid, Miles. I know it." Her temples ached. "You do not care, do you?"

"To be frank, no. I disliked your sister on first acquaintance and I like her even less now."

"Then you will not help me, sir?"

"Sir," Miles's servant interrupted. "There is a gentlewoman come who desires speech with you. She would not give her name."

Heloise said a prayer it might be word of Dionysia.

"Show her up," muttered Miles grimly. "And I promise you I will help you, *cariad.*"

Black Mechlin gauze shrouded the visitor's face. A widow, perhaps, with a petition, save that she carried no scroll or folded parchment. Virtuous certainly, for the blue-black robe embroidered with sable daisies enveloped her to the throat, and her fingers, clad in gloves of soft, expensive leather, rose to fold at her waist with nunlike briskness.

"Thank you," exclaimed the woman brusquely, as if his lady were only a servant. "Now, leave us, if you please. I wish to speak with Sir Miles alone."

Only after the door closed did she set back the veil to uncover a finely boned face of intelligent rather than beauteous mien. Her nose was not to his taste, and her upper lip was far too furrowed. The hollow cheeks hinted at asceticism but the lady's roundish, small eyes examined him with a disconcerting worldliness. Two-score years and childless, he hazarded, noting the lean hips and flat belly.

"*Y Cysgod.*" It was said correctly as if she was familiar with matters Welsh and of course she was. The hammer struck the anvil in Miles's mind—Margaret Beaufort, Henry Tudor's mother! She had buried Buckingham's uncle Harry some ten years since before taking on Lord Stanley as a husband. Miles looked afresh at her now, reminded of a raptor by the way the woman smiled.

"Not a *cysgod* at the moment, my lady," he replied wryly, glancing meaningfully to where his toes made contours of the coverlet.

"*May* I congratulate you on Harry's speech at Baynards Castle, Sir Miles?"

No, you may not, he thought, wondering how in hell she had found that out. He watched in irritated helplessness as Tudor's mother explored his demesne, glancing at his papers. "Why are you here, my lady?" If word reached King Richard that Tudor's *maman* had visited him at the Red Rose, the White Boar men would be watching him like hungry kites—if they were not already.

Margaret Beaufort paused in her peregrinations. "You know, I always wondered what my nephew's—well, nephew by marriage—capabilities are. I can see now." Was that supposed to flatter him? "A pity you are immobile, Sir Miles, and no longer have your hand upon Harry's leading rein." A bony finger prodded at the plate that had borne his dinner and raised the jug to sniff its contents. "Like fat, riches and fame can bring ruin to a person, if one does not have the backbone."

When she turned her back, he was able to glare at her, desirous of escorting her out.

"A pity, yes," his tormentor continued, "and just when you have reached the top of the mountain—well, almost." Miles held his temper, barely. Anchored by his injuries, he felt like a mouse being played with by a cat. "I am told Pen-y-Fan is usually stifled by fog and most days you cannot see a thing from the top—just like Harry. Does he merely want to rub the Woodvilles' noses in the mire? What was it that heretic Wycliffe wrote about the higher an ape climbs?"

The more you could see the filth of his hind parts. Miles's fingers itched to seize the handbell that lay behind his pillow but one could not throw things at a countess with the bastardized blood of John of Gaunt in her veins and a claim to the throne. She came back to regard him from the foot of the bed, coiling her fingers round one of the bedposts. "I know the story about you and Harry. He owes you his life, does he not?"

"And I owe him my livelihood, madam."

"What was it you actually saved him from—the cold?" Jesu, the woman could distort an act of quick-wittedness that other people respected into something to smirk at. "I truly am sorry about your leg." It was the way she said it. Everything this creature said had a layer beneath it.

And he reached the lowest layer. Christ protect him! So it had not been Hastings's people but her villains, garbed as Hastings's retainers, who had attacked him! What in God's name did she want? Suddenly he was afraid of being alone with her but—Jesu mercy, what was the matter with him? He could deal with any woman if he had to.

"Poor Hastings," she mused, as if she read his thoughts. "What an inconvenience he was to us all." Needle-stitching fingers stroked the pectoral cross of pearls set in gold that leaned obliquely upon her slight chest.

Miles had had enough. "Do you want an *amnestia* for your son, my lady? I can raise the matter with his grace."

"Oh, that is already done. Harry and I met, quite by chance, at the Red Pale, Caxton's printing works, you know." She was at the window now.

"Yes, I know," he muttered. Did she think him a country lout?

As if she was timing matters, she swung round, leaning back

against the mullion. "You were clever to nose out Stillington and you certainly presented very good arguments in your speeches, Sir Miles. A pity there is not more employment for kingmakers, but if ever you are impoverished, do let me know." Then she added, "You see, I do not believe that Gloucester's friends really want Harry's interference, so I should be much more careful in future, if I were you." Her glance slid from his face down the outline of his body.

Was she saying now that it had been Gloucester's men who had tried to kill him? Miles felt as though he was being forced to somersault his mind through hoops. Who in Hell had tried to rid Harry of his shadow *and why?*

"One day, Sir Miles, perhaps you will come to my way of thinking. There are so many wicked rumors around. King Richard III is such a good man—his speech on justice quite remarkable. In fact, I doubt we could have a better king, but some of the dirt must inevitably stick. The rumors are outrageous, are they not? As if our new and noble sovereign has murdered those poor little boys!"

Miles forced his fists to stay unclenched.

"And what nonsense about him being in love with his niece and intending to poison his wife. And yet that is what they are saying in the alehouses. *Calumniare fortites, et aliquid adhaerebit.*"

How much more putrescence could this woman ooze?

"Ah, you are so fortunate in having time to think at the moment. Make the best of such leisure, sirrah. Perhaps you would like to question your wife about who may have caused your injuries. She is very thick with Gloucester's henchmen. You know, I suppose, that it was Lady Huddleston who talked your wife into going to Brecknock and persuaded the fair-haired sister to insinuate herself 'twixt Harry's sheets."

It took all his considerable willpower to ask calmly: "How would you know that?"

"Because I interest myself in the activities of Margery Huddleston and her green-eyed husband. Ask your wife, eh? Adieu."

A cold hand touched his. He did not waste any gallantry upon it. "I trust you will not suffer any other misfortune, Sir Miles." At the door she paused. "Either you are not clever enough or you chose the wrong horse to saddle. I suspect both. Good day to you."

Miles buried his face in his pillow and swore sufficiently to make a stable hand embarrassed.

"How dare she treat me like a menial!" Heloise swept in, the epitome of outraged virtue. "What did that woman want with you? Jesu, you look like a wrung-out cloth."

"We need to talk, madam." His heavy tone needled her further.

"Dear God, is there much worth saying?" He watched her angrily pour out some mead and drink some down.

"Jesu!" He flung himself from the bed and, seizing her chin, stuck his fingers down her throat and forced her forwards. "Bring it up! In God's name, bring it up!"

A few minutes later, he drew her to his breast, wiping away the moisture from her eyes and lips. "It was meant for me, changeling."

Eyes wild with fear stared up at him from her ashen face. Wordlessly, she sniffed the pewter goblet before she slewed its contents onto the tray. No powdery slurry coated the goblet's pit or showed within the golden spill.

She dabbed her third finger in it and licked the moisture cautiously. "There was nothing wrong with it, sir." She poured more from the jug and carried the goblet to the daylight. "It smells well enow."

Avoiding further misuse of his damaged leg, Miles hobbled back to his hateful bed, cursing as if he had spoilt the mending. "Fetch me the map of the southeast shires, pray."

Clearly, nothing pleased her, but his lady obediently brought him the folded parchment from the coffer in the antechamber and he lay back upon the bed and unfolded the map across the sheet. It showed the locations of Harry's holdings.

"What is that?"

Heloise was running some kind of fur memento through her fingers. "Dionysia's rabbit's foot. Pershall found it on the stairs. She kept it for luck, Miles. It was always on her belt." Accusation whetted her voice.

He returned his attention to the map. "Tonbridge, Bletchingley."

"Bletch— Show me, Miles." The duke's holding lay east of Reigate, beyond Redhill, upon the pilgrims' route that wended from the east to Maidstone.

Closing her eyes and surrendering her mind, Heloise ran her finger back from Reigate towards the Thames. "Here." She opened her eyes. "Str—" The rabbit's foot in her other hand was making her fingertips pulsate.

"Streatham." Miles stared at her in amazement.

"Common meadowland," she whispered, closing her eyes, "a broad field stretching away from the king's highway and then beyond it a hill rising steeply into woods."

"Imagination. The same might be said of many hamlets."

Her eyes snapped open and she rubbed her hand across her throat as though her windpipe ached. "No. I must go there. I must."

"You will go nowhere. Not without me, lady mine. Are you lunatick?"

"Then send someone, I beg you." Her other hand joined its fellow at her throat. She swallowed painfully and sank upon the bed, her face grieving.

"All the way out there?" His peace of mind was shaken beyond his liking.

"Miles." Her voice was raw. "Please, *please.*"

Her desperation chilled him to the very marrow. "Very well, send your man Martin."

"It would ease my mind. Thank you."

Miles folded the map, his own throat dry now. He knew the highway. There was indeed a common in the vale, south of the straight, descending hamlet with its numerous inns and a Norman church dedicated to the patron saint of prisoners. Aye, he and Harry had once stopped for mass there; he recalled it had a crusader's tomb and a fine rood screen. And yes, he vaguely remembered thick woods rimming a great hill that rose east of the common and the shouts as an oxcart lost its flour sacks on the thin, ascending track that edged the field.

TWO DAYS LATER, MARTIN RODE BACK WITH DIRE TIDINGS: charcoal burners had found a woman of great beauty hanging from a tree in the woods between the hamlets of Streatham and Norwood. The priest of St. Leonard's had buried her outside the churchyard in unhallowed clay. There had been no jewelry but beneath her silken shift, they had found a paper with the words *Harrye, I love you and I alweys shalle.*

"Is it her writing, my lady?"

Heloise nodded, the tears splashing down her cheeks and trickling down her bodice as she felt the terrified pain in the parchment.

"I sent her to Bletchingley." His grace of Buckingham, High Constable of England, Grand Chamberlain, Justiciar of North and South Wales, and recipient at last of the vast Bohun inheritance, strode into the room. The charming artifice of the last weeks had been cast off, or was this, too, a disguising? "I loved her, madam."

Heloise could only stare at him blankly. The wreath of words dropped truth like wasted flower petals.

"Did you hear what I said, madam?" Buckingham's livid face seemed to float headless before her eyes. "I said that though your sister lay nightly in my arms, in the mornings she regurgitated what I had said like vomit." The duke paced to the window and turned, nostrils flared, the Plantagenet lip curled back in a lion's snarl. "How could she! I would have given her the world if she had asked it of me. I *needed* her. I thought that at Bletchingley . . ." The ducal chin rose with a mummer's timing. "Her escort said she stole away from them when they stopped for dinner. *She should have trusted me.*"

The void was empty of comfort. Heloise's stare did not absolve him and the duke needed retaliation. "How did the groom know where to find her?" he hurled the question at Miles. "I know you disliked the wench's influence, thought her an indulgence on my part, but . . . but the fellow says *you* told him where to search." The accusation hung across the air like a pointing finger.

"By Christ!" The oath spewed forth, drawn like entrails from a prisoner. Heloise watched Miles's hackles rise and lower. How could her husband buckler himself without confirming her arcane gift?

"Unhallowed ground!" protested Heloise, casting herself between them. "Unshriven! I—I pray you, let there be masses for her soul, my lord."

The distraction worked. Buckingham inclined his head, his understanding clear. "Certainly, my lady. Miles." Then he was gone.

Heloise let out a breath and turned.

The man upon the bed lay very still. "Were you afraid I would choose?"

"Yes." Her breath would have scarcely stirred a feather. "Yes."

Twenty-Four

As Lammastide drew close, bringing with it the possibility of plague, the nobility left the city. King Richard, Queen Anne, and their embarrassing excess of northerners rode off in splendor on a royal progress homewards to see their son made Prince of Wales before the delighted dalesmen. Buckingham lingered in London before trundling reluctantly back to Wales. A prisoner, too dangerous to be left in London, had been added to his entourage for safekeeping: Bishop Morton. Where else would Richard III bestow one of his greatest enemies but on his greatest friend?

Heloise's in-laws had been among the first to evacuate the fermenting puddles of London and cart their eldest offspring south to Dorset. They had lost one daughter-in-law and grandson to the pestilence, they did not intend to lose Miles's new wife and her potential contents, even if she were a Ballaster.

She behaved dutifully. Miles did not. With his seigniory reduced to a chair and footstool in his father's house, he became as unmanageable as Lucifer before the Fall. It was not just his injuries, but as if he feared the Buckingham cart might topple from the road unless he sat upon the driving board to guide the duke. Whenever Heloise tried to peel open what bothered him or probe the open sore of her sister's death, Miles closed up. When he was mended sufficiently to ride Traveller, he decreed a leisurely journey back through Heloise's dower lands to Brecknock, and everyone gave thanks except Heloise, who did not want to be anywhere near his grace of Buckingham.

At Hay-on-Wye—a day's journey from Brecknock (if the weather held), Miles briefly sloughed off his brooding countenance. His mood grew playful, drawing a sparkle from his pensive wife.

"Upon my soul, I do not know how you have borne with me, *cariad.*" He leaned across from Traveller's saddle. The kiss lightened her heart. They had relinquished sumpters and servants to Martin's care at their inn and were now alone on a mysterious excursion of Miles's devising.

Heloise's answer was sinful. "I have borne you a great deal, sir, I seem to recall."

"A holy day, changeling." He drew rein as an obliging sheep reluctantly rose from nesting on the bridle path. "A pilgrimage."

With August mellowing into September so sublimely, it was bliss to imagine that there could be more days like this, but the willow herb was slyly loosening its silken messengers upon the drowsy air and within the safety of the crawling ivy tendrils scarlet lords-and-ladies ripened poisonous berries on sappy poles.

The track, littered with rabbity pellets and ovine offerings, broadened out to include fresh horse dung, and a trio of wild ponies lifted their small heads from amongst the gorse bushes. Westwards, grazing land fell away gracefully, unfolding on a realm rimmed by the Black Mountains. To their left, a daunting grassy sward meadowed with nimble sheep rose at a narrow angle and, relenting halfway up, offered a path for cloven feet.

Miles dismounted and whistled, announcing his plan to squire his lady up Hay Bluff. An answering call came from a curly-headed shepherd boy, who scampered up from the lower tussocks to mind their horses. Well, if this was some personal challenge to test the skill of his bone-setter, Heloise hoped her lord won it, otherwise the villagers of Hay would be greatly inconvenienced. Lashing her wide-brimmed straw hat tightly beneath her chin, she doggedly followed him up the sheep track. The wind fought them at every step, but finally Heloise found herself triumphant on the decapitated hilltop with peaty earth echoing beneath her soles.

"Offa's Dyke," murmured her husband, as they stood side by side facing eastwards. He had to point it out to her. "Built from sea to sea, according to Asser's *Life of King Alfred.* If we go down this side of the hill, I can stand you in England and kiss you from Wales." His grin was as wicked as an outlaw's attacking a successful tax collector's cart. Had the moorland been drier or less wind-buffeted, she would have found her skirts swiftly invaded.

"I can tell you have tumbled on these slopes before." She leaned up and kissed him.

"Tumbled, hmm." Strong fingers drew her heart to heart. "Heloise, sweet lady mine, had I known you were such a stalwart, I would have assented at Bramley and earned ourselves a deal more pleasure."

"Who can give water to the horse, if it will not drink of its own accord."

"Impressive. Well, if you have folded your wings and such dry proverbs away, we might discuss, for hypothesis, what a mortal man might offer for thanks. It was too hazardous to bring a bowl of cream."

She laughed, running the tip of her tongue along her lips to provoke him. "Can you find Cupid's darts up here?" It was needful to pull away as she spoke, the words a dangerous underbreath. Veracity could have rough edges.

Firm hands turned her. "You need reassurance? I swear before God you are become the candle of my darkness and the pathway home."

The cadences were beautiful, but home to where? To Brecknock? And poor Sioned lying in the uncompassionate earth? Had she been but a taper lit upon this hilltop too?

"What, such a harsh mistress?" The frame of his hands left her. As if he read her mind, the silvery eyes gleamed. "I shall turn paynim before I reach Purgatory, an arm for each wife like an earthly pasha. You are unsated, I notice."

"I love you."

As if he could not bear the truth, he raised a buckler of words. "Do you now? Although I come umbilicled to Harry, *y Cysgod* glued to the soles of Buckingham's boots?"

"Miles!"

The guard lowered. "I thought you knew that, *cariad.*"

"Will the meaning wither if voiced? See—I love you, Miles. Hear me!" She flung her arms wide to the sky and shouted towards England, "I love him!" And she started running, running away from him, the tears gushing swifter. Running along the hill's haphazard spine until the breath was gone from her. Then she halted, her side aching, hating him for a little space. Perhaps she needed solitude, a replenishing, but her soul was heavy as if some tempest had begun its evil course.

Miles strode purposefully after his fey lady. She was standing like a monument, hands crossed defensively across her breast, staring westwards, the wind herding her skirts behind her.

"Changeling!" He turned her, tilted her chin, and kissed her questioning lips. "I was devoted to Sioned, but you, my darling, have the advantage of a man's love, not the pipings of a green boy."

"Did she share you with Harry, too?"

"You are unreasonable, I think." His hands kept her before him. A thumb scraped over her salt-dried cheek.

"Yes, and it shames me. I do not know what is wrong with me. Help me!"

"Changeling, changeling, matters have a way of working themselves out, given time."

"Like a splinter." Self-mockery fell like a droplet into the bitter sadness. His understanding smile warmed her heart, but not before she had glimpsed the self-doubt in his eyes. "Try," she whispered and wrapped her arms tight about him lest he disappear into the very air. "I cannot hold a shadow but I can love a man."

"Be patient." Miles did not know yet how to answer her but he was beginning to understand the question. "I do not know what I shall find at Brecknock. Stay with me, my heart, keep my feet on the earth." He lifted her in his arms, her thighs against his breast, and turned slowly, holding her like a beacon of defiance to east and west. "I love you, Heloise, and, God willing, I shall protect you with whatever strength I have. Give me the kiss of peace, lady mine." And he lowered her into the fortress of his arms. He would not unburden his fear to her, but at the inn he would bestow on her all the worship his body might offer.

"NED!" HELOISE, CAUGHT UP IN THE SCRABBLE OF LORD STAFford's limbs, even managed a pat for his full-grown dog.

"I knew you'd come back. I knew you would not forget your promise. Thank you for your letters." Set back on the cobbles, he bowed to her properly then offered his hand to his father's friend with a growing manliness. Heloise embraced Bess and then stared about her.

The garrison had increased and so had the number of servants and men-at-arms. If Miles had observed it already, he made no comment. His attention was harnessed by the black and white strip of fur that scurried across to arch its back against the dusty edge of his wife's riding gown. She bent to stroke Dafydd's crooning, then caught her husband's perturbed gaze and faltered. It was he who lifted the cat, glad of his leather-clad hands, and offered it to her.

"He missed you," babbled Ned, "but he kept the mice down in your bedchamber. You will come back and sleep in the nursery like you used to, please."

"I—I . . ."

"I do not think the new governess would be pleased to share a bed," Miles answered for her. "And married ladies are supposed to keep their husbands warm, and leaf fall is on us almost. Where is your father?"

The duke was hunting. It was Cat who hosted the board for dinner, better dressed now and in the London fashion—the new high constable had shopped before he quit the capital. Cat seemed amused by Heloise's new identity, though her women regarded *y Cysgod*'s wife right warily, but at least Myfannwy had been returned to her affronted kinsman.

"You realize we have the Bishop Morton with us," Duchess Cat warned Miles. "In the keep."

"A grave responsibility, your grace."

"He is very charming, Sir Miles. Although he is a prisoner, he does not lack for books and music. It is the least I can do for his kindness to my wretched nephew, *King* Edward." A wife's treason to speak so even if it was spoken softly.

Miles cleared his throat. "I assure you, madam, your nephews were well when I was last in London. The royal lodgings at the Tower are far more luxurious than those at Westminster Palace."

Especially since the duchess's sister had removed anything from Westminster that might fetch more than a shilling, thought Heloise. Instead she remarked, "Prince Edward had some malady in his jaw." And the conversation descended safely into anecdotal exchanges on toothache and diseases of the bones.

"A puzzlement," Miles muttered later in their bedchamber, having taken Heloise's brush from her maidservant and sent the girl away. "I have already inspected the garrison. The guard on the bishop is negligible." He paused as he drew the brush gently through her hair. "A cunning fellow, Morton, with a reputation for escaping. Put him in Hell and he will burrow out again."

Heloise, changing her rings, closed the tiny coffer lid. "Or?"

"Or he does not want to escape. And why does he not wish to?"

"Perhaps Brittany is not to his taste with the winter coming on. To flee is further treason and mayhap he enjoys the *serenata* by Cat's musicians."

"Or he is doing the serenading. Harry is due back." He leaned over and dropped the brush onto her velvet lap. "I shall go and await him like Dafydd the mouser."

"Rub against his boots?"

"Now who is being a cat? Something like that." His fingertips caressed her neck. "Meantime, it seems that we must jump from tussock to tuft. You know the proverb, 'Fields have eyes and

woods have ears'? Heed it until I have perused this place from
cellar to turret and the duke withal."

"I thought he was your friend."

"He is. So let us stay friends, *cariad*. Obey me, hmm?" With
a kiss upon her shoulder, he left her.

THE CIRCLE WAS JOINED, THOUGHT MILES, AFTER HE HAD
spent the best part of an hour catching up on matters. From what
Latimer and Limerick told him, the local nobles who had not
been to the coronation were foolishly treating the most powerful
lord in England as if the kingmaking had been a hiccough, a
little pothole in Castle Lane, and the sensitive new High Constable of England was finding his little castle somewhat stifling.

"What of Bishop Morton, your grace? No tunnels yet?" Miles
asked, edging Traveller up to Harry's horse as they rode back
from a special mass at St. Mary's Chapel next morning.

"I missed you, Miles." With a grin, the duke reined in beside
the town cross, signaling the rest of the retinue to continue up
Shepe Street. "Let us go down by the river and talk."

With two guards for escort, they turned off under Water Gate
and forded the Honddu's shallow surrender to the Usk. Dismounting, they left the others and followed the meandering path
of the riverbank on foot. The September sun was friendly, hot
enough for Miles to peel off his doublet and carry it hooked across
his shoulder. But there was no pleasing some; a stabbing heron,
disturbed among the sandstone boulders that littered the opposite
shore, flapped clumsily into the air, trailing its gangly legs, and
two aggravated moorhens scuttled into the reeds like outraged
dowagers. Harry sat down on the fallen tree that was accustomed
to their politics and, shielding his eyes with his hand, stared
across at the unperturbed sheep munching their way across the
meadow. It was the last glorious breath of summer and the leaves
were green and clinging still.

"You scarcely have a limp. Does it pain you, your leg?"

"Yes, sometimes." Miles gave a slow smile and shifted to give his limbs more comfort.

"Christ, Miles. I am so glad you are back." Harry struggled to free his arms from his cote and had to be helped. "Apart from a handful, no one here seems to realize I have just changed the course of history. You said you wanted to know about Morton. You should go and visit him—if you have several hours to spare. The man could talk anyone into an early grave."

"Then I had lief not. So?"

"So, he is a damnably fine conversationalist."

"So is the Devil, my lord."

"Aye, maybe they are brothers under the skin. To tell you the truth, talking with Morton has kept me sane these last two weeks. When I speak with him, it is as if I am at the heart of matters again. At least he appreciates what I achieved." So Harry had been flattered.

"Is he a Lancastrian at heart or a timeserver? Did you discover why he served Edward IV yet is so against Gloucester?"

"Aye, as tactfully as I could, and he asked me whether I remembered Aesop's fable about how the lion proclaimed that no horned beast should remain in his wood on pain of death."

Miles grinned. "What of it?"

"Well, in the fable one creature with a strange bunch of flesh on his forehead starts to run away and a fox calls out after him, 'Where are you going in such a hurry?'

"The creature replies, 'I neither know nor care so long as I leave the wood because of the proclamation.'

"'Oh, do not be such a fool!' exclaims the fox. 'The lion did not mean you. You have not got a horn.'

"'I know that well enough,' says the creature, 'but what if he calls it a horn, where am I then?'"

"Implying Gloucester will become a tyrant," Miles retorted wearily. Lord, what next? Too many winds had been blowing Harry's sails.

"Miles, Margaret Beaufort was prodigious friendly to me before I left London and Morton thinks he can persuade her to support me."

"In what?" Miles ground out, though he guessed the answer.

"He says . . . he says I would make a better king."

"That is insane. Forgive me, I mean no offense."

"Insane, is it?" The ducal lower lip jutted obstinately. "There was never a better time. The king is turning people out of office so he may reward his northerners, the Woodvilles are leaderless, and I have a claim to the throne. If I can unite all the discontents . . ."

"Your grace—" *Utter folly.*

"Hear me, Miles. Since April, you and I have proved that we can do anything we set our hearts on—in just one summer— and now it will be even easier riding since I have the manpower of Wales and no end of shires at my bidding."

"My lord, think hard before you take this step. You are the greatest man in England and the pillar of Richard's kingship. Together you and he could make this land of ours the envy of all Christendom. I would advise against this."

"Miles"—Harry set a hand upon his shoulder—"we have come further than we ever dreamt. There is nothing we cannot do. Most of England already thinks King Richard a tyrant. Are you with me?"

Twenty-five

Brecknock was humming like a summer hive but, like Dafydd, whose mice quota was efficiently down, Heloise was not part of the bustling. Nor was she part of the loving, save between the bedcurtains, and even then Miles's furrowed brow and taciturnity clouded the pleasure.

Something was wrong; the castle officers were tense, whispering in corners, breaking off conversations. Was it they thought her a witch? Had Buckingham buried rumors like caltraps to wound her? Imagination is a powerful enemy. Even when Sir William Knyvett returned from his new post as Constable at Castle Rising, bringing with him from Norfolk an excessive number of mounted men-at-arms, Heloise did not suspect the truth. It was finally a conversation, private—and obscure in places until she dissected it afterwards—between Sir William and her husband, that drove a crossbolt through the glass panes of her world.

She had not meant to eavesdrop but the two men, stopping on the allure outside the bedchamber she shared with Miles, must have thought themselves out of earshot.

". . . on paper, yes. Thomas Stanley's heir, Lord Strange, has promised ten thousand men from Cheshire."

"Ten thousand!" Awe laced her husband's astonished voice. "That is more than we can ever muster!"

"Aye, lad, but hold rein! Stanley is attendant on the king's person at present, you see, so we cannot be sure of his son's commitment, can we? It is right hazardous, Miles. Talk of the rising may have leaked out. . . . I had word before I came away that my lord of Norfolk has a standing army of retainers outside London and for what purpose, I can only guess. Kentishmen have long tongues when they have been at the ale, and if King Richard has sent for Harry . . ."

"The trouble is," replied Miles, "that with so many involved and all so far-flung, the chance of surprise is about as likely as Harry becoming Pope." The slap of fist must have been his for he exclaimed vehemently, "I make no secret of my misgivings, Will. God rot Morton! This is all his doing. And poor, silly Cat is taken in by the pair of them. Have you noted that? Upon my soul, I wish I had not tarried in Dorset. Godsakes, I could have talked some sense into Harry."

"I doubt it. He thinks he is Sixtus IV—infallible! You should have heard him at Oxford."

"What do you mean—at Oxford? What did he do at Oxford?"

"Only asked King Richard to betroth his son to one of his daughters. Old Dickon said no and I cannot blame him. Any fool could see that a foreign princess would be best, but of course Harry is out for a dynasty. And I thought: Dickon lad, you have just made an almighty blunder. If you had only said 'maybe' or 'I shall think upon it—' "

"—we might not be sharpening our swords."

Both men were silent then Sir William asked, "Have you told Lady Rushden, by the way? Or must I button my lip in her hearing?"

"Best you do. She does not know and neither do most of the household. With Harry's increased business as justiciar, we have managed not to arouse suspicion."

"Aye, happen you are right. Still might have some of Gloucester's agents in our midst, eh? Always reckoned Brian might have been one of 'em, and what about that other Ballaster wench, eh? Has Harry said aught more about her?"

"Oh, he believes that Nandik was telling the truth but he swears the quarrel was because she was with child by a northern lord. That was why he was sending her to Bletchingley—to have the babe and avoid the scandal."

"*Putain!* And he fancied himself in love with the greedy

whore. No wonder it smote him sorely. You had the better bargain, lad. All going well, is it?"

The unexpected silence chilled Heloise further, and unhorsed
Sir William too, for with embarrassment timbring his tone, the
older knight added, "Well, best not keep Harry waiting further.
He will be off the bench now."

Heloise sank against the wall, her clasped fists pressed against
her lips. The castle was not concerned with her—it was planning
a rebellion. Like the blind beggar healed by Christ, she saw now:
Buckingham was a Judas in ermine. This whetting of steel was
for battle with King Richard. *God rot Morton!* Miles had lost the
whip hand. It was Morton's evil tongue licking around the duke's
envy that must be driving this folly. And her sister, why had
Miles not told her what he had learned?

Jesu mercy, since cursed duplicity was a spreading puddle in
Wales, she would wade in too. After some consideration, she
pinned on her unicorn brooch and went to seek out the duchess
under the pretext of offering secretarial services.

The letter writing was over, Catherine Woodville explained,
but the postscript on her thanks was perturbingly naive: "I am
so relieved now that Harry realizes how much he has maligned
my sister. I am sure it is due to Bishop Morton's counsel—and
your husband's too—that has made him see sense, and Lady Margaret Beaufort has graciously interceded with her on Harry's behalf. My sister is still rather wary—would you not be, in her
circumstances?—but Dr. Lewis, the countess's physician, has
been visiting her regularly at Westminster sanctuary and kindly
carrying messages."

Poor, silly Cat is taken in by the pair of them! Dear God, Buckingham had as much intention of restoring the Woodville queen
to glory as galloping his horse up the spire of St. Paul's.

"So do you suppose his grace will manage to free your sister,
my lady?" Heloise asked, feeling her way. Even if the duchess's
depths were easy to fathom, one could not always see where the
potholes were.

"So he promises, once my nephews are rescued from the Tower."

Promises! Heloise thought later. Promises! From the fox who had sworn fealty to Prince Edward's kneecaps and then kissed his successor's cheek in coronation homage? King Richard was likely to be one of the worthiest kings that England had ever had—Heloise could testify to the respect in which the north of England held the man—and yet these greedy fools were out to topple him. When was this rising? No one had remarked her brooch, so what should she do? Find some means to warn the king? Or were his agents already aware of the conspiracy? And if they were . . .

Oh, God, Miles! She could not betray the man she loved to a hideous, public death. She must force the truth from him, make him see sense even if it broke the fragile ice of their marriage; but privacy was no easy matter in this crammed castle. Even in their shared bedchamber, the servants slept within snoring distance. But next morning, entering the great chamber on an errand for the duchess, she discovered him unlocking a carved chest.

He straightened up. His smile, a rarity now, almost melted her. "What are you doing here, changeling?"

"I came for this." She lifted Christian de Pisan's *The Treasure of the City of Ladies* from the wooden lectern on the small table.

Miles took it from her and opened it at random. " 'How a princess keeps her ladies in order.' What is this? 'They must not go about with their heads raised like wild deer.' Upon my soul, Heloise, should I be inspecting your forehead for velvety bumps?"

"That seems to be the only part of me you do not inspect, sir." The book, returned, was clasped to her ribs like a stomacher. "But so long as I meet your nightly needs."

The roguish smile, on leave for days, quirked his mouth. "Oh, prickly, are we? What is the matter, my love?"

It was important to sternly observe the swan tiles beneath her leather slippers. "I am sure you had rather not make a diagnosis."

A compelling hand tilted her chin. "Playing fast and loose? You have been casting daggers at me for days. You are not with child, are you?"

Heat rose unbidden into her cheeks. "No, thank—"

"Thank—what, God?" His silvery gaze hardened to sullen metal. "Have the duchess's women been frightening you with tales of childbirth? Do not heed them. You are too shrewd for that. I long to see you with child, *cariad*."

"And I should like to see more of you, sir, if you can ever spare the time to beget a child on me. Or am I to be hustled off to Bletchingley and murdered?" Blurted out, the truth lay in the air between them like some noxious vapor.

"God's mercy, Heloise!"

"Another matter you have not confided when you can spare the time. Was my sister's murder a hiccough that you took care of like Hastings's execution?"

He kept his gaze on her. "I did not see that you needed to think further ill of your sister. As for the rest, it cannot be otherwise and it will be worse." He strode back to the chest and lifted the great lid so that it was leaning against the wall. "I owe you an apology, Heloise. I was going to tell you tonight, but now will suffice." A defensive hauteur underscored his voice. "The king has summoned Harry to wait upon him at Nottingham so I shall be leaving in a few days' time. I regret I cannot take you on this occasion. The duchess expects you to remain in attendance upon her." So brisk, so cold. A clever half-truth.

"Do you suppose you shall be coming back?"

As if she had flicked a whip across his back, he tensed and stilled. "That is an extremely odd question," he answered without looking round.

"We live in extremely odd times," declared Heloise, drawing closer. "Three kings in one year and fools hoping for a fourth, I gather."

The intelligent gaze lifted from the assortment of coffered armor and he turned carefully, observing the adamancy of her folded arms. "So the bucket has hit the water, lady mine."

"You must be happy it was such a deep well. Dolt that I am not to have realized sooner. Are you going to butter me with reasons or is it not worth the bother? I daresay you did not want to make me anxious?" Do not lie to me, her eyes told him, and when he did not answer, she added, "Or am I supposed to be the king's spy like my sister was?"

"Are you?" That hurt.

"I am tempted, believe me, but there are too many trees in the valley for a hanging and I should not want the duke to lay the blame on you."

His smile reached only his lips. "No, there is that, I suppose."

"Miles, *please.*" Her heart was breaking as he turned back to his task. She loved him so much. Could beating her fists against his chest pump some common sense up to his brain? Would scathing anger serve? "Have you nine lives, sir, that you will waste this one? You cannot support the duke in such . . . such folly! Why not knock at the water gate of the Tower of London and ask for free accommodation straightway? I expect they will hang, draw, and quarter you if you grow persuasive?"

"Buckingham is in charge of the Tower of London," Miles parried pedantically, sorting through the metal pieces—fluted, embossed, and plain—dedicated to defending valuable aspects of the male anatomy. "I would swear that beggar de la Bere borrowed my cuisses last time we had a skirmish with the Vaughans."

Heloise did not care what protected his thighs. She was tempted to set her sole to his unprotected rear, tip him headfirst into the oaken chest, and hurl the key into the Usk. How could this intelligent husband of hers be so plaguey insane? "Sweet Christ give me patience, sir! King Richard has made your friend mightier even than Warwick the Kingmaker. Yet he is still unsatisfied."

Delightfully hoity as an outraged she-gull, his darling faced him. Miles fought down his usual reflex of kissing her to a standstill. Stubborn defensiveness did not serve either. "Cease raging, changeling! Yes, I expect he wants the crown. You said so weeks ago."

"Do not patronize me!" she snarled. "And supposing he does bring King Richard tumbling down? Who is next? Will he un-throne God?"

The bitter truth almost unmanned him. He wavered, sure of the honesty in her, wishing he might hush her in his arms, want-ing to fist asunder the wall that was rising between them. Torn between love for her and his commitment to Harry, he could only stare hollowly, unable to offer answers, desperate for her to trust his judgment.

"Miles!" His glorious, defeated Heloise hurled all in one last, desperate plea.

He flinched. She had not heard it but the trained soldier in him had—the unmistakable hiss of expensive fabric—and he knew who was listening. With a stride, he reached Heloise. One forefinger pressed upon her protesting lips; the other, gold-ringed, jabbed the air, for the iron handle on the narrow, studded door that clogged the stairs had not yet shifted.

"But this is no rebellion to rescue the little princes," she whis-pered, angrily ignoring his warning. Still in full sail with grap-pling hooks in midhurl, she knocked his wrist aside. "The Countess of Richmond wants to bring Henry Tudor across from Brittany."

"The countess wants the House of York vanquished," he re-plied hoarsely, his anger tortured into a cunning answer as he watched the iron circle tilt. "After that, we shall see."

The lady understood at last but she was more close to achiev-ing a hit than ever she would again. "And you and his grace purpose to go riding off into England, trusting to people that were enemies two months since." The sneer finally lifted the stop-per off her fury and she was spent; her gaze, too, sped towards that door.

He swiftly urged her away from that deadly inner door. "My

love, if you cease to trust me, we shall be destroyed," he whispered, and scoffed loudly, "You forget, madam, that my family have served the House of Lancaster since before Agincourt. We do not sell crossbows to both sides at once." Again he whispered, fiercely; *"React, changeling! We are in danger else."*

"Ohhh!" Heloise clutched the book with one hand, snatched up her skirts with the other, and stormed out into the great hall.

"Well done," applauded Harry, emerging like a wasp looking for treats. "Was that performance for my benefit?"

Miles gave him a tight smile. "Of course, if you insist on skulking perfidiously in the woodwork like a deathwatch beetle."

"Leave that." The duke waved dismissively at the tangled metal. "I have a spare pair of cuisses in my chest in the armory that will fit you. Come!"

Miles would have rather pursued his confused wife but he followed the duke out to the bailey.

"Cat is easily hoodwinked," observed Harry as they headed towards the guardroom, "but Heloise Ballaster is another matter. A pity you have not got her with child yet. It might give her something else to think about." Was that an oblique taunt?

"It has not been for want of trying."

His lord halted, the back of his hand against Miles's breast, and came to the point. "If she betrays us . . ."

"She will be betraying me." The ducal hand was coldly pushed aside. "I think you need have no fears on that."

"Wait, man!"

Chin raised rebelliously, Miles halted like one of his Welsh recruits with blatant reluctance. Harry gripped his shoulder, moving close behind him like a second Satan.

"Miles, be more cheerful. The crown is there for the taking. The Londoners believe the princes slain and Richard their murderer. This rebellion will be like taking a sweetmeat from a babe."

Not for the first time Miles drove the force of well-used arguments against such rock hard density. "A babe! Jesu, King

Richard has never lost a battle and you, your grace, have never fought one. If you lose . . ." He jerked his head round to find Harry unabashed. Did nothing weather that shiny resilience? "It is not too late to go to the king and tell him the rumors about you are all lies."

"No!" Harry spun him round completely so that their faces were level. "How many more times must I drum it into that stubborn skull of yours? Win all or lose all! I am the last lawful heir of Lancaster. The Yorkists are usurpers. They stole the crown from Henry VI's anointed head and murdered him in the Tower." Dear God, it was so pat now, as if Harry had learnt it by rote at Morton's knee. "God damn you, Miles, will you cry craven at this late hour with but a week to the rebellion?"

Avoiding an answer, Miles glared down at the flecks of saliva budding his cote's velvet nap. Harry mistook his silence for humility and let go, calmer now. "God is on our side, Miles. He must be or we could not have come this far. It is justice that I should take the throne at last and set matters right." The thin lips were a slash of defiance. "I will not change my mind!"

And if I change mine, thought Miles, what price friendship? "As you will, my lord," he answered with dignity, disliking Harry's smug triumph.

"We are like this, you and I." Brandishing crossed fingers, Harry blocked Miles's path. "Is it your soothsayer wife who is making you doubt me?"

Studying the wall above the duke's head, Miles answered haughtily: "The matter of her sister still is a running sore between us, but, of course"—his gaze slid down to examine Harry's face—"if it would please your grace to set her mind at rest?"

"Oh, but surely she trusts *your* judgment in the matter." The duke's knuckles playfully buffeted the looped knops of Miles's doublet. "Friend, if you cannot keep this new bride in rein, you will never have a quiet house. I hear you share her favors."

Miles had wrestled Harry but never in anger. Cold as an alabaster monument, he let his breath slowly out. "Your meaning, my lord?"

"Oh, I jest. I hear she keeps a familiar." The claws within the silky banter drew blood this time. It was so undeserved—so insane to threaten a loyal friend's innocent wife! Godsakes, Harry had better not aim any other shafts at Heloise's feyness!

With a control of temper that would have frightened servants, he managed an answer. "While we have mice disturbing our sleep, I think her wise. Is there some meaning I am missing?"

"No, I think you miss nothing and that is why I value you." Harry took a pace on and then swung back to face him. "Let her question Nandik."

"Nandik? I do not want that lecher anywhere near my wife." No, nor his table of planets and celestial concurrences!

The duke lifted up the simple gold cross he had taken to wearing of late, clouded the gold with his breath, and polished it against his stomacher. "Ah, but it was Nandik who provided the testimony that the whore I loved was spying on me, and it was Nandik I ordered to make the arrangements for her escort to Bletchingley."

"Why him?" Miles blurted out. "I could have handled matters for you."

"With a broken leg and married to the girl's sister! You think I ordered her death? Yes, I probably did kill her, for I gave Nandik a letter for the escort to give to her when she was too far from London to return easily. I cannot remember what I wrote but it is a wonder the words did not blister the parchment. I loved her, Miles. Perhaps my bitterness drove her to take her own life."

The entire truth? "And where is the letter now?"

"Ho, so the lawyer in you wants evidence? Burned, I am afraid. It was returned to me and I held it to the nearest candle. She had torn a scrap off the end to write her message." The red-lashed eyes watched him with feline inscrutability. "Now you may answer *me*. How did you know where to find her body?

What, has the cat got your tongue?" His grace's tone had grown wondrous smooth. "God's rood, Miles, do not tell me you already knew of Dionysia's treachery and that it *was* you who arranged matters!"

Miles had only one answer. "I would have done it properly." A careful bow and he walked away.

"NOT SPEAKING TO ME?" MILES ASKED, SHAKING THE FULL sleeves of his shirt into compliance so he might lean upon his elbow. His servant had removed his master's boots and outer garments and, drawing the bedcurtains discreetly about his knight and lady, retired to his creaking trundle bed. Miles was not ready to enter the sheets nor blow out the candle in the horn-paned lamp that hung above them. Within the honey-colored fabric cage that concealed them from their servants, Heloise, slender limbs folded beneath her, sat atop the sprawl of coverlet, protected in chemise and Holland petticoats.

"Is there anything worth saying?" she whispered. "Marrying a turnip would have made more sense. To think I actually wanted you to acknowledge me."

"Not now." His voice was heavy with warning and she complied sadly, watching him waiflike with an appetite that matched his hunger to seduce her. Protagonists in different corners, they fought a war with glances. He knew the lady slid her gaze across the loose laces of his shirt and coyly down, down to estimate his passion for her. And he wanted her, burned for her. Unclothing her with his eyes, he willed her across the samite fantasy of leaves and flowers, and when she leaned back in enticing resistance, he reached across, reveling in his masculine strength that might tow her into the harbor of his arms.

It was needful to smooth back the tumbled, elfin hair, plunder the sweet, surrendering mouth, and melt her to forgetfulness of all save him. His caresses, his kisses were now her kingdom. With a quiver and sigh, his beautiful Heloise succumbed to the passion he could summon forth in her at will. Her fingers tangled in his hair and slid down to conquer, wantonly coaxing him to a transcendent slavery in which he strove to drive her to unsurpassed pleasure. He became fire, aching to steep himself in her delicious softness so that he might forget the terror that racked him, that pulled reason from action by each slow, grinding hour. In love he took possession of her, each stroking thrust carrying them beyond the gates of Heaven itself until, male and female, they both lay sated and defeated in each other's arms.

And when he lay asleep, his arms a protective fortress about her, Heloise's tears silently trickled into the feather pillow. Trusting his judgment exacted a heavy price. Unless she could change his mind, he was going to ride with Buckingham to rebellion and a terrible death.

Twenty-six

Miles looked on with loathing as Bishop Morton heaved his huge bulk down the steps from Brecknock's keep. Treasonously liberated against King Richard's orders, Harry's newest counselor halted in the bailey and stared about him with smug satisfaction. Harry's rebel army was about to leave Brecknock.

Fifty mounted soldiers were saddling up, and beyond the castle walls, untidying the priory fields, four hundred foot soldiers, mostly Welsh, sweaty-shirted in their quilted jackets, were waiting morosely. Eleven wagons, bulging beneath roped canvas with breech-loading guns and cooking pots, weapons and ladles, tents and oatmeal, waited behind thick-limbed horses, while their shafts and wheels were checked again for damage. Sumpters, slung with armor, shifted their plumy hooves uncertainly beside the caparisoned destriers, their flanks already moist with sweat and drizzle.

Oh, to be sure, the rebellion looked well on parchment: two hundred English soldiers, coerced from cidermaking and carting sheaves, were appointed to meet the duke at Hereford. Breton mercenaries and Lancastrian exiles—the Channel winds permitting—were under sail with Henry Tudor. Their exorbitant professionalism had been purchased by the stolen treasury money, courtesy of Sir Edward Woodville. And it was hoped that when King Richard, yelling treason, came thudding out of his heartland, Margaret Beaufort and Lord Stanley's Cheshire retainers would close in. With God's good grace, the rebels hoped the king would be caught on the east coast between the claws of the two armies and scooped to oblivion or a beggarly exile. That was if the southeastern rebels battled successfully against the new Duke of Norfolk, who was guarding London and the reaches of the Thames.

With a heavy heart, Miles hastened up the steps to the battlements, casting an anxious gaze towards the south. Incandescent shafts of light were dappling the nearby hillsides greenish-gold but over Pen-y-Fan the clouds were purple, and to the east the Black Mountains were a sinister breaker frozen against a seething sky. The odds were that it would start raining before sundown and the road to Hereford would be churned into a mire.

"Miles."

His despairing lady was waiting, her lily cheeks veined with tears. *If only* . . . Oh, he had a cupboardful of those!

"My love."

Poor Heloise. She had used every persuasion short of destroying his kneecaps with a mallet to make him turn traitor, cursing his sense of duty and misdirected honor. But she had spent hours of loving labor stitching him a battle surcote, "to keep you safer from arrows." Had she sewn charms and spells between the silk layers? Miles glanced down at the family of roused sable snakes, with their golden flick of tongues, festooning his ribcase, and smiled at his seamstress.

What did one give a fey wife as a parting gift? He lifted the folded parchment from his leather purse and held it out to her. She must have felt the magic within for she opened it as though it hid a fragile crystal.

"Upon my soul, oh, Miles!" Her pleasure filled him with a delight beyond all price.

A four-leaf clover, kept through boyhood. "Three leaves for the Trinity, see. And the fourth, changeling?"

The sweet-sad smile Heloise beamed at him nearly destroyed his courage. "For our Lady or . . ." She watched the husbandly indulgence crinkle his eyes.

"Or your *tylwyth teg?* Who knows? But this is special, never wished on since its finding fourteen years ago."

"If you found it, then it is your right to do the wishing."

"Which I surrender to the mistress of my heart."

"Oh," exclaimed Heloise, love shining in her eyes, "then I wish—"

"No." He kissed her. " 'Tis ill luck to speak it. Close your eyes now." With his right hand holding hers, he watched as she turned her heart-shaped face with reverence to the distant hills, drew breath, and held it. It was the image he would take with him, the charm that would help him withstand the executioner's fire and the heated irons. Imagination, the pressure of her fingers, might have accounted for the tingle of reassurance, hope—God knows how else to describe it—that suffused his veins until it found his mind. Was this how a blessing felt?

"I love you," he whispered, raising his left hand to furl her cheek with tenderness, "I love you more than I can ever show you and whatever happens, remember that." Then he drew back from her and lifted a chain from about his neck. "This is the key to the coffer in our bedchamber. Within it is my will and sufficient money to keep you through the winter. Sell the other things if you need to." He still wore his rings. They might buy him a passage to Brittany or Ireland, or a last chance to speak with her before they hauled him out to the gibbet.

As if Heloise received that image from his mind, her beloved face went grey as ashes. Someone whistled at them urgently from the courtyard and suddenly her fingers were unpinning a brooch from her collar. He had not noted it before. A little unicorn.

"Would you wear this for me all the time, whatever happens?"

"Close to my heart, hmm." It was not to his taste. But how could he deny her? It was a struggle to fasten it to his shirt beneath his hauberk. His fingers trembled, his gaze misted, and it was she who finished the task. By the time she looked up, he had control again but his voice was ravaged. "I must go." He set a gloved finger beneath her chin.

Her eyes blazed defiantly now, as if she was willing him one last time to turn his cote. "King Richard speaks of justice. What does Harry Buckingham speak of but Harry Buckingham?"

It was true, except the harsh trumpets brayed and his esquire had started up the steps to fetch him. "Heloise, I beg you," he protested, gathering her against the freshly stitched Rushden serpents. "Sing a more loving song, my nightingale. Would you have me ride to war with your anger in my ears?"

She drew her head back, her lovely eyes shimmering like sunlight on water. "Promise you will come back to me, Miles, even if it is a hundred years hence, even if it takes all eternity. For I shall still be waiting for you and all my love is yours and yours alone."

With the unstudied grace that was so much part of him, he raised her hand to his lips. "If only in your dreams, my love. Whatever is within my power, I promise." And he was gone. Disabled by stinging tears, she listened helplessly to the ring of his spurs on each stone step.

"Miles!" Her strong, wonderful man turned. "Check the wheels of the third cart."

The raven eyebrows arched. "A premonition?"

"No." Her smile was watery. "I saw a fellow lurking by it last night."

Laughter creased the corners of his eyes. She would remember him thus. Even if they never met again, she would live out her life knowing that he had believed in her, loved her for what she was. The rope and the fire could not take that from her.

He is not coming back, is he? Risking the anger of *tylwyth teg*, she opened her mind, pleading desperately to see the future so she might arm herself against it. Her back braced against the battlement, she closed her eyes and waited for the unsteadying vision. Nothing.

Nothing looked down on her but the darkening sky. She had broken their rule and hers. Guiltily, shakily, she left the wall. The bailey was still full of soldiers and Miles was sitting astride Traveller. He saluted her, and pointed; the third cart had been pulled to the side and its load was being spread amongst the rest. Yes, this was where she needed to be, where he could see her, not trying to use her sight for her own selfish purposes.

Biting her lip, she stood stoically; garnering his image, reaching out her arms through the air, telling him she understood, telling him of her pride in him.

Buckingham's speech was brief; so were the tepid cheers that followed, before the sarsynett pennons and the fringed banners bearing the golden loops of cord, the flaring Catherine wheels, the swans collared with golden coronets, finally dipped like lances beneath the jagged teeth of the portcullis and were gone into the void. The courtyard slowly wasted its manhood out into the precarious world. The women, dabs of color against the somber doorways, withdrew, but Heloise, mute against the parapet, stayed, a drooping silken flag with nothing to move her until a small, sugar-sticky palm crept into hers.

"Do not cry, my lady," said Ned, Lord Stafford, responsibly, adding with a perfect imitation of Sir William: "It sets a bad example, you know."

NOT UNTIL HELOISE CREPT BETWEEN THE SHEETS MISERABLY that night did she discover a letter of love from Miles tucked beneath her pillow; but before she had leisure to read it twice, her bedroom door opened and a disgruntled Dafydd landed, paws braced. The door shut abruptly and the cat, glaring daggers at her, attempted to remove his furry head from the inconvenient ribbon burdening his neck. Though he clearly blamed her, he permitted her to assist and at last she carried the ribbon to the candlelight. The tiny parcel which belled it contained a piece of thin rag with an ink message signed *E*. Emrys?

Leave Wales, lady of y Cysgod, arianlais, as you value your virtue and your life, your devoted servant, E.

She sent for Martin next morning and, as a contingency, gave him a little of the money from the coffer and bade him discreetly take Cloud and his hackney for stabling at the priory, and then see if he might find Emrys. The news Martin brought back later from the town was disturbing. The able-bodied men who had been lying low to avoid recruitment had not yet returned. Why?

IT WAS RAINING STEADILY BY THE TIME THE DUKE'S COMPANY reached Bronllys but already there had been several suspicious incidents. Someone was deliberately slowing them and today was Monday and they needed to be across the Severn well before Saturday, October eighteenth, the day decreed for the common rising.

When Harry's destrier stumbled and the Llanddew blacksmith's lad muttered that it was a portent, the duke ordered the poor wretch to be hanged from the nearest oak. Miles protested but the double mischief was done. The Welshmen were all at it then, cursing their betters and babbling of misfortune. One man swore by his very soul that he had glimpsed an ugly *gwyllian* astride a forked branch. Not a hanging offense, thank Heaven, but the men started to scan the roadside for St. John's wort to keep the dwarves away, and a whole sheath of prayers went flying off to Saints Alud, Brychan, and Cynog. Then a Newport halberdier made a sign against the evil eye at Nandik and the scholar edged his horse closer to the duke. Miles uncharitably wished that they would pull the fellow from his horse and dispatch him quietly behind the hedgerow, for yesterday, to please Harry, Nandik had seen a king's death in his astral charts.

Matters could not be worse, Miles thought. The rain ran relentlessly down the sloping nape of his helm, trickling onto his lower back. Grey fog swallowed up the hills, the trees along the road were ghostly shadows, and the sky ahead was bleak. Ditches overflowed, horses stumbled in the hidden holes; wheels jammed in the squelching furrows and the complaining drivers had to cut sodden brushwood to wad the ruts so the horses could haul the carts onto solid ground. Staybraces broke; a sweep-bar jammed. The first of the food wagons unaccountably fell sideways, blocking the road, and the oatmeal became a porridge far too soon. A wheel came off a weapons cart.

Miles, whose soldiers had inspected each cart before they had left Brecknock, rode down the columns with his carpenters plunging after him to check again. Past Glasbury the wagon with the mended wheel had not caught up.

And the straggling column was growing thinner.

IT WAS NOT THE THUD OF A STONE CANNONBALL AGAINST Brecknock Castle's wall at first light next day which woke the sentry, but the unperfected weapon's explosion as it killed its gunners.

Heloise, roused by the alarum bell, held a large square of cered leather over the disbelieving duchess to keep the rain off as they stood above the gatehouse watching the trebuchet being hauled up Castle Lane. A mounted knight was bawling orders at the enemy archers and billmen assembling along the banks of the Honddu.

"Should we not shoot them or hurl boiling pitch on their heads or something?" Catherine demanded as the acting constable arrived red-faced to join them.

"Yes, I suppose so," he panted. "It is the Vaughans, madam. They have just delivered a message demanding the garrison surrenders you and the children, or they will bombard us. They have requested your person too, Lady Rushden."

"Jesu!" muttered Catherine, flouncing swiftly downstairs out of arrow range and mustering the few officers left to her in the great hall. On a head count, they had more musicians and children than soldiers.

"Sirs, how many of you could handle a bow?" Heloise asked, and when all the musicians cheerfully raised their hands, she had to explain that it was longbows she had in mind.

"I hardly think a few shawm players and a couple of lutanists are going to be much use," she fumed to the despairing constable. "We could garb everyone in the discarded livery and spare helmets. They might think we still have a reasonable garrison."

The garrison commander's messenger to the duke, dispatched

to advise him of their plight, had already been apprehended and displayed by his captors from across the moat as a wriggling tangle of thrashing legs. And Buckingham's army was marching further from them with every hour.

"My lady," the constable muttered, drawing Heloise aside some half hour later, "her grace is talking of surrender. It is important that Lord Stafford does not fall into their hands. King Richard, as you know, is a man for hostages. We must hold out as long as we can."

"He would not harm the child."

"No, *he* would not, but the Vaughans nourish a bitter hatred of the duke and the child may suffer for it." She tried not to think of such horrid possibilities. "I also mislike it that their request includes you, my lady."

"I think you had better see this message. Someone sent it me last night as a warning." Heloise watched the commander's growing concern.

"Christ have mercy, *virtue!* They will rape you, madam." A reprisal against *y Cysgod.*

"How long can we hold out, then?" She tried not to show her fear; it was necessary to be practical.

"A day or so, perhaps longer, with God's grace. A week if their bombards are ineffectual, and providing no one within the castle betrays us."

"If . . . if we could light a huge bonfire on Pen-y-Fan, would his grace see it, do you think?"

"If our forces are still in the vale, he might, but the mist is too heavy." His tired smile was polite. "But, my lady, can you imagine the likelihood of getting a man out of the castle alive, let alone heaving timber up to the beacons and keeping it dry in this deluge? Or that the duke could even send sufficient men back to investigate? He will have enough labor to make Hereford, let alone return here."

"So we need some means of sending Lord Stafford to safety before the castle is taken. What if we were to disguise one of the other children in his clothes and let him be seen with her grace upon the battlements, and meanwhile smuggle him out to his father? I have horses stabled at the priory."

"Yes." He rubbed his fingers across his upper lip. "That notion has merit. I will think on't."

MILES SHELTERED IN THE PORCH OF ST. ANDREW'S AT BRED-wardine and felt sick to the bone. Behind him in the church, resting their sodden feet, his men's faces showed it too—water-soaked brigandines wrapping rusting metal around hearts en-grained with mold. Courage there might be still, but it would go puff like toadstools, leaving flabby shells of emptiness. Was it only on Harry that God was pouring out his wrath? Was the sun shining on Tudor's sails out in the Channel or on Woodville blades taken down from the walls at Ightham or Maidstone? You could not hurry through mud. What if the fleet were becalmed; what if . . .

"A word with you, Miles." Knyvett set an urgent hand to his shoulder, drawing him down to the churchyard gate. "Bad news. A messenger has come from the prior at Brecknock. The Vaugh-ans have looted the castle in the king's name and taken her grace and the children prisoner."

"Godsakes!" Death scraped his fingernail down Miles's spine. "My wife, is she—"

"The fellow did not know, Miles. Rest easy, the duchess will let no harm befall her."

"Cat could not defend a sand castle!" Miles slammed his right fist against his palm. "Heloise is . . . is vulnerable." Vulnerable enough to be hauled to the stake. "They know how to hurt her." He angrily shook off the older man's restraining hand. "I must go back."

"Oh no, you shall not!" Knyvett spun him back to face him. "By Christ, man, if *you* leave, the entire army will desert."

"Maybe they should!"

"Miles, *Miles.*" Knyvett shook him. "Wait until you know

more, eh? You always had a cool head. Don't lose it now. That
is better. Now, listen to me! It sounds as though the Vaughans
were all ready to lay siege the instant we were two days' march
away. By St. George, we are in dung to our necks! Do you see,
if King Richard has knowledge of *our* plans, he must know about
the rising in the south. Now come and hear the messenger for
yourself."

God have mercy! Dung indeed! One of the duke's scouts had
already brought warning that Sir Humphrey Stafford, the king's
man, was felling trees along the road to Hereford and setting
bowmen to hold the bridges. A second scout had reported back
that Hereford had shuts its gates and the king had issued a proclamation of a pardon to all deserters and a reward of a thousand
pounds for Harry's capture.

Harry was still interrogating the elderly messenger from
Brecknock.

"Trapped!" growled the duke. "Humphrey Stafford's men have
been stalking us, picking off the slow ones. Sweet Christ, if this
news from Brecknock leaks out, we shall lose the rest of them!"
He hit his mailed fist against the tree. "They knew! The Vaughans knew! Was this your wife's doing?"

Miles gulped at the sudden accusation. Heloise could be straddled by some vicious whoreson or left for dead among the smoldering ruins and Harry had the gall to . . .

"No!" Miles turned his back, his fists clenched. The leash of
service around his neck was straining fit to break.

"No?" sneered the duke. "If they can set a leech beneath my
underbelly, why not yours?"

"Are you demented, my lord?" Miles swung round, the train-
ing of years harnessing his icy rage. "King Richard only needed
to set watch on the Beaufort woman's messengers to know something was afoot. A rising planned from Wales to Kent?" His tone
grew scathing. "Christ Almighty, it has more holes than a pau-
per's stocking."

"It could have even been you!"

Miles's hands slammed against Harry's chest, sending him crashing back into the tree trunk. The ducal armor jarred against the lichened, pillar-thick trunk and his grace of Buckingham slithered downwards to land in a painful straddle across the roots. The kernel of the old Harry showed in a brief crinkle of a grin as Miles pulled him up.

"Perhaps you had better hang me," Miles suggested dryly, brushing the leaves from the skirt of Harry's hauberk. "It might be more convenient than being ripped apart at Smithfield. Is there a map to hand, friends?" He jerked his head round at de la Bere and Sir Nicholas Latimer, who had come instantly to intervene. There was appreciation in the younger man's expression.

"Of course, Miles." De la Bere drew a leather-wrapped package from his breast. "Shall we return to the shelter of the porch, your grace?"

His grace, jarred in the place where Satan would fasten a tail on him, was sulky and, for once, silent.

"What the men need is action, food, and a place to dry out, not necessarily in that order," observed Miles.

"Or pay." The smooth voice of Morton insinuated itself into their midst. "I have just been doing a count. Buckingham, the men are falling out like the hairs in your comb."

ON FRIDAY EVE, WITH NED—DISGUISED AS A GIRL IN COIF AND skirts—huddled against her back like a baby creature clinging to its mother's fur, Heloise hit her crop on a broad front door and hoped she had reached the village of Weobley. It was not worth dismounting to shelter beneath the overstorey; the entire road in front of the house was sheeted with water and Cloud's hooves were awash. Bess backed her horse away, staring up at the carved gables. "I saw a movement up there at the side window. Smite again!" But it was Benet who slithered off from riding pillion and splashed stolidly across to hammer his fist upon the shutters.

"We are seeking the castle," Heloise told the hard-faced creature who tardily came. Beyond the narrow crack of the door, she
could smell griddlecakes and the steamy warmth of a kitchen.

"Up there, past the Salutation," muttered the woman cryptically, abruptly closing the door on them.

Around the next bend, they found a prosperous village of half-
timbered houses, but only the smoke, curling from each chimney
pot, moved in the drizzle. At the end of the street squatted a
tavern displaying a scarlet lion below its dripping garland, and
beyond the next corner, candles flickered behind the shuttered
windows of a second hostelry with a unicorn sign, but there were
no army wagons crowding the side lane.

In her male garments, Heloise had no heart to brave either
establishment nor dared she send slow-witted Benet. She let Ned
scramble across to Bess's arms and, dismounting, let herself into
one of the tiny gardens. The indifferent cottager gave them directions; the castle lay beyond the alehouse. Instinct told her that
this was not the answer, yet she dared not let Bess know that it
was not just the highway churned by an army's tramping feet
nor any villager's counsel that had led them to Weobley, but her
own fey instincts homing on Miles.

The path turned out to be only bridle width and little used,
but they kept going for a hundred paces more to discover only
tumbled stones. Naught but nettles and hawthorn reigned here
now.

"Oh, mercy," exclaimed Bess, close to weeping, "we shall be
benighted soon."

Heloise clambered up the grassy mound. Mayhap she might
see some campfires, though weather like this could swallow up
an army.

"Let us go to the church as we arranged and see if Martin is
come with any news."

At least there would be some brief refuge from the rain,
Heloise sighed, as they led their horses past the preaching cross
and drew them beneath the shelter of the church's southern

porch. Bess set Ned to counting the flowered panels above her head, while Heloise ventured in. The door latch echoed loudly in the semidarkness. A light moving to the left of the chancel behind the rood screen glimmered palely on a knightly tomb.

"Martin?" she called as she drew a cross of water on her dripping forehead and distractedly genuflected. Her voice sounded feeble in the eerie, pillared gloom.

The voice that answered came from above and she nearly swooned with the shock of it. A taper flared; a thin parson stood upon the rood screen beneath the great wooden cross, his intimidating flare of nostril and eye sockets lit from below. Heloise rallied; out came the gasping half-lie of Brecknock's farms and castle being torched and the need to seek the child's father who was with the duke's retinue.

But it seemed they had found help. St. Miles, the patron saint of lost armies and other movables, had answered her prayers. The priest, now he could see she was no pilfering soldier, came down from his refuge. Yes, he told them, an army had entered the village and then gone east to seize the empty manor house belonging to Lord Ferrers, a Yorkist lord. Perhaps they would like him to guide them there before nightfall? Hungry, shivering in their wet clothes after a day spent searching, all the while anxious to safeguard Ned's health and freedom, the two young women and Benet were at the end of their strength but what was half a mile or so more? At a side altar, Heloise lit all the prayer candles so Ned might warm his little cold hands while they waited for the parson to bridle his mule.

Perhaps the saints were warmed by the child's courage also, for Martin arrived back from his scouting, red-mired and sodden. The news was bad: the high road to Hereford was held by King Richard's men.

"But be of good heart, my lady. They have insufficient numbers for a battle yet."

*   *   *

WOONTON DEVEREUX WAS HARDLY THE JEWEL OF LORD FERrers's barony. The outline in the gloom was of an unembellished building in a sloping field flanked like a mother pig by a progeny of byres and barns. Judging by the noise and flickering lights, it was populated by more than oxen. They had found someone's army.

"Who comes?" Pikes challenged them.

It was then Ned inconveniently asserted himself: "I am here to speak with my father, his grace of Buckingham," he announced, snatching off his shameful female cap and veil before Heloise could stop him. "Go and announce me, sirrah. Straightway, if you please!" It was such wondrous mimicry of his father that one of the sentries saluted.

Green timber was smoking Ferrers's hall. Heloise wiped her stinging eyes and gaped. It was like stepping through some hunting pique-nique held in Hell. Scores of half-clad men crammed tight as flagstones lay amidst a mess of drying jackets and prostrate weaponry. The offensive stink of the overused garderobe fermented in air already musty, and the vapor from a hundred breaths oozed down the bare, speckled walls. Some knave whistled and poor, tired Bess found herself whooped at on all sides with bored hands tweaking her hem. The furore grew and the women almost tumbled through the solar door that Sir William Knyvett flung open to investigate the hubbub. The noise died in an instant.

"The Vaughans have taken Brecknock, my lord father," exclaimed Ned in his piping voice and was snatched inside by his father like a pipit seized by a sparrowhawk.

"Did you have to let him blurt that out in front of them?" exclaimed Buckingham, shoving his son to dry before the blazing fire, and then he realized who else stood behind the tall, hunched parson.

Another time Heloise might have succumbed to crazed laughter, for against a firescreen of glistening hauberks and steaming quilted jackets, the duke, stripped down to a rust-stained shirt, was fish-eyed with astonishment. He did not recognize her. She stood smiling foolishly at her husband, her hose crusted with mud, perspiring profusely into Miles's third-best shirt in the steamy heat, with her dyed, hacked hair dripping onto spreading stains across her padded shoulders. There had been little point in changing into the simple robe she had brought with her.

"Oh, my God!" said a beloved voice, disturbing the good parson's equanimity, and Miles's arms lifted her shoulder high as though she had won a tourney. His shining hair was tossed back, his cheeks dark with the growth of beard, his eyes ecstatic.

Bess, however, was eyeing the empty platters. "Would it be possible to feed Lord Stafford?" she asked, conscientious to her fingertips and with a little self-interest too.

"Yes." Buckingham's voice emerged in a strangled squeak; he had noted his son was shorn of curls and wearing skirts. "Yes, yes, Pershall, see to it."

"Come to the fire, Elizabeth." De la Bere conducted the bedraggled young woman to the hearth as though he were a Westminster courtier escorting a foreign princess.

"I do so enjoy a family gathering," observed Morton, his cathedral voice unpleasingly acrid. "A pity that it will be over so soon."

Twenty-seven

"Trust Harry's rebellion to meet with the worst floods in the Marches in living memory!" Miles muttered wearily to de la Bere as they stood side by side glaring at the perpetual rain. Noah would have been sympathetic: bridges broken, villages destroyed, beasts carried away, and one carter swore he had seen a wooden cradle in the midst of the Severn torrent and heard the babe within it mewling piteously.

For nigh a week, Harry's dwindling army had played at dice, consuming all Lord Ferrers's fowls and oxen and then high-handedly demanding food from the nearby farms, their presence becoming as loathsome as the morning smell of a fox in a fowl yard. As for Harry, cut off from the other rebel leaders, and with Brecknock looted by the rabble he despised, he left Miles to deal with the complaints and, like an oppressed crustacean, withdrew into a shell of self-hatred.

"Aye, matters could not be much worse," replied de la Bere.

The instant the rivers were passable, the king's supporters would send a battle force to take them and every man in Herefordshire and Powys would be out duke-hunting, let alone their own men. Thank God, their soldiers did not know yet that they could earn land valued at a hundred pounds or else one thousand pounds in coin as a reward for Harry's capture.

And the surly, restless army was no place for the women. Miles longed to keep Heloise beside him but it was wiser to lodge her with Bess and Ned at the closest religious house with a detachment of reliable soldiers camped at a discreet distance, but how long could he keep any of them safe?

It was on Tuesday as the funeral bell of St. Peter's tolled across the stubbled cornfields that the wind changed from south to west; God drew the clouds back like a curtain to the east and the rain ceased. Harry—whether he liked it or not—Miles decided, had to be pricked out of his downward spiral for some unpleasant decisions. He took it on himself to fetch Ned and the two women back to the farmhouse early next morning. They deserved a say in their future and there was not much time.

He returned to the farm with the child before him on Traveller to find Harry had been roused by the arrival of another fugitive from Brecknock.

Sir Thomas Limerick had materialized as a tonsured cleric, complete with ass, upon their doorstep. He had escaped to the priory during the looting.

Miles listened to his report in the solar with a heavy heart. At least Morton was not in the chamber to hear the catalogue of woes. The English Vaughans and the vengeful Welsh had been through Brecknock Castle like an attack of dragons. They had set fire to chancery and counting rooms. The rent rolls, tally sticks, register of writs, the inquisitions, and the rest were all ashes and it would take years to reestablish the accounting, let alone justify the collection of any rent.

"So the Welsh have won after all." Sir William, like a weary grandsire, set Ned down from his lap. The child, absorbing every word as Limerick told his story, was staring at his father's lackluster eyes while his fingers mischieved his small dagger in and out of its scabbard. Cheeks dimpled in calculation, the tiny fingers continued their play.

"Stop that!" snarled Harry, riled to perfection; and simple Benet shambled from behind Bess's skirts and told the boy, "M-must not p-play with knives, my l-lord." The dagger was taken and dropped into the depths of Benet's tawny sleeve.

"It is all up with you, Harry, lad," declared Knyvett, resting on his age like a stick. He spoke for all of them. "But the boy here is a different matter. If the House of York were to tumble, this child and Henry Tudor are all that is left of the old dynasty, and for all your hand-in-glove stuff with my Lady Margaret and that oily bishop out there, I would not trust either of 'em out beyond kissing distance." He stood, his mind made up. "Whether you will or no, I am taking Ned away as far as I may until you have resolved matters with the king."

The duke started in protest and then, meeting the expressions of the rest, let his shoulders sink. "Do what you will," he muttered, leaning against the wall beside the fire, chewing on his knuckle.

"There are my lands at Kynnardsley," offered de la Bere. "Your grace?" The duke shrugged.

"Then go with them, Dick," Miles exclaimed, taking charge. God knows, they could not remain here prevaricating. "No argument! Only you can ensure your people give them the shelter they need. Bess must go too but it is her choice, of course. Take William ap Symon. He is a good man in danger and quick-witted." Meeting the younger man's nod, he swung round on his wife.

"My lady?" Heloise looked up from the hearth where she was sprinkling powdered ginger into gispyns of cider. She poked pensively at a floating clove and raised her hazel eyes to Miles.

"I will stay with you, sir," she replied huskily, and then reached out sadly to Ned.

Miles clenched his jaw; the sour knowledge that he now might never live to share the joy of parenthood with her made his voice brusque. "Your removal must be done stealthily, Dick, for if the remainder of our force learn that his grace is sending his son away in disguise, we shall lose the rest of them." He unscrolled an ink-smudged vellum map and frowned at its shortcomings; they would be no worse off with sticks and mud.

"What do you recommend?" De la Bere joined him and they stood together at the casement discussing where to cross the River Lugg.

"Tomorrow, then." Harry looked round at his heir as if desperate to hold him, but crippled in affection; the pucker of lip was not enough to entice the child to him.

"No," asserted Sir William. "Tonight!"

"So be it," decided de la Bere, his eyes on Bess. "Are you agreed, Mistress Elizabeth?" Nodding like a seeded windblown reed, the girl's calf-like gaze was selective.

"I would speak privily with his grace. I pray you all give us leave." Miles glanced round at the others for obedience, but his smile for his wife was moist-eyed.

It took him two hours to talk sense into Harry before he finally sought out Heloise. He found her in a field beyond the overtramped meadows, perched upon a stone wall, her hose-clad legs dangling beside a creviced harebell, and her face turned to the sun like a priestess's. Plucked yarrow and nettles, herbs for wounds, lay by her thigh. Behind her the hacked corn blazed defiantly golden.

He sighed deeply, knowing he might not live to see another season's sowing. "This is foolish, my love," he muttered, leaning his forearms upon the higgledy stones. "I would have you stay close where I may protect you."

"So what is decided?"

"Well, I have persuaded Harry to put on Benet's well-worn homespun and go north with Bannastre and Pershall."

"Godsakes," whispered Heloise, laughter a relief. "He could have worn that for the coronation and built a church with the savings."

Miles smiled at the irony. "Aye, it took much persuasion. God grant the shabbiness will save him. Bannastre has a farmstead outside Wem and they are going there. We shall put clouts on their horses' hooves tonight and lead them forth. Maybe when the hue and cry dies down, Harry can take ship for Brittany and go to Henry Tudor."

Heloise bit her lip. "And what of us?"

"I will hold matters here for as long as I may."

"Hold matters!" She gripped the wall angrily. "And how shall you do that, pray, when their own commander deserts them?"

"Take that look off your face, changeling. If my Lady Huddleston or Queen Anne were in such danger, my darling, you would do the same as I."

A huzzah reached them across the meadow from a cluster of soldiers bent over dice. "You are risking those poor fools' lives as well as your own, Miles," she muttered. "Why not tell them to flee and save themselves?"

"Of course I shall, *once* Harry is safely out of Herefordshire."

"Harry this, Harry that. I have had a surfeit of Harries. What of us, Miles? We should go to the high sheriff at Hereford and beg King Richard's mercy."

And what if he call it a horn, where am I then? And Heloise, what if they named her a witch? "Is that what you want? And supposing your wondrously perfect king says no? Lord Hastings did not have a trial."

"No, you and *Harry* saw to that."

That insult was taken on the chin. "Oh, my love, I do not know the answer. I am doing what I believe is right." He lifted her wrist to his lips. "Forgive me, I have brought you nothing but misfortune." Gentle hands drew him to her lap and he was grateful for her forgiveness. Winding his arms about her, Miles turned his face to the sun, the wool of her hose against his temple. "I do not want us to live in beggary in some cursed foreign land." Bitter tears tasted upon his lips. "What is Tudor to me? Lancaster, York—what does it matter, if only some king will let me live in peace with you? Christ forgive me, this is all my doing. It was I who whetted Harry's ambition."

"Are you that important?" answered Heloise. "Then I shall come hand in hand with you to Hell. Oh, Miles, my love, Harry's is a mean spirit. A covetous man with self-interest as his Bible." Reaching out a loving hand, she caressed the dark, cropped hair, hewn for a battlehelm. "Where are the honors that you deserve?"

"They would have come but for this folly. He is my friend for all his faults. I shall do this last service for him and then what God wills shall be." He carried her hand to his lips. "Come, I shall take you back to your lodging."

Oh, let us all leave, she pleaded silently, raising her face to the boisterous clouds. About her the rustling beauty of the hedgerow promised peace beyond all earthly trials but there were cruel ways a man might die and a woman also. The pain is transitory, came the comfortless answer.

Heloise blinked back her tears, proud of Miles Rushden's nobility of nature. His courage and sense of duty were breaking her heart but she adored him the more.

"Oh, my love," she whispered as she took his hand.

NEXT MORNING AT BUCKINGHAM'S BIDDING, HELOISE WAS fetched by Martin to Woonton Devereux and bidden by Latimer to attend his grace in the solar. So the fickle duke had changed his mind. With misgivings, she entered to discover Buckingham alone, a sinister, armed presence in the dim light. The casement shutters were drawn but the upper lights allowed a scrape of sun, and the duke's engrained helm—expensive German steel, which had never seen battle—glinted blue with insect luster. The visor was up but he had his back to her, pouring over the map.

"Your grace?" If annoyance had edged its way into her voice, she did not care. She had no stomach for any more niceties. It was ludicrous to curtsy.

What now? She doubted reinforcements were on their way. Rhys ap Thomas with a leek in his helm and a surfeit of apologies for not joining their force at Brecknock? Was she to be parceled up and sent somewhere with Benet to guard her virtue while he and Miles were slaughtered fighting back to back?

"Lady Rushden. Forgive the dim light but I have a megrim." Buckingham's voice was distorted by the high chin piece of the gorget that was one piece with the breastplate. Failure had not extinguished his mocking tone. "What is to be done with you?"

"I might enlighten you after further discussion with my husband, when I can find him."

Buckingham ignored her peevishness. "I sent for you, madam,

because Sir Miles and I have agreed that you should be escorted to the nuns at Hereford without delay."

"Like this? Oh yes, I am sure the nuns will take me in. Does your grace have any other good ideas, such as embracing me to your metal heart, your usual strategy when we are alone in bed together?"

That made the helm turn; her clash of gaze with her husband's steel stare could have made sparks fly. "How did you know?" Exasperation hardened his voice. "I thought if I could fool you . . ."

"You could fool the rest out there," she finished for him. "But if Pershall is gone, will they not smell the conspiracy?"

"Not if they have seen him in Limerick's peddler disguise saddling up for Hereford."

"How very imagin—" The door rattled open before she could finish and Miles abruptly swung away to lean against the chimney breast.

"I trust I am not interrupting?" Bishop Morton heaved his great bulk past the doorway. "I take it no word has come from our allies while I have been napping?" He lowered his grossness onto a frail chest, which groaned in protest.

"What, still here, Morton?" sneered Miles hoarsely. "I wonder you have not dissolved out of sight like salt in water."

"I have been tempted. I am afraid God's hand is against you, my son, and one really must take notice of His opinion."

Heloise glared at the fat face. Not a flicker of sympathy was there. Morton was as unmoved by the whole business as a rock beset by turbulent sea.

Miles raised a despairing hand to his eyes and half-turned. "Should you not say 'against us'? Your God is not so clement to you either, Bishop."

Morton gestured with philosophical acceptance. "What is adversity? My hide is tough but a younger skin pricks more easily. Where is your boy?"

"Where are the princes?" retaliated Miles, with a shrug.

He had meant nothing by it but the answer shook him—the indifferent, despicable answer: "Well, you should know the answer to that, my lord high constab . . ."

Miles swung round violently and the bishop saw black lashes sketching eyes that had never been a Stafford blue. Morton swallowed and would have risen but hands as powerful as talons grabbed him by the neck of his cassock. "This is what you wanted, is it not, you traitor?" he sneered in a low growl. "You and Margaret Beaufort. You have picked us off, one by one, with your sling shots.

"Are the princes dead, then? Are they? By God, if I had been Richard of Gloucester, I would have lopped you on the log that Hastings died on." He jabbed at the clerical windpipe with his thumbs, itching to squeeze the air out of that huge throat. "You lying, stinking Caiaphas, you would not have recognized our Lord even if you had met him. You would have crucified Him and laughed."

"Sirs, hush!" Latimer anxiously let himself in and leaned against the closed door. Miles, meeting the chamberlain's warning, let the bishop subside onto the sagging wood, watching with distaste the thick ringed hand crawling up through the furrows of flesh to rub at his throat.

Morton's eyes, like stones, did not change. "Alack, Rushden, what a pity you were not born to miniver. The people might have crowned you, unlike the overreaching Harry who took my bait so easily. Let me give you some good advice, dear boy. Was it not our esteemed friend Caxton who wrote: 'More is worth a good retreat than a foolish abiding'?"

"Get your overstuffed carcass out of my sight!" Miles snarled. "Curse you to Hell for the evil your foul viper's tongue has wrought!"

"Jealous of my influence, were you, you young hypocrite? Buckingham for king? Dear me, you are so naive in Wales. Your mediocre friend even believed me."

"Sir Nicholas, in the name of my 'mediocre friend,' lock up

this priest before I commit murder, and let no one speak with him."

Heloise let out her breath as the door closed, her eyes glassy. "What did he mean?"

"Jesu, changeling, I am trying to make sense of this too." For a while, Miles was silent, staring into the embers of the fire, and then he cursed.

"Tell me, Miles." The syllables were forced.

"Harry told me last night that he sent the queen a warrant a week ago to take the princes from the Tower during the rising. He could do that as High Constable. It was to be proof of his change of heart. Nay, do not condemn me. I have only just found out. Cat knew, apparently."

Heloise sank weakly onto the oaken chest, feeling as though her lifeblood had just drained out through her boot soles. "Who—" Her voice was hoarse. "Who carried it?"

"Margaret's creature, Bray, one of Morton's many visitors." At her silence, he continued: "Harry intended the Woodvilles to rise with him to crown the boy and then when the princes were found to be missing from the Tower, he hoped to rally all King Richard's enemies behind him instead."

"Including Henry Tudor?"

"Tudor is due to land on the Dorset coast and Harry was going to pretend to support him as the Lancastrian claimant for the crown."

"Pretend?"

"Yes, hoping King Richard would annihilate Tudor. Then Harry intended to bring Richard down. I could not stop it. I advised him against it over and over—but it was all in hand before we returned to Brecknock. Believe me, I never knew about the warrant until today. *Heloise!*"

She was cursing Buckingham for all eternity. Had he ordered the boys' deaths or had Margaret Beaufort used the warrant to give her agents access to murder them?

"Good friend Harry, whose giddy head is so easily twisted by flattery," she spat out. "He has made it so easy for them. Do you not see? That evil bishop and Tudor's poisonous mother have just pulled away the main prop of King Richard's throne."

"Yes, but—"

"Oh, God have mercy! Those foul rumors about King Richard wanting the princes dead. I just hope the king had the sense to send those children north while he was out of London." She hit her fist against her palm. "I hope your *Harry* dies like a dog in a ditch and goes to Hell. He has left you as a whipping boy, do you not see? We have no future, nothing, Miles. Oh, upon my soul, I hope King Richard can mend the damage that wicked fool has caused!"

"It is my fault."

"Still singing the same old tune, sir?" She sprang to her feet. "Christ's mercy! Will you make him a gift of your guilt as well? He is not worth it, Miles. He never wa—"

The knock at the door silenced her and Miles strode to the hearth, folding his arms, his back sullen. Latimer came in and bowed, with Nandik skulking in his wake.

"It is the necromancer, *your grace*." Obeying the twitch of Miles's fingers, he beckoned Nandik in.

The swagger was gone. Cringing like a dog afraid of a stick, the fellow fell on his knees with a fawning whine. "Your grace, I crave permission to leave. I am in fear of my life from your soldiers."

"So you were wrong, man." Miles managed a whispered imitation of Harry's voice.

"Your grace, the weather, I—"

"Do you imagine I went on your word, you cur?" Miles spat out contemptuously, lifting his face to Ferrers's greyhound badge carved upon the chimney breast. "I kept you by me because you fed me praises."

"A fellow must make a living where he can, my lord. I could not rise except—"

"—except by stealth and feeding on men's dreams," Miles

finished for him. "Get you gone, you fool! You will be lucky if they do not burn you."

Latimer started forward as Nandik flung his arms around the greaves protecting Miles's shins, babbling, "My lord, return to Brecknock. Say you heard of the rising and were setting out to crush it. Your grace, it was not all lies. I swear the king must die. The planets speak the truth. Another hand may slay him and your cause may prosper!"

"A murrain on your cursed prophecies!" snarled Miles, slamming his palm against the wall. "Go!"

"Fool!" Latimer grabbed Nandik by the back of the collar and forced him out.

"What in—" Miles's strong hands framed Heloise's shivering body in an instant and gathered her close. "Changeling?"

"Oh, Jesu, I am sure he was speaking true, Miles. This time he was speaking true."

It took courage to maintain the pretext of the duke's presence. The second day, Miles commanded everyone to leave and the loyal remnant fled throughout the twilight, some to seek pardon, others to crawl in stealth along the ditches and hedgerows back to Brecknock. Heloise ordered Martin back to her family with letters of farewell, and by dawn, Latimer, the last strand of the spider's web of fugitives spreading out from Woonton Devereux, was on his way. Bishop Morton had bribed his way out of the cellar the day before. Only Miles, Heloise, and poor masterless Benet were left.

The priest from Weobley bravely visited them and they gave Traveller and Cloud into his care. Miles wished he might surrender Heloise and Benet to the good man's protection but he might as well have tried to push aside a fortress—two fortresses!

The sheriff's men arrived at nightfall, entering the unbarred hall in astonishment to find Buckingham's undented armor, stuffed with cushions and moldy arras, propped in the solar, staring vacantly, and only three people slumbered fitfully by the fire.

A half dozen men-at-arms contained them in a circle of naked steel while some score looked on. With a sword tip pricking at her throat, Heloise was hauled to her feet. Simple Benet crouched, frightened and moaning, beneath a pointing blade. Miles unscabbarded his sword and proffered it, hilt first, to his captor.

A visor was tipped back and its ruddy-cheeked, sweating owner rasped, "I am the undersheriff of this shire and I hereby arrest you for treason against the king's grace. Rushden, is it?" He consulted a list and checked the serpents on Miles's surcote. "We might get forty pounds or more for you, sir."

"All d-deserters are pr-promised a pardon," Heloise protested as her hands were tied.

"Didn't desert, did you?" guffawed the man who held her. "Didn't come to us."

"A woman," chuckled someone, divesting her of her dagger as he tweaked her breast. "This traitor's whore. Here's sport before breakfast."

"This is the lady Heloise," snarled Miles, with such authority that they recoiled. "King Richard's ward. Lay hands on her and I promise you, he will have you hanged."

THEY BLOODIED MILES AND BENET WITH FISTS AND SABATONS before they took them to the lord high sheriff at Hereford—it was really Buckingham and the higher reward they wanted. Not until they threatened to force Heloise down and rape her, one by one, did Miles, his lips swollen and bleeding, tell them that the duke had fled to Ross, and thence to the Severn estuary. The high sheriff took them bound to Gloucester and from there the journey became nightmare days of galloping roads. Heloise lost account of the blurred villages they rode through, the towns where she was spat upon, or the cellar doors that were nightly locked upon her. She was kept apart from Miles. No earthly chains, however, could fetter her mind, and with all her mental strength she willed courage and love across the air to him.

They were brought finally to Dorchester, a frosty, sloping shire town that lapped a Dorset crossroads and straddled the road between Salisbury and Bridport. The east wind licked keenly around Heloise's limbs like a master's whip as the Hereford men drew rein at a church halfway down the hill of the high street to ask directions.

Miles could have told them. He guessed now as they spurred down to Stinsford and rode up the Blandford Road through Yellowham Wood towards Pydeletown. Athelhampton? Aye, here was Will Martyn's newly built gatehouse with its oriel window but—sweet Christ have mercy!—Miles had thought to dine here once more, not die where his family had supped as guests! Would the soldiers camping beneath the canvas against the boundary greystone walls hang him on the morrow? Tears of shame pricked at his eyes and, damn it, his hands were tied to the saddle.

Heloise, ordered to dismount outside this unfortified manor house, did not mean to be defiant. They needed to haul her from the saddle and stand her up like a wooden doll, for her ankles, frozen from the long, cold ride, lacked grist to hold her and treacherously twisted, dropping her like limp sackcloth.

"Help her, you whoresons!" roared Miles, struggling to free his bonds from the saddle pommel so he might dismount. "Have you no pity!" A handful of dirt hit his cheek and then the soldiers and a scrabble of children were pelting him like a murderer. Miles answered in a snarl of local brogue that Heloise could not understand.

"Jesu, not more mouths to feed," muttered a Dorset voice. "Who comes now? By the saints! *Rushden?*" A gentleman in a Yorkist sunnes-and-roses collar stepped down into the muddy courtyard, his eyebrows arched in horror at Miles's disheveled state.

"In with her!" ordered the high sheriff before Heloise could hear more. Poleaxes prodded obedience. She limped through an arched portal into a warm world that was tawny with candlelight and redolent with the male scents of ambergris, musk, and horse.

Behind a linenfold screen, she caught the luscious smells of roasting meats and her empty belly pleaded. Everywhere, men's faces stared at her. Dazed, she could only blink at the jeweled hats and chains of office as her captor rasped out his purpose, and then, like a miniature Holy Land sea, the throng stepped back, leaving her exposed.

Ahead, to the right of an oriel window whose glassy crests tossed bands of vermilion across his hands, a man sat alone upon a cushioned chair of estate beside the hearth—the new king. Cord-du-roi secretaries bent before him on stools, hunched over their writing boards. The hall hushed, the only sound the scratching on parchment as they finished their sentences and set the empty quills back in the inkpots. Richard III looked round and his face froze in the world-weary expression of a man who had once thought he could trust people. Then, slowly, his icy mien thawed as he recognized his wife's maid of honor beneath the riding cloak, improper in her broadcloth cote and muddy hose.

"Heloise," he said with compassion, his gaze rising from her bound wrists to the shameful magpie hair.

Silently cursing her lack of grace, she hobbled forward to where the sheriff crouched before the king, and fell willingly to her knees. "Sovereign lord," she answered huskily.

"Unbind her," the king ordered; but someone said, "Search her sleeves first."

Loosened from the cruel leather, her hands felt jabbed by a hundred evil needles as the blood oozed back like unclogged rivulets. Dear God, why had they not brought Miles in? Jesu! Hastings had been given little time before they killed him!

"Your highness," she pleaded, "Have mercy on my husband." She searched his face, willing him to forgive. "He wrote the words that made you king."

"And another traitor spoke them," answered King Richard. "Is Rushden here?"

The sheriff rose. There was a rattle of harness near the door and her bound husband was hauled into the king's view. She longed to run across and necklace her arms about his neck with love and pride, but she might serve Miles best by a quiet dignity. His gaze searched her out and bestowed upon her such love as she had never dreamed of.

"The traitor, Sir Miles Rushden, your highness."

Traitor? Here was no haughty, defiant rebel but a man who knew his own worth and owned up to error. Yet there was not one iota of forgiveness among the king's men. They were staring with animosity at a prisoner who looked more Welsh than English: his black hair wildly tousled, the unfashionable growth of beard limning his jaw, the dribbles of mud spattering his surcote, and the rearing perfidious serpents. Miles was not given a chance to make any reverence, but was flung to his knees.

Desperate at the king's feet, Heloise beseeched humbly, passionately, God's mercy, as she felt the hatred intensify and insinuate itself between the White Boar men like an ugly wraith. Her prayers, pagan and holy, searched desperately for someone to listen.

"Hang, draw, and quarter the cur, sire!" It was Sir Thomas Stanley, married to the treacherous Countess of Richmond, rattling his loyalty—saliva and brandished fist an insult to the air.

"Make an example of him." The lethal proposal came from Lord Lovell and the room became a Tower of Babel as each man brandished his loyalty. Heloise, willing King Richard to forgive her lord, felt the cold November air from the open door. She turned her head and the babble ceased. With a creak of studded leather, Sir Richard Huddleston, like a player, strode into the heart of the hall and paused, absorbing the triangle of players before the king, his glance ironic before he made obeisance to his royal brother-in-law. *Help us,* Heloise implored him silently.

"And have you anything to say, Sir Richard?" Curiosity softened the king's face.

"It would surprise you if I had not, my gracious lord. Do you need my unworthy opinion? A great deal of mud seems to have been cast already." Huddleston's mocking glance examined Miles but then, as if he could not stop himself, his gaze was drawn to Heloise as she huddled at the king's feet. Surprise slid across his features.

You owe me for Dionysia's life! her eyes and mind told him. So does your king! You must save Miles! In God's name, you must!

Silent and stern now, Huddleston strode across to King Richard and, moving behind the royal chair, stooped. As he spoke quietly to the king, the white enamel brooch on his beaked hat reflected the light. A horse? No, a unicorn! Margery's brooch had been a unicorn!

It meant something, something she must do! Heloise strained to hear what he said while her mind stumbled through this deadly twilight to find the answer. Upon a tapestry among mille-fleurs, another little unicorn gleamed snowy and golden in the fading light. The faeries were with her; the answer was close within her grasp.

"Let him be tried straightway!" Stanley, like a plump gospel saint behind the king's other shoulder, seized the hall's silence, determined to herd their opinions into a verdict. "What say you, Rushden? We can hang you in the corn market in Dorchester, your entrails drawn out and your body quartered and sent to the four corners of the realm as a warning to all traitors. Shall we invite your old father to watch?

"Cat got your tongue, then?" he gibed the prisoner. "Answer us!"

"A trial is not needful, Stanley. Yes, I am guilty." Miles's voice was steady as a rock despite the waves of hate breaking upon him. "I did what I believed was right and I am answerable for it, but *loyaulté me lie*." It was perilous to cast a king's personal motto back at him. The furrows in King Richard's brow deepened at the ambiguity.

Stanley jerked forward. "Obedience to the king transcends fealty to rebels." He angrily seized a fistful of the captive's hair, forcing his face up, and Heloise felt the stab of Miles's pain. "You stink with treason, Rushden!"

"Holy Paul! Let others speak!" His liege lord reined him in with calm authority, but the earl let go with such violence that Miles almost fell forward on the hearth. "Rushden," declared the king, "you are fortunate that someone has already testified on your behalf." Mutters of disbelief fidgeted the listeners but King Richard held up his hand to silence them. "We have been informed that the prisoner did everything to dissuade the traitor Harry Stafford from his evil path."

"Jesu forbid we should pardon such a villain!" protested Lovell. "Am I going deaf, sire? He has just admitted his guilt! Let him be hanged!"

King Richard's gaze searched the crowded room. "Will you still speak for him?"

Heloise, frantically seeking a merciful face, gasped as de la Bere pushed forward from the back. The embarrassed reddening of his skin went ill with its blond roofing and, with a swift, shameful glance at Miles, he bowed. "Yes, sire, I still attest to his worth."

Someone else growled. Miles had flinched as though a cruel hand had lashed him, and de la Bere's face flushed darker. The young man clenched his jaw, declaring, "On his return to Brecknock in September, Rushden never ceased to warn Buckingham against this course. But the duke's mind was set."

De la Bere—the informer who had sent the warning to the king? *Dick de la Bere?* Heloise's mind was reeling. Surely not? The honest charm, the boyish chivalry, and all the time . . . Oh, dear God, it was Dick who had taken charge of Ned and . . . and they had blithely sent the child and the others with him—with him into a trap! Heloise stared appalled, the solid earth shaking beneath her feet. Was Sir William taken too? And where was Ned?

She felt the shame of being duped flooding through Miles. If his fists had been free, he looked as though he would have struck the younger man in pain and bitter fury. Curses were on his tongue. *Do not speak,* willed Heloise, *Dick is making amends and trying to save you.* To prevent him answering, she blurted out:

"L-Lord Stafford? What ha—"

"He is with Mistress Bess. Quite safe, my lady." And was Bess corrupted too? Had the entire household been wormed through with treachery?

"But the traitor still drew sword against you, sire." The High Sheriff of Herefordshire spoke in self-interest, thinking of the glory and forty pounds.

"And the woman is a necromancer. Buckingham surrounded himself with them."

Heloise started, shocked. Incredibly it was Piers Harrington who spoke, the esquire she had spurned at Middleham.

"No!" exclaimed Miles hoarsely. "Hang me if you must, but acquit my lady."

"Acquit?" Harrington snarled derisively. "I suppose God turned her hair grey."

The high sheriff nodded. "We have a witness who will testify she has familiars."

"Who?" snarled Miles.

"The man Benet."

"But he is a simpleton," exclaimed de la Bere, and Miles, meeting Heloise's panicked face, was turning ashen.

"With no reason to lie, then!" Lord Stanley bawled.

"Stop, please!" exclaimed Heloise, beseeching King Richard: "My gracious lord, if they must have a sacrifice, let it be me. God knows I have lived with fear and suspicion all my life."

"Dear me, my liege," said Huddleston clearly, at the king's elbow, "this eagerness for block and faggots prates of a wondrous love between these two."

"Then burn the pair of them," snorted someone.

"May I speak, sire?" Heloise raised her palms in supplication. "I can prove my lord's innocence."

"Then do so, Lady Rushden." The regal eyes were insistent.

"Sir." She turned to Huddleston. "My husband wears the unicorn." She heard a hiss of breath from him and met his gaze resolutely. "Upon his shirt against his heart."

Stanley was nearest. He gleefully yanked a fistful of shirt up from beneath Miles's breastplate. "By the lord, he does, see! So what of it?"

The air seethed between the king and his closest friends. Unprivileged, Stanley looked from one to the other but it was the king who understood. "Sir Richard Huddleston?"

Heloise turned the full force of her mental anguish on Huddleston but knew his strong mind scarcely acknowledged it. The surprise had been controlled swiftly. All of the king's men were gazing at the knight bannaret and he in turn was studying Miles.

"You mean I have to decide for you, my lords?" He unfolded his arms.

"I think you should." Heloise's voice was husky, her syllables weighting her husband's life and knowing as well as he did that the power of life lay within his gift. "But let me make it easier for you. Draw your dagger, sir."

Mouth taut but green eyes curious, Huddleston slid his dagger free. "And?"

"I pray you cut away the serpents, sir."

He tossed the haft into his other hand and approached Miles. De la Bere held out a hand to assist, but it was the guards, at a nod from Huddleston, who thrust their prisoner up on his feet. For a long breath, the two men stared at one another. Then Huddleston grabbed the neck of the surcote taunt, pricked the dagger into the argent silken membrane, and drew it down.

"No, deeper," Heloise commanded, and Miles, dazed, rallied and understood. Gratitude shone like glass, and love, intense and selfless, knelt at her feet.

Beneath the silk and its buckram interlining, murrey glinted. As though he were skinning a wild beast, Huddleston sliced the outer layers away. A cloth-of-silver boar, with feathery fetlocks and delicately curved tusks, glared out from beneath its ragged covering. The room gasped in unison. Stony interest serifed King Richard's mouth. It was his badge.

Please! Heloise cried silently to Huddleston. *I love the man. Give him back to me. Can you not see the courage in him? He stayed true till the last.*

The silver and emerald gazes, male and unfathomable, leveled, locked, and held. Heloise's heart raced, frantic, close to despair. Did Huddleston have the intelligence to see Miles caught upon a tide greater than he had the power to hold? Was there any mercy or imagination behind the agile mind? Time dragged its feet before Huddleston spoke at last: "I believe, sire, that you should grant this man a pardon."

"*Believe?* Or know?" questioned King Richard chillingly, and stood, making his own examination of the planes and chiseling of the prisoner's face.

"*Believe,* sire. I pray that will suffice. How can any of us know what truths may lie within another being's soul?"

As if the room drew breath again and every man with it, they waited for the King of England to disagree. Richard Plantagenet's head was bowed as though a heavy, twisted cord had been wound by some cruel torturer around his temples. When he finally raised his face, the betrayal by his greatest ally was visible in the bleakness of his gaze. Defiance, however, tilted the strong jaw. Bitter words sliced through the hushed air like an axe:

"That most untrue creature is dead. Let that suffice!"

Buckingham dead! Heloise felt the bleak, despairing scream of Miles's soul. Dark lashes briefly curtained her husband's hurt before he tilted his face to his merciful judge and said, "God forgive him. His greatest enemy was himself."

King Richard looked upon the redeeming unicorn badge and lifted sad, knowing eyes to Miles's face. "Shall you indeed mourn him? I fear me no one else will."

"You are fortunate to escape with a fine," exclaimed Huddleston, entering the bedchamber at the Antelope in Dorchester just as Miles finished cleansing himself. The bannaret snapped his fingers to his manservant to carry away the soiled napkins and the ewer. "What is it you need to know, Rushden? Can you not bury the dead? After that performance of wifely devotion, Heloise deserves a husband, not a mourner-in-chief."

"I want to close the door and bolt it," Miles muttered, rubbing a thin grub of ointment into a smarting wrist, and waited.

"Hearsay." Huddleston shrugged and handed him the clean shirt on loan from Athelhampton's owner.

"I should like to hear also." Heloise, bathed and warm in a borrowed gown of blue fustian, slid off the bed to stand behind Miles, her hands like a priest's stole scarfing his collarbone.

"A fellow named Ralph Bannastre betrayed your duke."

Words, his playthings, failed Miles now. He swallowed, head flung back; his fingers slid across Heloise's.

"Mytton, High Sheriff of Shrewsbury, arrested Buckingham in the orchard of Bannastre's farm at Wem, and brought him down to the king at Salisbury to be tried. He willingly confessed and provided the names of all the conspirators—except you, Rushden. He would not name you."

Miles turned within his lady's arms and gathered her to him for comfort, tears spilling down upon his collar.

"And King Richard spoke with him?" Heloise asked softly, cradling her lord's cheek against her own.

"No. The king was gracious enough to grant him an audience but our guards found a dagger in Buckingham's sleeve."

"What!" Miles jerked his head round in disbelief.

"God have mercy!" Heloise exclaimed, gripping his arm. "Miles, Ned's dagger! Remember? Benet took it and put it in his sleeve and then the duke disguised himself in Benet's clothes."

He closed his eyes painfully, his hand finding and locking with hers.

"I doubt it would have made much difference," said Huddleston sympathetically. "He was beheaded next day on the Feast of All Souls."

Miles tried not to think of the axe, of Harry's lifeblood bursting out. "And . . . Bannastre received his thirty pieces of silver?" Bitterness timbred his voice.

"The king permitted the wretch one of Buckingham's holdings in Kent and right unwillingly too. The man was an utter Judas." Huddleston's tone was scathing. "Loyalty is a precious commodity."

"Yes, it is." Looking upon his lady, Miles stroked his knuckles tenderly down her cheek. "Wait, Huddleston." Sir Richard had reached the door. "Which manor in Kent was given to Bannastre?"

"Yalding. Is that significant?" And not waiting for an answer, he left them alone.

Heloise slid onto Miles's lap as the door closed. "*Is* it significant?"

"Not anymore," he sighed wryly. *You stubborn fool, Harry, if only you had given Bannastre Yalding.*

"Miles?"

"Oh, Heloise, it will not be easy to throw a handful of earth on Harry's memory and just walk away." But it must be done. "Changeling," he whispered, settling her head against his shoulder and bestowing a kiss upon the tip of her nose, "it was because of you that I was pardoned."

"Nonsense," she murmured, snuggling against him. "King Richard and Huddleston recognized your courage to do what your conscience told you was right. I fear me that if Buckingham had stood in the king's shoes today, he would not have pardoned you."

"No." His cheek stroked against her silver hair, thankful her bright soul had become his anchor. "God forgive me," he whispered, shielding his eyes as if the deity could see his shame. "I am guilty of such arrogance, Heloise, believing I could mold Harry's soul into greatness. Such a waste. He could have helped make Richard's reign a golden age." But kind hands soothed his brow and peeled away his fingers. "Oh, dear Christ, I hope Knyvett and Latimer will trust to the king's mercy too."

"I am sure they will be forgiven, and you, in turn, must forgive de la Bere. He did what he believed was right and he protected Ned. Duty and honor are hard masters to serve."

She let the silence heal, and, entwined, they sat staring into the flames, the only sound in the chamber the crackling of the logs.

At length she stirred, leaning back so she might see the glow of candlelight upon his face. "Miles, I—I had a dream last night but I do not know what it signifies."

"Tell me, *cariad*." His acceptance warmed her more than the fire's heat.

"I was standing in Brecknock market looking up at St. Mary's but it was quite different. There was a tower upon it. And someone I knew stood beside me. He had the look of Buckingham and yet it was not he. Now why should I dream that?"

"I do not know, love." It was comforting nevertheless. He carried her fingers to his lips. "Thank you for all your understanding, Heloise. It took great courage and trust to stand by me these last weeks."

"Courage, no? You said to me once, remember, that I was happier hiding behind a mask. Well, that is over now. I am not afraid anymore. Seeing you standing there facing death so bravely gave me so much strength, Miles, strength to believe in myself."

In husbandly fashion, he tidied a lock of her damp hair back so he might see her face. "It was always there in you, Heloise."

Their foreheads touched.

"Oh, a murrain on this," she protested, laughter kindling within her. "I shall build a monument to you if you build one to me."

"You can have two, changeling."

Hazel eyes chastised him and then they grew more mischievous. "Shall I tell you a secret? De la Bere is going to marry

Bess. Shall I tell you another secret, *Cysgod?* There is still a place in this fickle world for an honest friend like you. Light a candle for Harry's soul and then turn to the sunlight." Her arms clasped him firmly. "Will you walk hand in hand with me into the future?"

"Yes, *cariad.*" His arms enfolded her. "With all my heart!"

Historical Note

Since most of the people in this story actually lived, I can tell you that de la Bere did indeed marry Bess, and Sir William Knyvett was granted a pardon, wed one of Buckingham's aunts, and later became the steward of the Countess of Richmond's household. Nandik was arrested for treason and sorcery but reprieved in 1485. Thomas Vaughan became steward of Brecknock. Catherine Woodville married twice after Harry's death.

Buckingham's treachery had immense repercussions. With his most powerful supporter gone, King Richard reigned for only two more years. Because of the mystery surrounding the disappearance of the princes in the Tower, Richard became the most controversial ruler in British history. At least the Richard III Society exists to remind the general public that Shakespeare's version is Hollywood Tudor style—great theater but hardly accurate, and there is no contemporary evidence of either a hump, a limp, or a withered arm. The bail system and the College of Heralds, both introduced by Richard, are still with us.

The Countess of Richmond, a successful organizer, saw her son crowned as King Henry VII, and became the most influential woman in England. Bishop Stillington assisted at the coronation of Henry VII. Morton, though later a cardinal and Archbishop of Canterbury, is mainly remembered by posterity for his taxation policy—"Morton's Fork."

Ned, third Duke of Buckingham, was executed by King Henry VIII in 1521—the year after his tower on St. Mary's Church in Brecknock was completed. He always kept a spare set of accounts with him—an emotional legacy from the sack of Brecknock?

Sir Richard Huddleston became Constable of Beaumaris Castle and Chief Forester of Snowdonia. Richard and Margery's son was abducted by his future mother-in-law, so Miles's abduction is not just a fictional invention. The story of Richard and Margery Huddleston's romance is told in *The Maiden and the Unicorn*.

I owe an apology to the late John Dokett, Gloucester's chaplain, for making him a fire-and-brimstone churchman rather than the quiet scholar he probably was, and I have to admit that the building of Athelhampton might have been still in its earliest stages in 1483.

The Northamptonshire tale of "Skulking Dudley," whose daughter put on armor to defend her father's honor, provided me with the inspiration for Heloise.

Traveller, though fictional, became acclaimed for his snowy coat and was in great demand for his procreational abilities. Dafydd moved to Bramley, where he terrified generations of local vermin, until he passed away peacefully beneath a rosebush at the age of thirteen.

Brecknock (Brecon) Castle is in ruins but you can stand beneath the wall of the great hall and stare out over Brecon. A wall and tower in the grounds of the Castle Hotel are accessible to the general public and there is a picture in the hotel which shows some of the fortress's former glory. The hall of Crosby Place was moved, stone by stone, to Chelsea and is now privately owned. Athelhampton Hall is open to the public on certain days.

Acknowledgments

Thank you to the following: my writers' group, especially my good friends and fellow writers Elizabeth Lhuede and Chris Stinson for their wise and useful comments and Delamere Usher, who took me to the races in search of a horse like Traveller and helped me with the final draft; Joan Kollins for keeping me on track with Heloise's clairvoyant ability; Michael Spencer for his help with the heraldry; Dr. Peter Davies for his help with Stillington's condition; John Sidebotham for advice on the roads and rivers of the Welsh Marches; and Geraint Rees of *Y Gronfa,* the Welsh Cultural Foundation of Australia, for checking my Welsh— *diolch, Geraint!*

Thank you to those who offered advice while I was researching in Wales, especially the friendly staff of the museum at Brecknock and Geraint Hughes, Dean of St. John the Evangelist Cathedral, Brecon. I am grateful to Elwyn John, Archdeacon of Brecon, for providing information on St. Mary's.

In England, thanks to Felicity and Don Head of Milton Keynes for research on Stony Stratford; my honorary aunt, Denise Lyon-Williams, for a useful discussion on the Welsh; Ralph Dean and Mr. and Mrs. R.W.A. Langton of Lacon Hall, Wem, for information on Ralph Bannastre; Pam Chant and Sally Martyn; and my father for suggesting Athelhampton.

Much deserved thanks to my editor, Christine Zika, and my agent, Jill Grinberg, and to the organizations of Romance Writers in America and Australia for their perennial support and encouragement.

And not to be forgotten: Stefan (Perth and Nice) and Sasha (Zurich) who were the right age to be an inspiration for Ned; and a thank-you purr to Cagney Coe, a feline of San Rafael in

California, who absolutely insisted in appearing in the story as Dafydd.

The Powys poetry extract is from "Elegy for Gruffudd ab Adda" by Dafydd ap Gwilym in *Medieval Welsh Poems,* translation and commentary by Richard Loomis and Dafydd Johnston (New York: Pegas Paperbacks, 1992). The latter also contains a more scholarly version of Dafydd ap Gwilym's poem "May and January."

Isolde Martyn

Isolde Martyn

The Knight and the Rose
0-425-19305-5

A vibrant tapestry of love, betrayal,
and political intrigue—inspired by a
real-life medieval court case.

"A lovely medieval, rich as
a stained glass window."
—Jo Beverley